MONTEZUMA'S PEARL

Just inches below the surface lay the treasure that would change my life forever. It stared up at me as calmly and quietly as the morning paper, yet little did I know that it commanded worlds. It was barely visible on the dark sandy bottom, and I should have just turned quietly and innocently away. But that was impossible. My eyes were transfixed like Adam staring at the apple.

The sea was my alluring Eve, offering up the fruit of knowledge. Something inside me said I must take it. Perhaps it was just natural curiosity or the lure of sunken treasure. Or perhaps fate itself was fulfilling a promise made centuries and cultures ago.

But it was already too late. The sleep of centuries had ended. The adventure had begun.

MONTEZUMA'S PEARL

DAVID LEE JONES

AVON BOOKS • NEW YORK

MONTEZUMA'S PEARL is an original publication of Avon Books. This work has never before appeared in book form. This work is a novel. Any similarity to actual persons or events is purely coincidental.

AVON BOOKS
A division of
The Hearst Corporation
1350 Avenue of the Americas
New York, New York 10019

Copyright © 1995 by David Lee Jones
Published by arrangement with the author
Library of Congress Catalog Card Number: 94-96278
ISBN: 0-380-77383-X

First AvoNova Printing: March 1995

AVONOVA TRADEMARK REG. U.S. PAT. OFF. AND IN OTHER COUNTRIES, MARCA REGISTRADA, HECHO EN U.S.A.

Printed in the U.S.A.

RA 10 9 8 7 6 5 4 3 2 1

For Paula, all of the Gregoires,
and the people of Baja

Acknowledgments

Having shifted gears again and gone off-road into this new story, there are new people to thank for their contributions, whether they know it or not.

First, as always, my wife, Paula, for taking care of me, the house, our daughter Rosemary, and a million other things. In case you're wondering, I take care of the yard, a couple of dozen houseplants, various bills, our two Chevys, the garage (currently filled to overflowing with home improvement supplies), and our Labrador, Daisy. I also pick our daughter up from preschool every day.

Paul and Barbara Gregoire, my in-laws, for treating me like a son, showing us Baja on a budget, and planting the seed of this story in my head.

Michael Larsen and Elizabeth Pomada, my agents, for believing in these wild stories.

Chris Miller, my editor at Avon, for her usual expert editing and story advice.

Frank Dorland, master crystallographer, who spent six years studying the life-sized Miller-Hedges crystal skull found in Latin America in the 1920s, upon which this story is based. There are three known life-sized pure rock crystal skulls in existence, all believed to be Aztec in origin. This tale is about the fourth, as yet undiscovered.

One who looks
Into the Eyes of God
When the shadow
Sleeps
Receives the power
of the Sun

. . . Aztec Legend

Fame is an anxious trumpeter
Astride a winged steed,
Hastily announcing one's arrival
And departure
In the same shallow note

. . . author

Introduction

Treasure

Every treasure carries a promise and a curse. The promise is always great wealth, worldly or spiritual, the curse invariably ruin or death. Knowing this great truth and little else, we are ill-prepared for the battle that wages within us upon discovering hidden treasure. We find the lure of fantastic wealth intoxicating, completely irresistible, and are drawn helplessly into its magnetic field. Unable to walk away, we must follow fate to the very center of the battlefield.

What strange and powerful forces are at work in this world and beyond to keep treasures buried for so long at the bottom of the brooding, quiet ocean? What makes the sea change its mind after centuries of silence and spill forth its secrets? Perhaps time itself, the keeper of all secrets, is finally ready to reveal its bounty, to cast its powerful, magic spell.

Sunken treasure often lies in shallow water, just below the surface, waiting to be discovered. Sometimes it only takes a shift in the tides, or a footprint on the ocean floor, to expose the cache of kings. The sleep of centuries can be guarded by only a thin watery sheet. And sometimes, in a rare bold moment, the sheet slowly slips away, and treasures that hold the secrets of the universe are revealed. When that happens, there is no escape, no putting the bounty back. Whatever curse or good fortune awaits the finder must be endured, regardless of cost.

Such is the story of Montezuma's Pearl.

1

Discovery

Mexico: Present Day

As my wet, bare foot touched the hard, curved ridge, I instinctively pulled back. But it was already too late. The sleep of centuries had ended. The adventure had begun.

Just inches below the surface lay the treasure that would change my life forever. It stared up at me as calmly and quietly as the morning paper, yet little did I know that it commanded worlds. It was barely visible on the dark, sandy bottom, and I should have just turned quietly and innocently away. But that was impossible. My eyes were transfixed like Adam staring at the apple. I stood motionless for a moment in the midday sun, baking on that nearly deserted beach in a tiny fishing village on the Gulf of California.

The sea was my alluring Eve, offering up the fruit of knowledge. Something inside me said I must take it. Perhaps it was just natural curiosity, or the lure of sunken treasure that sent me back to camp to fetch my shovel, or perhaps fate itself was fulfilling a promise made centuries and cultures ago.

I stared down at the hard-edged object beneath six inches of water, knowing I'd have to act fast. The tide was coming in quickly and would soon be up to my waist. By the time the tide went out again, my find could be buried forever in sand. Of course, it could have been only the ridge of a rock. There were plenty of those along the wide, flat shore, but it had the feel under my foot of a shell: the biggest one I had ever encountered.

I dropped to my knees, reached under the water, and ran my hand cautiously over its bony surface. There were two curved ridges exposed in the sand, each about a foot long and parallel to each other, like the matching flutes of a giant clam.

This far north on the gulf the tide went out a half mile, and I was a full quarter mile from camp. The situation didn't look good.

Making a valiant but vain attempt, I sloshed and ran back to grab the small camp shovel leaning against the Winnebago, counting my strides and sighting a line so I wouldn't lose the spot where the shell lay buried.

Just my luck to be alone, I thought. My wife and our two-year-old had gone the ten miles into town, and had taken the jeep. Maggie, our five-year-old yellow Labrador, went along for protection.

Shovel in hand, I charged over to the half-finished stucco shack the campground owner called home. But Mr. Zapata had gone off to check on his goat herd or something. I was alone, and the tide was coming in fast.

Tossing the shovel aside, I rummaged around under the motor home and came up with a hammer and a tent pole, then dashed back down the little sandbank to the water.

By the time I squished my way back through the thick, dark sand and sloshed through the rising tide, it was already too late. The shell had disappeared under two feet of water. I stood dejectedly over the spot where the ridge should have been. Was I even looking in the right place? Had I miscounted my steps? Was it ten yards to the left? Maybe it was a little farther out? I couldn't tell.

With the water lapping at my knees, I picked a spot and drove the tent pole into the sand, knowing the shell had to be nearby. Driving the pole down to three feet, I turned and left, wading back to shore, catching my breath, and getting thirsty for a beer.

Back at the campsite I opened the cooler and pulled out a bottle of Corona. I sat in a lawn chair with my feet resting on the foot-high rock wall that separated the hard, flat campground from the beach sand, which sloped twenty yards down to the water. In an hour the tide would be almost lapping the wall.

I thought about being alone. There was the wonderful peace of solitude, but what I really needed was someone to share my find. Even if we couldn't have done anything more than mark the spot as I had done, at least I would have had someone to share in the excitement. Sure, it was probably just a worthless shell fragment half-buried in the sand, but then again . . .

I finished the Corona, ignored the ten pounds that had settled in my stomach from the laziness of having a desk job back in LA, and grabbed another beer. This wasn't the stomach of the six-foot, 180-pound state wrestling champ of my high school days. That was seventeen years and many dreams ago. Back then I had two career choices, steroids or anonymity. The steroids could have gotten me on the cartoonish wrestling circuit, but I also wanted to live past fifty. So I wrestled a little in college, and got a degree in business instead. But I was not in the mood for too much of life's regrets that afternoon. There was some serious daydreaming to be done.

Popping the top, I laughed at the irony of the situation. The ice in the cooler had all turned to water, and the last dozen bottles of what started out as a case the week before floated and clinked together like glass buoys in a miniature ocean.

It was the beer that sent Ellen to town. She was to get ice and do a little tourist shopping. Sure, the fridge in her parents' Winnebago worked, but it was still stuffed with food, even after a week. She always brought enough to survive a month after a nuclear disaster.

The case of Corona for eight bucks was irresistible, and essential for relaxing in the warm sun of late October. Fortunately, the drinking hadn't ever gotten quite bad enough to cost me the marriage. I couldn't afford to lose Ellen, or Susie, our miracle baby.

Two beers later, with the tide mostly in, and sun above the palm frond umbrella, I imagined unearthing a whole giant clam, prying open its huge, thick jaws, and pulling out a satiny pearl the size, weight, and perfect shape of an undrilled bowling ball. I saw myself paying off the house, quitting my job as contracts administrator at the defense plant, and opening Hansen's Hardware—a mom-and-pop place with our dog on the porch, a Coke machine, and maybe even a gas pump wrestling circuit, but I also wanted to live past fifty. So I wrestled a little in college, and got a degree in business instead. But I was not in the mood for too much of life's regrets that afternoon. There was some serious daydreaming to be done.

Popping the top, I laughed at the irony of the situation. The ice in the cooler had all turned to water, and the last dozen bottles of what started out as a case the week before floated and clinked together like glass buoys in a miniature ocean.

It was the beer that sent Ellen to town. She was to get ice and do a little tourist shopping. Sure, the fridge in her parents' Winnebago worked, but it was still stuffed with food, even after a week. She always brought enough to survive a month after a nuclear disaster.

The case of Corona for eight bucks was irresistible, and essential for relaxing in the warm sun of late October. Fortunately, the drinking hadn't ever gotten quite bad enough to

 2

Sacrifice

"Home again. Home again," I said as my two-year-old ran to me from the jeep, repeating one of her favorite nursery rhymes. Susie was twenty-five pounds of blond hair, blue eyes, and wonder in a pink T-shirt, diaper, and lots of sunscreen.

"No, Daddy," she frowned and pointed her finger at me. "*This* is not home. We live on Wa nut Pace."

"That's right," I said excitedly, pulling her up into my arms. "We do live on Walnut Place. What'd you and Mommy buy in town?"

"Mommy ... Mommy got ice. They didn't have any woons."

"No balloons? Well, we'll get one back in the States."

"Daddy?" she said as I put her down.

"What, sweetheart?"

"I have a poop."

"Yes." I wrinkled my nose. "So I smell. Let's get you changed."

I reached for her hand and took it in mine. Off we went to the motor home for a diaper. Afterward she climbed down the steps and marched over to Ellen.

"Mommy, Mommy. Daddy smells funny."

"I know," Ellen said with a frown. "He's been drinking again."

As I came down the steps, Susie turned to me and pointed. "Daddy, *you've* been drinking again."

"I know, sweetie." I turned and glared at Ellen. She was sitting in a lawn chair under the palm leaf umbrella, still wearing her electric green one-piece swimsuit, and a gold cross and necklace. "What's for lunch?"

She put her long slender legs on the edge of the card table, pushing a box of camping stuff aside with her feet. She brushed a strand of her short blond hair from her face, rubbed the ridge of her small freckled nose, checked her nails, and started in on me.

"Well," she said sarcastically, "you're probably not hungry now anyway. How many *cervezas* did you have?"

"Only two," I defended, looking at the waves lapping the shore, higher with every motion. "You shouldn't have been gone so long."

"I swear, Jack," Ellen scoffed, "I can't leave you alone for an hour ... Look," she added, watching me sit on the rock wall with my back to her, "I know you're on vacation, and not driving anywhere, but ..." She walked over and put her arms around me. "I just want you to eat something if I cook it."

Our Labrador had gotten jealous and dashed over to me for some petting. I stroked Maggie's short, yellow coat. Her tongue fell out of her mouth in warm satisfaction. Susie joined me on the wall, mimicking my pose of looking out to sea.

"You see how she copies you," Ellen said, not mad, but firmly in my ear. "You don't want her ..."

"El," I interrupted, "I'll throw all the beer in the trash if it'll make you happy. I just can't talk about this anymore. Not since ... Look, I'm burned out on the subject. I *know* it's a disease, all right? I know what happened to Dad. I'll throw all of it out right now if you want."

"Not if you're going to buy another case tomorrow. It's got to be a clean break, once and for all."

I grabbed her hands around my neck. "Cheeseburgers," I ordered. "Potato chips and all."

"Cheez burgers!" screamed Susie. "With Sesame Street buns."

"With sesame seed buns," I agreed, kissing Ellen's slender wrists. "I'll get the soda."

"I don't like soda," Susie said, frowning. "I want juice."

"Apple," I answered, tossing a sandy tennis ball for Maggie. She tore after it as if it was treasure. Ellen got up without saying a word and headed for the Winnebago. I didn't have to turn around. I could feel her smile.

"Mommy! Mommy!" Susie shouted, running after her. "I want ... I want to get the Sesame Street buns. Wait, Mommy! I want to help!"

I got up and walked to the cooler on the other side of the motor home. With great determination, I grabbed all the beer bottles and set them on the wall. Feeling like an ancient Aztec priest making a blood sacrifice, I carefully popped the top off of one and ritualistically held it up to the sun overhead.

Then, in grand fashion, I slowly turned the bottle over and offered the precious liquid to the Earth. When I finished emptying all of the Coronas into the sand, I stuffed the bottles in their cardboard box to be returned for deposit.

I felt good, proud of my little gesture. I would try it once again—go dry. It would be sparkling water and soda the rest of the week. Heck, they even had Diet Pepsi in town now. It wouldn't be easy, but I made a decision then and there to try harder to hold on to the family, before I blew it once and for all. Letting Ellen go would've been tough. Susie would have been impossible. Shoot, I didn't even want to give up Maggie.

Scooting the case of empties under the motor home, I could hear Susie say from inside, "Mommy, Daddy poured out the beer. He won't smell funny anymore."

"I know," Ellen said. "Daddy only smells funny when he drinks. Let's just hope . . ." I heard the fridge open. "Here, Susie. Go take Daddy a soda."

"Okay," Susie answered. "*I'll* take Daddy a soda."

When Susie got to me she shoved the Diet Slice my way. "Hee er, Daddy, drink this. *You* won't smell funny anymore."

I picked her up, smoothed her short, fine hair, and kissed her cheek. Setting her down, I whispered in her ear. "Okay, sweetheart. Tell Mommy I have a secret. Tell her Daddy found something in the ocean today. Tell her I think it's buried treasure. Can you remember that?"

"Yes. You found something in . . . in the ocean."

"And what was it?"

"*Bear reed trez were.*"

"Good girl." I beamed with pride at her grasp of the language. She turned away when I tried to kiss her again. I grabbed my toothbrush from the glass on the card table and walked to the shower at the far end of the campground. Susie was climbing the motor home steps, repeating *Bear reed trez were* to herself.

The ocean was still climbing up the beach, pushing my find farther underwater, and putting my daydreams to an end, while an unexpected afternoon was about to begin.

 3

Shell Game

Over burgers and buns, sodas and chips, we talked of family, vacations, and such. Ellen never mentioned what Susie must have told her. I was sure she got the message. As good as we had gotten at understanding two-year-old talk, there was no question of interpretation. That only left the likelihood of Ellen's style in such matters.

She loved to underplay this sort of thing. Got it from her

dad, the actuary, and her mom, the IRS agent. The family approach had always been black suit mortuary to all questionable reports of instant wealth. Money was made only through long protracted efforts, preferably behind a desk. Instant wealth, such as winning the lottery or wild stock speculation, was to be avoided at all costs. The Protestant work ethic was alive and prospered in her family, especially since the eighties had come and gone with the stain of shame on the stock market. So the source of Ellen's demeanor in such matters was well established. Attitude may not be inherited, but it can certainly be learned.

My dad, in direct contrast, had been a jazz trumpeter before his liver gave out from the booze. His avant-garde style reminded me of Miles Davis—brilliant, but barely understandable for the pop music set. Doc Hansen's style was considered by the experts to be expressive, sometimes to the point of excess.

I barely knew my mom. Lung cancer took her when I was four. Dad raised me alone after that, and never got over Mom's death. The cigarettes took her; the bottle took him.

As a physical kid, I took up wrestling to deal with my family problems in some outward way. I was even a bouncer at the club where my dad played in LA before my pursuit of a business degree at Cal State. College was where I met Ellen.

Six years into the marriage brought us to Baja for our annual family vacation, this time without her parents. Her dad was recovering from prostate surgery that October.

"Daddy found *bear reed trez were*," Susie said over brownies for dessert.

"I know," Ellen answered, nonplussed, then turned to me across the table inside the Winnebago. "So, what's this *buried treasure* you've been telling her about?"

"Oh," I shrugged. "It's probably nothing, really. Just some big shell in the sand out there."

Her expression changed. She stopped chewing and swallowed her brownie, then chased it with her usual glass of nonfat milk.

"How far out and how big?" she asked.

"Quarter mile. That's my guess. Straight out. It looked

like the ridge of one of those giant clams you see in B
movies about sunken treasure. I could only see the top. It
was underwater and the tide was coming in.''

"So," she added nonchalantly, cleaning brownie off Susie's face. "You going to be able to find it again?"

"Sure, I marked the spot with a tent pole."

"Tent pole? Great. Now we'll probably have to buy my
parents another one."

"Sea's not that rough right now. It'll still be there this
afternoon."

She got up and took the dishes to the sink.

"This ... shell," she said coolly. "Was it open or
closed?"

"Closed, tighter than an actuary's books." I turned in my
seat and looked at her over my shoulder. "Ellen, it's big. I
know it. And it's got something inside it. I can feel it."

"Who made you psychic of the week?"

"Okay, so I don't feel it. So what? Even if it's empty,
it'll still make a great shell for our collection."

"If it's not all broken up. Look, when you buried the
tent pole, are you sure you didn't drive it into the shell and
break it?"

"I don't know. It was under two feet of water by then."

Ellen shut off the faucet and put her hands on her hips.
"Was this before or after the *cervezas*?"

"Ellen, that's not fair and you know it. But if you must
know, I was sober at the time."

"The tide will be out this afternoon," she said, wiping her
hands on a dishtowel. "We can go look then."

"Yeah, I just hope it's where I marked it."

"Yeah," she mimicked me, "I just hope the tent pole's
there."

4

Invisible Touch

The afternoon was heavy with waiting and hot wind. We spent a lot of time slow-tanning beneath layers of sunscreen before an onshore breeze pummeled us with heat and sand. We took to the water to cool off and clean the sand off the sticky parts of our bodies.

When it came to sun protection, I never needed as much as Ellen or Susie—the fair-skinned set. I already had a little bit of olive tint to my skin. They were white as washing machines. My hair was bushy and black, as were my eyebrows, chest, and mustache, though a few strands on my chest were beginning to show the transformation to gray. My high school yearbook said I had the rugged good looks of an outdoorsman crossed with a soap opera star—whatever that meant.

Ellen and I had met on the track at Cal State, where my wrestling scholarship got me in, despite mediocre grades. I had been doing laps as part of my workout when I was passed by a serious set of legs attached to a good-looking coed. I took off after her like she had stolen my wallet. It shocked me when she beat me to the finish line. When she finally slowed down I grabbed her arm to congratulate her. Still catching my breath, I asked where she learned to run like that.

"I thought you were chasing me," she said, exhaling, and we laughed about it.

We started out together running on that track. And though we may not have been Olympic running material, we both had athletic scholarships that got us through college, and we ended up walking down the aisle together.

Ten years later Susie came into our lives, just when we had almost given up on having children of our own. I didn't think much about it when Ellen got some fertility pills from the doctor, but I'll never forget that morning she came to the table with mist in her eyes. When she said she was pregnant, I cried for ten minutes. We were finally getting our turn at parenting. That was three and a half years and a lifetime ago.

Later that afternoon in Baja we filled the hole of anticipation with bouts of swimming. That was before the stings started.

We were splashing about and tossing in the waves close to shore when the water grew suddenly warm and green. A strange current had drifted in from somewhere. To the east storm clouds gathered across the gulf, while we enjoyed the rush of warm water.

Maggie had been paddling next to me and suddenly yelped. A minute later Ellen and Susie had both screamed and scrambled to shore.

By the time Maggie and I joined them, Ellen had a line of pink welts on her arm that looked like instant poison oak. Susie's were on her leg. Maggie had the same thing on her hairless belly. Something was out there.

Ellen carried Susie to the motor home for some lotion while I stayed at the shore, studying the water. Visibility was pretty good for about ten feet, but the wind was getting stronger and stirring up the bottom. Maggie began to bark.

I kept waiting for the theme from *Jaws* to start playing, but there was only the rushing wind and crashing waves. They broke up into whitecaps, smashing hard on the rocks and shells that lay strewn along the shore.

Scouring the water for my foe proved futile, so I turned to leave. The wind picked up harder, flinging the clothes off the makeshift clothesline we had erected between the Cristo-sized palm leaf umbrellas that marked the campsites.

Halfway up the slope I turned and called to Maggie. She wouldn't leave the beach. She stood her ground along the waterline and barked at the ocean. Slowly, I made my way down the gentle slope to the spot where she planted herself. The barking didn't stop until I reached her side. Searching the water again revealed nothing. It was choppier than ever, breaking wildly on the sand and lashing at my feet.

I grabbed Maggie's chain collar and got ready to drag her away, but she still wouldn't budge. "Come on, girl," I ordered, pulling at her chain. "It's only the ocean. Whatever was out there is gone. Let's go."

She refused to move, and began to whine. I reached down and picked her up—eighty pounds and all—and started up the bank. That was when she growled at me. She never did that, even when I took chicken bones away from her. Then she did the impossible: she nipped my arm.

It startled me so much that I dropped her. She ran back to her spot. I gave the ocean one last look, rubbing my arm and following Maggie's intense stare into the surf.

Ten feet offshore, in a patch of warm, green water, floated what looked like a transparent baseball threaded with a thin line of purple. It pushed part of itself out the back, pulled it in, and pulsated forward, towing foot-long purple strands behind it.

I ran to the motor home and checked on Ellen and Susie. They were fine, considering the welts. The pink lines of blisters had turned darker, but weren't getting worse. Susie was a trouper, barely complaining. Ellen never said a word.

Quickly describing what was in the ocean, I grabbed a blue plastic bucket and dashed back to the shore. Maggie had moved down the beach, following the course of the intruder.

I waded into the water, dodged a couple of waves, and with a quick motion scooped my prey into the bucket, then carried it back up the hill. This time Maggie came with me.

Setting the bucket in the sun, I studied the little sea monster and then climbed into the motor home. Ellen was gently rubbing another layer of ointment on Susie's leg. I motioned for them to come.

Once outside, Ellen held Susie in her arms and looked down. "What is it?" she asked.

"That," I said, watching it pulsate against the side of the bucket, "is a jellyfish."

"*Yellyfish*," Susie repeated. "I want down. I want to see it."

Ellen set Susie down, warning her not to put her hands in the water, then looked at me. I stared at the eight-inch welt on her arm.

"I didn't know they had jellyfish in these waters," she said.

"They don't usually," I answered. "But from what I read in one of those tourist magazines, it happens sometimes." I looked out to sea. The dark clouds across the gulf were moving north. "The storm must have swept them in ... Maybe they're the guardians of some secret treasure," I added in a fake dramatic tone.

"I think you swallowed too much salt water out there ... Well, at least now we can have peanut butter and jellyfish sandwiches," she added, making light of the situation.

"Oh boy," Susie said, and talked about it the rest of the day.

By the time the tide finally went out again, all signs of the storm had vanished, including the wind. It grew as calm and quiet as a public library.

I went off to take a shower in the tiny block bathhouse about six o'clock. The cool water spurting from a bare plastic pipe overhead felt good and washed off the itchy salt water. I was just coming out to resume the search for my treasure when something caught my eye as it raced across the muddy sand a good quarter mile out. A dune buggy was heading straight for the spot where the tent pole was planted.

 5

Making Tracks

I was too far away to do anything but yell, and even that would have been faint and distant. All I could do was stand by helplessly as the bloodred dune buggy screamed across the wet sand.

From the campsite, the tent pole looked needle-thin, sticking out of the sand. Then I lost it completely as the sun sank behind the rocky mountains in back of me.

Quickly grabbing some binoculars from the motor home, I watched as the dune buggy roared straight ahead, shooting sheets of water skyward with its big knobby tires.

The driver was dark haired and deeply tanned, massed with

muscles, and wearing only a pair of cutoffs. His long, thick black hair blew behind him like a horse's mane. I couldn't make out his features very well, but he almost looked like an Indian brave—young, powerful, and fearless.

Suddenly, he slowed and stopped behind the tent pole. Then, without getting out of the dune buggy, he grabbed hold of the pole, stepped on the gas, and let the acceleration pull it out of the sand.

I didn't move, figuring his dune buggy tracks would mark the distance from the beach, and knowing the pole had been planted directly in line with the campsite. I should be able to use the Winnebago and buggy tracks to put the spot in my imaginary cross hairs.

Ellen came out of the motor home and stood next to me.

"What's he doing?" she asked. "That's Dad's tent pole . . . Hey!" she shouted. "Bring that back!"

The driver looked over at us as he pulled away. Then, seeing my binoculars focused on him, he turned the wheel and began to circle back.

"Good," Ellen said, making a sun visor with her hands. "He heard me."

The Indian crossed over the spot where the pole had been planted and began to make random reckless turns, squirting up sand and water with his tires and waving the tent pole over his head like a spear. He kept circling, grinding an irregular pattern into the soft sand and shallow puddles. Then he began to widen the pattern, spinning and cutting in great arcs.

"Come on," I said at last. "He's trying to blot out his tracks."

"But he's making more," Ellen said, confused.

"Exactly," I replied, running down the hill with the binoculars in my hand. "He's hoping we won't find the exact spot I marked." As Ellen caught up I added, "By the time he's finished, we'll only have a sand bog out there—unless he hits something with one of those tires."

"Why would he do this?" she asked. "Does he know about the shell?"

"I don't know," I answered, hitting the wide, flat moonscape of wet sand. "He must have been watching me from somewhere."

"But how would he know what's out there?"

"Probably figures I drove the tent pole in for some reason. I'll bet he thinks we'll give up looking in a couple of days and just go home. Then, he'll come back and dig it up. A big shell could bring a lot of pesos in town, even with nothing in it."

A hundred feet out the sand got muddy. We sank to our knees with each step in some of the softer spots. The dune buggy kept spinning.

"Nothing doing," Ellen said, watching him make one last turn and speed away. "That's our tent pole. I'm not going back without it."

I lifted my binoculars and watched as the roaring red machine disappeared down the beach. It was pretty well splattered with muddy sand, but I could read small white letters painted on the rear fender: BAJA BUGGIES.

When we got to the erratic pattern of tire tracks, it looked like an impossible task to sort out the set we needed, but I wasn't through yet. I began to walk south in the direction from which he had come.

"Where are you going?" Ellen asked, now petting a very muddy Maggie at her side. "He went the other direction."

"Yes," I answered, undaunted. "But if we get to the edge of this mess, we'll find the original tracks he made coming in. Then we can follow a parallel line until we get in front of the Winnebago. That's where we'll start digging."

I turned around and looked at her, and then at the tip of the sun as it sank below the mountains. "But we'd better hurry. It'll be dark soon, and in less than six hours the tide will be in again."

"And if we don't find it by then?" she asked, shielding her eyes from the last of the sun's rays.

"We can always use a lantern tonight before the tide comes in," I suggested. "Besides, we've still got another tent pole to mark the spot."

"Nothing doing," she said angrily. "We're not going to leave *another* one for him to steal."

"All right." I shrugged. "I'll find an old two-by-four behind one of those empty tourist houses along the beach. Or we can always count our steps."

"Jack," she said, trying to keep Maggie down. "If we

don't find it tonight, promise me you won't spend all day tomorrow digging out here. It'll be our last day, remember? I want us to enjoy it—together. You said you wanted to go into town before we left to finish buying souvenirs, and I want to check out that resort south of town for my parents." She gave me a concerned look. "Besides, look how red your forehead's getting. You could use another hat."

"What's gotten into you all of a sudden?" I asked, studying the tire tracks.

"It's . . . I don't think it's safe anymore camping on the beach down here. Especially . . ." She looked at the wild pattern like it was something out of *Chariots of the Gods*. "Especially after *this* . . . I'm sorry," she added, trudging back toward camp, "but I just don't think it's safe."

"You mean for Susie," I agreed. "Okay, so we don't have a gun in the motor home, but at least we've got . . ." I looked at Maggie, panting and playing in the muddy sand. "Never mind," I added, shaking my head. "You're probably right. I'll make you a deal. If we don't find my shell tonight, I'll forget all about it." I glanced back at the camp. "And speaking of forgetting . . ."

"Oh, my God," Ellen said, slogging faster toward camp. "See what you made me do? I forgot all about Susie. What if that maniac circles back while we're out here and . . ."

"Ellen!" I yelled to her back, now twenty yards ahead. "I knew we shouldn't have rented *Cape Fear*. Now everything makes you paranoid."

"Somebody's got to act sane around here," she shouted, not looking back. She picked up speed on a harder patch of sand. Suddenly she screamed, "Look! Somebody's got her!"

Shielding the last rays of sunlight with my hands, I glanced toward the campsite and saw the familiar old straw hat and tall, lean figure of Mr. Zapata. He stood on the low rock wall, holding Susie in his arms.

"It's only Zapata!" I yelled, but Ellen raced on, having nowhere near my twenty-twenty vision and having left her prescription sunglasses in camp.

"It's Zapata!" I repeated, but she and Maggie were fifty yards ahead now. Only her own eyes from close range would convince her. I squished on behind, carefully counting my steps, knowing I was on my own in the clam dig now.

Once back at camp, Ellen was holding Susie like she had just been returned by a police officer after being lost at the mall. I was about to grab the shovel when the look on Mr. Zapata's face stopped me cold. It was not the unstressed happy smile he sported most of the time, despite his dirt-poor condition. His expression was deadly serious, and he had something to say.

 6

Montezuma's Pearl

"*Malo*," Mr. Zapata spit out, pointing with a bony crooked finger at Susie's welts. "This is a very bad sign."

"Ah," I answered, waving him off. "That's just a jelly-fish sting."

Mr. Zapata stared toward the spot where the mess of tire tracks had dug up the beach.

"Oh that," I said. "Nothing to worry about. Just some local looking for buried treasure. He won't be back. But if he does come . . ." I waved my shovel. "He'll be too late. I'm going out to dig up that shell, or whatever it is."

"This . . . shell," he said gravely. "Is it *muy grande*?"

I nodded and sat on the wall, then put on my work boots for digging.

He moved in front of me and motioned with his hands. "She is curved?"

"Yep," I replied, tying one of the boots. "Sure is."

He bent down and gently squeezed my shoulder, then sat down on the wall next to me. "There is a legend," he began. "It has been passed down for hundreds of *años*."

"Look," I said quickly, starting to get up. "Tell me after dinner. I've got a shell to find."

"No," he said gruffly, and forced me back down with his

hand. I was surprised by his remarkable strength. He had to be at least seventy, and was bone-thin, with skinny legs and arms. His hands seemed to have their own strength, at least for the moment. I couldn't have gotten up without knocking him over, so I decided to let him talk.

"Listen first," he went on, motioning for Ellen and Susie to take a seat on a nearby beach chair. "Then you can do what you like. But it is my duty to tell the legend. And yours, *amigo*, to listen."

Ellen had a concerned look on her face. She sat down in the beach chair, guarding Susie with her arms. Maggie curled up on the sand at Mr. Zapata's feet. The sun was gone for the night. Overhead, about in line with my treasure, a single star was emerging against the violet sky. Mr. Zapata took a deep breath and started his story.

"I have lived on this beach all my life, and my father's father before him. When I was little, my grandfather would point to that star—the first of the night—and tell me the legend.

"It started centuries ago, when Aztecs walked the Earth. It was a time of magic and mystery. The world was ruled by priests, magicians, and sorcerers. They predicted battles, disease, famine, and times of plenty.

"It is said that the greatest of them all was Montuca. He was son of a great sorcerer and high priest to Montezuma himself. In all the kingdom, Montuca was the only one who could move the gods and goddesses of nature. The sun and wind gods were his servants, and the goddess of rain bowed to him. He even ruled over the greatest of all, the Earth goddess. The Aztecs prospered by his hand. They thought their kingdom would stand forever.

"Then there came out of the east a white god. He came in ships and brought men in helmets on horseback. They carried invisible spears of fire. This new god was welcomed into the kingdom as the great savior of mankind descended from heaven. But he turned out to be a false god."

Zapata told us that according to Aztec law, only Montezuma and Montuca were allowed to know the holiest and most secret powers. But Montezuma thought Cortés was a god straight from heaven. In order to gain the favor of this

new god, he took Cortés to the sacred temple, where he
ordered Montuca to demonstrate his power over the elements.
That was Montezuma's fatal error. He showed Cortés the
magic.

Montuca did not want to do it, knowing the magic was
a sacred gift from nature and must not be shown to anyone.
He did not believe Cortés was the savior of the Aztecs,
and feared that he would steal the magic and use it for his
own gain. But as Montezuma's priest, and servant of the
people, he brought the wind and the rain to the temple that
very night.

Cortés was overwhelmed and intoxicated by the power of
the magic contained in the most sacred idol in all of the
kingdom—so powerful that whenever its name was mentioned, it was always in whispered tones. It was known as
the Eyes of God. Cortés wanted it for himself. For with it,
he knew he could rule the world.

He left that night with a plan—to capture the magic for
himself. He would place Montezuma under arrest, using false
charges, appoint himself ruler of the kingdom, and make
Montuca succumb to his will, using the magic for his own
ends.

The next day Montezuma was imprisoned, and Montuca
ordered to show Cortés how to work the magic. Montuca
stalled, saying the moon must be new to hand over such a
secret. That was two weeks away.

While Cortés waited, Montuca conspired with his closest
aides to escape with the magic. But one of them turned him
in, seeking the favor of the new god. Montezuma was executed to secure complete power for Cortés.

Soldiers returned to the temple fourteen days later to take
the magic, fighting resisters along the way. Everyone at the
temple was killed, except Montuca. He was wounded, but
escaped on Cortés's horse, taking the Eyes of God with him.
He was to hide it until the Aztecs could rise against Cortés
and regain their kingdom.

Mr. Zapata lifted his hand and pointed across the gulf.
"The legend says," he continued, "that Montuca made it to
the north, close to where the shore comes around to the Baja
side. He rowed a boat across, almost making it ashore. But

Cortés's men were in pursuit and caught him in the water. As the invisible spears of fire entered his heart, he gave the magic to the sea.

"The legend says a giant shell, placed there by the mother of nature, opened to accept the magic. To many, she was the most powerful of all gods and goddesses—even more powerful than the sun god. For she is at work even while he sleeps, and it was she who gave the magic to the Aztecs.

"The shell was never found, but the legend says that the time will come when a descendant of Montuca will discover the magic. And with it he, or she, perhaps, can rule the elements if they so choose. And in so doing, rule the world."

"That guy in the dune buggy," I said after a long powerful silence, "looked like a native Indian."

"No," Mr. Zapata said forcefully, waving me off. "You are the one who found the shell."

"But I'm not Aztec," I objected. "And how do you know it's the right shell? No offense, but I've never heard of this legend of yours. The history books don't say anything about it, as far as I know."

"History," he said, still looking out to sea, "is always written by those in power. The rest is considered to be only tall tales. But the legend survives the historians. It is said that written records were destroyed by Cortés himself to protect the magic until his men found it and returned it to him. But he died with the secret, as did Montuca. It is said that on certain nights Montuca's ghost has been seen walking the shores of Baja, looking for the magic he left in the sea so long ago."

"Sounds like a ghost story to me," I laughed. "How can you be so sure that what's buried out there isn't just another giant clamshell?"

"Such creatures of the sea are never found in these waters," he assured me. "They exist only in the reefs of the great oceans. They cannot live in these shallow, sandy waters, and certainly not so close to shore. Only the mother of nature could have placed it there."

He turned and stared me straight in the eyes. "The shell, and the magic in the Eyes of God, are meant for you, and you alone. You must not let anyone steal it. You must protect the heritage of our people.''

''I told you I'm not Aztec.''

''How do you know? Have you done your . . . family tree, as you say?''

''No, I haven't. But I'm sure that—''

''When you return to your country, I am certain you will find Aztec blood in you. The legend does not lie.''

''How can you be sure it's not just a shell fragment? Or even if it isn't, that what you talk about is inside?''

Ellen laughed suddenly. ''Jack, *you're* the dreamer. Dig up the darned shell. Then, we'll see.''

''But I thought you said . . .''

''Noon tomorrow,'' she winked, looking at both of us. ''If you don't make the legend come true by then, we leave with or without Montezuma's Pearl.''

''You make fun,'' Mr. Zapata said somberly, pointing at Ellen. ''Because you are afraid of the truth, the power. But ask yourself how you knew the name of a sacred object known only through Aztec legend.''

''Ah, I probably heard it in town somewhere.'' She shrugged. ''Wait a minute. Didn't you just say it was called the Eyes of God?''

''The Eyes of God lie within Montezuma's Pearl,'' Mr. Zapata answered, slowly getting to his feet. ''That is all I can tell you.''

''Then let's get started,'' I said, standing up with my shovel and heading down the hill.

Mr. Zapata grabbed my arm. ''As with all treasures,'' he said gravely, ''it comes with a warning and a curse. The warning is the stinging fish.''

''And the curse?'' I asked, not really interested, but wanting to get started.

''Power,'' he said, ''as always. Once you get it, you may not be able to give it up, even if you want to.''

''Maybe,'' I answered, joking. ''But right now I'd settle for a pearl just big enough to open a hardware store.''

I turned and headed for the beach, forgetting that I'd need a source of light to find the spot. But since I had counted my steps, it didn't figure to take all that long. As soon as I uncovered the shell, I'd drive the jeep out, hook up the winch attached to the front, and pull it out of the sand. What could have been simpler?

 7

Motorboat

I made my way out to the confusion of tire tracks and marked my line, then started digging. Naturally, I was knee-deep in wet sand by the time it got dark. Ellen took pity on me and trudged out with the Coleman lantern, swinging it in one hand and carrying Susie on her opposite hip.

The lantern was aided by about a billion stars overhead. They crowded in close to watch me dig, which I did in an ever-widening pattern down a foot deep. When fatigue and disappointment began to overtake me, I resorted to stabbing the sand with my pointed shovel to see if I could hit anything solid. I didn't, even after several hours. Too stubborn to quit, I dug on until the tide came in around midnight, even though it had seemed hopeless by ten.

Ellen and Susie had retired to the motor home at nine, so I dug the last three hours with Maggie, who lay beside me when she got tired of helping me scoop up sand with her paws.

Feeling more relieved than disappointed when the tide finally swept over my feet, I came in, not even bothering to mark the spot. Besides, I had unearthed an Olympic swimming pool–sized sand pit, and stabbed another area the size of a football stadium. It just wasn't out there.

I marched off to the shower and rinsed myself and Maggie off, knowing we had at least given it the old college try. It shouldn't have been too surprising that Maggie and I didn't find anything. The ocean moved so much sand around on a daily basis that it could easily hide a shell buried up to its flutes.

Too tired to think about it further, I looked in on Susie, snuggled up for the night on the sofa. She had a firm grip on her embroidered bear blanket, and a pacifier plugged into her little round mouth.

I crawled into bed and collapsed next to Ellen, shoving Maggie to the foot in the process. Just before I dozed off for the night, something caught my eye out of the bedroom window.

A star shot across the night sky with incredible speed, leaving only a faint light-echo of itself for a second. I thought about Andy Warhol saying that in the future everyone would be famous for fifteen minutes. Well, these flaming streaks were noticed for less than a second. For all of their speed and light, they were no more than a moment's entertainment to us.

Finally, I slept, and drifted into a dream. Some kind of ancient Aztec priest was running. The heat of the midday sun burned overhead, and a round object was bundled tightly in his arms. Blood dripped from a deep wound to his shoulder.

A lead ball from a musket had caught him in the left shoulder, tearing a hole clean through it. His servant had wrapped the wound with cloth before being executed with the others. All lay bleeding out life on the temple floor, except for Montuca, high priest to Montezuma.

When the tall Spaniard who fired at him stopped to reload, Montuca saw his only chance. He grabbed the most sacred idol in all of the Aztec kingdom from its pedestal and slipped out the back of the temple. Using the secret passage, he fled on foot, the heavy round object wrapped in cloth under his arm.

As he ran for the far exit to an ancient city, the sinking weight of the heavy bundle wore down his strength. I could hear his thoughts as clearly as if I were there.

If I can just make it past the last gate, he thought, *I will be safe from the invisible spears of fire. I must protect the magic from the powerful, pale warriors. Yet even with their helmets and chest armor, they too are only human.*

I could feel the pain in his shoulder deepen. He could only

bear it if he carried the magic in his right arm. Despite his youth, he didn't feel young anymore. Age had arrived too soon after the invaders.

Approaching a row of adobe huts halfway from the temple, he stopped and leaned against the mud wall of a dwelling and listened to the battle behind him. He never got used to the thunder of the fire spears the intruders carried, and winced as gunpowder exploded in the distance.

The pain had caught up with him. Suddenly he grew dizzy, and his head began to spin. The world became a blur.

A moment later I jolted awake. Hours had passed. The first hint of light was just beginning to paint the eastern horizon. Maggie was scratching at the door, wanting out.

She almost broke through the screen door before I got there, and started whining very loudly. Getting up, I tried to shake off the sleepiness as my hand turned the doorknob.

"Shhh, Maggie," I whispered. "You'll wake the baby." But she couldn't control herself, and flew out of the door as soon as I flung it open. She was down the steps instantly, bolting for the beach.

Wiping sleep from my eyes, I realized that it was still night—five in the morning, according to the clock over the oven. It was cool and dark outside, but the darkness was softened by a sea of stars overhead, though the moon was new.

I climbed down the steps and looked toward the beach. The tide was well on its way out, and a faint light was just beginning to glow slightly on the horizon, signaling the coming dawn.

Maggie disappeared in the near darkness. But something along the horizon caught my eye. A bright light flickered in the distance. It was much too low in the sky to be a star, and much too close to be one of the all-night shrimp boats that worked the gulf ten miles out.

A shadow moved against the light as Maggie charged it at full speed, barking into the night. She dashed to one side to avoid a large puddle, and when she did a shadowy figure moved behind the bright light. Someone was out there.

Running for the beach, I could see that whoever it was

had come by sea. A small outboard bobbed in the distance, just offshore.

The dark intruder quickly grabbed a shovel and rope, doused the lantern, and ran. Maggie was only a hundred yards from him, and gaining fast. The man reached the water, wading frantically. Maggie was swimming after him, suddenly only twenty yards behind. The small, skinny man was wearing one of those safari hats, with a shirt and shorts to match. Despite being weighed down by the gear he was lugging, he made it to the boat. He tossed everything in and climbed over the side, making the boat bob and barely beating a swimming Maggie.

I was only fifty yards away when he reached over and pulled the cord to the outboard. It wouldn't start.

Sensing what was about to happen, I yelled for Maggie, who was swimming next to the boat, barking and scratching at the side, trying to climb aboard. But it was too late. The small, thin figure outlined against the coming hint of daylight had given up on the outboard motor for the moment and was digging around in the boat. Suddenly, with a sure move, he came up with a pistol.

Maggie was still at it, scratching the wooden sides of the boat and barking loudly enough to shatter glass.

"Maggie! Maggie!" I shouted with all my strength, trying to save her. Luckily, she turned and swam back to shore. The man wasn't finished. He fired a few rounds at her, making small hard splashes in the water where the bullets hit and sank.

The intruder put the gun away and went back to the pull cord, firing up the engine in a couple of tries. He adjusted the throttle and slowly lowered the whirling blades into the water, moving swiftly away into the coming dawn. Moments later he was out of sight, speeding away at a pretty good clip.

Maggie had reached the shore, and came trotting back as if she had just chased a seagull off the beach. She was wet, panting, and happy. I shook my head and went back to camp, followed by the glowing light of the rising sun.

I glanced quickly at the spot where the man had been digging. It looked exactly like the spot where the tent pole had been, but it was hard to tell. Whatever the man had been exploring had been submerged by a pond that had been formed by the receding tide. All traces of my work had washed away, nature smoothing over the sand I had so ferociously dug up.

Once back at camp, I rinsed the sand off of me and Maggie again and headed back to bed. Luckily, Susie had slept through the whole thing. The motorboat and gunshots had been far enough away so that she didn't get startled in her sleep. The same wasn't true for Ellen, who always slept a mother's sleep—one ear open for the cry or whimper of a waking or restless child.

"What was *that* all about?" she asked, her voice sleepy and muffled by her pillow. "Sounded like some boat out there. And those loud bangs! I thought they were going to wake Susie."

"Go back to sleep," I suggested, deciding to watch the sunrise instead of climbing into bed. "Just some fishing boat run aground. I went out to help, but he got it in the water and took off."

"And those loud bangs?"

"His engine backfired a couple of times when he turned it over. They never keep those things tuned-up down here. Can't afford to, I guess . . . He's gone now," I added, turning to leave. "Get some sleep. The sun will be up in an hour or so."

She didn't say another word, and was soon making sleeping sounds again. I was glad she didn't press me for any more answers. It only would have upset her if she knew someone else was after our treasure. But who? And how can news travel so fast in a part of the world that is virtually devoid of mass media? Maybe he was working with the Indian I had encountered earlier. But if that were true, why did he come alone? And how did he find it? Don't tell me someone else saw me digging up the beach? Actually, that was possible. Anyone having a lantern out as far as I had could be seen for miles. In fact, when I was out digging earlier, several dune buggies had raced past on the beach, but always close to shore.

Anyone seen digging out there could only be thought of as a clammer. There were plenty of those up and down the beach. The year before, Ellen and I had dug up a couple of dozen and she had made clam chowder. But all of them were small—some no bigger than a baby's hand. Mr. Zapata was surely right. These murky shallow waters were not suitable for giant clams.

Even if it looked like I was a clam digger, no one should have known I was after a big one. But now there seemed to be at least three people who did know: Mr. Zapata, who shouldn't have told a soul; some muscle-bound Indian in a dune buggy, unless he was just drunk or horsing around; and some skinny guy in a safari hat.

I finally gave up thinking about it and watched the sun come up, letting the warmth and light wash over me like a shower. It gave me strength. I was, however, mentally burned out on digging for treasure. Whatever was out there could stay put as far as I was concerned. There were just too many people looking for it, and at least one of them had a gun. I wasn't prepared to deal with that.

It was a good day to be our last day in Baja. We would go into town and buy the last cheap souvenirs, including a hat to replace the one that flew off my head on the highway. We could even check out that resort for Ellen's parents, and start packing that afternoon for the drive back the next day.

It all seemed routine enough, like a normal way to end a vacation. But later that morning I was to learn a lot more about vacations. How they come and go, and how they end.

 8

Vaca Cion

Vacations are good for sky watching, and this one was no exception. It was cool at sunrise in late October, so I bundled up in a sweat suit and watched the rays creep over the horizon until the big yellow ball hit the sky full on. Afterward, as the troops began to spring to life, I made some Taster's Choice on the Coleman to warm up my insides.

As soon as the hot water hit the coffee crystals, Maggie was out of the motor home and on top of me, knocking a dog-sized hole in the screen door in the process.

I just stood there and stared at the hole, knowing a new screen door would be added to our shopping list when we returned stateside to the suburbs of LA, unless Ellen would let me get away with a patch job. Her parents would have picked up the tab with only a few questions asked, but we didn't like owing them money. We even paid back the down payment they loaned us for the house as soon as we were able to refinance.

That was when Ellen was working. She had been laid off from the accounting firm for months, and still couldn't find a job, even in accounts payable. Things were tough in the nineties, so we had to adjust. It was hard on us because Ellen's paycheck had gone for the mortgage on our three-bedroom tract house. But now her unemployment was only a fraction of that, so we borrowed from my unimpressive salary to make ends meet.

We were surviving, but saving was out of the question. It hurt because we were both nuts for paying off credit cards immediately and having no bills other than were absolutely necessary. If I hadn't put a new roof on the house myself, we would've been in deep dog stuff.

I credit Ellen for being the financial analyst in the family, despite my business degree. She was the one who got me out of debt before we married. For that, and Susie, I was most grateful.

At the sound of the crash through the screen door, Ellen got out of bed and stood over the gaping hole Maggie had made.

"Great!" she said. "A new screen door is going to cost a fortune. Now *all* the bugs can come in."

"El," I said, trying to smooth out the situation, "there aren't that many bugs down here, unless you count the red ants. Besides, I've got a roll of screen in the garage at home. All you do is cut out a piece and stick it in. Pretty simple job really."

"Well," she agreed, nodding from the other side of the hole, "at least you're a good handyman. We've saved a little there. Things are going to be tight until I find work. We probably shouldn't have come on this vacation at all, but after eight months, a person needs a rest from job searches and headhunters.''

''Why couldn't it have been me that got laid off?'' I protested. ''I could've started a fix-it shop and spent more time with Susie.''

Ellen came out of the motor home and shut what was left of the screen door. ''One of us has to be employed someplace where they pay medical,'' she reminded me. ''Otherwise, a broken leg could wipe us out. If my parents hadn't insisted we take the motor home, we wouldn't even be here.''

''Cheer up,'' I said, making a grand gesture at the campground. ''Staying at the Baja Biltmore only costs forty dollars a week. Even *we've* got that much.''

I had forgotten my coffee, which was starting to cool off, and that meant only one thing. But before I could turn around and grab my LA Raiders mug off the card table, Maggie started after what she had charged out of bed for: my coffee.

She always waited until the steam stopped rising, then she would begin lapping it out of my mug, dipping her tongue in and slurping away. It was the slurping that caught my attention, but by the time I got there, it was too late. She had finished all but a few drops in the bottom.

I never took the time to see if she liked it black, or whether it was the milk and Equal that made it so irresistible, but one thing was sure: she was a coffee dog.

By the time I got another cup ready, Susie was up and crawling through the new doggie door Maggie had made.

''Look, Daddy!'' she said. ''Maggie made a *hoe el*. I can go through all by myself.''

I got up and ran to the screen door, catching Susie as she tumbled out of the hole and into my arms. She laughed happily.

''Let's do it again, Daddy! I want to go through the *hoe el* again.''

I poured another mug of coffee and checked the hole for sharp edges. Then we started playing in it. By that time Maggie's belly was home to another mugful, and she was starting to get hyper from the caffeine. Pretty soon there were three of us playing in the hole while Ellen made pancakes on the stove.

We ate breakfast and cleaned up, then made sure Mr. Zapata would be around to watch the campsite while we went to town. He was, so we locked up and climbed in the old army jeep.

Ellen never said as much, but I could tell she was glad I had given up on my impossible dream of finding that shell. By the time we headed down the dirt road to town, I almost had myself convinced that it wasn't even a whole shell, just a small worthless fragment. I couldn't count how many times a shell sticking out of the sand had turned out to be just a broken piece. It was all too common. Yet somewhere deep inside, my brain still harbored the hope of real treasure.

We headed south and rolled into town at nine in the morning. San Bajamos was a small fishing village by nature, but its location a hundred miles south of the border made it an ideal target for tourists to hit on summer weekends.

The main downtown area was a series of stucco and adobe shops that were one block off the beach. It wasn't a modern mall, and wouldn't warrant a spread in *Architectural Digest*, but it was low-key, safe, and pretty clean.

The north side of town slammed into some rocky hills. Just below them, and a few blocks out of the downtown area, squatted what was their equivalent of a housing tract, but on a very tight budget. Dirt roads and yards surrounded rows of single-story block, adobe, and tin houses, many without glass in the window frames. Worn-out people came and went slowly. Skinny kids wearing ragged clothes played stickball in vacant lots. Scruffy dogs showing ribs wandered the streets searching for a handout. It was third world poverty.

By contrast, south of town sat all the *gringo* condos and resorts complete with swimming pools, riding stables, and tennis courts, pulling in the rich tourist trade.

In between, as if holding two fighters apart in the ring, stood the old-town souvenir shops, halfway between famine and fortune.

Once we hit the tourist strip, we got a couple of dumb T-shirts to prove our vacation was real, haggled with street vendors for some very good silver necklaces, and bought a swordfish carved out of some dark polished wood. Then I spent way too long looking for a hat, finally settling on what must have been the Mexican equivalent of a Stetson.

It was a tightly woven and bleached straw hat, complete with Indiana Jones styling, and a colorful cloth band that tied in the back, proudly announcing SAN BAJAMOS! GATEWAY TO THE GULF. It even had a sweatband and liner. Okay, so I blew seven dollars. But I was happy, and some poor cart vendor got dinner all week for a family of twelve.

We were all set, or at least I was. Ellen still had some stuff she wanted to bargain for. So I left her and Susie in one of the better air-conditioned shops and decided to take one last stroll on the boardwalk.

Maggie and I walked along the hand-poured sidewalk. The narrow, uncrowded beach sat quietly on one side; noisy, packed taco stands on the other. I was all set to say my good-bye to the town. All set, except some skinny Mexican girl wearing a faded blue checkered dress and nothing else came skipping along the low block wall that divided the beach from the street. She had a noticeable gap in her white front teeth, and calluses on her bare feet, dirty from the streets. She looked about twelve years old, and was slim and dark, with long straggly black hair and deep brown eyes. When she reached us she jumped off the wall and began to pet Maggie.

"What's her name?" she asked in very good English.

"Maggie," I answered, relaxing the leash a little. "And I'm Jack. What's yours?"

"Vaca," she said without looking up. "Vaca Cion."

"That name sounds familiar." I bent down. "Where have I heard it before?"

"It means vacation in your language." She let Maggie lick her face.

"Ah." I laughed. "No wonder I've heard it before. What a clever name for a pretty, young girl. Your parents must be very creative."

She looked up at me for the first time. Despite her worn dress and bare feet, she had a noble look about her. Perhaps it was her high cheekbones, or those bottomless brown eyes—or the teeth. Despite the gap, they were straight and white, like miniature sheets of copy paper. Poor girls never had teeth like that. I stopped staring when it occurred to me they could be false, and looked toward the water.

"Jack," she said, a sudden softness in her voice. "So you think I am pretty? Pretty girls fetch a lot of money, even in this poor village."

"I ... uh ..." Things were getting out of control, so I jerked on the leash and dragged Maggie away. Ten feet down the sidewalk I stopped, realizing it was naive of me to be embarrassed. Reaching into the back pocket of my shorts, I pulled out my wallet, producing a five-dollar bill. I turned and held it out to her.

"Put that away," she ordered, quickly getting to her feet and looking around suspiciously. "Or you'll get us arrested. We must be ... as you say ... discreet."

"Look," I replied, exasperated, folding the bill in my hand, "I don't want anything. I just thought you could use a new dress."

She walked over and reached out for me, holding my outstretched fist in her hands, then looked up and down the block. The street was half-crowded with tourists and locals, but no one seemed to be paying much attention. They probably saw this kind of thing every day, and couldn't afford to care.

"Jack," she whispered, looking into my eyes, "the jail down here has a dirt floor, cockroaches as big as burritos, and guards on the roof with shotguns. It's not a place to spend your vacation ... Come," she added, pulling slightly at my hand. "I do not live far from here. Come to my house. I have something I must tell you."

"You know I can't do that," I replied, getting nervous. "Look, if I give you twenty dollars, will you leave me alone? Wouldn't you rather just keep it for yourself instead of splitting it with the police for turning me in?"

"I don't work for anyone," she said, almost angrily. "But there's something you must know. It's about ..."

"Jack!" Ellen yelled, coming down the boardwalk with Susie. "Look what I bought!"

The girl glanced quickly at them, still fifty yards away, then back at me. "We will meet again," she promised. "There is something I must tell you. It's about your vacation.

There's been a change in plans. You can't go back to . . ." She looked at Ellen and Susie. "I must go now." She stood on the tips of her toes, and before I could do anything reached up and kissed me on the cheek. A warm glowing sensation rippled through my face, and then it was gone. She looked over her shoulder once more and ran away, disappearing down the street among the tourists.

I stuffed the five-dollar bill in my shorts as Ellen let Susie go, twenty yards away. She ran to me and I picked her up. She smiled and hugged me, then showed me her little silver necklace with teddy bears on it. When Ellen got there she said, "The necklace was only five bucks. Who's your girlfriend?"

"Her name's Vaca. She wanted to pet Maggie."

"I'll bet that's not all she wanted," Ellen said sarcastically.

"Ellen, please. You know I'd never—"

"Just kidding," she replied, pushing Maggie down. "Obviously, she didn't realize she'd be wasting her time on you. Did you tell her it wasn't your time of the month?"

"Thanks."

"Daddy, what's not your time of the month?"

"Mommy's just being silly," I said, rolling my eyes at Ellen.

Susie looked at her. "Mommy, *you're* being silly."

"Yes," Ellen said, setting her shopping bag down. "I know. Anyway, we're through here. Let's head out to that resort and get some lunch there. Then we'll go back to camp." She looked at her watch. "It's too late to do any digging anyway. The tide will be in by now."

"Oh, that." I sighed. "Look, I'm trying to forget about it, all right? I'm sure it was just a broken shell anyway. I'm not that lucky, remember?"

"Oh, I don't know," Ellen winked. "You seem to be doing okay with the native girls."

"Where's the jeep?" I asked, purposely changing the subject. "I've got to get out of here before anything else happens."

"Good idea," Ellen agreed. "You're starting to turn red, even with that overpriced hat on. Let's hit the road before you give all your money away."

"I didn't give her any money."

"No," she said, patting my back. "But you would have. You're a sucker for a hard luck story."

We left and headed out of town. On the way we passed the Baja Buggies shop, but I knew I'd better not stop. There was too much to deal with already. Better just to leave town quietly and get the vacation over with while things were relatively calm.

On the way south I couldn't help thinking how foolish it had been to offer that girl money. Ellen was right. I was a sucker for a down-and-out story—or any story for that matter, even an impossible one like Mr. Zapata's.

 9

The Last Tourist Trap

When we got past the last resort a dozen miles south of town, it looked like it was time to turn back. The Baja Bonita was nowhere in sight. That was the name of the place on the promotional brochure Ellen got from her parents. As retirees, they were always getting stuff like that.

The glossy, carefully photographed pictures showed some grand Mexican paradise on the gulf. The brochure guaranteed fifty percent off your first stay. Well, it looked like we would get a hundred percent off—because all we were staring at were cacti, sand, and the road out of town.

Then I saw something on the side of the road and slammed on the brakes. A billboard lay flat on its back, wooden legs broken off at ground level. It wasn't the first one I had seen that vacation. I had almost forgotten that the one to Mr. Zapata's campground had also been knocked flat the afternoon we first arrived. We were all set to stay at Ellen's parents' regular campsite when I noticed the sign down on the side of the road. I told Ellen maybe it was deserted and we could stay for free, and at first it was true. But the next morning Mr. Zapata showed up in his pickup truck. We almost left, but he grinned and said we could stay for half price if we didn't mind cold water in the shower. The motor home provided plenty of hot water, so we saw it as a deal. But lately it was looking like a mistake.

My mind came back from my thoughts and there we were, parked by our second downed sign. Maybe this one would bring better luck.

Maggie and I climbed out of the jeep and walked over. Staring at the sign, I confirmed it to be the marquee for our potential resort.

For a moment I thought about telling Ellen it said something else, but we needed some lunch, and the sign still had fresh paint on it. Maybe some kids had knocked it over, or some sneaky fraternity brothers wanted the place all to themselves and leveled it.

The sign pictured a family relaxing around a huge swimming pool. The parents sipped margaritas while a couple of kids and a family dog played in the water. Well, at least it looked like our kind of place, though I doubted whether dogs would really be allowed in the pool.

As I walked back to the jeep my stomach growled, and a cold drink sounded awfully good. I could pass up a beer pretty easily after a week of sipping suds, but a margarita like the huge bathtub-sized one painted on the sign was going to be hard to resist.

Climbing in the jeep I said, "That's our resort, if we still want it."

"*We* still want it," Susie said, repeating my words.

"Let's give it a try," Ellen agreed. "If it's open, they're probably desperate for business with that sign down." When I didn't say anything, Ellen went on. "Look," she insisted. "This ticket says we've got a complimentary meal coming. Free is free."

"What? No cheap luggage? No plastic camera? That's usually what these time-share rip-offs bait the hook with."

"Just let me do the talking," Ellen insisted. "You're a pushover, but you know what a hard sell I am."

"Yeah," I agreed with a nod. "They'll be lucky to get a peso tip out of you."

"How far is it?"

"Apparently just down the road." I shrugged. "Half a mile it says."

Maggie jumped into the back with Susie and we pulled off. As advertised, in a half mile the road came to a sharp left and headed toward the gulf.

A quarter mile of new asphalt later we dipped down a little hill and there it was: Mexican-style elegance in a two-story hotel, slowly working its way down a steep slope toward a secluded beach.

We pulled into the parking lot out front, eyeing an unfinished fountain and six clay tennis courts. As the only car in the lot, we almost left, figuring the place was closed. But before we could exit, a bellhop dashed out of the front door. He wore a pressed white suit with a red stripe on each pant leg, and a desperate expression. He ran for the jeep as though we had discovered him shipwrecked on a desert island.

"*¡Abierto!*" he yelled, waving his arms frantically. "We are open!" He screeched to a halt in front of the jeep. I had to slam on the brakes to avoid hitting him. Standing directly in front of the radiator, he said with a practiced smile, "*¡Hola, amigos!* Welcome to Baja Bonita." If he could have seen his badly stained teeth, maybe he wouldn't have smiled so widely. "Come in," he insisted. "We have special today."

Ellen and I looked at each other. My stomach growled loudly.

"Food," I said to the bellhop. "Do you have a restaurant?"

"*Sí, señor.*" He smiled. "*Muy grande.* You can have whatever you want. *Cervezas*, margaritas, tacos, enchiladas." He looked at Maggie panting from the noonday heat. "Dogs okay," he added.

Without saying anything, I put it in reverse and backed right up to the entrance. The bellhop ran over and opened the hand-carved wooden front door. Thankfully, he didn't put out his other hand for a tip. We filed in, including Maggie on her leash, and worked our way toward the restaurant.

The inside was equally impressive. Mexican tiles covered every inch of the floor. New stucco walls lined the interior, each one hung with dramatic, bullfighter oil paintings framed in heavy wood. Occasionally, a carefully placed potted palm or spineless cactus accented the museumlike interior, illuminated by a discreet track-lighting system.

As we passed the reception desk, a beautiful teenage Mexican girl looked up from doing her nails and smiled nervously. She had to make an extra effort not to frown as Maggie strode by on her leash.

The bellhop ran ahead into the kitchen and came out with a distinguished silver-haired maître d'. He wore the same starched white suit but a more controlled smile. We were whisked away to a sunny terrace filled with frosted glass tables, bright blue umbrellas, and potted palm trees. The terrace overlooked a sparkling Olympic-size swimming pool. It was carefully inlaid with colorful hand-painted tiles in the pattern of a Spanish cross, reflecting from the bottom of the pool.

After we were seated, the maître d' handed us Americanized menus, urging me to try their bathtub margarita. A glare from Ellen led to my reluctant decline of his offer. I had iced tea instead.

Chips, salsa, refried beans, and chicken enchiladas later, it was time for a tour of the place, led by Ernesto, a tall, slim, dark character with black hair and long fingernails. He was smooth, saying they were closed for remodeling, but we were most welcome to look around, even stay if we liked.

Besides the stunning pool and new tennis courts, there was a riding stable with some pretty fair colts in case we wanted to gallop along the beach, which was immaculate, though narrow, and packed with fluffy white sand.

On the way back up the hill we got the bad news: a hundred dollars a night, but reduced to fifty thanks to Ellen's brochure. We promised to think about it, but our only intention was to relay the message to Ellen's parents once back stateside.

Then something caught my eye near the riding stables. There was a little corral of blood-red off-roaders. A painted sign stuck in the sand matched the lettering on their fenders: BAJA BUGGIES.

I left Ellen to check out a deal for her folks, providing the hotel was still in business the next season and her parents liked the terms. Then, with Maggie in tow, I scooted down to the dune buggy corral.

After she decided it was okay to leave Ellen and Susie, Maggie began pulling me down the hill. I dropped her leash and she stopped. Then we went through the same routine until we reached sand.

Some large guy with kinky gray hair, a double chin, and huge sweat stains under the arms of his Mexican shirt was working on one of the buggies. At least he had it in the shade of a palm tree. Otherwise, he might have passed out from heat exhaustion.

Without looking up he waved a screwdriver over his head. "Ten dollars for all day," he said without any accent. "Two dollars an hour."

"What happened to that one?" I asked, watching him turn the screwdriver on a carburetor jet.

"Some guy foolin' around," he explained, still not looking up. "Got salt water in the lines. She'll be fine. This sort of thing happens all the time. We tell 'em to take it easy in the water, but how ya gonna enforce something like that ... That's what they come down here for," he added, looking up and smiling. "To get drunk and raise hell.

"Ed Masters," he said, standing up and sticking out his hand. "Came down here from El Paso five years ago. Never went back. What'll it be? An hour, a day, or something in between."

This guy was obviously *gringo* material, but deeply tanned from years in the sun. His Mexican shirt was almost big enough for him. His ragged cutoffs used to be suit pants, I figured, before he called it quits stateside.

"Right now all I need is an answer," I informed him. "Could you tell me who rented this one yesterday? It could've been the same idiot that almost ran me down."

"If I was to do that," he said, grinning through crooked teeth, "I'd be violating client confidentiality. Then I'd lose what little business there is this time of year." He tossed the screwdriver into a dirty wooden toolbox. "Besides, I got another one of these rentals in town. Could've been just about anybody."

"Anybody that looks like an Indian wrestler," I said, petting Maggie.

He looked sharply at me and began to wipe his hands on a shop rag. "Ah, that one," he said. "Well, I'll tell you this much. This *is* the buggy he rented. Wasn't stayin' at the lodge here, though. Came in driving one of those hippie Volkswagen buses you used to see back in the sixties. I figure he was looking for drugs. He parked the bus in the lot. Paid cash, including a thousand dollar deposit so I'd trust him, and that was it. Except . . ."

"Except what?"

"He had one of those fanny packs stuffed with bills, thousands mostly. Must have been a hundred grand in there. That's how I knew it was a drug deal. Nobody carries cash like that around."

I frowned. "So how would he get back across the border? A hippie bus is bound to be searched."

"Airport's only a mile from here," he said, bending down to scratch Maggie. "He'd have someone fly it out. When they check his bus, they won't find a thing. The money will be converted to dope. The dope'll be on a private plane, and he's home free. Happens all the time." He motioned up the hill toward the hotel. "How do you think they could afford to build the Taj Mahal here?"

I pressed on. "Look, he must have left you a credit card for collateral. A thousand bucks wouldn't pay for one of these four-wheelers."

"American Express," he replied. "But I reckon it's stolen." He stood up and looked me squarely in the eyes. "Look, do yourself a favor, *amigo.* Don't mess with him. They carry guns, and not for shootin' holes in beer cans."

I thanked him and headed back up the hill with Maggie. Soon we were saying good-bye, promising to come back with Ellen's parents next year, which nobody believed, and then we were off. It was time to head back to camp for our last afternoon in Baja. With any luck, it would prove to be uneventful.

On the way back we spotted someone hitchhiking along the road, just a half mile from the fallen resort sign. She was wearing that faded blue checkered dress and a big smile.

I passed her, trying not to look back. It didn't work. Ellen reached over and popped the jeep out of gear to get my attention. The engine raced, so I pulled my foot off the gas and coasted, waiting for Ellen to say something.

"Give her a ride," she insisted with a sly grin. "It's dangerous for a young girl to be hitching out here . . . Go on," she added, slapping my arm. "We'll squeeze her in the backseat, unless you want her to sit on *your* lap."

"All right," I said, slightly perturbed. "I'll prove to you once and for all that she didn't get any money, or anything else."

I slammed on the brakes and skidded to a stop, then shoved it into reverse.

"Get in," I ordered, as we pulled up alongside. "My wife wants to ask you some questions."

 10

The Vacation Goddess

"So, we meet again, *Señor* Jack," Vaca said with a wry smile. She looked at Ellen and raised her eyebrows. "Mrs. Jack, *buenos tardes*. How can I help you?"

Ellen climbed out without saying a word and squeezed in the backseat with Susie, her car seat, and Maggie. Then she motioned for Vaca to sit in the front. "Please," she said with mock courtesy. "Hop in. It's dangerous to be hitchhiking way out here."

"Oh no, *señora*. I'll sit in the back. It wouldn't be proper for . . ."

"I insist," Ellen interrupted, motioning to the vacant seat next to me.

Without further argument, Vaca sat in the front seat, even fastening her seat belt. As I pulled away, I kept waiting for the other shoe to drop. It didn't take long.

"So, *señorita* Vaca is it?" Ellen asked pointedly. "It's a hard life down here, no?"

"*Muy difícil, señora.* Very hard." Vaca looked at Ellen over her shoulder. "But people do the best they can with what they have. They are poor here. But you know that." Vaca got a serious look on her face as I put the jeep in third gear. "But that's not what you want to know," she continued, brushing black hair from her eyes. "And the answer may surprise you."

"Oh," Ellen sighed, "nothing surprises me anymore. How much to leave us alone?—In American dollars."

"Money is not why I am here," Vaca said seriously. "Though it certainly must play a part in this."

"In what?" I asked, slapping the steering wheel. "Ellen's right. Stop beating around the bush and tell us what you want."

"What I want is not as important as what *you* want," Vaca said coolly.

"Stop talking in riddles," Ellen ordered.

"She's talking in riddles, Mommy," Susie chimed in.

"And what was that remark earlier about my vacation plans changing?" I asked.

"I can see that the time has come to tell you," Vaca said, facing the road ahead. When no one answered, she explained, her eyes never leaving the asphalt.

"You may have figured out already that I am not from here," she began. "Though I may look like it a little. I am dressed this way so as not to attract unnecessary attention. It is true, however, that my name is Vaca Cion, just as I have said. I am . . . I am goddess of vacations. It is my duty to watch over tourists."

"Okay, I'll bite," I said, giving her a sideways glance. "But why, out of millions of happy campers in the world, have you selected us to pick on . . . and just what does a vacation goddess do anyway?" I looked over my shoulder at Ellen, who could only roll her eyes.

"As I said," Vaca continued, undaunted. "My job is to look after tourists. Sort of what you call a guardian angel. You were picked because I was on my way back from Acapulco, and this little fishing village seemed like a good place to rest up before going on to Palm Springs."

"But why us?" I asked again, pointing around the jeep. "Why us *specifically*?"

"The pearl," she said, finally looking at me. "It changes everything."

I pulled over and skidded to a stop, shoved the jeep into neutral, and threw up my hands. "Oh no," I said, looking up at the sun. "Not another one. Look, if everybody wants that seashell so badly, why don't one of you just go dig it up and leave us out of it. This whole thing is getting too complicated for me. I just want to go back to the States to my little suburb of LA, *and,* believe it or not, I almost *want* to get back to work. At least everything there makes some sense." I looked down at Vaca. "So, if you don't mind . . ."

"That would have been fine," Vaca interrupted. "*Normally* . . . You see, part of my job is to make something happen toward the end of vacations that makes people want to go home. Haven't you ever noticed that?"

"Go home," Susie repeated. "I want to go home now."

"We will, sweetheart," Ellen said. "We're going home *right now*. As soon as this *señorita* here gets out of the jeep."

"Very well," Vaca said sharply. "I'm sorry to bother you with such a crazy story." She unfastened her seat belt, climbed out, and started to walk away. When she got ten feet in front of the jeep she turned and said, "But you're going to have a hard time leaving with that flat tire."

Just as she uttered the word "tire," the high-pitched squeal of air rushing out of road rubber filled the air. I got out and examined the front tire on my side and, sure enough, there was a pencil sized hole in the sidewall.

"Wait!" I yelled to her back. "How did you do that?" She just kept walking.

"Don't mess with her," Ellen said. "Just change the tire. She could be a witch or something."

I gave Ellen a curious look. "El, you don't believe in that sort of thing, remember?"

"I know," she answered. "But something's not right here. Everyone's acting weird—like one of those 'Twilight Zone' shows. Look, just change the tire and let's get out of here."

Funny how Ellen could accept the unusual if it seemed like a well-known TV show, I thought, but not otherwise.

"All right," I agreed. As Vaca walked away, I spent ten minutes changing the tire, and listening to Susie say, "Mommy, Daddy's changing the tire now. It's broke." The rest of the time I spent fighting off Maggie's wet tongue. Ellen finally threw a tennis ball she found stuck under the seat, and that kept Maggie busy long enough for me to finish.

After that, we barreled off down the road. Needless to say, it wasn't long before we passed Vaca again with her thumb out. When the jeep got twenty yards past her, there was a loud blam. The tire that had just been changed had blown and I was fighting the wheel. I finally got the jeep off to the side of the road, but now we were fresh out of spares and still miles from town or camp.

Getting out, I told Ellen to wait while I trotted back to town, but then changed my mind. Vaca had reached the rear of the jeep.

"I don't know how you did it," I said through clenched teeth, "and maybe I don't want to. But could you please just leave me and my family alone? That flat could've gotten us killed, little Miss Vacation Goddess. If this is your idea of fun, well, it's not funny. And as far as your pearl goes, you can take that lousy clamshell and—"

"I'm truly sorry," Vaca said, with a sympathetic glance. "But I had to get your attention." She rested her arms on the flat spare bolted to the back of the jeep. "Look, this tire's fine. Put it back on and let's go to your camp. I'll explain on the way."

"Don't be ridiculous," Ellen said, glaring at Vaca. "That's flat and you know it. If I didn't have the baby here, I'd . . . How old are you, anyway? Don't you have parents?"

Vaca pointed skyward. "They're in heaven, *señora.*"

"I thought so," Ellen smirked. "A homeless waif. Look, we're not the rich tourists you think we are. I don't even have a job. Go pick on someone else, okay?" Ellen turned and looked at me as I stood on the side of the road in front of the jeep. "Jack, give her a twenty."

"What?" I protested. "Nothing doing. You're the one that said no money, remember?"

"That was before the tire trick. Pay her off and get rid of

her. It's still five miles either way, but somebody's bound to come along any minute. Let's just wait here."

It was just our luck that no one came along for the next half hour. Vaca refused to leave, and finally got out the jack and handed it to me. When I gave her an incredulous stare, she just told me to squeeze the spare bolted to the jeep—the one that had the hole in it. I knew all the air was out of it, but she talked me into it anyway, like someone asking you to squeeze her muscles to prove her strength. As soon as I touched the tire, my eyes grew big. It was as hard as Arnold Schwarzenegger's biceps.

I examined it more closely, inch by inch. There was no sign of a hole. I called Ellen over and she did the same. Finally, we looked at each other and I shrugged. Vaca just stood there as if to say *I told you so*. She bent over and petted a panting Maggie.

"Either she's related to David Copperfield," I said to Ellen, "or she *is* the Vacation Goddess . . . One more," I said, turning to Vaca. "One more trick and I'm ready to believe."

"Jack," Vaca said, raising her eyebrows, "just change the tire. Trust me. I'm on your side." She sounded like a personal injury lawyer about to take my case and fifty percent of the settlement fee. I looked up and down the road, turned, and glanced across the desert in both directions. There was not a soul in sight. Then, faintly in the distance, the sound of a vehicle came from the direction of town.

"We wait," I said. "See if this guy stops." I walked into the middle of the road and waved my arms emergency style as the vehicle approached. It was some kind of tan-colored Range Rover, and it wasn't slowing down. When it got twenty yards from me, Ellen screamed and I jumped off the other side of the road onto the shoulder, rolling over several times and slamming against some spiny cactus.

Getting up, I brushed myself off, picking a few spines out of my forearms. Ellen and Vaca pulled out the rest, including some stuck in my seat. As they did I remembered the Rover had Baja plates, and the face of the driver had looked familiar for the split second I saw it. It was the guy in the boat. I was almost sure of it. Behind that safari hat and wire-rimmed shades was a thin, deeply tanned and muscular face with a pencil mustache. I wasn't positive, but it must have been him. Who else would try to run me down?

"Anybody get a look at that license plate?" I asked.

"Baja," Ellen assured me. "Naturally." She looked at Vaca. Neither of them had gotten a lot of details, but Ellen had read an insignia stenciled on the side of the door.

UNIVERSIDAD DE MÉXICO

Strange, I thought. But at least it was something we could tell the authorities at the border. Not that they would do anything, but it would make us feel better.

I changed the tire and we all climbed into the jeep. "Vaca," I said at last, "who was that? Surely anybody who can fix a flat knows who's trying to kill me. I've already figured out why."

"Yes," Vaca agreed. "It's for the pearl, of course. I didn't get a good look, but that must have been Professor Hardwick. He owns one of the treasures."

"One?" I asked. "How many are there?"

"There are known to be just four in the entire world," she informed us. "Only three were ever found . . . until now. The Museum of Mankind in London has one. A private collector in Canada has another, Professor Hardwick has the third, which he stole from a museum in France . . . And you"—she gently put her hand on my shoulder—"have found the fourth."

"Then there were *four*," I repeated, "not just the one as Mr. Zapata said."

"The others are copies," she said. "To use as decoys. They, too, were solid crystals, carved by men and discovered centuries later in archaeological digs. But only the one covered in pearl holds the true magic, holds the Eyes of God."

"But what are these Eyes of God? And what is made of crystal? I thought it was pearl."

"A giant clam," she told us, "like an oyster, makes a pearl by covering over irritations. It could be only one grain of sand, or something much bigger. A pearl was found once that weighed fourteen pounds. It came out of the heart of a giant clam such as the one you discovered. The treasure is now covered in a protective layer of pearl."

"What is it?" Ellen asked, suddenly taking great interest. "What is covered in pearl?"

"A life-sized replica of a human skull, carved out of pure rock crystal by the hand of a goddess. It has been infused with the power of nature—the power to control earth, sunlight, wind, fire, and water. The power lies in the eye sockets carved into the skull. They are the Eyes of God, or so the legend says."

"Well, pardon me, *señorita*," I interrupted. "But if you're a goddess, then you should know. Do these so-called eyes have power or not?"

"I don't know," she said wistfully. "It all happened before my time. All I know is that it was a gift of nature to Montezuma's priest."

"I hate to be rude," Ellen said from the backseat, "but Ms. Goddess, how old are you anyway?"

"As old as vacations themselves," Vaca replied matter-of-factly, looking at Ellen in the rearview mirror. "Ever since people began to venture from their hometowns to get away from the drudgery of work. I was created to watch over them while they were away, especially ones whose vacations come with danger." She looked straight at me.

"The only danger for me," I stated, "is if I keep searching for that pearl. Well, I'm not. I'm going home. I don't want any part of this anymore. Let's just leave this legend to the Aztecs and that will be the end of it."

Vaca disagreed, repeating what Mr. Zapata had said about there being some Aztec blood in my veins, proving the pearl was to be discovered by a descendant of Montezuma's people. Whoever looked into the eye sockets under the noonday sun received the power to control nature.

"Naturally," she said at last, "there's a curse."

"Power," I said, "according to Mr. Zapata. But it doesn't matter. I'm not digging up anything. Besides, I don't even know where to look anymore."

"That's one of the reasons I'm here," Vaca said. "Mother Nature asked me to help you find it. She told me I'd have to show you where to dig after you gave up. She doesn't want the magic to fall into the wrong hands. Evil could be done if someone sinister could control the weather—natural disasters and all that. I don't think I have to spell it out for you.''

"All right," I said, slowing down for our turn down the road to camp. "Why did Mother Nature pick *you* to help me out, anyway? What's in it for you besides a break from the crowds in Palm Springs or averting some airline disaster for a bunch of traveling tourists?''

Vaca smiled. "I accepted this assignment because I needed something good to put on my résumé," she said sarcastically. "Maybe I can get a better job in the Goddess Corps." She brushed her hair back with her hands. "I'm getting tired of the tourist business with all the complaining about ruined vacations. I feel like a dentist. Nobody's happy to see me.''

"All right," I said. "I deserved that. But can you just give me a hint why you're doing this?''

As the jeep hit the dirt road to camp, I waited for her reply.

She took a deep breath and began. "Very well. But promise not to laugh.''

"Laugh? Look at me. My whole life's a cliché—burned-out ex-jock staying in a job he doesn't like just to raise a family. Vaca, nothing's cornier than that. But I love them. That's why I'm doing it. Love is beyond what people think. And it's a matter of survival. It's either keep slugging it out at work over some boring job, or homelessness. So, I'm going to keep going to that lifeless place until I win the lottery or something else comes along.''

"Fair enough," she agreed. "Here's my story. Believe it or not, I'm here to help Mother Nature. I love my job and I enjoy helping people, even if they don't know I'm there. I see how happy they are when they're home safe and sound. The whole underlying purpose of vacations is so you can recharge your mental batteries and go home refreshed. People just love to be home again. A lot of them say they'd like to vacation forever, but most want to be home. My job is to see that some of them—the ones in great danger—*can* return home.''

"And do they all make it?" I asked in a calmer tone.

"No," she admitted. "Sometimes I'm too late to avert disaster. The powers of darkness are great, and I can't be everywhere at once. Like everyone else, I must live with my failures.''

"What are your limits?" I asked outright. "Besides only being in one place at a time?"

She told me that she couldn't change coming events, only try to do things to help people avoid disaster. She considered the *Titanic* one of her greatest failures. She was busy helping a snowbound ski party when the great ship went down.

A lot of times she heard about people in need just before they were in great danger, often only moments before someone was about to fall off a slippery cliff or board a doomed airline flight, and sometimes she didn't make it in time. She did have some interesting powers, but they, too, were limited. She could get tourists out of foreign prisons by picking locks and diverting the guards. She could do mechanical repairs and cause engine failures to keep planes grounded. She could occasionally get airline flights changed, delayed, and rerouted. Nothing showy or major, but little things that could keep some souls out of trouble at times. It all had to appear as just chance or circumstance. At present, my family was her top priority, especially since Mother Nature, whom she greatly respected, had asked her to look after us. But she wasn't allowed to inflict harm. That meant she couldn't bring violence to the thieves and thugs that stalked tourists all over the world, just try to foil them or have them arrested.

"What about Mother Nature's powers?" I asked. "Are they unlimited, or what?"

"I'm afraid," she shrugged, "that even she has limits. At her height, she could dominate the elements—earth, wind, fire, sunlight, and water." Vaca got a reverent look on her face and went on, telling me that Mother Nature had taken a five-hundred-year leave from Earth after giving the skull to the Aztecs in the beginning of the sixteenth century. She had tremendous powers then, but now they extended just a small distance from her body, perhaps only twenty yards or so.

She had put all of her powers into the skull except just enough to keep herself active until her return.

"That's why it's so important that the skull doesn't fall into the wrong hands," Vaca reminded me.

A long heavy silence filled the air, a silence I broke when my thoughts spilled out of my head.

"My god," I said. "The power to control nature is in that skull."

"That's what I've been trying to tell you."

The rest of the trip was pretty quiet, just the engine, wind, Susie repeating parts of the conversation and saying she was hungry, Maggie licking the hot air, and Ellen mumbling something to herself about Mother Nature. We rolled into camp and skidded to a stop in front of the motor home. As we got out of the jeep Ellen pulled me aside. It was time for a strategy session. I made sure her back was to the Winnebago. That way she wouldn't see that the screen door had been carefully removed from its hinges and was gone.

 11

Right Place, Wrong Time

"So, what do you think of little Ms. Vacation Goddess?" I asked Ellen, already knowing the answer.

"The same as I think about all of this," she replied, shaking her head. "In a word, *weird*. I don't know what's going on, but you almost got run over back there. So, let's not play Indiana Jones, all right? This is getting to be too dangerous, especially for Susie. I'm not staying another day in this place. So here's the deal: we dump the girl, hook up the jeep to the motor home, and ride off into the sunset."

"You're willing to wait until dark, then?" I asked. Vaca had definitely gotten my attention. I didn't believe in her exactly, or the whole Montezuma's Pearl bit, but whatever was out there was obviously worth something, and judging by the way everyone was acting, there were enough riches buried in the gulf to duck out of the rat race forever. Despite the danger, I had lied to myself about forgetting the treasure. It had become irresistible. Especially when I thought about that gray metal desk and the windowless walls waiting for me back at the plant.

"One hour," Ellen said, holding up her index finger. "No more. I'm going in and pack up. Be ready to go when I call." She turned and grabbed for the screen door. "What's this?" she shouted. "Now the screen door's gone." She twisted the knob to the regular door. "Well," she added over her shoulder. "At least it's still locked."

"Kids," I explained. "Probably looking for something to sell. When they couldn't pick the lock, they probably decided to steal what was left of the screen door."

I turned and motioned for Vaca, who was sitting in the sand playing pat-a-cake with Susie. "Okay, Junior Goddess. Let's go. You can show me where this thing's buried."

"Jack!" Ellen yelled, coming down the steps to get Susie. "I thought you were giving up." When I didn't answer, she added, "Never mind, but if you find anything, anything at all, it rides in the jeep. And if anyone pulls us over between here and the border, let them have it. Is that clear?"

I looked at Vaca and shrugged. "Whatever you say, El. But we haven't found anything yet."

"Yeah," Ellen said, picking up Susie. "And with any luck, maybe you won't."

"What's that supposed to mean?" I asked, turning half-way around.

"Look, the only reason I'm letting you go out there again is because if I don't, I'll never hear the end of it. You'll be telling people how *I* let the big one get away for the rest of your life. Well ..." She stroked Susie's hair. "This is your one big chance. But you'd better get going." She looked at her Timex. "You've only got fifty-five minutes left."

"Well," I replied, turning to Vaca, "what are you waiting for? Grab a shovel and let's get going." She bent down next to the wall and began digging with her hands. A few seconds later, she produced a new shovel, the good kind you'd find in a True Value hardware store. She stood up and swung the shovel over her shoulder like a rifle, handle pointing skyward.

"Junior Goddess Vaca Cion reporting for duty, sir," she said with a salute. "Ready for the digs, Captain."

I returned her salute with a disbelieving look at the shovel and grabbed one for myself from behind Mr. Zapata's place. "Tide looks like it's out far enough," I said on the way down the slope to the beach. "March."

We slogged out a good quarter mile, with Vaca leading the charge. Maggie and I followed a few steps behind. "This is the spot," she said at last. Before I could sink a shovel into the sand she added, "But not the right day."

"What?"

"Never mind," she said. "We'll mark it with my shovel."

"Look," I asked, frustrated. "When *is* the right day?"

"Monday. Today is the Sabbath. We should rest."

"Rest? I almost got killed, and you say we should rest?"

"It's only until tomorrow. The pearl is to be found at dawn, when the sun is low in the morning sky."

"That's just great," I said, trying to keep Maggie down. "But you heard Ellen—one hour." I looked at my watch. "Less than forty minutes now."

"We have until tomorrow," she insisted, shoving the blade of her shovel into the wet sand until it stood straight up.

Maggie took off after a seagull, and we were alone. I looked out to sea, then back at the camp. One of those heavy, illuminating silences descended upon us. I began to feel dizzy and strange. Suddenly, I found myself staring straight into Vaca's eyes. My whole life began to flash before me. Only it wasn't my *whole* life, just the vacations.

I was a kid at the lake with my dad, fishing in a canoe. All I caught were empty beer bottles Dad tossed to my end of the canoe. Then summer camp faded in, and five years had passed. I was standing in the woods with my friend, Billy Ogam, watching a cub fish in a cool mountain stream. We had to run like hell when the cub's mom came after us. I could feel my heart pounding in my chest.

High school came next. I was in the Long Bar in Tijuana, challenging some *gringo* to a tequila-drinking contest. I won that battle, but lost the war when I passed out afterward and got a case of the heaves for three days.

Next I had met Ellen and we were on our honeymoon to Cancún, Mexico, climbing the steep Mayan pyramids. I lost my balance, and almost fell to my death, but grabbed a chain bolted to the steps for wobbly tourists and hung on until I could get upright.

A second later I was diving off the side of the road as that Range Rover barreled past. Then the vision vanished as quickly as it had appeared, and I was back in the real world, standing and staring at a smiling Ms. Vaca.

Still a little fogged up from the spell she had somehow cast, I shook my head to try and clear my mind. Eventually, everything came back into focus.

"What in the ..." The words began to erupt from my mouth. I stopped them midsentence, realizing I was at her mercy. "Oh, never mind. I don't want to know how you did it."

"Jack," she said softly, and grasped my hand. She was as warm and brown as fresh toast. "Let's go back to camp."

"Fine," I agreed, and started for the Winnebago. "But Ellen's not going to buy waiting until tomorrow, unless you show her your trick."

"I can't," she said, perturbed. "It took all the power I had for one day. Maybe some other time," she sighed. "But don't worry ..." She reached up, placed her free arm around my waist, and gave me a friendly hug. "You're not going anywhere just yet."

We sloshed in silence most of the way back, but at one point I had some questions.

"Am I really Aztec?"

"It's better if you find out for yourself."

"Do you think you'll get a promotion for this?"

"I sure hope not."

"Why not?"

"Can you keep a secret?"

"Nope."

She laughed. "Doesn't matter. Nobody'll believe you anyway. You may not know this, but Mother Nature says she's thinking of retiring. She's quite old now, and nearly exhausted."

"How can she be exhausted? She's been on vacation for five hundred years."

"Actually, I'm afraid I didn't make myself clear. She hasn't really been vacationing. With what limited powers she has left, she's been working hard on some other planets in faraway places of the universe. Planets that might become like Earth someday. I think she's overworked herself the last half millennium to make up for what she couldn't do here. She hated leaving, but a promise is a promise. I know it hurt her to stay away for so long. I could see it in her face the last time I spoke to her.

"When was that?"

Vaca ignored my question, telling me instead that Eartha was about to return, and that just *seeing* how the Earth had gone downhill since she had left made her tired.

"She said taking care of the Earth was hard work, even before man got hold of it. But that now it was becoming almost impossible. Eartha thinks that even if she comes back with full powers, it may still be too late to fix the planet."

"Why wouldn't *you* want a job like hers?" I asked. "It sounds like you could help a lot more people. With your youth and some added powers, I'll bet you could do wonders for this tired planet."

"Granted that somebody's got to fight for the environment besides Greenpeace and the Sierra Club, but *I'm* certainly not ready for the big leagues yet. Taking Mother Nature's place would be out of the question for a minor goddess like me. Besides, I don't think I could handle that much responsibility right now. Why, some days it's all I can handle to help a few stranded tourists. I can't even imagine diverting a hurricane or something. Besides, you don't just put in for goddess jobs. God chooses you."

"Which one?"

"You know, the only *real* one. The rest of us are called gods and goddesses, but we're really only helpers."

"So," I joked, "what comes with the nature job besides smog, deforestation, and polluted rivers?"

"Oh, the usual," she joked. "Company car, cellular phone, airline upgrades. That sort of thing."

I stopped walking, turned and faced her. "Okay, I'm sorry I asked. But can't she just go poof and disappear in a puff of smoke?"

"Geez, Jack. This isn't the Disney Channel. While on Earth she lives in a body just like you and me."

"Then," I asked, "you wouldn't take a promotion even if God asked you to?"

"In that case, there'd be no choice. He usually doesn't take no for an answer."

"But you wouldn't ask for it, would you? You're a rare bird indeed. The people I work with can hardly wait to get their hands on any small amount of power."

"Except you," she said. "You just want out, don't you?"

"You got it. But I'm not in a position to save the Earth. Look, think of how many more people you could help if you did get the job."

"*That*," she said forcefully, "is the only thing that would make me volunteer on my own. But even if I did, I'd miss not helping people one-on-one. . . . Say, you're a pretty good salesman. You can present a point with the best of them."

"Naw, all I've done is negotiate a few government contracts for my company. Big deal."

"Don't be so modest. It's not everyone that can negotiate with the government. You've either got to be a super salesman, or a heck of a lawyer. . . . But I'm still not considering it, for your information," she added, reading my face. "Besides, when did you care so much about the Earth?"

"I've got a two-year-old who has to live here after I'm gone. I owe her some kind of Earth to live on—preferably, a healthy one. . . . Look, I'll make you a deal. No more sales pitches for the keeper of the Earth. But if I persuade Ellen to stay, you agree to get her and Susie out safe and sound."

"I'll do the best I can," she said, raising an eyebrow. "Let's shake on it."

Vaca put out her hand, and I took it in mine for a good shake. "But . . ."

"But what?"

She smiled. "Ellen isn't leaving without you, and you're not going anywhere."

"Oh, great. Now what have you done? Somebody else going to try and run me over? . . . Look," I added, starting up the slope for camp, "you can do whatever you want to me. But don't . . ." I grabbed her shoulders. "Please don't endanger the baby."

"Jack, I'm doing everything I can. You must trust me on that." The look on her face was sincere.

"All right," I agreed. "Apparently there's no choice at the moment. . . . Hey," I added, getting an odd thought, "you ever been skiing?"

"I've been to all the resorts. Lots of tourists, broken legs and all that."

"No, I mean actually racing down the slopes on a set of skis. It's wild, especially on the expert runs."

"When would I ever have time to learn? Usually, I'm so busy trying to keep skiers from killing themselves that I've only had time to watch."

"But wouldn't you like to try it? Just once? See what it's like to be human? Have some fun?"

"Sure, it does look like a lot of fun. I don't get too many vacations, though. Last one was ten years ago. Had to save the cruise ship I was on from sinking in a storm. Oh, well, comes with the territory, I guess."

"Okay, here's the new deal. You get us, *all* of us, out of this in one piece, pearl or no pearl, and I'll teach you to ski."

"Sure, but—"

"Look," I added, reading her expression, "humor me. It's about all I can offer you for helping me out of a tough spot. Unless you'd like some wrestling lessons."

She just gave me a look. "Vaca," I added, "I can't take something for nothing from anyone, goddess or not. If you won't accept my gift, then—"

She reached over and hugged me. "Aztec boy," she said to appease me, "you've got yourself a deal. If I can get some time off."

Suddenly, Maggie came running back and got all jealous, nipping at my leg. I yelled at her. She had never done that before, and now twice in two days.

Vaca said she was going into town for the night, and marched off into the desert. Just before she disappeared over a sand dune, she turned and yelled over her shoulder.

"Remember! The treasure will be yours tomorrow if you want it."

She didn't wait for a reply. It wouldn't have mattered. There was nothing left to say. Even though I had been impressed by what seemed to be some kind of hypnotic trance she put me in, and the fix-a-flat routine with the jeep, it still never occurred to me she could actually be a goddess. I went along with it just to see if she would reveal something of her motives, though I did like her imagination and warmth. Yet her motives almost seemed clear. Like everyone else, she wanted the treasure. I couldn't blame her for that.

As she disappeared into the desert, I just wondered what else she had up her sleeve. I watched until she was completely out of sight. The setting sun caught her at the top of the dune, and opaqued her out like a ghost ship on the horizon. It was time to talk to Ellen.

Once back at the motor home, it was apparent that Ellen wasn't in a discussion kind of mood, so we got ready to leave instead. I would save my let's-wait-until-morning speech until the last minute, hoping for a break in Ellen's mood. Vaca had assured me there was nothing to worry about, but I had my doubts. An hour later we broke camp, stuffed everything into the motor home, and prepared to leave.

Mr. Zapata wasn't around. He had taken his beat-up truck to town or something. So I stuffed the forty-dollar camping fee into an envelope and slid it under his front door. Ellen hooked up the jeep to the tow bar behind the Winnebago and we were off—almost.

When I climbed behind the wheel of the motor home and turned the key, we were greeted by dead silence. Either the ignition switch had suddenly gone, or something was amiss.

Getting out and popping the hood revealed the problem. The two front batteries were gone. A quick check on the one in the rear produced the same results, but with an added bonus, the portable generator was gone as well. Next, I lifted the hood on the jeep. A battery-sized hole stared up at me.

Ellen and I talked about our predicament at great length. We figured that the batteries from the Winnebago had been swiped while we were in town and probably sold for cash. Ellen had been so busy straightening up inside and watching Susie that she hadn't even tried any of the lights or noticed that the clock had stopped. But what about the battery in the jeep? The only explanation was that Vaca had been working with an accomplice and lured me out to sea while someone stole the Delco Freedom under the hood.

Ellen was busy in the motor home and must not have noticed that either. No surprises there. In LA a whole car could be stripped in five minutes or less. A battery was a snap. Yet, it wasn't the usual cut-the-cables-and-run job. Not only had the hood lock been carefully picked on the Winnebago, as well as the one in the rear compartment, but in all cases the cables had been carefully removed with a wrench, as if the owner had just taken them out for a charge. The jeep was the same—no damage, no violence. Regardless of the careful work, Vaca was obviously at the heart of it.

With the sun long gone behind the mountains, I had three choices: hitchhike or jog to town, trot along the beach until I found someone or a phone, or wait until morning. Then it would be light again and Mr. Zapata might be back. No way was I going to leave Ellen and Susie alone now. We decided that at daybreak I would check the resort five miles down and have someone take me into town for some new batteries.

Maggie and I sat outside most of the night. I was armed with a shovel in one hand and a kitchen knife in the other. Ellen and Susie were locked in the motor home. Sometime after midnight I drifted off and was doing fine, until Maggie woke me with wild, frantic barking.

 12

Camp Warrior

Out of the purple night appeared an Aztec warrior. Approaching on foot from behind Mr. Zapata's house, muscles shining in the starlight, he was dressed to impress. A silver belt buckle bigger than a cowboy's adorned his waist, holding up a leather loincloth. Around his neck dangled a miniature carved crystal skull. A multicolor beaded headband supported an array of wild bird feathers atop his head, fanned out peacock style. His dark cheeks were painted for war, with streaks of red, yellow, and blue ground into his skin. His savage stare bored into me as he clutched a crude spear with a pointed rock tied to the end.

Maggie was unimpressed, despite the authentic costume, and took up her fierce barking posture in front of the big umbrella twenty yards from the intruder.

There was something familiar about him, but I couldn't quite put my finger on it. I wasn't sure whether to laugh or get scared, but when he raised his spear like he was going to run Maggie through, I grabbed her.

A flashlight flipped on inside the motor home. I looked over my shoulder for an instant and saw Susie's and Ellen's faces in the bedroom window. At least they hadn't come out.

The warrior didn't speak at first, so I broke the ice.

"Who are you and what do you want?" I asked, holding Maggie's chain as I crouched in front of the umbrella.

He answered slowly, in a deep powerful voice. "I am the ghost of Montuca, high priest of the Aztecs. I have come for my birthright."

"And just what is that?" I asked, playing along.

"The pearl," he replied in reverent tones, resting the spear in the sand, pointing the sharp end toward the stars.

"Oh, no. Not another one."

When he saw me shake my head in disbelief, he added, "It belongs to my people."

"The Aztec Empire is dead," I reminded him, holding back a growling Maggie. "You'll have to come up with a better story. Costume's not bad, though."

He remained undaunted. "I am the guardian of the pearl," he said. "Do not make me use my powers."

"And ..." I smiled. "Just what powers might those be? If you're going to impress us with flat tires, you'll have to take a number. Somebody's already beaten you to the magic show this week."

This perturbed him. With a frustrated look, he growled, "Just go. I beseech you, before I turn the ocean to ..." He suddenly grew calm, almost apologetic. His expression softened, and he slowly paced the campground, looking out to sea.

"Jack," he began again, "I know your weakness for liquid spirits. You are strong now, but the time will come when the temptation is great, when you will wish for the spirits to soothe your soul. Please do not test my powers of persuasion. For when you are weakest, and your head is spinning with spirits, I will take the pearl. You will give it up without a struggle. Make it easy on yourself." He turned and glanced over his shoulder at Ellen and Susie as they stared out the window. "And your family," he added.

He turned my way and opened his arms gracefully, as if to embrace me. "Please, just leave this place, before it is too late. Go back to your . . . oaks, your Sherman Oaks, your life in America. You do not need the riches and curses of the world. You have a family. Go home, Jack. While you still can." With that he turned and walked away.

I must admit, his speech was almost moving. I wasn't sure how much he knew about me, but either this campground was a magical place that attracted goddesses and spirits, or the people I'd met of late were the best actors south of Hollywood.

First Vaca, and now *this* character. Not sure of what to make of him, and lost in thought about his promise to get me drinking again unless I left town, I accidentally let go of Maggie's leash. Sure enough, she bolted after him.

Eighty pounds of muscle and yellow fur came up behind Montuca's ghost. Before he could do anything, she grabbed his loincloth in her teeth. I was too stunned to move, so I just sat there.

Ellen quickly pulled Susie from the window after she yelled, "Look, Mommy. You can see his buns!"

That caused me to laugh involuntarily, but it didn't last very long.

The warrior was suddenly kneeling down, petting Maggie. Our good old guard dog was licking the midnight intruder to death. Montuca turned and gave me a look that confirmed that Maggie was no defense, and that he could have run her through in a second with the spear clutched in his other hand.

That look, I figured, was his last warning for us to get out of there and back to our cul-de-sac in Sherman Oaks, where life made some sense. It might have worked, except that over my shoulder a beam of light suddenly poured out of the motor home window, and was illuminating Montuca's ghost.

Susie had somehow gotten hold of the flashlight and was intending to shine it on Montuca's buns. She sure was giggling. But instead of catching his buns, she got his chest, arms and face. That cleared things up a little. For in that moment I could see quite plainly that our ancient Aztec warrior had a vaccination mark on his arm.

A minute later he was up and gone, disappearing into the dark night. Maggie came trotting back, her solemn duty of making friends with total strangers now finished. Soon, the sound of an engine firing up in the distance broke the near silence. It sounded like the kind of engine and muffler combo that comes with a dune buggy.

As it raced off, I discussed the incident with the women. Ellen accused me of showing Susie the flashlight trick, which I categorically denied, saying she must have picked it up from the day-care we used when Ellen was out on interviews. It was hard to suppress a grin about the buns incident. I tried, but with limited success.

The vaccination mark didn't mean anything to Ellen. She hadn't been fooled in the first place, and still wanted to get on the road in the morning after my battery run. Darn; I should've asked Montuca's ghost for some help in rounding up some batteries, especially since he wanted me gone so badly. Oh well, another missed opportunity.

Things quieted down after about an hour, and I went back to my lawn chair outside, falling asleep again about 3:00 A.M. It was only the sun blasting in my eyes that woke me the next morning.

As I jolted awake, something caught my eye. The screen door had been neatly screwed back in place. Climbing into the Winnebago, I checked on the women again, and noticed a note stuck to the steering wheel. Thankfully, Ellen and Susie were fine and hadn't heard or seen a thing. Apparently, neither had Maggie. That seemed impossible. The note said simply:

> *Today is the day.*
> *Best wishes,*
> VC

Not trusting anything, I checked around the motor home for bombs or whatever looked suspicious. When I popped the hood, the batteries had returned. Even the ones in the rear and the jeep were back, along with the portable generator in the rear compartment.

We were baffled, but it was time to get out of there. I cranked the engine over and threw it into reverse. Just as we began to back out I saw Vaca's shovel stuck in the sand, way out by the waterline—but it caught me funny.

Grabbing my binoculars, I focused on it as best I could, then left the engine to warm up and ran for the beach, despite a shouting Ellen.

Maybe I was pushing my luck, and maybe my vision was shot from fatigue, but what I saw was a chance to get back to the States all even. The luck was going good that morning, so I ran for the needle-shaped object sticking out of the sand. Halfway there my hunch proved right. It wasn't a shovel.

Seconds later a feeling of foolishness and danger began to overtake me. I should have gotten the hell out of there. What was I doing? I kept slogging through the sand anyway, knowing that any sane person would turn back. But just then it couldn't be done. Not as long as that tent pole was staring me in the face.

 13
Clam Dig

A couple of minutes later I was at the tent pole, which was stuck in the sand at the same spot from which the Indian had taken it. At least it looked like it. The tide wasn't coming in yet, so the pole wasn't underwater.

When I grabbed it, a warm tingling sensation raced up my arm, as though it had been asleep and was just waking up. I shook off the strange feeling and grabbed the pole again.

Pulling it out revealed just the tip of an old shell a few

inches below the surface. It was enough. I dropped to my knees and began digging like a dog. This time the ocean wasn't going to take my treasure away. By the time Maggie joined me in the dig, I had exposed the top half of a giant clamshell, nearly four feet long and three feet deep, judging by what I had uncovered.

When I got about two-thirds of the way underneath, I looked it over carefully. It was a soft shade of silver-gray, and covered with hundreds of little volcano-shaped barnacles, so sharp that I cut my hands a few times by digging too close to them.

I foolishly made some attempts to pull it out of the hole Maggie and I had dug around it. But it was way too heavy and the hole kept filling with seepage until it resembled a saltwater moat around the upright clamshell.

Looking up I saw that the tide had just begun its slow creep to shore. It would pick up fast, but luckily was still a couple of hundred yards away. That gave me only fifteen minutes to get the shell ashore.

Ellen finally came trudging toward me, carrying an excited Susie.

"Mommy! Mommy! Daddy's found a shell! And it's a *biiiig* one. I want to see it."

Before Ellen reached me I met her twenty yards away and explained that I'd have to hook up the winch on the front of the jeep and pull the shell out. No, I hadn't tried to pry it apart, though it had looked quite dead. And yes, I would try not to damage the shell.

While digging around it I'd noticed there was no living tissue lining the large matching curves of the flutes, just a half-inch-thick, bony shell welded tightly together by time and the sea.

Ellen suggested I get the crowbar out of the motor home and try to pry it apart first, in case the jeep got stuck in the muddy sand. "Just be careful," she warned me, "not to break the darn thing to pieces. We still don't know if anything's inside it yet. It could be just an empty shell, and our only treasure—besides those tacky tourist souvenirs.

"To tell you the truth," she added, carrying Susie over to look down into the moat, "it'd be a lot less trouble for everyone if it *is* empty. Then maybe we wouldn't have so many uninvited guests.''

Deciding not to comment until I saw inside it, I suggested that it would be best for the shell and us to drag it ashore before the tide came in. Ellen agreed after looking at the incoming tide. She wasn't prepared to lose it again, or to lose me to the insanity of the situation if the sea swallowed it up again.

Once at the jeep, I loaded the backseat with shovels, a pick, and tools, then drove back out. The sand was so soft in spots that the jeep started to sink a couple of times, even with four-wheel drive, but I managed to maneuver it to safety and parked ten feet back of the moat.

Ellen stood over the hole while Susie circled it recklessly, screaming and laughing with glee. The clam still sat straight up in the muddy sand pit. I kept expecting to hear an ear-shattering sound come screaming out of it, like that monolith on the moon in *2001*, but all remained pretty silent except for the distant sounds of campgrounds two miles in either direction, and the lapping of the tide, now only a hundred yards from us. No time for elaborate plans and speculation; we had to act immediately.

I reeled out the heavy steel cable coiled about the winch and wrapped it around the midsection of the shell, but not before protecting it with layers of beach towels normally reserved for jeep seats. Then came the moment of truth.

"Everybody back," I ordered. "Way back. This Goliath weighs a couple of hundred pounds at least. If it breaks loose and pops out of that hole, somebody could get hurt."

Ellen picked up Susie and obeyed, stepping back fifty yards. Maggie circled the pit, suddenly barking as though the mail carrier had come. It was just our luck that a small crowd of onlookers from the other campgrounds had gathered along the shore. When some of the tourists and locals began to slog out toward us, I told Ellen to head them off.

"Just how am I supposed to do that?" she asked.

"I don't know. I guess you'll have to think of something."

"Thanks," she said, rolling her eyes and starting for the beach, "for giving me the easy job. Have fun with your shell."

She turned and made for shore with Susie in her arms, while I worked the electric winch and yelled at Maggie to shut up.

Technology proved to be stronger than nature this time. An old dead shell proved to be no tug-of-war opponent for a winch with its thick steel cable. The shell broke free of its sandy mooring with a couple of strong tugs of the cable, without pulling the jeep apart in the process.

After it cleared the moat, I got out and examined the shell, making another foolhardy attempt to heft it into the backseat. It proved to be too heavy and awkward to manage. Actually, I probably could have heaved it into the backseat with a couple of old wrestling moves, but if I screwed up, I could break off some of it, or destroy my back in the process. No thanks.

As near as I could tell under the towels and cable, it was undamaged, a perfect three-foot-high and four-foot-wide specimen with no splits or cracks. I wanted to keep it that way. At least until I got it opened.

Glancing up at last, I noticed that Ellen was giving a tour guide speech to a group of a dozen curious onlookers, as if she were the curator of a recently constructed open-air beach museum—except that she must have announced that it wasn't open to the public yet, because when she pointed my way, everyone dispersed rather quickly.

In five minutes the beach was clear and I was dragging my treasure ashore, with the jeep in reverse all the way, just ahead of the advancing tide. I had to be careful not to get stuck in a couple of places, but the gods were kind that day.

I got the shell dragged up on the beach and over the low rock wall onto the flat campground beneath the umbrella. By that time it was pretty well covered with sand, and didn't resemble the fine fluted specimen I had started out with, but rather a giant breaded chicken breast instead.

After I shut off the jeep and made a victory gesture toward the ocean, I asked Ellen what she had said to clear the beach so quickly.

"I just told them you discovered some toxic waste," she said with a grin.

"And that worked? What would they care down here for?"

"Look, Jacques Cousteau. Take your head out of the sand. Pollution is a global issue now. Nobody wants to be somebody else's dumping ground, even a poor defenseless country like this."

"Yeah," I nodded. "Guess you're right. Remind me to cut a check to Greenpeace when we get back to the States." I looked up and down the beach, and then scanned the hills. The coast was clear.

Unfastening the clam from the wire cable and removing the sandy towels, I filled some buckets with salt water as the tide came in and washed it off. It was still in one piece, and sealed up as airtight as an old Volkswagen beetle.

Once I got it positioned on the sand under the umbrella, I spent the next hour trying to stick knives and other sharp objects between the flutes, but it wasn't going that well. It just wouldn't cooperate. So I decided to get a chisel and work at the base of the hinge. After all, it wasn't held together by living tissue anymore, only by time and calcification.

This proved to be an excellent idea. I was able to drive a wood chisel into the hinge with some well-placed blows from a three-pound hammer. Ellen gave me a nod that signaled she had forgiven me for bringing a whole toolbox full of assorted wrenches and stuff on our vacation. I always liked to travel prepared for the unexpected, and this certainly qualified as such.

I carved a crease along the foot-long hinge between the shell halves and, with one final blow, drove clean through, popping the hinge apart.

Then it became relatively easy to inch my way around the shell with the chisel and a flat-bladed screwdriver—like working a stuck lid off a paint can. When I finally etched my way along the great curving flutes and completed circumnavigating the clam, it was time to open nature's treasure chest.

Crouching on my knees, I reached over the clam and grabbed the hinge halves, now almost a quarter inch apart. I looked at Ellen and she gave me a smile of approval. Slowly, as I lay sprawled out over the clam, I worked my fingers into the hinge. By now I was sweating profusely from the midday heat.

The shell suddenly created some kind of suction and closed down hard on all my fingers; only my thumbs were outside the hinge. My fingers were already swollen from heat and work, and now were being cut off from fresh blood. The suction increased as I tried to pull them out. My fingers were gradually being crushed.

"El!" I yelled. "I'm stuck. See if you can get a screwdriver in the side of this thing!"

She quickly grabbed a flat-bladed screwdriver and wedged it in the side between the shell halves, then drove it home with a hammer. I could wiggle my fingers a little, but I couldn't pull them out. Ellen tried to reposition the blade, but now the screwdriver was stuck. The suction increased again and my fingers began to grow numb.

"Get the crowbar!" I yelled. "This damn shell's trying to kill me."

Ellen picked up the crowbar lying on the sand nearby and dug it into the side of the clamshell, but she couldn't get it in far enough to wedge it open. My knuckles were turning white, my face deep red.

"Okay," I said, looking wickedly up at Ellen, "no more Mister Nice Guy. Get the three-pound hammer and drive that crowbar into the side. If we break this thing, we break it. But I'm not giving up my fingers without a fight."

Ellen was getting tense, but was still pretty calm considering the circumstances. Luckily, Susie was in the motor home fast asleep, while Maggie paced back and forth, whining at my predicament and occasionally stealing a lick on my face.

Ellen lifted the hammer back with one hand and prepared to slam it into the curved end of the crowbar. If she could drive it in far enough, she could stand on it. Maybe her weight would open the shell far enough to free my fingers.

The instant she crashed the hammer into the crowbar I gave it my best yank. It separated a little. She tried it again. It moved a little more. I could almost wiggle my numbing fingers. On the third blow a loud crack rang out, so loud that it echoed off of Mr. Zapata's house. Ellen looked at me with worried eyes.

The shell had split, right at the seam. The halves were free, though still sitting one atop the other.

I slowly pulled my bloodless fingers out of the clam and had Ellen wiggle them for me one at a time until I got the feeling back. Luckily, none were broken. I wanted to slug that shell, but didn't want to bust a knuckle, so I kicked it instead, which only hurt my foot through my work boots.

Then, when all the color had returned to my fingers, I reached over, grabbed the top half of the shell by the free hinge, and pulled.

At that very instant Maggie let out an ear-shattering bark, and the ground beneath me began to shake.

 14

Earthquake

It was an earthquake all right; everything was shaking at once: houses, umbrellas, the motor home, and the ground. As a Californian, I was used to this. Everyone I knew in LA did one of two things. They ran or they froze. Ellen and I were freezers. That is, we both always stood our ground unless we were under something top-heavy, like the palm frond umbrella. It was shaking wildly back and forth, right over our heads, while the ground beneath us rolled like someone was shaking out a carpet.

Maggie held on like a dog on a surfboard, ready to ride it out, but then got scared and squirmed her way under the motor home.

Immediately our attention turned to Susie in the Winnebago, as it rocked from side to side. The wheels even came off the ground. In an instant Ellen and I were on our feet, making our way like sailors in a choppy sea toward the motor home.

Ellen got there first, and was on the bed at Susie's side by the time my feet hit the steps. As I steadied myself in the doorway, the palm frond umbrella crashed behind me, just missing the Winnebago.

"El! Get Susie and let's get out of here before this thing tips over," I shouted as the motor home went up on two wheels, rattling dishes inside the locked cupboards. But just after I said it, suddenly it was over. The earthquake had stopped as abruptly as it had started.

The motor home still pitched from side to side, but it was slowing down. A few seconds later, all was still.

I stood and watched as Ellen held Susie for a long time, then took my turn holding my little girl, who wrapped her legs around me and said, "The ground was moving, Daddy. I got scared."

"So did I, honey. Daddy got scared too. I was worried about you."

Afterward, I surveyed the damage. None of the vital parts of the motor home appeared to be damaged, just some loose maps and papers had gotten scattered everywhere.

Once outside, I rolled the huge umbrella away from the Winnebago and called for Maggie. I could hear her whine, but her chain wasn't rattling. Wherever she was, she wasn't moving. In the excitement, I had forgotten where she had hidden.

Instinctively, I got down on my knees and, sure enough, she was crouched under the motor home, shivering with fear. She wouldn't come out, so I had to crawl in after her.

Getting her calmed down took a couple of good long hugs. Then we crawled out together. I picked up a tennis ball lying in the sand and tossed it across the campground. When Maggie tore after it like it was a neighborhood cat, I knew she was all right.

It wasn't until then that I took a good look at the campground. Several of the umbrellas were down, and some of the beach houses that lined the back of the narrow strip of packed sand had broken windows. Mr. Zapata's house had lost half the roof when it collapsed. The bathhouse had a wall that had fallen outward, and the chicken coop had burst open. A dozen hens were running everywhere, enjoying a rare taste of freedom. Maggie was after them in an instant. I had to tie her up to keep her from chasing them.

Half an hour later I was just stuffing the last of the chickens back in the coop when Mr. Zapata came barreling down the dirt road toward camp, making a dust cloud behind like smoke from an old train. He swung around the corner and pulled up alongside the chicken coop.

"¡*Dios mío*!" he shouted, hands on his head. "*Señor* Jack, what has happened here?"

"Don't tell me you didn't feel that earthquake," I said, latching the door to the chicken coop. "It must have wiped out half of San Bajamos."

"¿*Cuándo*?" he said, wrinkling his brow.

"Half hour ago," I answered, turning to face him. "Took me that long to get all these cluckers back in the henhouse."

"Jack," he said, adding a deep level of sincerity to his voice, "I just came from town. There was nothing. The ground there was still as—" He looked at the ocean as it crept in slowly toward camp. "As the sea," he said, gesturing toward it with his arm.

Indeed, the water was coming in quietly. Fortunately, the tide had been too far out during the earthquake to make a mess of things. But when Mr. Zapata looked out to sea, something else caught his eye. Suddenly his expression changed, even as I began to insist that San Bajamos *must* have felt such a big quake—one that had destroyed half the campground.

Mr. Zapata wasn't much interested in my speech. His eyes were glued to the giant clamshell lying on the sand. It was sitting there as calmly as before, except for the first time I noticed that something was different about it. The top half of the shell had shaken itself halfway off.

With the umbrella out of the way, the sun shone down directly on the shell, and even in the bright glare of the midday sun, there seemed to be something glowing inside the shell, returning the sun's light, and its power.

Mr. Zapata and I approached the shell slowly. When we got there, now joined by Ellen, holding Susie, and Maggie, everyone stood by speechless, staring into the bottom half of the shell at the large, luminous, satiny pearl lying there as stately as a crown jewel on a velvet pillow.

There was nothing else inside the shell; microorganisms must have scrubbed it clean. There was just the nearly round, soccer ball–sized pearl sitting against the pink shell.

A cloud drifted across the face of the sun, making an umbrella of shade over the campground. It *was* true. The pearl was glowing with a soft light, tinted with light pink as it reflected off the inside of the shell.

I crouched and carefully lifted the top half of the shell free the rest of the way, setting it aside on the sand. It was warm.

Then, with a glance at the others, and a quick look around to make sure the ground wasn't going to start shaking again, I slowly reached into the shell.

When my fingers got two inches from the pearl, I could feel some kind of electricity emanating from it, but I couldn't stop. My fingers went the last few inches, and suddenly I was touching it.

Warm, tingly electrical impulses filled my hands and slowly crept up my arms and shoulders, but I couldn't let go. The feeling reached my neck, and then my whole head began to tingle. The world faded away. The vision of the Aztec priest took its place as he staggered down the streets of the ancient city, the round heavy object still in his arms.

It was the year 1520, and Cortés had just taken the capital. That was why Montuca had escaped with the sacred object. The word of Montezuma's death had spread quickly. Villagers had either joined the fight against the white warriors, or fled in panic. Everywhere people ran wildly in the streets. Women carrying children poured out of the city to try and save a generation that could come back and conquer Cortés.

Montuca wouldn't be easily recognized in the excitement, having shed the feathers worn only by the high priest, and all his other garments except a coarse loincloth and the bandage. That and the thick crowd in the streets would help. But he was tired from the long escape tunnel, and was weakened by loss of blood.

As he labored down the chaotic streets, the weight of the sacred object was killing him. Yet whom could he entrust with its power? Who could be the keeper of the magic? Who would use it for the good of the people? Everyone who had come to know its power was dead, except him.

If he tossed it into shallow water, surely it would be discovered quickly. But he was too weak to dig a deep hole, and there was no time for that. The Spaniards had most likely secured the city and would soon be combing the countryside and the canals surrounding the capital, rounding up all remaining Aztec officials for imprisonment, slavery, or death. They must not find the magic. They must never gaze into the Eyes of God.

The legend had said that the holy magic must never see the sun, the light of day. For when it did, the mother of nature would return and take back the magic, then disappear for thousands of moons. But if the magic was discovered by invaders, they might use it for great evil.

Montuca leaned against an adobe hut to rest. He closed his eyes for a moment to pray for strength, and the world faded away.

The vision before me vanished and I was once again holding the pearl. The sun had emerged from behind the cloud and Mr. Zapata's hand was on my shoulder.

"The pearl is *magnifica*," he said in reverent tones, kneeling over me and making shade with his body. "The power inside is even greater than its beauty. But you must be careful, *amigo*. You are the protector of the magic now. You must see to it that it doesn't fall into evil hands. And that what's beneath the layers of pearl must *nunca, never,* see the sunlight, especially at midday, unless—" He paused, then: "The quaking of the Earth was just a small sample of its power."

"I understand," I said, still shaken from the vision. I let go of the pearl and the electricity subsided. "Come on," I added, trying to stand. "Let's drag it under the motor home."

"Stay there," Mr. Zapata ordered, but he didn't have to. I had fallen over the shell in my dizziness.

"Jack," Ellen said. "Are you all right?"

"Never been better," I said sarcastically. "Except maybe after winning the state wrestling title."

"Yeah," she scoffed. "I can see you're normal. Your sense of humor is still intact."

Mr. Zapata was back with a Mexican blanket from his truck. He helped me up and we wrapped the pearl inside it, being careful not to touch the milky surface, or expose it to the sun. Then, when we had finally secured it inside the blanket, we tied the ends together at the top.

I changed my mind about the pearl's destination after explaining to Mr. Zapata that the motor home seemed to be a target for thieves and such. Then I picked up the pearl in the blanket and carried it to Mr. Zapata's house, feeling a dull pain in my left shoulder. Yet I had never injured it.

Carrying the pearl to his half-demolished shack like a father holding a newborn, I set it down under a wooden crate that served as a lamp table in a part of the living room that still had a ceiling. The crate still had the word FRAGILE stenciled across its side, and THIS END UP pointing at the dirt floor.

Ellen and I washed off the shell, and decided we could stuff both halves in the booze-smuggling compartment under the bed in the motor home. I wouldn't be using it this year.

We ate lunch and discussed our escape plans. They were simple enough. The pearl would be switched with the shell in the booze compartment for the ride home. The shell, beautiful as it was, would be our going-away present to Mr. Zapata. Maybe he could get enough to fix his house by selling it to some rich tourist in town.

He only took the shell after our repeated insistence. When we got ready to go he handed me our precious cargo, and some advice to go with it.

"I know you wish to take it back to the States and cash it in for, as you say, big bucks. But remember this: What's beneath the protective layers is far more valuable than the pearl. And you must know also that the legend says it will never leave Aztec land. As to whether that extends to your Sherman Oaks ... Well, maybe once, but no more."

"What do you mean?" I asked, puzzled.

"To put it simply, you'll never get across the border with it," he insisted. "That's the legend ... But go ahead," he added, handing it to me and waving good-bye. "You'll see for yourself."

With that, I stuffed the pearl in the hidden compartment and got behind the wheel. The motor home started and we rolled off down the dirt road, waving good-bye to Mr. Zapata and our wild, wonderful vacation.

15

Roadside Distraction

It was a hundred miles to the border, which meant only a two-hour drive. We would be there long before sunset, barring any unforeseen circumstances.

I debated with myself whether to tell Ellen about my dream and vision of the Aztec priest, but decided it would sound too crazy, so I just kept it to myself.

We did discuss our treasure riding under the bed. Between us we couldn't come up with a good story if the border police decided to take the Winnebago apart. Obviously, we didn't bring the pearl into Mexico, and would have a heck of a time convincing anyone that it belonged to us. Finders-keepers was one thing in the States, but some border guard was bound to claim it "for the people of Mexico" unless we came up with more than a hundred dollars cash and some overloaded credit cards to pay him off. We'd probably have to surrender the pearl.

All of the talk about being found out led me to get suspicious. I began to spend a lot of time looking in the rearview mirror to see if we were being followed. But it wasn't the view behind the motor home that provided the adventure that day. It was the view in front.

About fifty miles from the border on that lonely two-lane highway, an old Volkswagen van was broken down on the side of the road. The engine compartment was open and a hand-painted sign on a piece of cardboard was stuck in the back window. HELP! STRANDED AMERICAN!

I should have known better. Even as Ellen ordered me to slow down it began to smell like a trap, but it was too late. By the time I recognized the van as the one at the resort, I had pulled over and stopped.

Still, it wasn't too late to pull back on the road and get

out of there. Except Ellen said, "Jack, go on. See if we can help. It's dangerous down here."

"All right," I agreed. "But that looks like the van owned by that wild Indian, the one in the dune buggy." When she gave me a confused look I added, "You know, the one with the buns."

"Buns!" Susie yelled from her car seat. "Mommy, I want to see the buns."

Ellen thought about it a moment, then looked at Susie. "Okay," she said to me. "Maybe we'd just better get out of here before—"

Suddenly the Indian came out of the passenger's side of the van and threw up his arms in a surrender motion. He looked more normal in a pair of faded Levis with holes worn in the knees, cowboy boots, and a short sleeve safari shirt. He even had his hair pulled back in a ponytail.

Before I had sense enough to get back on the road, he was standing on the highway next to my open window.

"Look," he said, rubbing his chin. "I'm sorry about the tent pole. I drank too much tequila and made a fool of myself the other day. I didn't have the guts to apologize to your face, so I just put the tent pole back this morning. I hope you found it all right."

"Yeah," I said, relaxing a little. "We found it."

"What were you marking? A good clamming spot or something?"

"Sure," I nodded, grinning at the irony. "Got a couple dozen six-inchers."

"Six-inchers?" He raised his eyebrows. "That's not bad for around here." He looked at the VW van. "Well, if you could do me a favor when you get back to the border." He handed me a folded piece of paper. I took it automatically.

"Phone my brother," he added. "Tell him to come and get me. And bring a toolbox. Unless you've got a set of metric wrenches in the motor home here."

"What's the problem?"

"Fan belt's loose. I don't have any tools. Some locals cleaned me out the other night."

"If that's all it is," I said, "a crescent wrench will fix it." I handed him the paper. "Here, you won't be needing this."

I got out and walked over to the side of the Winnebago, unlocked the storage compartment, and took out a small red toolbox. Then I followed him to the van. Sure enough, he had a loose fan belt, which was easily fixed by a crescent wrench and a little elbow grease. I was just wiping my hands off when he went into the cab, saying, "How much do I owe you for the—"

"Don't be ridiculous," I replied. "Glad to help you out."

"No," he said. "I insist."

Before I could stop him, he reached into the glove compartment and came out with a Colt .45, which he promptly aimed at my head.

"Now," he said with a wry smile, "let's have a look at that pearl."

Rather than waste time claiming I didn't know what he was talking about, I just cut it short.

"Don't have it," I said. "Zapata took it. Said it belonged to the people of Mexico or something like that. And *his* gun was bigger than that peashooter you've got. I think he's been watching too many Dirty Harry movies."

"Well, then, you won't mind if I have a look around ... Oh," he added, free hand on his heart. "How rude of me. I haven't properly introduced myself. Name's Chief Zephacan, God of Liquid Spirits. I've come to claim the pearl for my Indian friends."

"Well," I scoffed, "you could at least get your story straight. The other night you said you were Montuca's ghost. I should have known the fan belt story was a fake. So, tell me. What do *you* know about the pearl?"

He waved his gun at me and motioned toward the motor home. "No time for chitchat," he said with a smile. "Open up the motor home there. I've got some buried treasure to look for. And in case you're worried about the old Colt here ..." He stopped and aimed it at the front passenger's tire, then squeezed the trigger, blowing a hole in the tire with a loud blam.

"Don't get any ideas, *gringo*. There's five more pieces of lead in the chamber."

"All right," I agreed, somewhat subdued. "There's no need for violence. I've got a wife and daughter in there."

Ellen had come to the front to investigate the loud noise and the flat tire. She saw the gun and went back to protect Susie. When we climbed through the door she was curled up on the corner of the bed, holding our little girl.

"Could you please put that gun away?" she asked, both perturbed and scared. "We were just leaving."

Maggie didn't like it much either, and began to growl from her spot on the bed.

"Fair enough," the Indian said. "No point teaching the kid bad habits." He put the gun behind him and let them and Maggie outside. I didn't dare take a swing at him, though I wanted to. It was far too dangerous. On her way out the door Ellen turned and looked at me.

"Show him where the pearl is, Jack," she said. "We've only got the one spare, and none on the jeep, as I recall."

I glared at Ellen, but knew he'd have taken the motor home apart until he found it. She had to tie Maggie up by the jeep, since our faithful dog had broken into a barking fit over the intruder.

Out the window I watched Ellen carry Susie into the brush to get as far away from the gun as possible. I was glad for that. Then, going straight to the hiding place, I pulled out the pearl, still wrapped in the Mexican blanket. It looked like a hobo's sack without a stick.

Once outside, I handed it over and said, "Here, now please leave us alone."

"Nothing doing," he answered, frowning. "Open it."

I stopped cold. "You know it can't be exposed to the sun."

He looked up at the sky. It was three in the afternoon. "The legend says only the noonday sun," he reminded me. "That was hours ago."

"Look," I protested, "that's not what *I* heard. It's only *worse* at noon. That's all."

He tossed it to me, keeping the gun aimed at my head. "I said open it. I'm not leaving without the real McCoy."

"What if I take it inside the motor home? Then we don't risk another earthquake."

He cocked his gun. "The next thing you hear will be a loud bang," he said with a smirk. "It will also be the last. Unless you open it right now."

I sat down between the motor home and the Volkswagen van on the dirt shoulder of the road. The pearl was nestled in my lap. My fingers carefully untied the knot at the top. I purposely made a little patch of shade with my new straw hat, then opened the blanket enough to show him the top of the pearl. That wasn't good enough. He wanted to see the whole thing, and arguing was only going to get me in deeper. So I unfolded the blanket and sat with the pearl on my lap. It rested comfortably in a soft, pink luminous light of its own creation.

The afternoon became unnaturally quiet. Maggie had stopped barking. That bothered me. What was she up to? My suspicions were confirmed a moment later.

Just as the Indian nodded his approval at the pearl, there was a flash of motion near the back of the motor home. Maggie had chewed through the leather part of her leash and was free, racing at full speed toward the Indian.

He saw her out of the corner of his eye as she rounded the motor home in full stride, just twenty feet from making her leap at his neck. Her eyes were intense, her growl fierce.

He spun to fire, and when he did I moved instinctively to save my dog. The pearl hit the ground with a solid thud. Instantly, I was on top of the Indian, knocking him flat on his back. The gun went flying.

I got up and started looking around frantically for the gun, not sure where it had landed. It must have flown over his head into the bushes. Good. I was pretty sure he couldn't outwrestle me, and knew he was no match for Maggie, who was getting ready to tear him apart.

She never got the chance. Just when she got to him there was a blinding flash of light and a sudden powerful wind came up off the desert, driving Maggie under the motor home, and knocking me flat on the ground. It was howling and pitching sand in my face so fiercely that I had to cover my eyes with my hands to keep from having them gouged out. My hat was long gone.

Minutes went by with the wind ripping through the desert, pressing me flat on the ground. All I could think about was Susie and Ellen out there, but I couldn't move. I couldn't even see. I was being sandblasted.

Finally, after what must have been five minutes, it stopped. The air was as still as a lake without ripples. I got up, spit sand out of my mouth, and looked around. The Winnebago was still behind me, and the jeep behind it, but the VW van and the Indian were gone, along with the pearl.

Maggie crawled out from under the motor home and we dashed off together into the desert. I ran wildly through the brush, desperately calling for Ellen and Susie. Fifty yards away, they were safe. Ellen had seen the thick sandstorm come up along the road, but it didn't come near them. I was baffled, because it had hit from that direction—right where they were sitting, playing in an open patch of sand.

On the way back to the motor home Susie wanted to know if that mean old man with the gun was gone. I looked around for the Colt .45, but never found it. I had to cut my search short, having a flat tire to fix. But just before giving up on the gun I saw something lying in the dirt on the side of the road. It was a piece of pearl about the size and shape of a small sand dollar. I wouldn't have even noticed except that it was glowing soft pink. When I picked it up, it was warm, and had a faint, faraway tingle to it.

I was just bending down to change the flat when an old farm truck skidded to a stop alongside the motor home, then raced away after dropping someone off. It was Vaca, and she had my hat.

 16

The Mouths of Babes

"Hi, there," Vaca said with a big smile. "How's it going this afternoon?" She looked at the jeep hooked up to the motor home. "You're not leaving, are you? You've only been here a week."

"Ten days," I answered, staring at my hat in her hands. "But it seems like a month."

"Hey," she went on. "Aren't you *having fun yet*? As you *gringos* say."

"Well," I replied, gesturing toward the front of the Winnebago, "we'd be having a lot more without this flat tire. Say, as long as you're here, why don't you see what you can do?

"Come on," I added with a sweeping motion. "Lay your hands on this tire and heal it. That seems to be your specialty, other than getting us in over our heads with this pearl. . . . If you know so much," I added, making a grab for my hat and missing, "why didn't you just tell us some Indian was going to come along and take it away. And thanks for scaring everyone half to death. That Aztec had a gun, and I have a two-year-old here. Couldn't you think of a nicer way to—"

"Jack," she said, finally handing over my straw hat, "I'm sorry. I can see you're upset. I didn't know about the gun. Honest. I don't know *everything*. Besides, it was supposed to happen this way."

Still upset, I slammed the hat on my head and paraded back and forth, complaining that if we were never destined to have the pearl, then why put us through all of the torture of discovering it? I went on about that sandstorm and how it could have blinded someone.

"I didn't create that wind," she said seriously. "It must have been the pearl. Did you expose it to the . . ."

"He made me unwrap it," I told her, cooling off a little. "It hit the ground when I jumped on him." I reached into the pocket of my Big Dogs shorts and pulled out the piece of pearl. It still had a pink glow about it, but was beginning to fade.

"Jack," Vaca said grimly, squeezing it closed in my hand. "The skull is now exposed. I just hope this isn't a piece that covered one of the eyes. Because if it is, there will be nowhere to hide if Warren taps the power."

"Warren?"

"The Indian, as you call him. His name is Warren. Warren Gates. He—"

Susie had stuck her head out of the motor home. "Daddy, I want to go home now. Mommy says to make her fix the *tie-were* so we can go home."

"Okay, sweetheart. Vaca says she's going to fix it for us, *right now*. Then we'll be on our way."

Susie turned to give Ellen the message. Vaca bent down, put her palms on the tire and closed her eyes. Slowly and silently, air began to fill the tire as the motor home rose a fraction of an inch at a time until it was back to level. The tire was hard and full again. Vaca stood up and smiled. "Bullet's still in there," she said. "But it won't hurt anything. It'll just rattle around a little. One more souvenir for you and the family."

She reached down to pet an excited Maggie, who had come over for a belated greeting. Vaca noticed how black her hands were from the tire. I told her to wash up in the motor home and finish her story about Warren while we took her back to town.

"I'm not going back to town," she said over the sink. "Besides, you don't want to head in that direction anyway. Border's north, as I recall."

"That's fine with us," Ellen said, concerned, handing her a towel. "But where are *you* going?"

"Wherever that pearl went," Vaca said. "And I'm sure it's headed for the border right now."

"Yeah," I chimed in, then added in a fake dramatic voice, "but it will never leave Aztec land."

"Exactly," Vaca said, sitting on the couch. "That will make it easier to find. It's got to be between here and the border."

"And just how do you propose to get it back?" I asked. "Make a hole in one of his tires? Maybe you two could have a contest blowing holes in each other's tires. Except you don't have your own wheels. You'd have to borrow ours, I guess. How many flats can you fix in a day, anyway?"

"Jack," Ellen said, looking at Vaca, "I think it's time to trust her. If she wanted to do us in to get the pearl, she could have done it long before now. We could have woken up this morning with a dozen flats, counting the jeep and the spares, and no pearl at all. Instead, it must have been Vaca who got the tent pole back and re-marked the spot where the pearl was buried for you, then got all our batteries back, if I'm not mistaken. Now, after some maniac steals the pearl, Vaca turns up in time to get us back on the road. It wasn't her fault that wild man laid a trap for us. She can't be everywhere at once.''

My jaw dropped half a foot. I tried to talk, but the words got tangled in my throat. Here I was the one who had befriended Vaca, believed in her enough to get us the pearl. And now, just because I was mad about losing it, Ellen goes and takes Vaca's side, steals her away from me just like that. I couldn't believe it.

''Well I'll be a certified public accountant,'' I was finally able to spit out. I stared at Ellen, still in disbelief. ''El, I thought you didn't believe any of this. Why now, all of a sudden?''

''Simple,'' Ellen said, looking at Susie playing with blocks on the bed. ''It was Susie's idea.''

I sat down at the breakfast table opposite Ellen and Vaca seated on the couch. ''Okay, go on. Explain Susie's idea. It probably makes as much sense as anything else.''

Ellen took a deep breath and began. She reminded me that she and Susie went to Sunday school at the local church. One of the things they teach the children is that there are guardian angels that protect people, especially little kids. They do this for folks who need a little extra help to get through difficult times. Sometimes angels show up just to get people out of danger. On special occasions, when the danger is great or the person really lucky, the guardian angel can be seen performing small miracles.

Ellen had explained to Susie that Vaca had fixed the flat because she had a special touch, one that nobody else had. This was enough for Susie. That was her miracle. ''I can see her, Mommy,'' Susie had said. ''*Baca* is our *guard-we-un* angel. She came to help us.''

Ellen thought about it. She was raised in the church and was still a believer. What Susie had said had touched something inside her. There was no other explanation. Since *people* didn't have special powers, Vaca was not a person. She was an angel, our guardian angel. And because the danger was great, she had come in the flesh to help us out. Calling herself the Vacation Goddess was simply Vaca's way of explaining that she was the guardian angel of tourists. She had even said as much. Ellen could accept that, and did, with a little help from the mouth of a babe.

"I know it sounds crazy," Ellen said, staring at me. "But if you went to church once in a while, it might not seem so wild after all."

"Well," I said, "goddess, angel, sorceress. It's all the same to me." I looked sheepishly at Vaca. "Look, I'm sorry. I was just mad about losing that darned pearl. All I could see was quitting my job and being happy. Now all that's gone in an instant."

I shrugged. "Ah, what the hey. Maybe losing it's for the best. If that pearl really has all those powers, it's starting to sound too dangerous to deal with." I glanced at Vaca. "It's not radioactive, is it?"

Vaca laughed. "No, its powers are all natural."

"Yeah," I said sarcastically. "So are earthquakes and hurricanes."

"That's why we have to get it back, before . . ."

Susie ran up and grabbed Ellen's leg, then pointed up at Vaca. "You're our *guard-we-un* angel," she announced. "Can we go home now?"

"Sure," Vaca said with a smile. "You can go home now."

"Are you going with us?" Susie asked hopefully.

"That's right," I answered for Vaca. "She's going with us. At least until we get to the border."

"Palm Springs," Vaca corrected me. "I have papers." She patted a front pocket on her dirty dress.

"You'd better," I said. "The last thing we need is to get caught at the border smuggling illegal aliens."

"If it really bothers you," Vaca said, "you can let me off when we get there, and I'll make a run for it. That's the latest thing these days."

"Fine," I said, not really paying attention. Then, climbing behind the wheel and firing up the engine, I turned to Vaca, sitting shotgun. "Now, who's this Warren fellow, and what does he have to do with all of this?"

I pulled the motor home back on the highway and headed north.

🦎 17
Olympic Trials

"He's what you call a treasure hunter," Vaca informed me about Gates as she stared at cactus along the road. "According to my research, he looks for lost treasure. He usually waits until someone's discovered something and then steals it. So, I don't think he cares much about the pearl's powers. He just wants to unload it for cash and be on his way."

"Guess I figured that much. But how did he even know about the pearl? When he drove by in that dune buggy there was only a tent pole in the sand."

"As soon as you talked about it, the word was out," she answered authoritatively. "Once a secret is spoken, it travels in the air like dust in the wind. Some of that dust settled in his ears. And some in Dr. Hardwick's as well, I figure. That's why he tried to run you down the other day. That was him in the boat the other night, too."

Ellen was sitting in the back, doing a puzzle with Susie on the breakfast table. "At this point," she stated, looking up, "I think it's best we head on home. No offense, Vaca. I haven't changed my mind about you, but there's just too many people chasing this pearl. And I don't want to put my daughter in any more danger. So if it's all the same to you—"

"I understand perfectly," Vaca said over her shoulder. "And there is certainly no need to involve you in this any more than necessary." She glanced over at me. "Jack must decide if he wants to fight his destiny and go home to America, or live up to the legend and regain the pearl."

"Look," I said, raising my voice, "let me make one thing clear. This legend talk has been fun stuff, but let's cut to the bottom line. The only reason I want that thing back is to cash it in for a lot of loot. In short, my interest is purely

84

financial—the same as our illustrious Mr. Gates. I'm afraid we're more alike than you think. We're both mercenaries.''

Vaca read the look on my face, but didn't say anything at first. She just watched the road roll under the tires. Finally, when I had cooled off a little, she said, ''Money is not the worst of motives. Like other sources of power, it can be used for good. If I know you, Jack, your wife will have to keep you from giving it all away.''

''After,'' I replied, ''I get my hardware store.''

''Then I take it you're still in this?''

Losing control for the moment, I pounded the steering wheel. ''Damn it! That's *my* pearl. I found it fair and square. And I want it back. It was in my hands, and then he took it. I had him, too, until that stupid wind came up and made off with it. People have no right to take somebody else's dream. I lost a chance at going to the Olympics, once. And I'm not going to lose this, too, not without a fight.''

I looked in the rearview mirror. Everything that had any value to me was in that reflection: Susie's sparkling eyes looking for pieces of the puzzle, Ellen's loving concerned glance, even Maggie's tongue-wagging smile. Everything else was just material possessions, devoid of smiles and tears, passion and life. The pearl had captured my sense of adventure and greed, taken me in like a sucker bet. But if it took my family away, it was going to be war. That was one thing for which I would fight to the death.

Ellen met my glance in that silent reflective moment, and read my eyes like a headline. She knew I wouldn't leave her and Susie to go on a risky treasure hunt, at least not without permission, and dragging them along was out of the question. She knew also that the prize could set us free, at least financially. And she knew the danger. She wasn't afraid of the danger, but she would never leave Susie at her mother's for some crazy adventure, and taking a two-year-old on a dangerous ''Mission Impossible'' episode was irresponsible, to say the least. If I went at all, it would be alone.

Before she even spoke, I could read the message in her eyes. It was the same message she sent with her glance at me during the Olympic wrestling trials. We were in college and in love, and she traveled across three states with me on the team bus, putting up with the jabs and jokes of my team-mates. During the meet I took a bad fall in the semis, and sprained my back, but managed to defeat my opponent and make it to the finals. I was in a lot of pain, and we discussed my pulling out. The doctor had already told me not to wrestle anymore. He said my career was over.

Ellen sat with me in the locker room before the final match, the one that would decide the last spot on the Olympic team. She looked at me and said, "I'm going to marry you whether you go out there or not. But remember, you'll have to live with that *back* the rest of your life. I know it's only a sprain, and this means a trip to the Olympics if you win, but it could be a lifetime of endless back pain if you get hurt, or worse." She walked out and left me alone with my decision.

The team doctor came in. He couldn't even meet my glance. I knew what it meant. He had to disqualify me medically, saying it was just too dangerous risking permanent damage if I took another bad fall. He couldn't live with himself professionally or personally if he let me go back out and wrestle.

I lost my composure. My dream since junior high had been that moment. I quietly apologized, and then promptly tied him up and taped his mouth. He didn't resist. He knew the situation had made me crazy.

For a second I thought about opening his bag and giving myself a shot of painkiller, but it was out of the question. I wanted to win it fair and square, with no drug scandal.

Leaving him tied up on the locker-room floor, I went out and wrestled, sprained back and all. The pain was unbelievable; it almost tore me apart. But my strength and will to win were stronger. I won, barely, and immediately collapsed to the mat after the referee raised my hand in victory.

They took me away on a stretcher, and after the doctor was freed, they took away my championship. It was a big controversy in all the papers. There was even a segment on the local news, and for a while I was a minor celebrity, though Johnny Carson never called. I wasn't surprised at what had happened. I knew beforehand that everything would be taken away, but I had to prove something to myself, prove that for at least a fleeting moment in time, I was the best.

In a few months the excitement died down, and miraculously, so did the pain. It turned out to be only a very bad sprain, and never bothered me much unless I tried to lift a water heater or something, or sat in a car all day.

I took the dream as far as I could, but came up short, ending up with my second choice, a business degree and a contracts administrator job. The bad part was that I never got to wear a medal, never got to touch one, never even got to compete for one in the Olympics. But I *had* touched the pearl, and all of the feelings about the spirit of competition were coming back. It was my gold medal, and I had to have it. It still wasn't too late for the mid-life crisis Olympics.

Ellen knew all of this when she looked back at me in the rearview mirror. She saw it in my eyes. Not too many people get a second chance in life. Getting the pearl back and trading it for a lot of cash was mine. Owning my own business, however small, was about the only dream I had left, other than the treasure of watching a little girl grow up. That wasn't negotiable at any price, not for a thousand giant pearls. Yet there I was, willing to risk *my* life for a financial fortune. Somehow, though, it didn't seem that dangerous. It seemed like just another wrestling match.

Warren didn't scare me that much. What scared me was him around Ellen and Susie with that loaded gun. But if I could just get him one-on-one, in hand-to-hand combat, I'd take him for sure. At least I wanted to think so in that moment, soaked in the intoxication of impending glory.

"Why don't Susie and I take the motor home?" Ellen said at last, like nothing had happened between us in the mirror. "You and Vaca can take the jeep. That is, if your back is feeling all right."

"Back's fine," I said, smiling. Vaca gave Ellen a weird look. "Actually," I added, looking in the mirror again, "you might not believe this, but the seats in the jeep are more comfortable for long drives. They don't hit my lower back funny."

I pulled over and stopped by the side of the road. Vaca was still a little confused. I was glad for that: at least she didn't know everything about us.

We explained to Susie that Daddy had some business and would meet her and Mommy back home in a couple of days.

Maggie wasn't as easy. She had always been my dog. That's because I spoiled her, even risking being constantly yelled at for feeding her at the table and letting her on the furniture, especially the bed. So she came with me and Vaca.

There was a full set of hugs all around. Susie and I had the longest session. She told me to be careful, come home soon, and even managed a practiced "I love you," with Ellen coaching her on the sidelines. That was the toughest to take. Naturally, Ellen was still skeptical about my trying to be Indiana Jones, but since she believed in Vaca, it helped a little.

"Don't worry," I said, unhooking the jeep. "It'll be just like one of those dumb business trips I go on, except for no airplane flying to worry about. Just think of it as another contract negotiation trip. Only this time if I win, *I* get to keep the prize, instead of some corporation. I'll call in a couple of days."

Ellen loaded us up with a cooler full of food and drinks. After I checked the progress of everyone's welts and saw they were healing fine, it was time to go. Just before walking back to the motor home for the last time, Ellen turned and said to Vaca, "Take care of him for me, will you? He *needs* a guardian angel. And make sure that he eats. When he gets excited he stops eating. And no booze, remember?"

"Thanks, Mom," I said. "See you when I get to America." I was as happy as a kid camping overnight in the backyard, and just as naive.

It didn't even faze me when Ellen said, "If he pulls that gun again, surrender. I'm not ready for single-parenthood."

She came back and consulted with Vaca, asking if she could somehow wreck the gun if Warren decided to fire on us.

"Don't worry," Vaca said. "I can do more than blow out tires if I have to. Guns have a way of jamming out here, especially when dust gets in the barrel."

Ellen felt better, if only a little. She gave me one last hug like I was a cop going off to a bad neighborhood. "I'm not letting you go unless you stop somewhere and get some protection," she said, pulling away to look at me. "I'm not promoting violence, but if he sees you with a weapon, it might discourage him from trying to shoot."

"But if I don't have one," I replied, "he's got no *reason* to shoot."

"Just promise. It'll make me feel better."

I promised and she went back to the motor home. Vaca, Maggie, and I sat in the jeep and watched as the Winnebago pulled back onto the highway. Just before it got out of sight Susie appeared in the back window, waving good-bye. We both waved back, I more frantically. Vaca gave me a compassionate look when she saw my face. It was scary all right, because at that point none of us knew if we'd ever see each other again.

I straightened my hat, started the jeep, and put it in gear. "Okay," I said, wiping my eyes under Ray-Bans, "which way to the pearl?"

"North, of course," Vaca replied. "But not as far as the border." She pulled a bottle of mineral water out of the cooler at her feet. "I have a feeling it's not far from here."

"Look, as far as jamming this Warren's gun, I thought you didn't do dust storms?"

"I just wanted to make her feel better. Besides, I didn't say that. All I said was, I didn't do the one that brought me your hat."

"Then who did?"

"Who knows?"

"So, could you jam his gun with flying dust if you had to?"

"How do I know? I've never tried it before."

"Then forget the pearl. It'll have to wait for us to catch up. Which way to a gun shop?"

18
The Deal

"So you want to fight violence with violence," Vaca responded to my request for directions to the nearest gun shop. "But do you really want to risk getting shot at for a little money?"

"A lot of money," I corrected, shifting into high gear. "What's inside that pearl has got to be worth a fortune."

"Then you don't really think it has powers? What about the earthquake, and that dust storm?"

I turned and smiled, closed-lipped. "What I think, Ms. Vaca, is that for all of your twelve years you are a very mature person. Maybe people grow up fast down here, but the way you talk and act like an adult is beyond just plain street smart. You're obviously very gifted. My theory is that your parents could not keep up with you and took you to a special teacher, someone who knew how to develop your mental and psychic abilities."

I took a deep breath and continued, reminding her that I didn't believe in goddesses and guardian angels, but believed in the mind's unlimited power. I'd had a few samples of it during my wrestling days in college. Like a lot of sports, wrestling isn't just brute force. It's mind over matter. Or in the case of my last bout, mind over pain. After I won that last match, the team doctor told the press that wrestling with that sprain was like competing with a broken arm. No one could believe I didn't scream during the match. But Muhammad Ali once fought with a broken hand. Sure, it hurts, but after a while you go beyond the pain. It doesn't come back until the match is over. Mind over matter.

"The way I've got it figured," I told her, "is that your teacher helped you develop your mental abilities." I patted her shoulder. "But it's a shame, really."

"Why?"

"Someone who can make and fix flats is a novelty. But someone who can control the movement of the Earth and the wind is a sorceress." I stared at her. "Vaca, you're wasting your talents chasing pricey artifacts; you could be a tremendous asset to the world. What's money when you can control the elements? You could help people. For all I know you can bring rain. Have you ever tried to stop or divert natural disasters? You could save lives, communities, countries maybe. I'm sure they'd pay you a lot for that."

"Good," she said, smiling. "We're making progress. You don't believe I'm a goddess yet, but you do believe in my powers."

"Yep," I said, nodding. "That I do. But why—"

"Make you a deal. You just believe in my powers, and I'll help you get your pearl back."

"Is that the deal?"

"Almost."

"Uh, oh. I knew it. Hey, I thought we already had a deal."

"We do. That *is* the deal. And here are the terms. I lead you to the pearl on one condition."

"What?"

"Once you get it back, you test the legend."

"You mean—"

"We peel off the layers of pearl and expose the crystal skull. Then, in the noonday sun, you look into the Eyes of God."

"What will that prove?"

"If you are Aztec, the power that has been asleep in the eyes for nearly five hundred years will be transferred to you. Then you'll have power that will dwarf mine. You will have power over all of nature, not just the little things I do. You, and not me, can change the world."

"Aren't you Aztec?"

"No, I'm not an Aztec goddess. I'm what you might call in the Western European tradition. That's where serious vacations began in earnest."

I slapped the steering wheel. "All right, then. Fair enough. Since *I'm* not Aztec either, I've got nothing to lose. But here's *my* deal. After I do this noonday sun show—providing

I don't get blinded by the reflection—I have the right to do whatever I want with the pearl. Cash it in or whatever."

"You've got a deal," she said, and stuck out her hand for a shake. As we shook on it she started to tell me something about the pearl and the noonday sun, but I wasn't listening. Something had caught my eye in the rearview mirror. A blood-red dune buggy was screaming up behind me. There were two men inside, but before it got close enough for me to identify the passengers, my eyes glassed over and I was back in my Aztec priest vision.

Montuca's head cleared a little as he rested against the village wall, still holding the pearl, pain pounding in his shoulder. He knew there was only one solution, one way to the sea. But it was a long way off, and he was wounded and on foot.

He suddenly grew dizzy, almost delirious. With bodies bolting past him in the street, his desperation relieved him of his senses, and he acted purely on survival instinct. He did the unforgivable, knowing it would be his death, and hoping the sun god would forgive him. But it was his only hope now, for he could feel his body growing heavy, the blood saturating the bandage. His life was slipping away. His knees began to buckle, but with one last surge of strength he stood his ground.

The sun glared down directly overhead. Montuca was privy to the knowledge that the magic could be allowed to see the noonday sun under one condition: an Aztec would have to gaze into the eye sockets. This would give him the power in the skull, the control of nature. But it was to be done only if the skull were in great danger, and was known only to the high priest.

He pulled back the smooth cloth that held the magic. It was already speckled with his own blood, but the sacred object was still clear, pure and shiny. Montuca exposed just the very top of its luminous curved surface. He was about to gaze into the Eyes of God when a brilliant flash of reflected light blinded him for a second, and then faded as a cloud slipped in front of the sun. The pain surged up in him, and he had second thoughts. He was dying, and not fit to receive the power. He must save it for one who was ready and able.

With his consciousness ebbing, Montuca suddenly saw the image of his father, Techapan, the high priest before him, standing in the middle of the dusty street. He was dressed in his finest ceremonial feathers. His hands were empty and outstretched. Villagers ran through his body as if he weren't there, yet Montuca saw him as clearly as the dust in the street.

The road came back into view. I was still driving and, thank god, still in my lane. Something caught my eye on the side of the road and I slammed on the brakes, then backed up pretty fast. When the jeep covered a hundred feet in reverse, I stopped and looked out across the desert.

There was a set of tire tracks leading off into the scrub brush, heading northwest. They were a width and size that seemed somehow familiar.

"Well," I said, "is this the way to San Jose, or what?"

"If you're trying to say that these are Warren's tire tracks heading toward the border, then yes. That's them."

"Good," I said, putting it in four-wheel drive and heading off the pavement. "Then let's get going."

"And your gun shop?"

"No time for that now, *kemosabe*. These look like fresh tire tracks. Besides, we've got *your* powers. *I* can wrestle, and"—I looked in the back—"we've got a trained killer Labrador here. Worse comes to worst, she'll lick him to death."

"Well," she scoffed, "then what are we waiting for?"

"Just one thing," I answered, stopping the jeep and straightening my hat. "Before we go any farther. Are you responsible for these flashbacks I'm having?"

"What flashbacks?"

"Come on, don't play dumb. You know, the Aztec priest and all that."

"You're having the visions!" she beamed and hugged me. "I knew it. Oh, Jack, this is wonderful. You're *so* lucky."

"Lucky? I thought we were going to end up in a ditch back there. I don't know who was driving, but I was out of it for quite a while."

"When?"

"Never mind. Tell me about the visions. Why is it necessary for you to set me up with them? I told you I wasn't Az—"

"Damn it!" she shouted. "I'm *not* doing it. Didn't Zapata tell you?"

"Tell me what?"

"About the visions. He must have forgotten. The one who comes to claim the pearl has *powerful* visions. He can see the past. He will know what happened the day Montuca escaped. And he will know what he has to do to save the Aztec people, to save the world from white man's destruction. Jack, this is great. You cannot doubt any longer. Only you—"

"Vaca, we made a deal. Maybe I can't stop you from giving me these visions, but I said I'd look into the skull, and that's that. If nothing happens, then the game's over. Don't try to convince me with any more of these dangerous visions. We might get killed next time.

"And another thing. I'm sick of this stuff about white man destroying the Earth. Look, I'm just a regular guy who has a daughter he wants to inherit the Earth when he's gone. And it would be nice if it was in good shape when she does. I recycle bottles, cans, and plastics. Ellen even makes me compost our lawn and yard clippings. So, just give me a break on that account. I'm doing the best I can, or at least all I've got the energy for right now."

Vaca could see I was upset, and began calmly. "There's no point getting defensive," she said. "Besides, it doesn't apply to you. Aztecs are not considered white men."

Rather than respond to that one again, I just shut up and drove off into the desert with Vaca mumbling to herself about me saving the Earth. I can only imagine how our little hunting party looked: a washed-up wrestler turned mercenary, a twelve-year-old homeless girl with magical powers, and a happily ignorant yellow Labrador. All off to save the world, fearlessly charging into the sunset. Thank god there weren't any windmills to joust with in the desert. But there was something else waiting for us. Something more human, and infinitely more dangerous.

19

Twinkle, Twinkle

Hours later, as the sun was just starting to duck behind the mountains, we were still on the trail. Warren's tracks wound toward the border, all right, and also headed west, in the direction of the Pacific. From the angle they were taking, he must have been planning to cross somewhere between Tijuana and Mexicali.

"He must know somewhere to sneak that bus across," I guessed. "Unless he's planning to bribe some border guard."

"You left out a couple of things," Vaca pointed out. "He could be ditching the bus for another vehicle, or maybe an airplane. There's more than one way across the border." She read my face. "But cheer up. Like I said, he's not—"

"Yeah, I know. He's not leaving the country with that stupid pearl. Is there something you're trying to tell me here, or am I just dense?" Looking at the wry smile on her face set off something in my mind.

"Hey, wait a minute," I said, slapping the steering wheel. "You *do* know something, don't you? And for some reason you can't tell me. What is there, some law of lost treasure or something? This reminds me of an old movie where people talk in riddles. And until the hero figures out what they're saying, he can't find the treasure." Reading her poker face, I added, "Okay, I can take a hint. If you can't tell me, I'll just have to guess.

"If Gates can't leave with the pearl, then he's got to get rid of it here." I looked around at the dried-up scrub, bony trees, and cacti. "But where? Is there some secret cave around here? Can you tell me that much?"

Vaca informed me that she didn't know much more than the legend stated, but since the pearl's territory was limited,

Warren would have to unload it between where we were and the border. That meant—

"Of course!" I yelled. "He's going to sell it. Someone's meeting him out here and that will be the end of it. Wait a minute, just before that last vision someone was coming up behind us in a dune buggy."

"That could be just about anyone," Vaca said, propping her feet on the dash. "There are hundreds of those things down here, maybe thousands. This is where they hold the Baja 1000."

"Darn, if I hadn't zoned out back there, I could have seen who it was."

"So what? It doesn't prove anything, unless *you've* got mental powers now."

"Hardly." I rolled my eyes. "If I did, would I be listening to you?"

"Look, smart aleck. We're both on the same treasure hunt. Only for different reasons, that's all. Let's try to make the best of it."

"All right," I replied, turning a little red. "I'm sorry. All I was trying to say was that this whole thing is starting to look a little stupid to me. Yeah, I know I was all hot to tramp off across the Earth in search of ancient artifacts, but look around you. All we've got is a set of tire tracks to follow. I'm not even sure anymore if these are the right ones. There's probably ten thousand Volkswagens down here. Half of them are dune buggies and surf vans."

"Jack," she said, "it's too early to give up on this. Pull over and let's eat. You're tired and hungry, that's all."

I gave her a mean look, so she tried another tack. "Okay, then. Let me drive, but Ellen said you have to eat or you get cranky. I think she's right." She looked around. "There's nobody out here. So quit trying to be macho." She pulled out a box of chocolate chip cookies and held them up to my face. "Me drive. You eat."

I stopped the jeep and looked at Vaca, then at the sun as it slipped behind the ridge of a mountain. Shutting off the engine, I took the box of cookies and powered them down, with some help from Maggie and Vaca. Then we had sodas.

So much for Mister Natural Foods. But I felt better. Low-Blood-Sugar Man to the rescue.

Afterward, we decided it had been a long day, and made camp. Vaca thought I was trying to short her on the driving, but I promised to give her a turn in the morning. We rolled out some sleeping bags and made a little fire with broken brush. Vaca even wandered off with a flashlight and came back with some edible cactus. We burned off the spikes, sliced it up, and ate it. It went pretty well with the cookies, but would have been better for a main course, instead of dessert.

The dark purple sky was filled to overflowing with count-less stars, forming in constellations like the card section at a football game. We tried to name as many as we could, got a bunch wrong, I'm sure, and settled down for the night. We didn't talk much after that until just before dozing off. With Maggie groaning pleasantly at the bottom of my sleeping bag and my eyes closing to the brilliant array of starlight over-head, I turned to Vaca.

"Susie used to make Ellen and me sing 'Twinkle, Twinkle, Little Star' to her every night," I said. "She called it Pinkle Pinkle. I could sing it in my sleep. A couple of times I think I did. Boy, how she loved that song.

"How do you do it?" I asked. "I mean, how do you get along without a family, without someone to love. I'm so weak I probably couldn't even get through life without a dog."

"You really know how to hit a girl when she's down," Vaca groaned. And before I could apologize she launched into a little lesson on life for my benefit.

"Aren't we a pair," she said, almost with a sigh. "Win or lose, *gringo*, you'll go back to your family. And I'll go back to saving tourists ... It's not that bad really," she added. "But you got me thinking. It would be nice just once to have my own vacation."

I reached over and hugged her, sleeping bag and all. "I'm still taking you skiing," I said. "It's even more fun than you think. Coming down a slope at sixty miles an hour, skis barely touching the snow—the feeling is incredible. There's nothing like it. The only time I felt higher without being drunk was carrying my daughter to the nursery after she was born. Those sparkling eyes looking up at you are brighter than stars. I thought I'd died and gone to heaven.''

Before Vaca could stop me I launched into a long, boring proud-father story about the firsts that are solid gold to parents: the first smile, word, step, and so on.

"I shouldn't even be here," I said at last. "I'm pushing my luck. We got everything we wanted with Susie. We never even had a boy's name picked out. When the doctor came in at the last minute to assist, he mistakenly told us we had a boy. 'No, it's not!' I shouted. 'That's the umbilical cord you're looking at tangled between her legs. That's our little girl!' ''

I went on about how beautiful she was, how smart, and how she'd need her brains to take on the world. Like a lot of fathers, I wanted her to do better than I had done with my life. It didn't look like that part would be too hard if she had good parents around, especially a sober father.

"Maybe we *should* forget all of this moneygrubbing," I finally said. "I already have more than most people in the world. And with your talents, so do you. Could be we *are* just pushing our luck. If I'm not around for Susie, she'll be no better off than I was. I'm not saying single parents can't raise kids, but Ellen could use some help once in a while. I gotta be good for something.

"Besides, I just want to be there for the rest of the firsts: report card, the school play, all of it . . . Vaca, did you make up the part about your parents being dead because you ran away?''

"They're not dead, just in heaven. My only regret is not having an actual childhood. How about you? Any regrets having Susie? Any at all?''

"Besides dirty diapers, temper tantrums, all-night crying sessions, constant messes, and pouting? Can't think of a thing.''

"Doesn't any of that really bother you?''

"Love kind of drowns all of that out somehow." I looked at Maggie curled up on top of my sleeping bag. "Take Maggie, for instance. I still love her, even after she's just eaten what the neighbor's cat left.''

"Oh, that's gross.''

"No," I disagreed, tickling her through the sleeping bag. "That's life."

We had a major tickling match after that, laughing until our sides split. It felt good to let off steam. Then Vaca got serious, telling me that sometimes it's okay to be a little selfish in life, but the matter of the pearl wasn't one of them.

"Unfortunately," she stated, "there's more to life than just what *we* want. I know this is beyond you right now, but just think for a moment. If the pearl really is magic, then its powers can change the world."

"I'm sorry, Vaca," I apologized, leaning back on my sleeping bag. "But I don't believe in magic. It's just fun for the mind as far as I can see."

She watched a star shoot across the sky at incredible speed, then told me that magic is just what we don't yet understand. Electricity was magic until Edison came along. Now everyone accepts it as a part of everyday life. I should think of the pearl as just another power source. If we could harness it, maybe we could stop the world from falling apart. Even if we could only slow the destruction down a little, it might give the Earth time to adjust to man's changes, and humans time to think about what they're doing. That might be a bigger contribution to my daughter's life in the long run—to everyone's sons and daughters.

"Look," I said. "I'm tired. Let's get some sleep and talk about this in the morning."

"Deal. See you in the morning."

With that we dozed off. When I awoke the next morning, the sleeping bag next to me was empty. Vaca and the jeep were gone, along with Maggie.

20

The Big Blush

My eyes followed the tire tracks farther west, wondering whether she had taken off after Gates with Maggie, and whether she had decided to ditch me. The disappearance of my dog came as no surprise, since she would jump in the jeep or my Saturn back home anytime anyone made a move to go anywhere. What Vaca didn't know worked in my favor, and that was that Maggie wouldn't get too far down the road before she would start to whine for me. Vaca would either have to turn back or wrestle Maggie out of the jeep, the way I had it figured.

I put my sandals on and hiked behind the jeep tracks, which paralleled the VW tracks. About a mile into my nature walk I came to a small downgrade. Directly at the bottom, in a small patch of sand, sat Vaca and Maggie. My dog immediately saw me coming from a couple of hundred yards away and jumped out of the jeep, bolting for me in her usual friendly, excited way.

By the time I got to the jeep, Vaca was revving up the engine and spinning the tires, which were now up to the middle of the wheels in sand.

"Got a problem, lady?" I asked, leaning on the spare tire, and dodging sand spitting up from the rear wheels. "Why don't you just go poof and make the jeep pop out of the ditch you've created?"

She stopped revving the engine and took it out of gear. The sand spitting stopped. "I thought this was an all-terrain vehicle?" she asked, frustrated.

I walked around the driver's side and she scooted over to the passenger's seat. "Normally it is," I answered, pushing my hat back on my head. "But you have to have it in four-wheel if you're going to be driving in deep sand."

"Wait a minute. I thought you put it in four-wheel way back at the road?"

"Did," I said sharply. "But I took it out again before we went to bed last night. I figured if somebody went joyriding, she might not notice."

Putting it back in four-wheel drive, I eased on the gas pedal and slowly pulled out of the small pit she had created. Maggie hopped in and we circled back toward camp.

"So," Vaca said. "Didn't trust me, huh?"

"Seems like it was a good idea. I didn't want you getting lost out here."

She crossed her arms and put her feet on the dash. "If you ask me," she said, "somebody just wanted to make sure he wasn't getting left out of the treasure hunt. Well, for your information, Mr. Trusting, I was just taking it out for a morning spin. I figured it might be my only chance to drive. Men always hog all the driving. Some kind of macho division of labor thing or something. Besides, I got tired of listening to you and Maggie snoring. At least *she* woke up when I got ready to leave."

Back at camp we ate some stale donuts and drank sodas. Our provisions were about half-gone. Only some cheese and crackers, a handful of sodas, and a bag of Doritos remained. We were supposed to have stopped at a store before leaving the main road, but totally forgot when we spotted the VW tire tracks leading into the desert.

All was not lost, though; we still had emergency rations in case things got desperate. There was a pool of melted ice in the bottom of the Playmate cooler, and half a twenty-pound bag of Purina Dog Chow in the back with Maggie. I was sure she'd share it with us if it came to that, but an effort would be made to avoid that option, even if it meant more cactus eating.

The map in the glove box said there was another road thirty miles farther ahead that split off toward Tijuana to the west, and Mexicali to the north. That should mean civilization, or what passed for it in Baja, which was usually a broken-down town with dirt farmers and goatherds. But because of tourists, there would be *gringo* supplies, maybe even a shower. It had become clear that we both needed one, and some toothbrushing as well.

After breakfast, we shared my toothbrush and kept heading west, following the constant impression of tire tracks. Hours later, with the sun almost directly overhead, we got out to answer the call of nature.

I went into the desert on the driver's side, and Vaca went the other way. When I returned, she wasn't back yet, and I had taken my time. Getting worried, I took off after her, telling Maggie to go on ahead and find her. Maggie didn't really understand, so I coaxed her along with a tennis ball that was stuck under the seat of the jeep.

A couple of hundred yards from the jeep Maggie darted behind a big bush. Vaca screamed. I ran up a small rocky hill, dodging lizards, and caught up.

Vaca was frozen in place. She was standing up, still with her faded dress on, but her underwear was down around her bare feet. Maggie had already come back to me, awaiting further instructions. When I got within twenty feet of Vaca I saw the scorpion.

It stood with its tail up, looking ready to strike, just inches from Vaca's right foot.

"Vaca," I said as calmly as possible, "don't move. I'll be right there."

"I . . . I can't move," she said in a frightened voice. "Jack, I'm scared."

It was the first time she had ever sounded like such a helpless little girl. It almost threw me at first, but I shook it off and quickly made plans. If I charged, the scorpion might sting Vaca before I got there. Throwing a rock and missing would have been a major disaster. That left one thing in my mind: Maggie.

I grabbed her by the collar and led her around behind the scorpion. We were ten feet away. The scorpion was still studying his victim, preparing to strike. A sting out here, miles from nowhere, could be fatal. I had to act fast. It was a gamble, but everything was at that point. I was relying on Maggie to create a quick distraction and not get stung in the process.

She pulled hard on the chain, ready to charge the scorpion

at full speed, the way she charged cats across the street at home. Maggie always chased the ones who ran, but stood her ground if they stood theirs. I was relying on that reaction—only this was far more dangerous than an old house cat. I was relying on Maggie's speed, size, agility, ferocious bark and growl, hoping she would frighten the scorpion into a quick retreat, long enough for me to grab Vaca. This was not entirely untested. Maggie was so quick that cats rarely were able to get in a strike against her. She would dart back and forth with incredible ease, teasing the cat, and retreating fast enough to avoid the claws. She even tried this once with the mailman. I heard the commotion out in the front yard and came running. There was Maggie, barking up a storm and ducking the mailman, who had emptied half a can of Mace into the street trying to squirt her. He never even came close. She was way too fast. As soon as I called her she came running, but they made us put the mailbox on the curb after that.

If Maggie got stung by that scorpion, I would hate myself. But if Vaca got stung, I'd never forgive myself. There was no choice. I had to act immediately.

Maggie made a hard pull on the chain and I let her go. In typical fashion she charged the scorpion. A second later the scorpion turned to protect its flank, staring into the eyes of a wild dog. Vaca was still frozen in place.

Suddenly, the scorpion darted straight at Maggie from two feet away. Instantly, Maggie backed up and barked, then circled, now fitting herself between Vaca and her attacker. The scorpion became defensive, holding its ground and spinning to guard against a darting Maggie.

I saw my opening, and went for it. Two seconds later I had scooped up Vaca and raced to safety twenty feet away. Maggie was still circling and barking up a storm. She wanted to play, but I couldn't chance a lucky strike at her nose by the scorpion.

"Maggie!" I yelled at the top of my lungs, and she came running, tongue hanging happily out of her mouth.

Vaca threw her arms around my neck. "Jack," she said at last, "those things scare me to death."

"Me too," I said, returning her hug. Then I set her down.

"But before we go any farther, could you pull up your pants. I don't want anybody thinking . . ."

"Jack," she said with an amused grin, "we're in the middle of nowhere. Who's . . . Look at you. You're turning red. You're embarrassed."

"Just pull your pants up and let's get out of here."

Back at the jeep she thanked me for saving her, but I reminded her that she owed her rescue to Maggie and the cats back home on our cul-de-sac. They had given Maggie lots of practice in dodging pointed things.

Vaca promptly gave Maggie a big hug, and put up with a lot of licking in the process. Afterward, Vaca let Maggie sit on her lap until she got to be too heavy to hold. I mentioned that we'd better find that road, get some supplies, and clean up before we went any farther.

"I'm sorry," Vaca said with the sun overhead. "But provisions will have to wait. Look." She pointed to another set of tire tracks that had come from another direction and caught up with the VW, following along as we had done. They were the size and shape of a dune buggy, but that wasn't all.

Up ahead, maybe only a mile over a small hill, a thick column of black smoke was rising from the desert. And for a moment, there was a slight, almost imperceptible movement of the tall cacti all around us. They were swaying gently from side to side, the way things do after an earthquake.

 21

Desert Fire

We covered the ground to the smoke in good time, but it was a pretty bumpy ride. Maggie fell out of the jeep a couple of times and had to race to catch up. Naturally, she thought this was great fun. But the column of smoke was getting thicker and blacker as we got closer.

From a hundred yards away we could make out the vague

features of a Volkswagen van, black smoke billowing from the engine compartment. It had that look. The one that says that in a minute at the most, the whole thing would become a tiki torch.

We pulled up to within fifty feet and skidded to a stop. Either Warren was making off on foot, or had rendezvoused with his partners and was gone. That would explain the other set of tire tracks, which stopped beside the van, and then took off again on a direct route east toward the main road we had left behind a day ago.

"Well," I said, getting out. "Looks like we lost him. And from the angle those tracks are taking, it can't be more than a couple of hours back to the main highway."

"Unless he's still in there," Vaca said seriously, standing beside me.

"Now, why would he still be—"

"Ever heard of the good old-fashioned double cross? That van's on fire for three possible reasons. It caught fire from some electrical short. It was burned to signal its location to his partners. Or he's been double-crossed and he's still in there."

"Naw," I said, watching as flames began to grow higher than the roof. "There's nobody in there. Besides, the pearl wouldn't be inside, anyway."

"If Gates *is* in there," Vaca said, starting for the burning van, "he's the only one that has any clue to where the pearl went."

I grabbed for her arm, but it was too late. She was running, and was halfway to the van before I caught up to her.

"Get off me," she said, as I tackled her to the ground. But I wasn't going to let her up—wasn't going to, except Maggie had caught up and started licking me so fiercely in the face that I lost my grip.

A second later, Vaca was up and gone while I tried to hold off a playful Maggie. By the time I broke free, Vaca was pulling the driver's door handle and fighting the heat and smoke billowing out of the backseat. She yanked it open with a yell and more smoke poured from inside the van.

Vaca stood fanning the smoke with her hand and backing up a little. When I got there I found out why. The door was as hot as a stove top. Vaca had gotten burned. Cursing myself for letting her get away, I looked inside the van. Much to my amazement, there was Gates stuffed on the front floor on the passenger's side. He was unconscious, but possibly still alive.

With fire roaring in my ears, I pulled off my shirt and wrapped it around my hand, raced around to the passenger's side, and pulled open the door. Flames and choking smoke had engulfed everything but the front seat, but it would be only a few seconds more before the whole thing went. It might even blow up.

Grabbing Gates by the shoulders, I pulled him out of the van and backed up fast to fifty feet away, coughing all the way. My eyes burned from the smoke, which was so thick that I couldn't see Vaca on the other side. Maggie ran back and forth, whining desperately. She was worried about Vaca. Just as Maggie disappeared around the front of the van, now completely consumed in black smoke, it blew.

The blast knocked me down, and a shower of hot broken glass filled the air, shards landing at my feet.

I left Gates on the ground and ran around the front of the van. No Vaca, and no Maggie. They must have made it to safety. They just had to. The air was still filled with the choking, black smoke, but it felt suddenly empty. I could see for a couple of hundred yards beyond the smoke, but there was nothing but desert. My mind started to go. I ran around wildly, looking for a scrap of dress, a dog collar, anything at all.

The black smoke had been billowing almost straight up. But the wind, which had been nearly still, suddenly blew a huge puff of smoke in my face. I must have passed out.

The vision of Montuca appeared again. He stood in the street of the ancient Aztec city, staring at the apparition.

His father never spoke. He didn't have to. The look on his face said everything. It was the same look that suffused his face as he lay on his deathbed. He had whispered his last words to his son before joining the gods.

"The magic is yours now," he had said, barely audible.

"Use it well. Guard it with your life. You must protect our people, for the time will come when . . ."

The image of his father faded, but the words hung in the air like birds of prey. Montuca knew that as long as he had one heartbeat left, he must protect the magic. That would please his father and the rest of the gods. It must not fall into the wrong hands.

The commotion had stopped for a moment. The world had gone silent as a sleeping child. The cloud that had hovered overhead drifted slowly away, and the sun shone brilliantly again.

He quickly covered the magic with the sacred cloth as he saw something out of the corner of his eye, standing almost serenely where the image of his father had been.

A beautiful, golden brown horse shook his head at Montuca. A tear of joy welled up in his eyes. The gods had not deserted him.

My eyes opened, and I saw Vaca's face, blackened a little with smoke. There were small shards of glass in her hair. She held my head in her hands as I lay on the ground. One of them had a burn mark on it. She had a faraway look in her eyes, and a big, friendly smile. For a moment I thought I had died and gone to heaven. But then Maggie appeared and began licking my face. Welcome to the real world.

"Thank god," I said to Vaca. "You're alive."

"Of course *I'm* alive," she stated. "I'm immortal, but it's you we need. Get up, Warren's coming to."

"I thought we had an agreement," I said, sitting up. "No more Montuca visions."

"I already told you," she said, hands on her hips. "Those are not my department. I only do vacations." She made a sphere with her hands. "Past, present, and future. Group rates available."

"How can you joke at a time like this? You almost got blown up. Let me see your hand. You must have burned it on that door handle."

"It's fine," she said, hiding it behind her. "Now, come on. Warren's got some explaining to do."

"You're right about that," I said. "But he's not going

anywhere very fast on foot.'' I grabbed her other hand and led her back to the jeep.

"Where are you taking me?'' she complained. ''The pearl's getting away.''

''Look,'' I said, like a concerned parent, ''there'll be other opportunities. But I'm not letting you go on without wrapping that hand. It could get infected. I've got a first aid kit in the jeep. Let's get that hand cleaned up and—''

''Okay, *Dad*,'' she said sarcastically. ''But then we grill Gates. It's not too late to chase that pearl.''

''Boy,'' I said, wrinkling my brow, ''you just don't give up, do you?''

''Heaven,'' she stated flatly, ''doesn't like quitters.''

Back at the jeep we got the burn bandaged. All in all, her hand didn't look too bad. There was only a first degree imprint on her palm. But I wasn't taking any chances with it. We were hours from civilization, let alone a hospital.

As I picked the glass out of Vaca's hair, the smoke died down, leaving a burned-out husk of metal in the desert where the van had been. As it crackled slightly in the distance, the sound was joined by Maggie's low growl in the backseat, and the crunching of boots on the desert sand.

When we looked up, Gates was standing beside the jeep, rubbing his head.

 22

Tequila

''I know nothing I could say would do any good,'' Gates said, standing beside the jeep, trying to rub the pain out of his head. ''But thanks for saving my life, just the same.'' When I didn't say anything he added, ''Sorry, Mr. Hansen, for scaring the hell out of you and your family. But I only wanted to cash in the pearl, just like you.''

''Get out of here,'' I said through clenched teeth. ''Before

I jump out of this jeep and take your head off. You may think you're tough, waving a gun at a two-year-old. But I say that's just about the most cowardly thing I ever saw. You may have frightened my family, but you don't scare me, Tonto. If that damn wind hadn't come up, I'd have stuffed you in the front seat of the VW myself. I'm not even happy about saving your life. So take a hike. You can probably make the road by sundown.''

"All right," he said, brushing his long shiny black hair back and rubbing a smudge of soot off his face. "I deserved that. But it looks like we both got snookered. The old professor's got us fighting among ourselves while he gets away with the treasure. Oh, well. What do you care? Go back to California and mow your lawn. It's probably too late to catch him anyway."

"Where'd he go?" Vaca asked, ignoring me.

"He didn't say exactly," Gates replied, slyly. "At least if he did, it's slipped my memory." He reached over and petted Maggie, who had been growling low the whole time. She gave in immediately and licked his hand.

"Leave the dog alone," I ordered. "She's obviously a poor judge of character."

"Okay," he said, suddenly getting mad. "So I stole your stinking pearl. What did you expect? You think I'm with the Salvation Army or something? With the money the professor was supposed to give me, I could have given up this despicable profession and retired to Florida or something."

"All right," I said, starting the jeep. "Enough small talk. We're outta here."

Putting it in gear, I pulled away, leaving Gates alone in the desert. In the rearview mirror, I could see him walking slowly toward the main road. There was a decided limp to his gait, and he was holding his right leg.

A mile later Vaca reached over and popped the stick shift out of gear, racing the engine. I let my foot up off the gas and stopped the jeep.

"You got some sort of problem?" I asked, still mad at Gates.

Vaca turned halfway toward me in the seat. "Look, Jack.

Don't be so self-righteous. You're no better than he is.
You're both a couple of mercenaries, as far as I can see.''

"What do you mean?" I defended. "He pulled a gun on
my kid. How's that make us the same?"

"Neither of you gives a darn about using the pearl for the
good of the Earth. Why, you're no better than some industri-
alist that's polluting the environment while lining his pockets.
All the while, the Earth gets sicker every day.''

She got out and started to walk away. "Guess I was wrong
about you," she stated flatly. "I thought you might actually
try to use the power of the pearl for good. You don't care
at all, do you? You never intended to look into the Eyes
of God. You're filled with greed and self-interest, just like
everyone else.

"Well, then go ahead," she added, pointing her finger at
me. "Chase the professor on your own. But I'm staying here
with Warren. At least he's not lying about his motives.''

She turned and walked back toward Gates, still far away
and limping in the distance.

I slammed the jeep in gear and sped off. If she was going
to be that way, then fine. Let Gates take care of her. All of
this save-the-planet stuff was getting to be a little too much
anyway. I turned to Maggie for consolation, but she was
sitting up in the passenger's seat, whining.

I kept driving, and the whole mess caught up with me. I
couldn't leave Vaca out here in the middle of nowhere. Not
without food and water, not with a burned hand, and certainly
not with Gates.

Turning the jeep around, I went back a half mile to get
Vaca. I pulled up alongside and stopped.

"You want something?" Vaca asked, perturbed.

"So I ain't Mother Teresa," I answered. "Get in. You
can't be walking around out here with that hand.''

"Hand's fine. It's only a little burn.''

"Vaca, there are scorpions out here, remember?''

That got her attention. She looked around, but there
weren't any in the immediate vicinity. She quietly got in the
jeep. Maggie hopped in the back. When I tried to steer the
jeep toward the highway, Vaca fought me for the steering
wheel.

"What are you doing?" I asked.

"Let me drive."

"All right," I agreed, exhaling. "But no funny stuff."

We switched places, and she took off with a jerky start. She started heading back the wrong way, toward Gates. I kept waiting for her to turn around, but she didn't. I reached over, popped it out of gear, and turned off the key.

Vaca quietly and calmly explained that she wasn't going back to the road without Gates. We fought over this for several minutes. Finally, she reminded me that unless I was giving up the search for the pearl, we would need Gates. Chances were, he knew where the professor was planning to take the pearl, or at least where to meet him in case the professor had missed the rendezvous in the desert. That much had to have been preplanned.

I reluctantly agreed to take Gates back to the highway in exchange for the pearl's possible location. Nothing more. By that time Gates had come up alongside. I told him to get in the back, explaining that the price of a ride back to the road was what he knew about the pearl. He popped a sly grin, one that I didn't like, and we were on the road again.

All the way back to the main highway Gates grumbled that if he hadn't sprained his ankle, he wouldn't even need me. I told him if it wasn't for what he knew, he'd still be back there limping in the desert. Then I ordered him to tell us where he thought the professor had gone, but he graciously declined, saying his memory was a funny thing—like none other in the world. It always seemed to go blank out in the desert, and the only thing that ever brought it back was good tequila. *Sure*.

So there we were, hating each other and needing each other at the same time. Add to that a Labrador that was rapidly making too many friends, and the self-proclaimed Vacation Goddess, and we made an even funnier bunch than before. Like it or not, though, it looked as though we were going to have to stick together for the time being.

Naturally, I was dumb enough to believe Gates was going to tell us everything we needed to know after a bottle of tequila. And I suppose he believed he could ditch us as soon as he got to some kind of town. Vaca pointed out everyone's position just before our wheels hit the highway again. I stopped the jeep, but Gates wouldn't tell us whether to go north or south.

"Look," Vaca said, "this might sound stupid, but we all need each other here. We need Warren to tell us where the professor might have gone. We need you, Jack, for the wheels." She pulled a small piece of khaki cloth from her front dress pocket. "And we need Maggie to sniff him out."

"Where'd you get that?" I asked.

"Back at the van. The professor must have torn his shirt when he was ditching Warren here." She turned and looked at Gates. "Unless this belongs to someone else."

"There *was* somebody with him," Gates confessed. "That guy from the dune buggy shop. But he was wearing a Mexican shirt. I knew I shouldn't have trusted him. He's the one that knocked me out with a gun butt. He and the professor are partners. Guess they decided to cut me out of this one."

"And just what do we need *you* for?" I asked Vaca, half kidding.

"To stop you two from fighting, for one thing," she frowned.

"Fighting?" Warren said. "Hell, even with my bad leg I'd make refried beans out of *gringo* here."

"What?" I said. "You're just lucky I don't pick on those weaker than me, like some people I know. Why—"

"Will you two shut up for a minute?" Vaca ordered. "As I was about to say, Maggie will be good at finding the entrance to the professor's hidden cave. But I'm going to have to zero in on which mountain it's in. The range is twenty miles from the road, in case you haven't noticed."

"Mountain cave?" I asked. "So that's where he's going."

"Warren," Vaca asked, "where were you supposed to meet them if they didn't show?"

"Can't say as I get your drift."

"You may be greedy, but you wouldn't just drive out into the desert without having a backup meeting place. Too many things can happen out here. The way I've got it figured, the backup place is going to be within striking distance of Hardwick's hideout."

"Actually," Warren admitted, "I was supposed to meet

him alongside the highway. I waited there for an hour, but he never showed. So I took off across the desert for the border. Figured I'd sell the pearl in the States instead. The professor must have had me staked out, and decided it would be easier to dispose of me out in the middle of nowhere. Looks like he was almost right. But just how are you going to find this secret cave of his?" He looked at the outline of the string of peaks twenty miles off. "That range runs for hundreds of miles."

"Leave that to me," she said. "Now, where was that meeting place on the highway supposed to be?"

"Like I said," Warren answered, petting Maggie, "memory's gone. Only tequila can bring it back."

"He's stalling," I said.

"Stalling my eye," he defended. "Ain't anybody else at least thirsty? I'm getting dehydrated. And nobody's offered me anything out of that cooler lately."

I agreed that we could use some food, drink, and showers. We made a deal to get cleaned up and get going again. We'd have to find some little tourist trap along the road, one with a store and a shower. It was only three in the afternoon. Maybe we could still find the cave before dark.

"All right," I said at last. "At least point us in the right direction. Are you sure you'll be able to recognize the spot?"

"Can't say for sure," he replied, rubbing sweat off his forehead. "But I think there was one of those little white crosses on the side of the road."

"Great," I said. "There's only about a million of them on this road."

"Yeah," he said. "But the one I remember was south of here. Pretty close to San Bajamos. Can't be sure though, my memory's fuzzy on the subject. It gets dried-up out here."

"We know," I said. "Look, put a cork in it. We're heading toward anywhere south of here with tequila, tacos, and a shower. Then maybe your trick memory will come back. And Vaca," I added, turning toward her, "what's this about a secret mountain cave?"

Vaca got a serious look on her face. "That's where he's

going to try to relieve the skull of its power," she said, worried. "If he hasn't already."

"Is he Aztec?" I asked.

"No, thank god. But he's surely planning some means to make the skull release its power so he can harness it. He's a brilliant scientist."

"But wouldn't he wait at least until high noon to get the maximum effect?" I asked, concerned.

"That," she said, "is our only hope. But sometimes people can't wait for nature before they try out their own schemes."

I pointed the jeep south and rolled off down the highway. An hour later we came to a small, broken-down village, filled with cardboard and plywood houses and not much else— except for a small, hand-painted word on the side of an abandoned car: CANTINA.

 23

Cantina

Twenty feet from the rusted-out car shell, a small one-room adobe shack stood its ground against the elements and time. It sported two empty square holes in front for windows, some broken tiles accented with rusty tin for a roof, and crushed dirt for a parking lot; but to us it meant civilization.

We piled out of the jeep and walked past the worn plywood plank that functioned as a front door. No surprises inside. Some rickety tables and chairs, a solid dirt floor, and a beat-up counter with a badly cracked mirror behind told the rest of the story.

A tired, leathery old man emerged behind an opening cut out of the back wall. He greeted us wearing a tank top, shorts, and a warm smile. *"Turistas,"* he said, almost to himself. "Come, sit. We are *abierto. Open."*

Just as we were sitting down, a wide-body Mexican woman wearing a peasant dress wedged her way through the hole.

She clutched a straw broom that looked like something a witch had left behind, and immediately began to sweep the packed dirt floor.

When she got to our table, she gave us a hard look, and then threw a fierce glance at Maggie, now sitting at my feet. Figuring she wanted to sweep the spot, I grabbed a wobbly wooden chair nearby and shoved it next to me. Maggie got the hint and jumped up on the chair, sitting as proper as a queen waiting for dinner.

The woman didn't move. Her husband tried to talk to her in Spanish, but she wouldn't have it. She pointed the straw end of the broom at Maggie, and said something in Spanish to Vaca.

"Is there some kind of problem?" I asked Vaca, perturbed.

"No dogs allowed," Vaca informed me. "Maggie will have to wait outside."

I glanced down at the dirt floor, and then around the room. It wasn't as clean as Maggie's doghouse back home. I was tired, hungry, and cranky, and about to launch into a spiel about how Maggie was practically a person, but suddenly realized that I was the guest here. They didn't have a sign saying they had the right to refuse service to anyone, but they certainly didn't have to put up with an arrogant *gringo*. I was ashamed of myself. It may have been only a shack, but it was their castle. I was out of line.

"Of course," I said, apologetically, and took Maggie outside, tying her to a post with her dog leash and pouring her a dish of her dog chow.

Back inside, Vaca and Gates had ordered drinks, beans, and tortillas. It sounded pretty good right then, so I added my name to the list. A few minutes later the old man came out with warm cans of Pepsi for me and Vaca, and a bottle of tequila for Gates.

Everyone ate in relative silence, serenaded by Maggie's gentle whining outside, and some pop Mexican tunes featuring loud horns and accordions on an ancient radio that sat on one end of the counter. After second helpings we stocked the cooler in the jeep with more warm Pepsis, and a couple of dozen homemade tortillas. We even took cold showers out back one at a time, while wide-body mama washed our clothes in the sink. She had really warmed up after the dog incident, and even brought Maggie a couple of fresh tortillas as a peace offering.

We sat around in worn towels while our clothes dried on a clothesline. It didn't take all that long in the desert wind and heat. I looked at Vaca's hand, but there was no sign of a burn. It had healed completely. I just shook my head. Warren drank a half bottle of tequila and was getting a pretty good buzz on. He offered me some several times, and even teased me when I turned him down, calling me a teetotaling *gringo*.

"Sorry," I told him. "I promised my wife. Besides, I'm the designated driver."

"What are you doing here?" he asked, seriously. "This can't be worth it to you, risking your life for some wild treasure."

"Sure," I agreed. "I *should* give it up. But that's what you'd want. Then you'd have it all to yourself. You'd like that wouldn't you?"

"You son of a . . ." Suddenly, Gates lost control and was jumping over the table. He pushed it aside and it rolled away. He took a swing at me and missed. But before I figured it out, I was on the floor and he was on top of me. But not for long. The old moves came back and I was out from underneath. We rolled and wrestled on the dirt floor in our towels like two jocks in a battle for king of the locker room.

Gates was better than I thought, and stronger. Despite being bogged down by the booze, he almost had me a couple of times. I must have been getting rusty. Then, with a quick move, I was sitting on top of him, pinning his shoulders to the floor. Vaca came over and counted to three, just to show us how stupid we looked. The wide-body woman came out and poised her broom behind my head, ready to strike.

"When you two are finished fooling around," Vaca said, "get cleaned up. The sun will be down in a couple of hours. If we don't get started soon—"

There was a low rumble all around; the building began to shake. Tables and chairs tipped over. Bottles and cans rattled behind the counter. It only lasted for a few seconds, but it snapped us out of it. I sprang to my feet and headed for the shower. Turning to Gates on the way outside, I said, "Either there's a lot of quakes around here, or the pearl's nearby. We'll finish this later."

I grabbed his half-finished bottle of tequila lying at my feet, walked to the hole of a window, reached through, and poured the rest on the ground outside.

"You've had enough for one day," I said to Gates, and tossed the bottle into an empty oil drum outside.

We showered again, paid up, filled our canteens, got dressed, and headed out. Before we did, we asked if they had seen the professor or his sidekick.

The waitress's eyes got big. "He is evil," she spat out, standing by the doorway as we walked past her. "No one will go near his cave. Some have tried. They drove toward the mountain, but never returned . . . I warn you," she added, pointing a crooked finger at us. "Stay away if you value your lives."

"What about the police?" I asked. "Surely they know of him. Haven't they investigated the disappearances?"

"Paid off," she said disgustedly. "At the very highest level by the professor himself. There's even talk that he's working on secret projects for the government. Everyone officially denies he exists, and the existence of the cave. But two years ago caravans of earth-moving equipment rumbled right down this very highway and took off across the desert toward the mountains."

She went on to say that this went on for months. Heavy equipment coming and going, always under the cover of darkness. If people asked questions, they were told it was a classified government project and to say they had seen nothing. If they persisted with inquiries, they quietly disappeared. The local officials that were there now lived on the wealthy tourist beaches south of town. They drove Mercedeses and had caviar flown in. All of them had been paid off by the professor.

"But where did he get all the money?" I asked. "Surely a professor doesn't make—"

"Silver mines," the woman said. "That's what they say. But I don't believe it. I say he created the money himself. He is not human. He is from the land of darkness. He is *malo*."

"How do you mean?"

"He came in here once. Sat where you sat. Ordered *cervezas*. When I looked in his eyes to take his order, they were as black pits. And there was something else I will never forget. The dirty, brown irises in his eyes were turning slowly, like gears in a machine. He is not human, he is—''

Just then her husband stepped from the back room. *"Una loca,"* he said nervously. "My wife, she's a little bit crazy . . . Come on," he said to her. "Let them go."

She turned away, but over her shoulder she just kept repeating something in Spanish about *"muy malo."*

As we made our way to the jeep I asked Vaca what she thought about all of it.

"The silver fortune is true," she said. "And everyone knows about the cave. The officials aren't talking, but it's said he's experimenting with alternatative sources of power. I even heard his lab is built on a dormant volcano, and that he's trying to study it with high-tech equipment. See if he can revive it in a controlled way and harness the power."

"Isn't that dangerous?"

"Not nearly as dangerous as the power in the skull. He knows its power would dwarf even the most powerful volcano. That the skull was discovered near his cave is a godsend to him. He sees it as a gift of destiny to make him the power lord of this planet. That is his only goal.

"He has been given permission by the Mexican government to explore sources of power for the twenty-first century. At first he started out only wanting to harness nature's power. Wind machines, solar panels, and the like. But it was never enough. He wanted more. The idea of unleashing the power that lay sleeping inside a dormant volcano came to him at last. If he succeeds, he will be ruler of one of the most powerful energy sources on Earth. But it could wipe out this entire area. He's willing to chance it. Some say he's evil for tampering with nature, but others only believe that he's a mad scientist, or perhaps a futurist."

"And what do you think? Is he human?"

"That," she said, "remains to be seen. But we'd better get going. We're running out of time."

Our clothes were almost completely dry as we spun back onto the road. While Vaca dozed in the front seat, I demanded that Gates tell me the location of the rendezvous spot. He reluctantly pointed south, toward San Bajamos.

"Can't be more than twenty miles," he said.

"Good, now we're getting somewhere. Sounds like you're starting to sober up."

"Look, all I was trying to tell you is that if a man's got a family waiting for him at home, he's already got his treasure. Don't you think I'd trade my worthless life for that? Hell, you don't know when you've got it made. You're only out here to add to your fortune. But if you leave that wife of yours a widow, you'll have thrown it all away."

"Oh," I said sarcastically, "so *that's* why you took a swing at me. You've got a funny way of making a point."

"Okay, so the booze got the best of me. I was just trying to knock some sense into you. But I can see that's a lost cause. The rich get richer. Say, what do you think that skull's worth split three ways?"

"Enough for my needs," I replied. "Do me a favor, will you? Don't rub it in about me being a rich *gringo* leaving my wife and kid for some fortune. I'm just chasing my dream, same as anyone else would do. I feel bad enough without you reminding me every five minutes."

"All right, already," he said defensively. "I was just trying to—"

"Gates," I said, looking at him in the rearview mirror, "let's just forget it for now. Tell me what *you're* in this for. I mean, what are you going to do with the money?—besides retire to Florida."

"I'd tell you," he said, embarrassed. "But it's too damn corny."

"Corny? You're talking to someone who cried the first time he left his daughter. Now, *what's* corny?"

"This is pretty basic stuff," he said, glancing back at me in the rearview mirror. "But I'm looking to start a family. Kids, dog, the whole bit. Maybe even a cat."

"Any why can't you do that now?" I asked, puzzled.

"Who wants a drifter like me? I've gotten fired from every job I ever had. Ever since Vietnam I haven't been worth a damn. I just can't take orders anymore—at least not for very long. I figured the money from the pearl would give me enough to start a life of my own. One where I can be my own boss."

"What have you got in mind?"

"Anything where I can work for myself. Actually, I sort of fancy a gardening service. All I need is a truck, some tools, and a mower, and I'd be set."

"That can't take all that much money," I said. "Why haven't you done it by now?"

"First wife cleaned me out in the divorce. I'm still paying alimony. What's your excuse?"

"Well," I laughed, "as long as we're being honest. It's guts, I guess. Haven't got enough of them to just flat out quit my job and go for it. I could borrow on the equity on the house to start a business, but I'm chicken, I guess. I don't want to put my family in that much danger."

"Isn't that what you're doing now?"

"Yeah," I laughed again. "Never thought I'd be in the danger business. Guess I'm taking my fifteen minutes of fame now. That is, if we find this thing and get away with it."

"Hold it!" Warren shouted. "Stop the jeep. I think we just went by the spot."

"Are you sure?" Vaca asked, waking up.

"Yeah," he said. "I remember that the cross had a piece broken off one of the arms. We just passed it. Must be the tequila finally bringing out my memory."

"Naw," I replied. "Must be the sobriety."

I stopped the jeep and backed up. On the mountain side of the road, stuck in the dirt all by itself, was a two-foot-high painted white cross. A piece was missing from one of the arms.

 24

Flat Rock

With a little looking we found a fresh set of tire tracks fifty feet down the road, heading west toward the mountains. The tire marks looked the same as those we'd been following. Ones that went with dune buggies.

We followed along nearly straight ahead for fifteen miles, as the sun started to sink behind the low mountain peaks five miles ahead. It looked as if we were going to be able to trace the tracks right to the professor's cave. Gates couldn't resist commenting on this.

"So, with these tire tracks so easy to follow," he said to Vaca, "what do we need you for, anyway? We should be able to get right to his hidden lab with no problem."

"Yeah," I agreed, half kidding, and turning to Vaca. "Looks like we don't need you after all. Unless Mr. Aztec here starts another fight."

"Hate to spoil it for you," Gates said over my shoulder. "But I ain't Aztec."

"What?" I said in disbelief.

"I'm not from around here, and neither are my ancestors. I'm from Arizona. They call us Navajo."

"Navajo?" I said with surprise. "Well, where's the turquoise?"

Gates grabbed me around the neck and I almost lost control of the jeep. I got it stopped and sure enough, we were out on the sandy dirt wrestling again. Vaca got out and started walking straight ahead, toward the mountains.

I worked loose, stood up, and dusted myself off, thinking how much I missed a good wrestling match, and noting a small spike of pain in my lower back.

"All right," I said to Gates. "You win. My back isn't what it used to be. Here . . ." I held out my hand for a shake. "No more fighting."

Gates held out his hand and I pulled him up. That was the extent of the handshake. He watched Vaca walk away, now a hundred yards in front of the jeep. Maggie, anxious for a walk, had gone with Vaca when I wouldn't let her join the tangle of arms and legs Gates and I had made in the dust.

"And just where does she think she's going?" Gates asked. "Can't she take a joke? Hey!" he yelled at her, cupping his hands. "I thought we were all in this together!"

Vaca didn't turn around. She just kept walking toward the mountains.

"We'd better go after her," I said. "There are scorpions out here, and it'll be dark in an hour."

"Ah, let her go," Gates said. "The walk will do her good."

"Nothing doing," I replied. "She's got my dog."

We climbed back in the jeep. This time Gates got in front. I started it up and put it in gear. "Say, where'd you learn to wrestle like that?" I asked, impressed by his moves.

"Arizona State. I was the heavyweight wrestling champ."

"Small world," I said, shaking my head. "Wait, didn't I see you on TV in the '72 Olympics? Naw," I added, looking at him. "You can't be that old. You still look like you're in your thirties."

"Some people age slower than others," he assured me. "At least on the outside. But to set the record straight, the only wrestling I did in '72 was with the butt of a rifle. Uncle Sam took me in '69. Low lottery number and all that."

"That's right," I remembered. "You said you were in Nam. War was over by the time I came of age."

"War's never over for those who went," he said flatly. "Guess I told you I lost my respect for authority."

Up ahead, Vaca had stopped, as if waiting for a school bus. When we got within fifty feet we saw why. The tire tracks came to an abrupt end, right where they entered a twenty-foot-wide, rocky stream. They didn't come out the other side.

I pulled up alongside and they both got in the back. Maggie still dripped from the stream. I looked at Gates and he read my expression.

"Well, so what?" he said. "Flip a coin. Either they went upstream or down. Which way do you want to try first?" He glanced over his shoulder at Vaca. "Unless *you* think you're close enough to 'sense' the whereabouts of his hideout."

Vaca got a concentrated look in her eyes, and stared at the rocky mountains ahead with great intensity. After about a minute she stopped and pointed south. I crossed over and paralleled the stream for a full five miles.

Then, up ahead, a barrage of tire tracks came out of the stream on both sides. Evidently this was a popular crossing spot for desert dune buggies. On the mountain side we sat and stared at a dozen sets of smudged-out tracks coming out of the water and heading in all directions, half of them toward the hills. The stream had meandered west, so that we were only a couple of miles from the first set of foothills. I wondered whether it was close enough for Vaca to do her mental gymnastics.

I climbed out of the jeep and got down on the ground, trying to decipher the tire tracks, but the hodgepodge all looked the same to me. "Come on, Gates," I ordered. "Aren't you supposed to be able to tell tracks?"

"Ha," he laughed. "You've been watching too many old Westerns. It's not in my blood, you know. I grew up in a condominium. I could do better with tennis shoe tracks than those you're looking at."

Vaca sat in the backseat and concentrated again, then got out and carefully studied each set of tracks that led toward the hills. She bent down and put her hands on all of them. At last she stood up, and picked out a set.

Gates and I had no reason to overrule her. So, soon we were on our way, following the tracks toward the hills. Five miles later, with the sun almost down, the tracks stopped abruptly at the edge of a wide, flat, stony area that ran a hundred yards deep and paralleled the brink of a cliff face. It looked like a dried-out riverbottom, and disappeared in both directions as far as I could see. It was a good place to hide tire tracks. They simply disappeared on shoulder-to-shoulder river rocks.

We were almost out of daylight, so we decided to make camp until morning. We gathered a few sticks from dehydrated shrubs, and made a small fire. It was Gates's turn to cross-examine Vaca. She stuck to her story about being the Vacation Goddess, but Gates was just as skeptical as I was, figuring she just wanted to cash in on the pearl, like the two of us. He didn't believe any of the Mother Nature story, observing that treasures are always surrounded by myth, but in his opinion, not magic.

Like me, he figured Vaca had strong mental powers, stating that some old Indians he knew in Arizona had developed limited mind control, such as walking on fire. White men always called it magic. But he considered it mind over matter, or nature. He had heard of no one who had discovered how to control the weather, however, as Vaca had suggested. That was still out of reach, even for desert medicine men. But I could tell by the careful way he listened to her that it sparked his interest. If she could prove it to be true, he would definitely be impressed.

It didn't take long for his skeptical side to take over, though, and he ended up saying that Vaca was using whatever powers she had gained unwisely, to seek out a fortune, as far as he was concerned, and not for good, as she claimed. Nevertheless, Vaca still insisted that all she wanted was for me to gaze into the eyes of the skull at noon when the time came, and her job would be done.

In the end, Gates and I figured it didn't matter. As long as we split the booty three ways, Vaca could tell any kind of story she wanted. Gates pushed her a little, though, just to see how far she'd go to protect her story.

"So, let's assume you are this Vacation Goddess. Besides a few parlor tricks, what's the proof? And why does this pearl fall under your jurisdiction? Simply because Hansen here found it?"

"That's correct," she answered right off, staring at the stars overhead. "He was on vacation when he discovered it. Therefore, I'm responsible for the outcome. There's nothing to prove. If you don't believe me, it doesn't matter. As long as Jack—"

"Isn't there some kind of God of Lost Treasure or something?" Warren interrupted sarcastically.

"Actually, there is. But I'm doing Mother Nature a favor, remember? I told her I'd follow through on this. Besides, since technically Jack's still on vacation, it falls under my jurisdiction."

"Vacation?" I asked. "You call this a—"

"Let me get this straight," Gates interrupted. "Hansen here looks into this skull at noon, and gets power over nature. Is that it?"

"Exactly."

"Ha." Gates slapped me on the arm. "And you agreed to this? What if you go blind?"

"Why not?" I answered. "Nothing's going to happen just by looking into some skull eyes. Just a little reflection of the sun, I figure. It sounds like a small price to pay for my part of the fortune . . . Hey,'' I added, glancing at Vaca, "can I wear my Ray-Bans? I don't want to burn my retinas out.''

"Sure," she said, half kidding. "If the power can't penetrate a little UV protection, then we've got the wrong skull.'' She paused for a moment, and continued. "I realize neither of you believe any of this, but it doesn't matter. Just hold up your end of the bargain and I'll hold up mine. As soon as we do the eye test, I'll be on my way.''

"I wish I could believe that," Warren said. "But somehow it seems a little too innocent. You've got something up your sleeve, I know it.''

"Well," Vaca replied, "you'll just have to wait and find out. We haven't got the pearl yet." She paused for a moment, as if listening to a faraway sound. "But it's nearby. I can feel it inside that mountain ahead. With some luck, we'll be in by tomorrow morning.''

"Preferably," I joked, "before noon.''

The rest of the evening passed quietly. The next morning we drank sodas, ate tortillas, and scoured the huge rocky flat for any sign of tire tracks and for an entrance into the mountain on the side of the cliff. It was all pretty frustrating, especially since there were no tire tracks leading off the rocks in any direction along the edges of the large rocky plain.

At about nine in the morning, with despair starting to set in, we turned to our ace in the hole. We should have done it earlier, but everyone was so sure that we'd find some more tire tracks somewhere, or an entrance to the cave, that we just forgot about it. But finally, as Vaca thrust her hands into her pockets, she had the answer. She came out with the piece of khaki cloth left by the professor at the burned VW site.

Turning to Maggie, she held it out. "Here, girl. Looks like you're our only hope. See what you can do. Find the professor.''

Maggie sniffed it deeply, and got very excited. She began to bark and growl, and then put her nose to the rocks at her feet. Soon she was off, sniffing a trail along the edge of the cliff. We chased after her. A few hundred yards from camp, she stopped and pawed the rocks, then sat up and barked at the cliff face at a spot we had passed several times, but dismissed. There had been several rock slides along the cliff face, and this was just another of them. But a second look made it seem different somehow. It was a little bigger than the rest, stacking several large boulders against the cliff face as they fell from above. At the top a small trickle of gravel and dirt was still running downhill. Either the cliff was starting to go again, or this was a recent slide just finishing up.

A large gully had formed in the side of the cliff from where the rocks had fallen, and there weren't any big boulders sticking out of the remaining face that looked ready to come down. This had the look of a fresh rock slide, all right. Besides, Maggie's nose was irrefutable evidence. The entrance to the cave had to be behind those rocks.

I pulled the jeep about and we started hooking the winch around some of the bigger boulders. It took a lot of work and was a little dangerous at times, with rocks sliding every which way, but we were finally able to clear a person-sized hole between some of the bigger ones. Behind them, dug into the side of the cliff face, was a car-sized entrance to the mountain, complete with a fresh set of tire tracks leading inside. I put Maggie on the leash and grabbed a tire iron, remembering my broken promise to Ellen to get a gun. Warren took a fishing knife out of my toolbox, and Vaca my heavy six-battery flashlight. We squeezed through and entered the cave. When we did there was a slight, almost imperceptible rumble from somewhere deep in the mountain and the faint sound of water lapping.

It was twenty-five minutes to twelve.

 25

The Cave

Once inside, the cave looked normal enough. It was a car-sized tunnel carved through solid volcanic rock. Tire tracks dug into the ground-up rock floor confirmed that the dune buggy had entered here. All we had to do was follow them to their destination. That was part of the problem. If the professor was such a brilliant man, this seemed a little too easy. Besides, even if his secret lab was somewhere on the inside of the mountain, we didn't as yet have a plan to recapture the pearl. It would depend on what we found.

Five hundred feet into the tunnel we came to a fork in the road. Tracks led in both directions, but the set to the right were the ones we'd been following. Their markings were distinctive enough to tell them from the set on the left, which were from some other vehicle.

Just as everyone started off down the road to the right, I grabbed Gates's shoulder. I had something to say.

"Wait," I said in a loud whisper. "Let's take the other path."

Vaca turned and shone the flashlight on me, then away when she saw it was blinding me.

"Naw," Gates said, standing behind her. "The buggy tracks lead that way." He pointed with the knife.

"Naturally," I replied, raising an eyebrow. "That's exactly what the professor wants us to do: follow the tracks like birds eating bread crumbs. Then he's got us for sure. This smells like a trap to me."

I held back Maggie, who had been sniffing and pulling toward the right pathway the whole time. I looked at Vaca for support.

"They went that way all right," Vaca said, pointing down the right-hand tunnel. "It *could* be a trap." She waved the flashlight down the dark tunnel. "But let's face it, we don't know *what's* down the other way."

"No," I admitted. "But there's only one set of tracks going either way. So, obviously they both lead somewhere. Otherwise, the tracks would double back on one of these roads. Let's not make it too easy for them. I say we take the tunnel on the left. If they are waiting for us, it will be down the right road here ... Unless you two want to split up."

Vaca got a concerned look on her face. "Maybe that's not such a bad idea," she agreed, taking a deep breath of tunnel air. "That way if someone gets captured, maybe at least one of us can get away."

I stared at Gates, and he back at me. We still didn't trust each other.

"Yeah," I said. "And somebody could get away with the pearl and cut the others out at the same time." I placed the tire iron in my leash hand and pushed my hat back on my head. "I think we'd better stick together for now."

With that, we took off down the left tunnel. I had to pull Maggie at first, but then she got into it, and sniffed on ahead with no trouble, right in line with the other set of tracks.

A thousand feet later we came across a Range Rover, parked squarely in the middle of the tunnel, only a foot on either side for clearance. It had Baja plates.

We squeezed between the rock wall and the side of the Rover. Vaca and Maggie had little trouble, but Gates and I had a tough go of it. When I wiggled my way past the passenger's door, the insignia for the *Universidad de México* stared me straight in the face. This was the professor's all right. If there had been any doubt, it was gone now.

The engine was cold. It had been there awhile. I climbed through the open window and crawled around inside. Nothing was in there, except an empty bottle of tequila lying on the floor. It was time to move on, especially with Vaca, Gates, and Maggie standing in front of the Rover getting increasingly perturbed at me.

Their impatience was rewarded by a slight rumble inside the tunnel, and some small rocks falling to the ground. Then the disturbance stopped.

"It's ten minutes to twelve," Vaca reminded me. "If the professor exposes the pearl, this whole place could cave in."

"Wait a minute," Gates protested. "I thought it had to be in sunlight. This place is as dark as a sewer."

"Gates," I said, sticking my head out the window, "only *you* would know that. Look, we'll take your word for it, but who says the lab's in *this* tunnel, anyway?"

Vaca and Gates both looked at me. I wasn't making any sense. "Okay," I offered. "I'll make it simple. Where's the sun?"

"Cut to the chase," Gates said with disgust. "We're running short on time here, remember?"

Without answering right away, I climbed out the sunroof

and crawled on top of the roof. There was a good foot between me and the top of the cave. Vaca couldn't resist shining the light above me. I ordered her to hold it steady while I felt around with my hands along the top of the cave.

"If I'm not mistaken," I finally began, "that rumble came from sunlight hitting the pearl. I'm sure this tunnel eventually leads outside again, but following it might not lead us to the pearl. If the professor's going to keep people out of his secret lab, it's got to be *hidden* inside this mountain, and it has to be located where there's a hole in the roof for sunlight. I figure it's closer to the top of this mountain, somewhere overhead."

Suddenly, just above the driver's side, a section of rock on the roof of the tunnel gave way to my pushes. It was heavy and round like a manhole cover, but I managed to slide it aside. When I did, a flood of soft rainbow-colored lights poured down into the cave, spotlighting me on the roof of the Rover. They were accompanied by the deep sound of electrical hums, as though a power station was nearby.

"If you'll follow me," I said like a tour director, "we'll be entering the upper level now." I looked at Vaca and beamed. "All children must be accompanied by an adult, and pets must be on a leash."

"Well," Gates said, kicking the dirt with his boot. "I'll be a son of a—"

"Jack!" Vaca said in a loud whisper. "You're a genius. But how in the world—"

"Simple," I said. "You don't see any footprints down there other than ours, do you? That means in order to get out of here they either had to go through the side of the tunnel, or more likely, through the ceiling."

There was another slight tremor, sending baseball-sized rocks to the ground below. Vaca, Maggie, and Gates scrambled as best they could up the sides of the Rover. Luckily, no one was hurt, but by the time the shaking stopped, several large boulders had fallen all around the Rover, but not on it. The area just over the Rover was probably structurally reinforced, most likely to prevent just such an occurrence from burying it in heavy rock. The trapdoor to the cave, it seemed, was the safest place to be at the moment. And at the same time, depending upon what was waiting for us upstairs, it could be one of the most dangerous.

We climbed through the hole in the top of the tunnel and entered the upper level.

 26

High-Tech Noon

When all of us got our feet planted squarely on the next level, we were in still another tunnel. It dead-ended about ten feet behind us into a huge water tank that backed against the cave wall. That explained the freshwater smell when we first entered the cave. At the other end of the tunnel, facing due west, light was emanating in an alternating array of hues. As electrical groans pierced the air, the walls of the cave in the distance slowly and steadily cycled through the rainbow, as if being illumined by one of those ancient Christmas tree color disks turning slowly in front of a spotlight.

I told Maggie not to bark, though it might be tough to stop her if we ran into any trouble.

We began to walk toward the light and sound at the end of the tunnel, which rose about a foot for every ten. We were a couple of stories up by the time we reached the other end, which opened into a dome guarded by a corridor.

The corridor was ten feet wide and rimmed with a four-foot-high wall, which served as a railing around the interior of the cave. From the edge of the tunnel we could see that this part of the mountain had been carved out like the inside of a giant pumpkin. Only instead of a removable top, it had a slide-away ceiling that was opened just a slit at the very apex to let in a narrow band of sunlight, mixing with the rainbow of lights spraying up from below.

We were near the top of the stone dome, and from our vantage point could see that the corridor spiraled around and down, forming steps like some crude staircase in a Stone Age capitol building. The power hums were much louder now. They poured up from below, echoing off the rock walls like an amphitheater, and seemed to make the rainbow of lights dance on the cave walls. Something was going on down below, and I had to find out what.

I told the others to wait at the edge of the tunnel while I had a look over the wall. Vaca and Gates reluctantly agreed, but Maggie started whining when I looked both ways down the corridor and crawled across on my hands and knees. I was forced to signal Vaca to let Maggie come to me before she gave us away. When Maggie scrambled over, I held her by the leash so she wouldn't jump up on the wall.

Slowly, I inched my way up the wall and peeked over the top. I couldn't keep Maggie from joining me with her paws on the wall, but at least she wasn't barking.

Below, encircled by the rock wall that descended fifty feet to the bottom, was the lab. An incredible array of high-tech electronic equipment filled the room. Banks of power supplies, generators, signal analyzers and heaven-knows-what were backed against the round walls of the cave. A control room sat opposite me at ground level with large, smoked glass windows that reflected back the traffic jam of equipment across from it.

Center stage sat an aluminum platform, knee-high and twenty feet square. Out of its middle ascended a cylinder as high and round as a basketball hoop. It was made of brushed stainless steel and sported a dozen thick black power cords plugged in all around. It looked like some android octopus. The cords led to the stacks of electronic equipment lining the walls. High-intensity multicolored indicator lamps on various control panels saturated the room with the mixture of dancing lights, while piles of high-voltage generators polluted the air with their deep electronic groans. I pictured myself inside Hoover Dam when the floodgates let loose. It wasn't deafening, but it was the sound of sheer power.

Atop the cylinder a series of two-foot-long and foot-wide glass panels fanned out in a circle like petals of a giant electronic flower. They were a dull silver color, and appeared to be light absorbing, rather than reflecting. I made this assumption when my eyes were drawn to the center of the flower. There, in all its luminous glory, sat the skull, crystal clear, and sparkling with its own inner light. It was naked, having been stripped of its protective pearl layer.

Whatever power was emanating from its shining surface seemed to be absorbed by the panels and pulled down through the pedestal, which began to glow with a faint tinge of red, as if from heat energy.

Suddenly it became clear to me. The banks of generators and electronic equipment weren't powering the pedestal that held the skull. The skull was powering them. They were only being used to transform the energy to usable electricity. The skull's energy was being siphoned off, channeled into the pedestal and through the power cords. There seemed to be more than enough power to run the equipment, but where was the excess being stored?

I followed a large bundle of inch-thick wires from the base of the pedestal. They disappeared under a door at the end of the control room.

Suddenly, the slit of sunlight overhead began to shift. The roof was sliding to direct the light squarely onto the skull. Sunlight bathed the skull in brightness. The eye sockets became as white as molten metal. Energy poured out of the skull and into the pedestal in a stream of pure light. Banks of power converters began to overheat and pop their circuit breakers. One by one they all shut down. The energy kept coming. It couldn't be shut off and it couldn't be controlled.

The ground began to shake. Rocks unplugged from the ceiling and walls and fell to the ground. A couple of bowling ball–sized ones just missed me.

If the professor was in that control room, he'd better find a way to get that gap in the roof closed or the whole cave might go.

The shaking increased. The cave started to crumble, letting more rocks fly toward the ground. A small one hit my shoulder and bounced off. The staircase wall was starting to come loose. I held my ground, but over my shoulder Vaca and Co. were getting anxious. They wouldn't hold their positions much longer. We had to think of some way to rescue the pearl, but it was still the professor's move.

Vaca and Gates yelled at me. Maggie barked loudly and

ran back to the tunnel with the others for protection. By now the entire skull was white-hot and glowing like a sun. I thought it would melt through the pedestal or explode.

The waiting paid off. Just then the door to the control room was flung open and Ed Masters, the guy who owned Baja Buggies, ran out, still in a Mexican shirt and shorts. He made a desperate run for a crank stuck into the side of the cave. When he got there he began to wind it as fast as he could; rocks still fell from the ceiling and walls, some of them barely missing him, and some crashing on top of the equipment. A few hit the platform with tremendous booms, denting it considerably. One basketball-sized boulder just missed the pedestal. The cave was coming apart at the seams. Masters finally got the roof closed, and escaped through a side door.

The shaking suddenly stopped, followed by a long anxious silence, but the skull was still glowing a brilliant white from stored energy. It looked as if it could still explode at any second.

Everyone was now at my side, looking over the wall. We all knew we'd have to act fast. But how? It was still too hot to handle. We'd have to find a way to transport it without burning ourselves, or wait until it cooled down. By then the professor and his accomplice would surely be onto us, unless we'd been discovered already. For all we knew Hardwick could still be in the control room. We'd have to think of something, and fast.

We never got the chance to put any plan in motion, because before we could discuss anything, there was a tremendous explosion, like a dam bursting, and a great roar filled the cave. Suddenly, a wall of water was rushing at us from the tunnel. The water tank had burst wide open.

We all got up and ran down the spiraling rock pathway, but it was no use, the water was moving too fast. A six-foot wave of water was upon us by the time we were halfway down the staircase. I tried to grab Vaca and pull her up on the wall, but both of us got washed away. We didn't know whether we'd be drowned or crushed against rock.

I lost track of the others as the current pulled me under. By the time I got right side up again, I had swallowed a lot of water and taken some bumps on the rocky steps. The water had pushed me all the way downhill to the bottom of the cave, where my shoulder slammed into a refrigerator-sized piece of equipment. All power must have been cut, because otherwise I'm sure I'd have been electrocuted. My head popped up for air as the last of the water came down the ramp, flooding the floor three feet deep.

Looking around for the others, I found Gates clinging to the platform, banged up, but breathing. There was no sign of Vaca or Maggie. I wasn't really worried about Maggie—she was a naturally good swimmer—but what about Vaca?

I sustained a major bruise where my shoulder had slammed into the test equipment. Gates had blood dripping from his forehead. But still no sign of the others.

We were frantic. Gates and I swam, waded, and splashed our way around the lab in vain. Then, just as we were about to give up, Maggie barked and came swimming around some bobbing equipment toward us. She was towing Vaca, who had hold of Maggie's chain collar. When they reached us, I looked them both over. Vaca had some bruises, bumps, and a torn, soaked dress, but looked okay otherwise. Maggie was happy, healthy, and having a darn good time.

"Well," Vaca said, wringing out her hair and standing in three feet of water like nothing special had happened, "what are you two staring at? Somebody climb up there and get that skull."

Neither of us could say a thing. Here we had almost drowned, and she was ready to complete the mission.

I shrugged. "Why not? Can't jet ski in the harbor."

The lab was a mess—equipment flooded out, banged up, and bobbing at odd angles in yard-deep water. Gates searched the control room. He found nothing but a bunch of half-submerged monitors and switches behind the glass window, but he managed to wade out with a mop he pulled from a closet in the back.

"Great," I said sarcastically. "You go ahead and mop up. I'll watch."

"No, you dummy," he growled. "This is for knocking the skull off that pedestal there. The water should cool it off enough to handle in a couple of minutes. Then we scoop it up and get out of here before they come back.''

"Nudge," I corrected him. "That mop's for nudging the skull off the pedestal. We want it in one piece." I turned to Vaca. "Maybe we'd better let it cool down for a while, so it doesn't shatter from the temperature change when it hits the water."

"No need," she said, waving me off, and standing chest-deep in water. "Won't you *ever* understand? It's not some fragile piece of Waterford crystal. It was created by Mother Nature herself. It can take extreme heat and cold. Besides, we may not have much time. They're bound to be back any minute now to assess the damage. We've got to grab it and run."

"Yeah," Gates agreed, looking down at the water, now starting to subside. "Let's do it."

"All right," I said. "Come over here. I'll stand on your shoulders."

"Nothing doing." He looked at Vaca. "Let the goddess here stand on mine and we'll knock it off."

"Nudge," I insisted. "We'll nudge it off."

Without further discussion, Gates came over and Vaca sat on his shoulders. Maggie got excited at this, and began to bark. I had to shut her up before the professor and Masters came back and ruined our escape plans.

It actually took quite an effort for Vaca to nudge the skull off the pedestal and over the glass petals, but in a couple of minutes she had it over the top. It was still glowing when it hit the water, and steam roiled up around it. As I approached it a half minute later, the water surrounding it was the temperature of a hot bath.

I reached down into the water and hefted it up. It was warm, but had become clear again. Except now several bursts of white had formed inside it like stars in the Milky Way. Vaca was wrong. It was heat damaged, scarred on the inside. It still glowed with an inner light, but I wondered about its remaining power, and its value.

I held it in my hands, still marveling at its smooth shiny surface. There *was* a slight residue of power in it, but not enough to burn or shock me. It just felt warm and tingly.

Turning it over, I couldn't resist feeling the strong jaw-bone, rubbing my hands over the carved straight teeth. It was a flawless work of art; at least it had been.

At last I was pulled in by its spell and my own curiosity. I couldn't help gazing into the eye sockets. They seemed bottomless and beckoning, pulling me into the star bursts inside the cranium.

The world suddenly faded away, and I was five hundred years in the past, standing invisibly beside Montuca.

Gathering his strength, he staggered into the street, noticing that the pain in his shoulder had subsided for the moment. The blood had stopped flowing from the wound. If only the horse in the street would hold still.

Montuca approached, still weighed down by the round, stone-heavy object in the cradle of his right arm. But he was making it—one slow step at a time.

The horse was burdened with a saddle. That would make staying aboard its back easier, but the improbable task of mounting it lay ahead. Luckily, the horse stood its ground.

When Montuca reached the large powerful beast, he grabbed the reins with his free hand. The pain came back sharply, but he held on.

At the end of the street a low wall enclosed a courtyard. It was only ten strides from him. If he made it that far, he might be able to mount the horse.

Montuca studied the saddle. Instantly he knew there was only one golden animal with these saddle markings in all of the land. It belonged to Cortés himself. It seemed only fitting that it should provide Montuca's ride to freedom.

He staggered onward, the majestic horse in tow. Finally, nearly exhausted and ringing with pain, he reached the wall and set the bundle on top of it, carefully tying the cloth so that the magic would be held fast inside. The pain increased, burning like fire in his shoulder. The blood began to ooze again.

Montuca mounted the horse. It was the first time he had sat on one. He had neither time nor strength to dismount the beast and proceed on foot. He would manage as best he could. He had to.

Montuca turned the horse around with some effort and leaned over, snatching the knotted cloth with his good arm. He grew dizzy, but held on, slowly urging the horse in the direction of the sea.

"Jack," Vaca said. "We've got to move. I hear someone coming."

27

Escape Route

I came to my senses quickly. Sure enough, there were voices coming from behind the door that Masters had used for an exit.

All of us began scanning the place, frantically looking for a way out. There were plenty of rock walls, but there was a distinct shortage of escape routes.

"Warren," I said, using his first name for a change, "was there a door behind the control room?"

"Sure," he said, standing in a foot of subsiding water. "But it only led to a closet."

"Come on," I ordered, running for the rock steps. I had the skull under my arm like a soccer goalie about to make a free kick. "Let's go back out the way we came in. All the water's down here now, so we can't get washed away."

I glanced over my shoulder at the others, who just stood there with dumb looks on their faces. "Come *on*," I commanded in a loud whisper. "It's our only chance. They probably don't even know we're here."

"Well," Vaca agreed, standing at the foot of the stairs, "I suppose you're right. But what if they *do* know we're here and it's a trap?"

"Too late," Gates said, blowing by Vaca on the stairs and catching up to me. "The door's rattling. Let's take what's available."

Maggie dashed on ahead, leading the charge. We didn't quite make it to the top of the staircase before the exit door opened. Masters flung the door open so hard it banged off the wall. He flashed a shotgun wildly around the lab.

I hit the deck. Vaca and Gates followed suit. We still had a good fifty feet to the tunnel, but we could crawl on our hands and knees if we had to. The rock wall would hide us. And that's just what we did. Maggie even joined in, getting down low as if she were crawling on the living room rug, thinking this was all part of the fun. It wasn't easy crawling along, one small step at a time, trying not to drop or scrape the skull on the rock stairs, but I managed somehow. I even found my hat on the steps. It was a little wet, but otherwise undamaged. I couldn't resist putting it on as a sign of victory.

But just as we got to the top of the steps and nearly to the tunnel turnoff, a shadowy figure appeared below us, coming around the curve of the staircase, and shouldering that shotgun.

That was the bad news. The good news was that we had only twenty feet of flat ground to cross to reach the tunnel, and there were boulders in the path. They slowed us down all right, but when Masters opened fire, most of the burst hit the rocks behind us, except for the pellets that knocked the straw hat off my head.

I was even stupid enough to reach over with one hand and pick it up while Masters loaded two more shotgun shells into the barrels, then locked it closed again with a powerful snap. But he was too late. By the time he aimed and fired, we were all scampering into the tunnel.

Naturally, all he had to do was come on up the ramp, which he did, but that gave us enough time to make quick plans. I was about to launch mine when Warren cut me off, grabbing me by the shoulder.

"I was in Nam," he said soberly. "Let me wage this battle."

"Nothing doing," I said. "We're in this together, remember? I can't let you go out there."

"Don't be stupid," he said straight-faced. "Nobody's going out there and get shot. Listen up, here's the deal."

In less than twenty seconds Warren had given us our orders, cutting out everything except our planned actions. He was right. He did know what he was doing.

Masters was slowly making his way up the stairs, breathing heavily from the climb. When he got twenty feet away he stopped, shouldered the shotgun and aimed. This time we were ready. We had some ammunition of our own, and it was our turn to fire.

On my command Maggie barked and Warren shone the flashlight in Masters's eyes. I threw baseball-sized rocks at him while Vaca ran for the far end of the tunnel, the skull tucked under her arm.

One of the rocks hit Masters in the chest, and he fell backward over a boulder, firing into the ceiling and sending a shower of rocks down upon himself. In a few seconds he was buried beneath a mound of small rocks. I almost went after him to make sure he wasn't going to climb out of the pile and come after us, but Warren grabbed my arm.

"Let nature take its course," he said. "He got what he deserved."

"I wasn't going to save him," I explained, straightening my hat. "I was going to make sure he wasn't getting up anytime soon . . . Good," I added, staring down the tunnel. "Vaca must have found the exit. She's gone."

With that we gathered ourselves and made a run for the end of the tunnel. We had to dodge an obstacle course of boulders to get there. When we got to the end, the water tank had been split wide open. Jagged twisted metal stuck out of the side where it had blown. It was empty except for a few inches of water in the bottom. The rest of the water had drained through the round hole that led to the tunnel below, but the Rover wasn't beneath it. Instead, there was a faint light showing beneath us. I hoped it was daylight.

Warren went through the hole first, dropping to the ground below, then Maggie jumped into his arms. Just as I was lowering myself into the hole, a light appeared at the end of the upper level tunnel in the corridor at the top of the cave. It took a second for my eyes to adjust, but when they did I could see that it was a lantern. It swayed slightly as a thin, bony hand held it aloft.

The butane-powered light from it flickered, throwing distorted shadows on the walls of the cave, but the image of someone holding the lantern was crystal clear. The narrow, fierce stare of Professor Hardwick seemed as big as the tunnel itself. He didn't speak. He didn't have to. His dark, buckshot-sized eyes fired hatred into me from fifty yards away and two stories above me.

I returned his stare with as mean a look as I could muster. A strange thought entered my head. What I had seen in the lab was beginning to change my feelings about things. Suddenly, as if transformed by the danger and my vision of the skull pouring out all that power, I had come to realize there was more at stake here than a priceless artifact. If it was only a matter of money, Hardwick could have just cashed in the skull for a fortune and been done with it. Instead, he had invested a fortune in the lab. He obviously wasn't planning on turning the skull over to anyone. He had other ideas.

The look in the professor's eyes was not one of friendly competition over the ownership of lost artifacts. He had gone to a lot of trouble to tap the energy of the skull. It was a matter of the inexhaustible hunger for power. That was in his stare. And he wasn't going to let me get in the way.

I didn't want to believe it, and I didn't want to accept it. But having seen the skull's power with my own eyes, there was just no way to keep on believing we were on some ordinary treasure hunt anymore. At that moment, the adventure turned into a battle.

Just before I dropped to the ground below, Masters joined the professor at the end of the cave. He was badly bruised and scraped, but managed a mean, vengeful glare. Beneath me, on the wet floor of the cave below, Maggie barked anxiously, and Warren called out.

"Jack," he said. "There's a lot of fallen rock down here, but I see light at the far end."

"Vaca!" I yelled, and it echoed off the rock walls. But there was no answer, only the cold, heavy silence of the cave.

28

Potato Sack

I jumped to the ground below. A light emanated from the end of the tunnel opposite the direction from which we had entered. Tire tracks from the missing Rover pointed the way toward the source of light.

There wasn't a surplus of time to spend contemplating Vaca's whereabouts, so we marched ahead, calling her name every couple of yards. But there was no answer, just her name echoing off the tunnel walls from our voices, and Maggie's barking.

We had no idea whether Vaca had been caught and escorted away by some unseen accomplice, or had somehow fired up the Rover and found a car-sized exit. With her proven mechanical powers, that was a distinct possibility. The real question, though, was whether she was waiting for us outside.

Halfway down the tunnel the light grew brighter and much closer. A couple of hundred feet at the most, and we'd be outside.

Warren turned to me and asked, "Do you suppose she hotwired the Rover?"

"Ha," I laughed. "It wouldn't surprise me. She's quite a kid."

"That *kid*," Warren frowned, "just made off with our fortune. Whose idea was it to trust her with the skull anyway?"

"Mine," I admitted. "Who was I supposed to entrust it to, you? Don't be so suspicious. She's probably got the Rover parked right outside, waiting for us."

"Sure," he said, shaking his head. "And I'm Montuca's ghost. Let's face it. We've been outfoxed by a kid. A smart one, but a kid just the same."

I didn't answer. The conversation was leading nowhere. What we needed was proof one way or the other, and that would be found outside.

When we got to the end, sure enough, the tunnel led to the outside world. Both of us stuck our heads out slowly, gradually adjusting to the hot, bright sunlight, and looked around for any signs of the professor and his friend. Obviously, he wasn't just going to let us drive away with the goods, so we stepped up the pace once we emerged into broad daylight.

We exited from the tunnel on the other side of the mountain. It looked like the same old desert, filled with rocks and sand, and sparsely populated with cactus and dry juniper. There was no sign of anyone, but the tire tracks led straight ahead into the desert, abruptly stopping at the edge of a deep canyon.

We ran to the edge, some fifty yards away, and looked over. The canyon was a thousand feet wide and miles long, with steep, stone sides. Way down at the bottom, three hundred feet below, sat a very conspicuous pile of boulders. That must have been the dump site for the rocks the professor had carved out of the cave to make his lab. I was sure it started out as a natural cave in the mountain behind us, and he had enlarged it for his own purposes.

I looked back at the mountain, my eyes searching the rocks, but couldn't see the spot where the rollback roof should have been. It was too well camouflaged. I wondered if they were watching us from a secret porthole in the rocks, waiting to track our escape route. Even if they weren't, they were sure to be after us soon.

"Look," Warren said, getting my attention, and pointing to the bottom of the canyon. "Right there, between those boulders. That's the Rover. Or at least what's left of it."

I couldn't answer at first; my eyes were confirming the sighting. He was right. It could only be the wreckage of the Rover gone over the side.

"I'm going down," I said, starting over the steep cliff, but he grabbed my shoulders and pulled me back. Before I knew it, we were engaged in another wrestling match, tangling around in the dust. Needless to say, Maggie was getting her licks in with her tongue.

"Don't be stupid, Jack," Warren pleaded, still grabbing at me. "If she's down there, she couldn't have survived the fall. It's three hundred feet to the rocks. She's too smart to go over the edge. I'm sure she bailed out beforehand."

"I don't know," I said, getting him in a headlock. "Her driving's not that good. Maybe she didn't jump out in time."

"Nonsense, she's probably heading for the jeep right now."

We stopped wrestling and looked at each other. "The jeep!" we said in unison, both having the same thought: the Rover was her decoy and she was on her way back to the jeep, maybe even rolling off toward the highway with the skull.

Both of us jumped up and ran for the front side of the mountain. Just as we got around the corner, the jeep was staring us straight in the face. Behind the wheel sat Vaca, with a smile as big as Baja.

"Hey, *gringos*," she said, "want a ride to town? Five bucks each, unless you want to meet my sister. Then it will cost you extra."

"Vaca," I said, "we were worried about you. *I* thought you might be at the bottom of that canyon."

"Don't be silly. I'm—"

"Wait," Warren said. "What's that noise?"

"Sounds like a dune buggy to me," I answered, my eyes getting big.

"Yeah," he said. "And it's coming from the other side of the mountain. Hey, we're outta here."

"Not so fast," Vaca said, watching me dust myself off. "Jack, where's your hat?"

"Crap," I replied disgustedly. "Probably back at the edge of the canyon."

"Great," Warren said, rolling his eyes. "Now they'll be onto us for sure."

"Jack," Vaca said with a sly grin. "You just may have made the perfect mistake."

"Now, just what is that supposed to mean?"

"Come on," she said, motioning back toward the canyon.

"Follow me. Let's hide behind the rocks along the edge of the mountain. If I'm not mistaken, they'll find the hat lying at the edge of the cliff. They'll figure we were too excited about our getaway and didn't see the canyon coming up on us. It'll look like we went over the edge. They'll head down the canyon looking for the skull. And when they do, they're going to be in for a big surprise—especially when the dune buggy joins them."

"Vaca," I said, "you're brilliant."

"Shut up," Warren said. "Let's get to the rocks. I want to see if they take the bait."

We made our way to the large boulders that lined the foot of the mountain and worked our way around the corner, but near enough so that we had a clear view of the edge of the cliff, just fifty yards away. As advertised, my hat was sitting ten feet from the canyon, right between the tire tracks that ended so abruptly where the canyon began.

A bloodred Baja Buggy carrying the professor and Masters rolled up from inside the mountain and stopped. Masters got out, picked up the hat, and put his finger through the buckshot hole in it. Then he tossed it on the ground and looked over the edge of the cliff. In a second he motioned for the professor to join him. We silently cheered them on, barely able to contain our excitement. The moment was ours.

In a few minutes, Masters had driven back to the cave and returned with a very long rope, which he hooked to the front of the dune buggy. He wedged large rocks under the four tires. Just as he was putting the last one in place, the professor lowered himself down into the canyon, using the rope. Five minutes later Masters joined him.

Slowly, proudly, we emerged from the rocks, walked past the dune buggy and stared down. The professor sat on a ledge two hundred feet below. Masters hadn't waited for him to reach the bottom. He was already a hundred feet down himself. When he stepped onto a large flat rock to rest, I nodded to the others, picked up my hat and put it on my head. It was time to say hello.

Maggie was the first to greet our competitors. When she barked, both men looked up sharply. All of us waved. Both men quickly let go of the rope and stepped back on their respective rocks, hugging the side of the canyon as best they could.

Deciding it was time for a vehicle inspection on the dune buggy, I motioned the others back from the cliff. When they stepped aside far enough to be clear of any danger, I removed the rocks from the four wheels, took it out of gear, and released the hand brake. We all lined up behind and rolled it over the cliff. It went airborne for several seconds before crashing miserably onto the rocks. The professor and Masters were shaken, but unhurt.

We all waved one more time, wondering how they would manage to get out of the canyon. It was time to head back to the highway, and the *kid* had earned the right to drive.

Vaca told us how she hot-wired the Rover, and showed us a potato sack she had found that held the skull, sitting on the floor of the front seat. Naturally, under the pretext of wanting to admire it, I started to open the sack. Vaca reached over and held my hand to stop me.

"Jack," she said, "don't fool with Mother Nature right now. If you want to feel the skull inside the sack, go ahead. But I don't want it exposed to sunlight any more today."

"Fair enough," I agreed, slipping my right hand inside the sack. It was the skull all right. It felt smooth, and still in one piece. I traced the teeth with my fingers just to be doubly sure, and when I pushed my thumb gently into the eye sockets, they felt warm, tingly, and electric. I half expected to see another vision of Montuca.

I held on to the skull for the longest time, until Vaca hit the highway and turned toward San Bajamos, saying we were going to her place for the night. She drove through the poor part of town, past tin and cardboard shacks. On the last dirt road that dead-ended on the side of a rocky slope, she pulled over at an abandoned adobe hut. A tin roof covered about half of it, while the doors and windows were made entirely of air.

"Come in," she said. "This is my current residence."

She held out her hands and I reluctantly turned over the skull, still inside the potato sack. When I did, the tingling stopped. I thought again about all of the visions I had been having and how they seemed to tell a story—how the Aztec high priest had escaped with the skull. But the story wasn't finished; Montuca hadn't made it to freedom. The ending would have to wait, though, because the visions had stopped as well as the tingling.

Meanwhile, Vaca reminded me of my promise: that at noon the next day I would look into the Eyes of God.

"We'll talk about it after dinner," I said. "I'm starved. Now, where's the nearest taco stand?"

 29

Sundowner

"You Americans are the hungriest bunch of people I ever saw," Vaca said, shaking her head. She looked at Warren. "And I suppose *you* want to eat also?"

"Now that you mention it. Too bad all they got is Mexican food down here. I sure could use a Big Mac."

"There's still some tortillas in the jeep," Vaca offered, and, seeing our sagging expressions, added, "All right. Come on; I know a place where we can get some steak fajitas."

"Hey," Warren said with a nod, "that's more like it."

We arrived at the dirt floor restaurant and ate like starved tourists. While I gulped down my third Pepsi, Warren finished off his fourth Corona, chiding me for having cola and steak. Not wanting to get into another wrestling match, I dropped the subject. We paid extra to use a cold shower behind the place to get cleaned up, and headed back to Vaca's.

On the way out the door, a dirty Mexican boy ran up to Vaca and told her to hold out her hand. Thinking he was playing, she closed her eyes and turned over her palm. When she did, he let a handful of dirt run slowly through his fingers into her palm. Surprised, she opened her eyes and gave him an odd stare. He whispered one word and ran outside, disappearing into the desert.

On the way to the jeep I asked her what that was all about, and what was the word.

"Eartha," she said, getting a very serious look on her face. "It's what the locals call Mother Nature. The boy was trying to tell me she's back. I'm afraid we're in for some rough weather."

I looked up at the sky. "Looks like sunshine to me," I said, happy and full of dinner.

From behind us Warren, who was half-lit, interrupted. "It's part of the legend," he smirked. "If no one claims the power of the skull for the Aztec people within three days after it's been uncovered, Mother Nature herself comes to Earth in the flesh."

"Fine," I said, playing along. "Then the power over the elements returns to nature, where it belongs anyway. Well, that's all right with me, but—"

"Unfortunately," Vaca said, climbing into the jeep behind the steering wheel, "the legend also says that Mother Nature must not only take back the skull, but then cannot intervene again for five hundred more years."

Warren climbed into the back seat. "That's fine." He smiled. "She can do whatever she wants with it. *After* we sell it to the highest bidder."

"No!" Vaca shouted, turning around and glaring at Warren. "You'll get your chance. But not until Jack looks into the eyes tomorrow at noon."

"Agreed," Warren said, holding up his hands defensively. "But I don't want anybody's grandma butting in, claiming to be this Eartha."

Vaca turned back around and started the jeep. "That kid was a messenger," she said. "He was trying to let us know that Eartha's on her way here. That means we don't have much time. I just hope she gives us until tomorrow."

I couldn't say anything. All I could think about was the vision of the skull sitting on that pedestal in the lab, pouring out power. No one said a word all the way back to Vaca's.

After the sun went down, a bitterly cold wind came up and howled through the doorway and window openings. It got so frigid at one point that all of us were shivering. A shining sliver of moon came out. Maggie gave in to her

ancient urges and howled away. It took awhile to get her
stopped. When I went outside to bring her back in, Vaca
joined me.

"She's here, isn't she?" I said softly over my shoulder.

"Yes," Vaca confirmed. "We've only got until tomorrow
at the most."

"I want you to know that I didn't believe," I confessed,
"until today at the cave."

"I know," she answered, putting her hand on my shoulder.
"But I was sure that once you saw the power, you'd change
your mind."

"When I saw that light pouring out of the skull, I had to
ask myself. If this is only a legend, then where is that power
coming from? And why did the professor set up such an
elaborate mechanism to harness it? This has to be for real,
and the professor's playing for keeps."

Vaca explained that the professor knew he couldn't stare
into the eyes and gain the power: It would only blind him
because he wasn't Aztec. His fancy equipment was trying to
harness the power of nature with modern technology. He was
trying to trick the skull into releasing its power by placing it
at the center of his artificial sunflower, the pedestal setup.

Although a scientist, the professor was also an amateur
anthropologist with a fascination for ancient artifacts and
magic. He had studied many of the ancient Aztec rites, and
even recreated some of the more secret, sacred ceremonies.
It was rumored that he had once engaged in human sacrifice,
though no one could prove it. He knew there were four crystal skulls, but only one with power. He gained permission to
study two of them, and stole the third. All proved devoid of
power. The fourth and final skull had yet to be found.

The professor believed that the Aztec high priest infused
the fourth skull with magic—that Montuca himself had mas-
tered the power over the elements, and then told the legend
makers that the power was put inside the skull by Eartha so
as not to draw attention to his own supernatural abilities.

The professor also believed that Montuca had cursed the
skull, so that only someone with Aztec blood in his or her
veins could secure the power again and rule the elements,
and in so doing, rule the world.

In short, the professor believed Montuca was a sorcerer of the highest order. But he believed too that the power could somehow be released and harnessed. An ancient Aztec poem was the key. The poem said that the energy of the sun was captured in the heart of the sunflower. The poem itself had always been dismissed as superficial, only extolling the nutritional value of the sunflower seed. But one night the professor, high on tequila, had a vision.

In his vision he saw a field of sunflowers, turning themselves upward toward the heavens, collecting the sun's energy like solar panels. In the center was a single giant sunflower, ten feet tall and five feet across. In its center was the skull, receiving power from the sun and storing it in its enormous petals. As it did the wind blew, the Earth shook, and ancient volcanoes began to boil. When he heard that the fourth skull had been discovered, not twenty miles from his cave, he saw it as a sign. All he needed was that skull to fulfill his vision. He learned of Warren through Masters, and they struck a deal. Warren was double-crossed and the rest was history.

It occurred to him that if he could create a sunflower with the skull at its center, he might be able to release the sun's energy that Montuca had stored in it. He knew from the legend that the noonday sun activated the power inside the skull. The petals of his flower would be panels to collect that energy. If he could siphon it off, he could capture the magic.

He thought his artificial flower could fool the skull into releasing its power. He also knew of the danger of such a release of powerful energy. And how difficult it would be to control. His idea was to transfer the energy to the petals and then store it in a specially constructed chamber, one that wouldn't let in light, or let out energy. It would have to be strong enough to hold the skull's power and not break. He had already constructed such a chamber to store volcanic energy. So it was perfect, almost too good to be true. Yet it *was* true. Destiny surely had picked him to gain the power over the elements. No one could be allowed to stand in the way. The fact that entry into the skull's secret powers was guarded by the Aztec blood curse did not matter. He saw it only as a challenge to be overcome, or circumvented—as only a lock to be picked on a treasure chest holding unfathomable wealth.

Hardwick believed that, in time, he would learn to use the power. He wanted to control the elements, to be the high priest, and more than anything else, to rule the world. This was his chance. It almost worked, but the skull wasn't fooled. It knew the artificial from the Aztec.

"The poem," I asked. "How does it go?"

Vaca recited it from memory.

> Behold the flower shaped like the Sun
> Burning yellow and bright
> In its petals limitless energy
> Is drawn from the fireball in the heavens
> In its center lies the key to the Mother of Nature
> Its seeds hold the power of the Sun
>
> That which holds the power of the Sun
> Is greater than all of man
> The flower is the center of life
> And must be obeyed
> To worship not the flower
> Is to walk as an animal
> To be sacrificed to the Sun
> For its great glory
>
> Anger not the Sun and the seed
> For blindness and death await
> Those who heed not the warning
> Shadows shall fall over the Earth
> When Eartha returns again
> To claim her child

Not satisfied, I asked, "But what is the meaning of the poem?"

"It means that only when man respects nature, represented by the flower, and puts it at the center of his world, instead of himself, can he truly be called human. Otherwise, he is no better than a beast. We have been entrusted with the keeping of the Earth, but we must live up to the challenge."

"And what about human sacrifice?" I asked. "Wasn't that rather primitive and brutal?"

"The human sacrifices were symbolic, offering up man's most precious gift, his own life, his self-importance. It was believed that unless man gave up his own sense of greatness, he could not save the world. And thus not please God."

"And this special chamber—the one that lets in no light and can store the skull's energy. Where is it?"

"It has to be somewhere inside the cave. And judging from what we saw, the professor's already siphoned off energy from the skull. There's no telling how much he's got stored or what he can do with it."

"Or how much is left inside the skull," I added. "It looks damaged to me. But answer something: why was a crystal skull chosen to store the sun's energy?"

Vaca explained that to this day, besides being one of the cornerstones of modern electronic technology, quartz crystals are believed to have healing properties. They balance and channel electrical energy. People even wear small pieces of them around their necks to ward off infections and improve health.

"If crystals do have some healing properties," she speculated, "you can only imagine the healing power of a piece the size of a skull. It could, if used properly, go a long way toward healing the planet humanity has neglected."

Warren interrupted, behind us. "That's all good stuff for mythmaking, but as far as I'm concerned, the professor was just taking advantage of the crystal's scientific properties—using it as a sort of solar collector to recharge his equipment. That's all. The skull has no magical qualities. There is no such *thing* as magic. It was just an opportunity to run experiments with a good-sized chunk of pure quartz. Nothing more."

"Listen," Vaca said impatiently. "Believe whatever you want, but if what you're saying is true, he could have done that with the one he stole. As long as Jack looks into the eyes tomorrow, you can sell it, destroy it, or whatever you want afterward."

"What if it doesn't have any power left?" I asked. "After

what happened in the lab, it may be burned out. I still say it's damaged. And even if it isn't, there's—"

"You're not getting cold feet," Warren said, hand on my shoulder. "First, you refuse to drink with me. Now—"

"Nobody's getting cold feet," I said angrily. "It's just that *if,* and I did say *if,* the legend has some truth to it, it sounds to me that I could be blinded if I'm not Aztec. Hell, looking into that thing at high noon might blind me anyway. You saw all the light it generated in the lab."

"So wear your Ray-Bans," Warren smirked.

"Warren," Vaca criticized, "we're not talking about ultraviolet protection here. We're talking about—"

"Drop it!" I demanded. "I'll make my final decision tomorrow. It looks like the wind is finally dying down. Let's get some sleep."

"Remember," Vaca couldn't help saying, "you *promised.*"

"Yeah," I said. "But that was before the skull blew out the professor's lab equipment. Nobody told me I was taking on the power of Hoover Dam."

"Aw, come on," Warren said. "You knew what you were getting into. The sun is going to be up in a few hours, and if you don't do this, I'll . . . I'll—"

"Enough," I said. "It's my decision. And I'm making it tomorrow, promise or no promise. After all, it's my eyesight."

We went off to bed, and I dreamed about watching my little girl grow up. It wasn't until then that I realized how much I missed her and Ellen. There they were in my dream, looking at me and crying. Ellen held Susie up and she felt the bandages on my eyes, explaining that Daddy would never see again.

After that I had another dream. Ellen, Susie, Maggie, and I were sitting happily on the porch of a hardware store, somewhere in a small mountain town. Overhead the paint was just drying on the new sign. I looked up and could see quite clearly that the letters formed the words HANSEN'S HARDWARE.

I didn't know which dream was true. Maybe neither one. Perhaps only my fears and hopes were playing out their hands in a high-stakes poker game. And I didn't even like to bet.

When I awoke the next morning the sun was coming through the paneless window, blasting in my face. In six hours I would have to make another decision. But I had made one already, the instant I pulled myself out of sleep: to call stateside and talk to Ellen and Susie. To see if they made it back safely. I wouldn't ask them to decide for me; obviously they wouldn't want me to blind myself by practically staring into the sun. But I did want to hear the sweet sound of their voices once more, just in case I took the plunge.

 30

Moment of Truth

The next morning we all slept late, despite the moment of truth that lay ahead. Fatigue had finally caught up and conked everyone out until ten o'clock, including Maggie. It took some effort, but I talked Vaca into letting me phone home. We drove into town about eleven, found a telephone, and I made the call.

"Ellen," I said. "It's me, Jack. Are you guys okay?"

"Jack," she said. "Thank god you're safe. Where are you?"

"Still in San Bajamos."

"Did you find the skull? Are you in some kind of trouble? You sound worried."

"I'm fine. We've got the skull. I'll tell you all about it when I get back."

"When are you leaving?"

"This afternoon. Look, how's Susie? Put her on. I want to hear her voice. She's there, isn't she?"

"Sure, just a second. She's playing with her train set."

A long, anxious minute followed, seeming like half an hour. But if I could just hear her melodious little voice, it might give me the strength I needed to go through with the ordeal to come. It took some coaching, but finally, Susie's sweet voice came on the line.

"Hi, Daddy. Mommy said to *worry* home."

"Sweetheart, tell Mommy that I'll hurry home right after lunch. Do you miss me?"

There was a conference at the other end, then, "Mommy says she miss you."

"I miss you, Sweetheart, and Mommy too."

Ellen was back on the line. "Nice job," I said. "You almost got her to say she missed me." Ellen said she had called my boss and told him I was stuck in Mexico, but would be back in a couple of days. The motor home was working fine, and was I really okay? Was I feeding Maggie?

After I answered all of the above, it was time to say good-bye, though the words came with some reluctance.

"Well, guess I should get going," I said. "Just wanted to make sure everything was all right."

"Jack, promise you'll be careful. I want you back in one piece . . . Wait, Susie wants to say good-bye."

"Bye, Daddy. Mommy made me a new dress. It's blue."

"Bye, Sweetheart. I can hardly wait to see it."

I was about to ask her to put her mother back on when she hung up the phone. When I called back it was busy. Trying again didn't get me through, so I gave up and dropped the receiver on the hook.

Vaca and Warren, who had been standing right behind me, gave me concerned stares. I decided not to announce my decision until after breakfast. Thinking was better on a full stomach, although the answer to their stares was already inside my head.

"All right," Warren said, halfway through a chorizo at some taco stand by the boardwalk. "Enough suspense already." He looked up at the sun. "It's almost noon. Let's do it. Unless you've chickened out."

"Here?" I said, facetiously.

"Course not," he replied sharply, wiping beer off his mouth. "Vaca, does it matter where we do this? Besides not on a crowded street?"

"No," she said, exhaling. "As long as it's somewhere in the sun."

I looked across the street at the gulf, then up at the rocky slope that guarded it to the north, capped by a small stone building and a fifteen-foot-high, white cross.

Up there, I decided. "Top of that peak." I looked at Vaca. "Anything up there besides that shrine?"

"A few tourists," she said, running her hand through her black hair. "But behind it, on the gulf side, is a little ledge. Locals used to sit up there and watch the ships come in until someone fell. Now it's fenced off."

"Good," I said. "Nice and private. We can climb the fence, right?"

Vaca gave her approval and we were off, heading through town to the little dirt road that led to the shrine of Our Lady of San Bajamos. Once at the top we parked, noting only one other car, and hoofed it up the steep steps carved into the rock.

It was a tough climb, made more difficult by the midday heat and lack of wind, but I lugged the skull up the rocky slope, accompanied by Vaca and Warren. Maggie stayed behind to guard the car, especially after Vaca informed me it would not be a good idea to have her running wild at the shrine.

Sweat poured down my forehead, and a stain had developed on my back. My knees were starting to get sore and my head faint by the time we reached the top, reminding me how out of shape I had become since college, but I made it under my own steam. Warren didn't look much better. Despite his soldier-of-fortune attitude, he was breathing as hard as the rest of us.

The shrine itself was a rather simple affair, a small block building with a statue of Our Lady behind some iron bars to protect it from vandalism. On the way up we passed a couple of hardy yuppie types coming down, the father carrying a toddler on his back in a carrier. That left us pretty much alone.

The view from the front of the shrine reminded me of being at the top of a Ferris wheel. We could see the whole town spread out beneath us, including the harbor and the road out of town in either direction. Even from far away, it didn't look like a postcard tourist trap, at least not to me. It still

looked like a poor, struggling fishing village, filled to overflowing with clapboard houses and lean-tos. For a moment it
made me think about wanting to turn the skull over to the
peasants. After all, I had found it in their gulf. Then I thought
about the job I disliked waiting for me and reverted to my
finders-keepers attitude, but I was starting to weaken in my
resolve.

Vaca showed us the way around the rocky slope on the
side of the shrine, and we made it to the six-foot chain link
fence that said "No Trespassing" in Spanish.

Glancing around and seeing no one looking our way, we
climbed over the fence and navigated the rocks to the ledge
waiting for us on the other side. The gulf was spread out in
all its quiet magnificence, stunning and green against the dirt,
rocks, and sandy white beaches. But there was no time to
talk in breathtaking terms. It was a minute to twelve.

I looked up at the sun and down at the potato sack in my
arms. Reaching in, I ran my fingers over the skull's smooth
surface, now warm from the climb up the rocky slope. It still
had a tingle to it, if only slight.

As I pulled it out of the sack, the sun caught the top of the
skull and flashed a blanket of white light at me. Staggering, I
stepped back against the mountain.

The world faded away and a vision appeared, but this time
it wasn't Montuca. All I could see was Susie's bright radiant
face, saying that she wanted me to see her new blue dress.
In a few moments it was gone, but it left a deep impression
in my mind.

Turning to Vaca, I handed her the skull, still in the sack.
"Here," I said. "Take it. I'm going home."

Vaca didn't say anything, but Warren was beside himself.
"Come on," he said. "Don't chicken out now. Give it a
quick look and we'll be on our way. Ain't no big deal."

"Easy for you to say," I answered. "But you haven't got
a wife and kid at home."

We argued about it until he finally said, "Fine, go back
to your housing tract, but I'm taking this." He reached out
and snatched the skull out of Vaca's arms. Holding the potato
sack in one hand, he marched off. He didn't get far.

Acting almost on instinct, I jumped on his back and

brought him down. We wrestled on that ledge, only four feet wide and ten feet long. A few times we almost went over the edge. At last he managed to throw me off, then stood up, facing me from the far end of the ledge.

When he realized he'd have to let go of the skull or hit me with it, he let down his guard. It was Vaca's chance. She had snuck around behind him, and as he regripped the potato sack, she grabbed it out of his hand. When he went after her, I tackled him.

We were suddenly at it again, tumbling on the rocky ledge. Then he made a quick move and had me pinned down, shoulders to the ground. Except for my head hanging over the edge, I had been in this position many times before during my wrestling days. He was just where I wanted him.

He reached back to slug me in the face, and when he did he suddenly realized his blunder. In a second I could have flipped him over the edge to the beach three hundred feet below. It was an easy move, just like flipping someone off the mat in wrestling. But before I had time to think about it further, Vaca had swung the skull around inside the sack and hit him squarely in the back of the head. He crumbled on top of me, unconscious.

Pushing him off, I got to my feet, carefully pulling him back from the edge and rolling him against the mountain.

We left him there and made it back to the jeep. This time Vaca carried the skull. We both knew I had made my decision and didn't want to handle the skull again.

As I climbed behind the wheel, I said, "Where can I drop you off?"

"Take me to my place first. I've got to get something."

When we got there she ran inside with the skull. After five minutes I got worried, and went to the doorway. She was just climbing into the shack through the back window. The potato sack with the bulge in it sat on the dirt floor.

"What was that all about?" I asked.

"No more questions," she replied with authority. "You had your chance. Now it's mine."

Deciding not to pursue it, I headed back to the jeep. She picked up the sack and walked back with me.

"Well?" I asked. "Which way?"

"Just head north," she said. "I'll let you know."

She spared me the lecture about saving the Earth and all that stuff I couldn't afford to think about just then, and we rode on, mostly in silence. When we got to the turnoff for the camp where I had discovered the clam, she said, "Turn here."

"Where are you going?" I asked, frowning. "Warren will come here right after checking out that abandoned shack you were staying in."

"Doesn't matter," she said. "Tide's in."

"What? I thought you were going to find an Aztec to look in the eyes?"

"No time for that. Eartha's in town. We've got to get this thing back to the sea before she does something drastic."

We zoomed off down the dirt road and rolled up to the camp. Mr. Zapata's truck was there, but he didn't answer his door. So we decided to borrow his outboard and take a little cruise on the ocean. With the tide in, we easily pushed the boat into the waves and cranked up the engine. Soon, we were on our way out to sea. Maggie barked as if a burglar were on board.

When we got a quarter mile out I looked at Vaca. "Don't be silly," she said. "We're not dumping it here." She held up the sack. "This is for Mother Nature's eyes only. We don't want some dumb tourist stumbling onto it by mistake."

Two miles later she grabbed my arm. I stopped the engine. After the boat had slowed to almost a standstill, Vaca leaned over the edge and dropped the gunnysack into the water. When she did a hot wind suddenly came up and the sea got pretty choppy for a few minutes, almost tipping us over.

"All right!" I finally said, yelling at the sun. "You got your Eyes back. Now let us go."

The wind died down, but very slowly. On the way back to shore a tiny speck standing on the campground wall became larger. When we got ashore, someone was waiting for us.

31

Run for the Border

As we got closer to shore, the tall, thin, familiar frame of Mr. Zapata came into view. I wondered whether he had figured out what we had done, or whether he even cared. The answer was soon to be forthcoming.

He wasn't upset about our borrowing his boat, but he easily guessed the details of our little adventure. He came down and helped us drag the boat beyond the low rock wall at the end of the camp.

"You did the right thing," he said. "Returning the skull to the sea. It belongs to nature now." He looked at me and smiled, lifting the brim of his straw sombrero with his index finger. "Until another Aztec comes to claim it."

Vaca had a stressed-out and disappointed expression on her face. "I'm afraid it's too late for that," she said, heading for the jeep. "Come on, Jack. You can drop me off in town."

"Sure," I said. "You've probably got lots of tourists to get back to: scorpion bites, flats to fix, and all that . . . Say, you're better than I thought—a real pro at ending someone's vacation. You got me to go home with nothing except this new hat."

"It's not a vacation anymore," she said, gravely. "You'd better get across the border before someone shows up and claims the skull for keeps."

Maggie and I walked to the jeep and got in. Mr. Zapata stood on the wall, looking out to sea.

"Why?" I said, climbing behind the steering wheel. "You really think Hardwick will find it out there? Or do you suppose Warren got loose and was watching us with binoculars or something?"

"You've got a short memory," she said, frowning. "You know darn well what I'm talking about. Eartha's probably on her way here right now. And believe me, you don't want to be here when she comes back to retrieve it. She's not going to be very happy that no one claimed the power for the Aztecs."

"Then let's stay and talk to her."

"Jack," Vaca said impatiently, "you had your chance, remember?"

"Surely she wouldn't hold it against someone for just wanting to go home and raise a family," I said. "Instead of saving the Earth. Would she?"

Vaca gave me a blank stare.

"Okay," I agreed. "Enough. Let's get out of here. It's her world anyway."

"No," Vaca said, correcting me. "It's ours. Her job is just to try to keep it clean and safe. But it's too late now. She's come back."

"Wait," I said. "Is her five hundred years up already?"

"Not until the year 2000," Vaca explained. "But man—the professor—already made his attempt to gain the power she left in the skull, and failed. That may be the only chance man gets. Besides, the legend says she'll claim it within three days of discovery—and it's been stressed," Vaca reminded me. "She may need to take it back before it's damaged further, and the power released, into the wrong hands. She may have to intervene now, and not wait. Since the incident in the cave, it's a whole new ball game, as you *gringos* say. She'll probably be here any minute. And there's no telling what could happen if she unleashes her power on the way out of here for another five hundred years. It could be devastating."

Mr. Zapata turned slowly around, and when he did, all the blood seemed to have drained from his face. "You mean," he managed to spit out, "that Mother Nature herself is coming for it?"

"In the flesh," Vaca confirmed. "So if you'll excuse us, we'll be going now."

Mr. Zapata didn't wait for me to fire up the jeep, he ran faster than I thought he could for his truck, jumped inside, and slammed the door. He had it started and the tires spinning before I could even back up. By the time we made our way onto the dirt road to the highway, his tires had created a huge cloud of dust in front of us. I pulled over and waited for it to pass.

"Boy," I said. "You sure scared the tamales out of him with that Eartha story."

"What?" she said, almost angrily. "You mean you still don't believe in her?"

I shook my head. "After what I've seen lately, I'm not saying I don't believe in anything. Let's just get out of here while we still can."

Once at the highway I started to turn south toward San Bajamos when Vaca grabbed the wheel. "Now what?" I asked. "Not enough tourists for you in town?"

"Changed my mind about this place," she said, almost lightening up a little. "It's no place for a girl to be wandering around. Matter of fact, this whole country is starting to look a little dangerous to me. Go on, head north. You can drop me off in Palm Springs."

"Ah, I should have guessed. Some more tourists to work over. Tell me, do *gringos* and *gringas* believe in vacation goddesses?"

"Don't you?"

"I don't count," I replied, pulling onto the highway and heading toward the States. "I'm *un gringo loco.*"

The next couple of hours were pretty quiet, except once I asked how she was planning to get across the border. That, of course, was a stupid question. Although she'd lost her papers back at the cave, she'd just create a distraction and walk across. Naturally, she didn't want to endanger me, so I was to wait down the road for her. I hoped the cops wouldn't pick me up later for assisting an illegal alien to cross the border, contributing to the delinquency of a minor, and so on. Oh, well, at least if they caught me on the American side, they'd probably let me make a phone call.

At first I figured Vaca was just kidding me and would produce papers saying she was a runaway from LA or something. After all, her English was impeccable, and her manner sophisticated. It seemed to me that she couldn't have been raised in a shanty, not with those rows of perfect, white teeth. For all I knew, she was some kind of royalty slumming it for a week. She must have had one of those eccentric rich mothers who dabbled in psychic powers, and picked it up quickly and well. It had to be something like that. She wasn't just going to distract the border guards and dash across, was she? Surely she would make a phone call and some stretch limo would come to the rescue. Then the joke would be over.

My question was answered rather decisively when we got to the border. About a hundred feet from the checkpoint, she climbed out of the jeep and kissed me on the cheek.

"Meet me on the other side," she ordered, and disappeared into a crowd of people selling velvet paintings and plaster Ninja Turtles.

I got out of the jeep and started to run after her, accompanied by a cacophony of horn honks and yelling. Obviously, no one wanted my jeep holding up traffic. These people were anxious to get back to the promised land.

Forced back to my car by a couple of Mexican cops, I almost had to pay them off to let me go, but Maggie protected me with a growl. For a moment, though, there was a tense scene when one of the cops went for his gun to silence Maggie. I told him she was too tough for taco meat and wrestled her back into the jeep. Twenty minutes later, we were across the border.

I never thought it would feel so good to be back in the land of "M*A*S*H" reruns and McDonald's, but as the jeep rolled into California, I felt better immediately. Who needed sunken treasure when he had "Monday Night Football" and VH-1? Not to mention Kentucky Fried Chicken and Astroturf. I was so excited to be stateside, listening to radios next to me blasting out Madonna and Michael Bolton, that I almost forgot to pull over and wait for Vaca.

Finally, about a half mile into Calexico, I pulled into a money exchange and traded in my pesos for forty-seven dollars. I was rich by many standards, and besides, I still had a wallet full of credit cards to fall back on.

I climbed back into the jeep and waited for an hour, but there was no sign of Vaca behind me. Once, I almost got out and walked back to the border to look for her, but decided I could just as easily miss her that way as by staying in the car.

Another hour later, with the sun starting to sink in the

west, it occurred to me that she wasn't coming. She was gone, and I would probably never see her again.

I wasn't prepared for that, but my poor little rich girl dream was evaporating before my eyes. She simply hadn't made it across. Perhaps she never intended to. That kiss, innocent and quick on my cheek, could have been her last good-bye.

I started the jeep and pulled into traffic, dejected, but getting hungry just the same. Then I saw a McDonald's on my right just up the road, and pulled in. The drive-thru was clogged with cars, so I parked in a stall. When I shut off the engine it became evident that *I* couldn't eat, but Maggie could. She whined, sniffing the air for the sweet smell of burgers wafting from the grill.

"Oh, all right," I said. "I'll get you a Big Mac." I pointed my finger at her. "But only if you promise to chew, and not swallow it whole."

Reading her blank expression, I forced a slight smile and went on in, coming back with a couple of burgers for Maggie and a large Diet Coke for myself. No way could I eat. Maggie didn't have the same problem, and wolfed down the Big Macs in a couple of seconds. She even managed to get in a couple of chews. After finishing my Diet Coke I went to the rest room. I was just washing my hands when Maggie scratched at the door. Uh oh.

I opened it and she jumped on me like she hadn't seen me in a week. On the way out I apologized profusely for my dog's behavior to anyone who would listen. But Maggie still wouldn't calm down. I knew she liked burgers, but this was getting out of hand. Maybe she knew we were heading home.

Back at the jeep she would hardly stay in the seat, and as we pulled out of the parking lot she began to howl. We had just passed a playground for the kids in the front of McDonald's. Then I remembered how crazy Maggie was for the slide. When she was a puppy I held her in my arms and went down the playground slide for fun, and for some reason she loved it.

"Okay," I said, stopping the jeep and looking around. "But only once, and then we go."

Naturally, there were no dogs allowed, but we only wanted to go down the slide once. I needed something to cheer me up, especially since my head was beginning to feel like it needed a beer.

We went down the slide one time, then got chased out of McDonald's. The slide did cheer me up a little, but not for long. A mile up the road I got depressed again. Looking down at the gas gauge made me pull into a Texaco station with a convenience store. I filled it up and went in to pay. I came close to grabbing a beer next to the sodas. That scared me, but I made it out of there with just a Diet Pepsi.

Maggie began to bark big time and barged through the glass front door, jumping all over me. I finally got her calmed down, and headed out. But then she dashed for the jeep, and began licking someone sitting in the front seat. If it hadn't been for Maggie's wild behavior, I would have thought it was an apparition. That was the only reason I didn't reach out and hug Vaca. Instead, I regained my composure and nonchalantly got behind the wheel.

"What took you so long?" I asked, popping the top on the soda can.

"Seems nobody believes in goddesses these days," she said. "Even border guards. Too Americanized I guess. Look, you hungry?"

"A little."

"Good, there's a Denny's just up the road. What do you say?"

"Well, I suppose I could eat something."

With that I took off down the road. When we got there Maggie stayed in the car and we headed inside. I reached for the entrance door and then changed my mind. Grabbing Vaca, I hugged her hard and slow. "Damn it," I said. "Don't go scaring me like that again. I thought you were gone."

"I told you to wait for me."

"Yeah, but I didn't think it would take so long. Where *were* you?"

"It took a while. I had to blow a half dozen radiators to create enough of a distraction so I could start hoofing it. I made it all right, but you were nowhere in sight. So when I saw this gas station, I decided to wait for you to pull over."

"But what if I hadn't stopped here?"

"Don't be silly. Have you seen how much broken glass is

on the roads down here? You know what it can do to a tire under the right conditions.''

"Never mind," I said. "Last time I worry about you."

"Yeah, there's plenty else to worry about. We've got company.''

"What's that supposed to mean?"

"Tell you over dinner. I'm starved.''

 32

Home Again

Over burgers and fries, Vaca gave me the bad news. She had seen Hardwick and his sidekick cross the border into California. They were driving a new Range Rover.

"A lot of good that will do him," I said, downing a Pepsi. "The skull's at the bottom of the gulf now."

"He doesn't know that," she informed me. "Or he wouldn't be coming this way."

"So what?" I quipped. "Ma Nature's going to beat him to it anyway. I'd rather take my chances with her any day over that megalomaniac."

Vaca reached over and put her hand on top of mine. "Okay, I'll spell it out for you. He doesn't know where the skull is, but he knows we do. He'll find a way to get the information out of us."

"How? What can he threaten us with? You're not afraid of him, are you?"

She took a drink of water and set it down on the table. "There *is* a way to get it out of us. *You* have a family, remember?"

"What?" I yelled, and everyone turned around. "That son of a . . ." Without saying another word I jumped up, ran for the phone, and called home. All I got was the answering machine. I left Ellen a message to go to her parents', who had an unlisted phone number, and I'd call her there. I tried

to remain calm, but wasn't succeeding very well. Slamming down the receiver, I ran back to the table.

"Come on," I said. "Let's pay up and get out of here before he beats us to my place."

A minute later we were in the jeep and rolling off toward Sherman Oaks. Vaca understood that under the circumstances I wouldn't have time to drop her off in Palm Springs.

"Wait a minute," I said. "You never intended to go to Palm Springs, did you?"

"Sure I did, before I saw the professor. I—"

"Vaca, don't spoil it with a lie. Just come with me. I have a feeling my vacation's not over yet. I may need you still."

"Let's hope not," she said, but not very convincingly.

I broke the speed limit a bunch of times, but luckily never got caught, except by the usual afternoon rush hour traffic. That added another hour to an already four-hour drive. I stopped twice and called—once to home, getting the answering machine again. And once to Ellen's parents'. She had returned the motor home, but wasn't there. They didn't know where she was, probably shopping with Susie, they figured. Not wanting to alarm them excessively, I told them to have her stay there if she came over, I had a surprise for her. Feeling helpless, I hung up and got back on the road.

Finally, just after eight o'clock, we rolled down my street and pulled into the empty driveway. I hoped that Ellen was still out, or at her parents' as instructed.

Before running into the house, I dashed over and pulled up the unlocked garage door. My heart sank to the concrete. The Saturn was parked there, and the engine was cold.

In near panic I raced for the front porch, unlocked the door, and ran everywhere, Maggie right on my tail. No Ellen and Susie. They definitely had been home, because there were wet diapers in the washer. But they were nowhere in sight, and there wasn't a note. Maybe they just went out for a walk, I thought. Yeah, that was it: just a walk around the block.

The corner of my eye caught something. Both lights were blinking on the answering machine in the kitchen. The green one for personal messages, and the red one for incoming calls. Almost beside myself, I mistakenly pushed the incoming call button. There was the message I had left from the pay phone.

Then I pressed the green button, the one for personal messages. Ellen sometimes left memos on it for me when she went shopping or something. I hoped against hope that she had left a message saying she was at the supermarket or something. But that's not what played. It wasn't even her voice. It was Dr. Hardwick. His sinister, squeaky voice grated against my nerves.

"I won't waste time with niceties, Mr. Hansen. If you want to see your wife and daughter alive again, you will do exactly as I say. The skull will be returned to me by noon tomorrow. There will be no questions and no negotiations. I will call back tonight with further instructions ... And I wouldn't get any funny ideas about contacting the authorities. Because if I spot them coming, you will never see your wife and daughter alive again."

"That son of a ..." Vaca had reached out and hugged me from behind, stopping me midsentence.

"Jack, I don't know what to say. I'm really sorry. I didn't mean for this to happen. I'm—"

"Forget it," I said, sitting down at the kitchen table. "It's not your fault. I'm the one who had to go chasing some wild dream. I've done this to myself. Well, there's no choice now. We'll just have to try to fish that skull out of the gulf. That is, if it's still there. And if we can find the spot."

She sat down opposite me and I looked her straight in the eyes. "Look, we've got to find that thing," I said desperately. "You remember how far out we were, right?"

"Sure but—"

"*But nothing*. We know where we sank it was straight out from the campground. Two, maybe two and a half miles. We'll rent some scuba gear and go look for it. We've got to find it. We just have to. I'll kill that dirty—"

"Jack, I have something to tell you."

"Later, can't you see I'm thinking."

"Yes, but—"

I slammed my fist down on the table. "Damn! What if Eartha gets there first. Then what?"

"Then we—"

"Of *course*, we'll just have to get her to help us. She will help us, won't she?"

"Jack, there's more at stake here than—"

"Well, if she won't let us have the skull, we'll just have to fake it. We'll pretend to be handing over the skull to Hardwick, and then—"

"*Jack*," Vaca interrupted forcefully, "that's what I've been trying to tell you all along. But you won't shut up. I know you're upset, but just calm down and listen for a minute, will you?"

"Calm down? My wife and daughter have just been kidnapped and you want me to stay calm?"

"I've got the skull."

"You *what*? But I thought it was at the bottom of the gulf?"

She reached across the table and grabbed my hands. They were shaking with fear and anger. "I lowered a rock over the side of the boat." When I gave her an angry stare, she explained. "Jack, wake up. If it was for the money, I wouldn't be telling you this. I'd be living on the Mexican Riviera right now with the proceeds from the sale of the skull."

I shook my head. "But . . . why? What are you saving it for? Or should I say whom?"

"*You*," she said, looking away. "I came here to convince you it was your duty, your destiny, to look into the Eyes of God." She glanced back at me. "I can see now that it may be too late for that, but since I'm partly responsible for the kidnapping, I'm offering to give the skull back to you. There may be hell to pay, but I couldn't live with myself if I didn't give you a chance to decide for yourself."

"Decide what? Whether to look into the eyes? Vaca, I'm sorry, but I can't carry the world on my shoulders. I just want Ellen and Susie back. Mother Nature or whoever she is will just have to fight it out with Hardwick for the skull. I'm no hero, I told you that. I'm going to give it to him for my own selfish reasons. I want my family back, and that's that."

The phone rang, and I almost jumped through the roof,

but I calmed down enough to pick up the receiver on the third ring.

"Hello?" I said nervously.

"Jack," Ellen said in a tense tone, "we're fine. The professor says to meet him with the skull at his cave by noon tomorrow. He says if anyone follows you, it's over for all of us. Jack I—"

The phone hung up. I tried to get someone back on the line, but there was nothing but a dial tone. Finally, I slammed down the receiver and dashed out the front door. When I got to the jeep, Maggie was already in the passenger's seat ready to go anywhere, but there was no sign of Vaca. I ran back in the house, but couldn't find her anywhere. I even yelled her name a couple of times, but to no avail.

"Okay, Maggie," I said, standing beside the jeep, "where is she? We can't leave without her."

Maggie went over and sat by the open garage door, then gave out a bark and some whines.

"All right," I said. "I'll close the garage door." I reached up and grabbed the handle. When I did, there was a rattle of boxes inside the garage.

A few seconds later Maggie found Vaca behind some crates of garage junk. She was just coming down from a stepladder, with an old trumpet case in one hand. It was the faded, black leather job that had belonged to my dad. Everything I had of his was inside. I had only opened it once, and just seeing an old trumpet, closed it again.

"Vaca," I said, exasperated, "what on Earth are you doing? We've got to get on the road."

She ignored me, as if in a trance, then carefully placed the trumpet case on my empty workbench and popped it open. Same old horn. Big deal. Before I could launch further protests, she reached in and removed the trumpet, placing it delicately on the workbench. Without saying a word she pulled a utility knife from my pegboard of tools on the wall and sliced the purple velvet bottom right out of the case.

There, lying neatly on the bottom of the case, was an old black-and-white photograph of what must have been my grandfather, standing in front of a hardware store. He had his arm around a small, Mexican Indian woman dressed in a peasant dress. There was a boy standing between them.

Vaca turned it over and, sure enough, it carried the names of my granddad, his wife, Morning Star, and their son, Joseph Hansen, my dad. She turned it over and showed me that my grandmother was wearing some kind of necklace with a pendant. I studied it very carefully, even taking it out in the sunlight. There was no mistaking it. The pendant was a shape I had seen before in the windows of novelty shops. It was a piece of rock crystal, carved in the familiar form of an upside-down obelisk, held fast by a sterling silver clasp and attached to a chain. When the camera had caught it, it reflected the sunlight, and appeared to be white-hot with light and energy.

I couldn't speak, knowing what it meant. Finally, Vaca spoke for me. "Your grandmother was pure Aztec," she said. "You may only be part, but that's enough. Aztec blood still runs through your veins. This was the only way I could prove it."

As I turned to walk away, Vaca ripped out one of the velvet sides, and brought out something in her hand. As I lowered the garage door, she showed it to me. Sunlight reflected off its smooth surface, blinding me. Then it died down. But it left me with a definite impression of power.

When I climbed behind the steering wheel, Vaca reached up and began to put the silver necklace around my neck, crystal pendant and all. It glowed a soft shade of lavender. Grabbing her wrists, I explained that my mind was already made up about the skull. It was going to be traded for my family, and that was that.

Vaca said if I wanted her to hand over the skull, I must wear this piece of pure quartz crystal. It was my heirloom, my family gemstone, and my link to my heritage. And unless I did, she wasn't going anywhere.

"Fair enough," I finally agreed. "What harm can it do?"

She fastened it around my neck and it rested on my breastbone, lying gently against my skin. As I backed out of the driveway and sped away, there was a warm tingling sensation where the pendant lay. It was like a miniature version of the energy transmitted by the skull, my own personal power station.

We picked up some junk food at a 7-Eleven and we were off. As the moon rose in the east, we headed south toward the border. For a moment I thought I heard the faint but familiar sounds of a jazz trumpet playing softly in the distance. But it could have just been the wind.

 33

Back to Baja

It was pretty late by the time we crossed the border, and there wasn't much time to spare. We had less than twelve hours left to dig up the skull and deliver it to the professor. The roads are dark at night in Baja, with no streetlights, but we raced on over familiar turf and zoomed down the highway to San Bajamos. Vaca and Maggie got some restless sleep as I powered my way south. I couldn't have slept, even with Nytol, so it didn't matter to me that I did the driving.

At two in the morning we pulled into town and found our way to Vaca's shack. We climbed out of the jeep and went around back. I shone a flashlight while Vaca got down on her hands and knees beside a giant prickly cactus and began to dig. Maggie and I joined her shortly. But after much digging in the designated spot, we came up empty.

Vaca turned a stark white as she looked at me across the three-foot hole we had created with our hands.

"It's not here," she said in disbelief, but I already could see that. "Jack, I'm afraid it's been stolen."

"Now what?" I asked, throwing up my hands. "We're doomed."

She couldn't say anything, and I couldn't say any more. The empty hole had sapped all my energy, and in a matter of minutes, we were both curled up in sleeping bags on the floor of her vacant house. Outside one of the holes for windows a star flickered, as if ready to go out. A moment later, we were asleep.

At the first hint of dawn I sprang awake and shook Vaca.

"Come on," I ordered. "Let's get going."

"What have you got in mind?" she asked, stretching.

"Skull or no skull, we're going to the cave. We'll bring a rock in a gunnysack if we have to. But we've got to try to free Ellen and Susie."

On our way to the jeep a terrible wind came up and caught us in a vicious sandstorm. We were pelted by hard grains, as if being sandblasted. It got so fierce that it drove us back into the house. Sand still flew in the window openings, but at least we could huddle against the wall and avoid being suffocated by sand. By the time it died down a half hour later, the floor sat six inches deep in grains.

We finally made our way to the jeep, got enough sand scraped off the seats to sit down, and I turned the key. It wouldn't start.

I was furious, slamming my fist against the steering wheel. When I opened the hood, there was sand everywhere. The more I tried to clean it out of the carburetor, the worse it got. Finally, in complete frustration, I slammed the hood.

"Come on," I said, fuming. "Let's walk into town. See if we can rent one of those dune buggies. The show's not over yet."

It was eight o'clock by the time we made it downtown. Just as I suspected, the sandstorm seemed to be localized to just the few blocks near Vaca's place. As our feet hit the boardwalk along the beach, I turned to Vaca.

"Eartha has the skull, doesn't she?"

"It sort of looks that way," Vaca shrugged.

"You don't suppose we could borrow—"

"I doubt it."

"That's what I thought."

Without saying another word, I stepped off the boardwalk and walked toward the beach.

"Jack, where are you going?" Vaca asked behind me.

"Just leave me alone. Can't you see I'm upset?"

"That's understandable. But where are you going?"

"To the shore. I have something to discuss with nature."

"But there are bathrooms along the boardwalk."

I didn't answer, and she didn't follow. One by one, my

footsteps took me down to the waterline. The morning was brilliant and crisp. Waves gently splashed onshore. To my left was the rocky mountain capped by the shrine, and a little harbor with tired fishing boats. To my right the beginning of a long row of rich *gringo* condos wound around the edge of a continent. Behind me the shops of a struggling fishing and tourist village waited anxiously for business. And far behind, off in the distance, stood the mountain that held the professor's cave and the treasures of my life: Ellen and Susie.

How could I have been so stupid to think I could outwit an evil genius? An average guy like me, who had a middle-class existence, was no match for someone who specialized in the business of power. What was I thinking? This guy was even capable of taking on Mother Nature. I was lucky just to escape a few natural disasters once in a while. I understood nothing, and was capable of doing damn little on my own. But yet, I wasn't willing to toss in the towel.

When I reached the water, a flock of seagulls sailed over my head and blocked out the midmorning sun for a second as I gathered my thoughts and prepared my simple speech. When the seagulls flew on, I began.

"Listen," I said, staring at the gently breaking waves, "you don't have to remind me that I screwed up—that I was willing to sacrifice the Earth for my own gain. I'm not very proud of that right now, but it's the truth.

"I have very little to offer you. All I can promise is that I will fulfill my pledge. If it's not too late, I will look into the Eyes of God.

"Give me a second chance, that's all I ask. Maybe I don't deserve it, and maybe I'm a poor example to be representing the men and women of the Earth. But at the moment I may be all you've got to save this planet. You're certainly all I've got to save me from my situation.

"Your five hundred years of nonintervention won't be up until 2000, Vaca said. That's another five years to wait to see if mankind destroys the planet, another half a decade down the drain. And man can do a lot more damage in that time. But if you give me a shot at it, I promise I'll look into your skull now. Maybe another five years of trashing this planet can be averted.

"I can see that for me there's no other way out. You can blind me or whatever you want, sacrifice me to the other gods, I don't care. Just let my wife and daughter go.

"It's in your hands now. Strike me down if you like. But please, let my family go."

When I got up and turned around, Vaca was standing right behind me. She had tears in her eyes.

"Don't cry for me, Argentina," I said. "It's my own fault."

"I'm proud of you, Jack," Vaca said to my surprise. "That took a lot of guts."

"No, it didn't," I said on the way back to the boardwalk. "That was the speech of a desperate man. Any coward could have made it."

"Your head's full of sand. Cowards don't offer to sacrifice themselves for anybody."

"Yeah," I laughed. "But parents do. Let's just hope it works. Say, let's hit one of those taco stands along the boardwalk."

"You hungry?"

"Not very. But that speech dried my throat. I'm thirsty as hell."

We made it across the boardwalk and found a little taco stand that had a picnic bench with tons of hot sauce sitting on it. Some kind of taco were grilling on the fire. I didn't want to know what kind, especially with the look the cook gave Maggie.

I was depressed beyond consolation, feeling deep in my gut that my entreaty was in vain. I never felt so bad, sunk so low into desperation. I needed something to kill the pain before I confronted the professor. And I needed strength. In such a state I acted on instinct, very basic instinct. Without thinking, I ordered a Corona.

Vaca took it away from me and poured it out, giving me a minilecture about the evils of drinking, saying that if I wanted strength, it lay within, or I could draw on the power of the crystal pendant around my neck.

Beyond hope, I laughed in a grizzly way, and pulled the pendant off my neck, since I couldn't feel it buzzing anymore. Stuffing it in my front pocket, I ordered another beer.

When it came I grabbed the bottle and fought it away from Vaca. As I brought it to my lips, a voice spoke behind me. It was a voice I had never heard before, yet it had the familiarity of an old friend. It was frail, female, and elderly, but it was tinged with hope and warmth.

"Come on, Jack," the voice said, "don't spoil that beautiful speech by trying to drown out the pain. I need you sober, and in full command of your senses."

Vaca gasped and bowed her head reverently. Her sudden move made me set the bottle down. Even Maggie had crawled under the table and curled into a ball.

As I turned around to see the face of the voice, the crystal pendant in my pocket came alive with energy, sending a pulsating electrical storm through my pocket. I reached in and pulled it out. My whole hand filled with power. Then it raced up my arm and flooded my chest and head. Tingling with electrical power, I turned and looked at her.

 34

Mother Nature

Mother Nature had an elderly, distinguished face. Her skin was a rich walnut brown, accented with thick black hair that was streaked with silver. A long straight nose, a regal expression, and her sparkling brown eyes rounded out the picture. She was wearing a white Mexican peasant dress, hand embroidered around the neck and sleeves with blue and green thread. And there was something else, something I should have expected, considering the shape the Earth was in, but it never crossed my mind. She was sitting in a wheelchair.

Still, her noble bearing had all the power one would expect of a goddess. She looked at me as I stared at the wheelchair, which had an umbrella hanging from it. The handle and ribs were solid oak, the cloth forest green canvas.

"What did you expect?" she said with a laugh. "Olympic

material? Everyone ages, even us. My legs aren't so good anymore. Since I can't use my magic powers to intervene in earthly affairs, they've grown tired walking the Earth. But I'm doing what little I can. Mostly speaking to congressmen and women, and lobbyists of course. Sierra Club and Greenpeace have helped a lot lately, but they can only do so much.''

"I suppose that's where I come in," I said, thinking out loud. "You need someone to help balance the scales the other way."

"That I do," she said wistfully. "If it's not too late already. I'm hopeful, though, that there's still time to turn things around. But . . .''

"But what?"

"As you know, my five hundred years of staying out of the way won't be up until the year 2000. I'm afraid you may be right: Five more years of neglect might be the straw that breaks the camel's back. The Earth will probably be past the point of saving by then.''

"My speech *was* meant to get your attention, but only to save my family. What about all the things people are doing now? Recycling, reducing fluorocarbons, and all that?''

"All of them good things, but it may be too little too late. The Earth is dying. Polluted rivers, landfills, oceans, and air are crippling life here, not to mention deforestation.''

"Look," I said, exasperated, "I don't think I can take another long lecture about saving the Earth right now. Not that I don't care, but it's beginning to sound like a broken record.''

"Men and women can do almost anything," she said to my surprise, "including save the planet. Things are changing already . . . but the time for talk is over," she added, hardening her expression. "The time for action is here. Someone has to seize the power inside the skull and make use of it.''

I told her that even if I gained power over the elements, I might not know how to control it. What if I wiped out whole ecosystems and populations just trying to learn how to use it? She said that every job had a learning curve, and that I couldn't expect to be an expert at first. It might take a decade before I got good at it.

"By that time," I protested, "it may be too late anyway."

Her face stiffened. "Somebody has to try," she insisted. "And you're the best hope I've got right now."

"But what about all those recent sandstorms, earthquakes, and such? What do you call all that, computer simulation?"

"Small-scale parlor tricks," she scoffed.

"Okay, so you can't intervene directly, but there must be something you can do. I don't believe you can't move behind the scenes somehow. You can't just wash your hands and leave it all up to some . . . some average Joe like me to save the world. That's ridiculous."

Vaca grabbed my arm from across the table and looked at me. "Jack, you don't get it, do you?" She glanced over at Eartha. "All of her power, except for a tiny reserve to run her life, is in the skull. She won't tell you this, but when she left the Earth and promised not to intervene for half a millennium, she did the only thing she was capable of doing. She secretly made the skull and infused it with all her special powers. It was the only way to give mankind a chance."

"But why only Aztec blood?" I asked. "Didn't that limit the chances of someone civilized gaining the power?"

"At the time," Eartha said, "this land was only occupied by Spanish conquerors and Aztecs. Which would you let have the power?"

When I didn't reply, she finished by saying that her only mistake was to fall in love with a human, Montuca's father, and bearing his son. Seeing I was left speechless by this revelation, she continued.

"It's ironic—I fell in love with the very thing that may destroy this planet. Don't get me wrong, I didn't create the Earth, but I swore that I'd try to preserve and protect it. Five hundred years of leaving the Earth alone didn't seem like so long to avoid the scandal of loving a human and having his child. But even I could not foresee what would happen when humans consolidated their power. The skull was supposed to guide mankind in my absence, but twenty years after I created it, Cortés came and it had to be hidden, leaving nothing but 'civilized' men to care for the planet. Well, you can see what that's left us with. If there's no habitable world to live on, what good are all man's ideas and plans?"

"All right," I said, standing. "I'm ready now.. Where have you stashed the skull?"

There was a long, lonely silence. And then, with a sad expression, Mother Nature looked up and said, "I don't have it, I'm afraid. When—"

"What?"

"When I got to the spot where Vaca had buried the skull, it was already gone. But—"

"Great," I said, shrugging. "Now what?"

"You didn't let me finish," she said. "When I arrived, a fancy off-road vehicle was pulling away. It had two men inside."

"But why the professor's message to me at home?" I asked. "If he already had the skull."

"That must have been before they found the skull," Vaca conjectured.

"My god," I said. "That means they've got everything. Quick, we've got to rent a dune buggy and get to the cave before it's too late."

"Why rent?" Eartha said. "Your jeep's just around the corner."

I grabbed the handles of her wheelchair and raced off toward the jeep, hoping like hell it wasn't too late for my family and the world. Vaca and Maggie jogged along beside us. When we got there I asked Mother Nature where she found the power to fix the jeep. She just looked at Vaca.

"I could have fixed it before," Vaca confessed, "but then you wouldn't have met Eartha."

"Thanks a lot," I answered, helping Eartha into the front seat of the jeep. "No offense, ma'am. But will taking you along do us any good?"

"Experience," she said with a wink, "is sometimes the best weapon. And sometimes all you've got—apart from the power of your convictions."

"Say," I asked, "do you have anything I could use to get us out of this?"

She reached over and pulled the crystal pendant out of my pocket. "Your grandmother's," she said, slyly. "Wear it for her. Out of respect, if nothing else."

She placed it around my neck and locked the silver clasp.

When she touched my skin I could feel her vibrate with the same electrical energy as the pendant and the skull. It was very low voltage, but definitely there. I wondered if she was dying. Besides her tired legs, there seemed to be a tired spirit residing in her body, masked thinly by her sense of humor and quick wit.

It reminded me that I had witnessed several people retire from my company "to the good life," only to read their obituaries a few years later. It was always said that without meaningful work, they just lost the will to live.

Despite Eartha's mostly jovial mood, I could sense an inner resignation. It seemed to me that, like many others, she must have missed doing her real work. And if all of this crazy stuff was true, who was going to be the Earth's caretaker? God knows it needed one.

When I saw my reflection in the rearview mirror, I shuddered at the realization that destiny seemed to have picked me for the job. Me, Mr. Average Guy, fighting off polluters and land developers. The scariest part of all was that there might have been no better choice available just then.

All of it was too much responsibility and much more personal sacrifice than I would normally accept. But I didn't have time to think about it. Crazy as it sounded, like it or not, I had a world and a family to try and save, and not a lot of time in which to do it.

 35

Inherit the Earth

I had been doing pretty well suppressing my feelings about Ellen and Susie, but on the way to the cave they started to come out. It wasn't all that noticeable to the outside world, but as I stared ahead at the mountain containing the professor's cave, it turned into a backdrop like a silver screen.

There were Ellen and I, jogging on the track together, and

along the beach in the summer. It never occurred to me how magical those moments were, how symbolic it was to see us running life's race together, how happy and innocent it had seemed at the time. Despite the recent "economic upturn," we were struggling financially, but at least we were going through it together. That helped a lot. Loneliness is the great crusher of the human spirit, and companionship often the foundation of hope. So, with a little help from each other, we were making it.

We had my income to keep us afloat until Ellen got full-time work, and we had her level-headedness. Ironically, she was the one who let me chase my dream, and now look at what I had done.

In the vision projected against the mountain I saw Susie being born, and me carrying her to the hospital nursery, all aglow with the glories of fatherhood. In my mundane worka-day existence, she was to be my crowning achievement, my contribution to Western civilization. Like all parents, we wanted her to have the opportunity to become whatever she wanted, bolstered by our love and support.

Perhaps it was naive, or maybe just human nature, to want your kids to do better than you. Perhaps it was nothing more than just advancement of the species, but that desire to make a better world for your children had always served as a mea-sure of success for parents everywhere, and we were no exception.

It is no small thing that children will run the world some-day. The better equipped they are and the better shape the Earth is in, the better their chances to make it work. For us, and for parents everywhere, it wasn't the meek, but the chil-dren who would inherit the earth. As obvious and ordinary as it sounded, it was still our credo.

The scenes of Susie's short life kept coming, playing before me like a video on fast-forward, all blurry, but each one had its own significance. Susie in a high chair with her first burrito smeared on her face, Maggie gratefully eating most of it, when it landed on the floor. Susie standing beside our bed, saying she had a "poop" in her diaper. Those first couple of unintelligible words, and those first awkward steps all came forth from out of my memory's treasures in random order.

There were more: Ellen and me racing into Susie's room after that loud thump and picking her up off the floor, crying. She had fallen out of bed headfirst. And our great relief that she was all right. All three of us lying in bed sniffling from a cold Susie had given us, trying to keep the used Kleenexes away from Maggie. Me rocking Susie to sleep on a borrowed rocking chair, singing "Twinkle, Twinkle, Little Star" until I grew hoarse.

Susie and me at the doctor's with her second ear infection, and the nothing-to-worry-about glance from the doctor. Ellen and Susie making oatmeal cookies, watching the cookie batter bowl bounce off the kitchen floor. Maggie again to the rescue. Susie's first tooth, and chasing Maggie, who had stolen one of her dolls to use as a dog chewy.

Dozens more images of all three of us just being human around the house, being a family.

And finally, clear, still close-ups of Ellen's and then Susie's smiling faces. "I love you, Daddy," Susie saying in one of those rare, priceless moments. This time after I gave her chocolate ice cream and a bedtime story. And Ellen saying, "Yeah, you're a good daddy, when you're sober and not spoiling her." It hurt me a little at the time, but now it was like music to my ears.

The images faded and I was back staring at the mountain, wiping a little bit of moisture from the corners of my eyes. The irony was that now, even if I saved my family, I had promised to look into the skull. And if I gained the magical powers inside it, my life would surely change forever.

Odd questions popped up. Would I still have to work? I supposed so, unless I was able to trade in the skull for a large sum of cash. Sure, that was it. Then my life would consist of cavorting around the globe, averting natural disasters wherever possible, and channeling the forces of nature where they would do the most good. I would have to make major decisions about the environment. Many people would be unhappy, but the good of the Earth was at stake.

And what of the professor? He wouldn't take all of this usurpation of power lying down; he'd come after me. Which meant either I'd have to go into hiding, or I'd have to eliminate him. No—I couldn't do that, could I? Yes, I could, especially after he kidnapped my wife and daughter.

I wasn't a violent person, even as a wrestler. It was always more physical ballet than a brutal match. The object was always to outmaneuver your opponent, not destroy him. But I wasn't a saint. The thought of Hardwick possibly torturing my loved ones brought out my deepest desires for revenge. If he had harmed them in any way, he would be killed. At least, that's how I felt. Desperate times call for drastic measures. This qualified as defense of my family, and perhaps the world.

There was more. Even if I managed to have some sort of life in addition to trying to care for the Earth, one thing was certain: things had changed forever. And there was just no turning back. Who would have ever thought a vacation would lead to a battle to control the forces of nature, with me at the center of it? I never wished more strongly to be back to my normal, uneventful life.

Just before we got within parking distance of the cave, I had an ironic thought. For the first time I had an inkling of the torture that people who had been ravaged by tragedy must feel upon losing everything. But with one important difference: I could still do something about it, I hoped. Besides, what use could the professor possibly have for my family now?

I was so lost in thought that the cave came upon me sooner than expected. When I looked up at last, we were at the base of the mountain. There didn't seem any point in trying to sneak up on the cave, so I pulled up by our regular route and parked near the rock-piled entrance we had used the last time, sure that the professor had seen us coming from miles away.

We still didn't have a definite plan, but we got out of the jeep and picked our way through the boulders at the side entrance. It was a little tough getting Eartha through, but I held her arm and helped her while Vaca carried her folded wheelchair. Once inside, Vaca said she had an idea.

Before she could present it, the Earth shook a little, producing tremors exactly like the small localized earthquakes that had come before. I looked at my watch. It was twenty minutes to twelve.

36

Inside Job

Once we were inside the cave, Vaca said, "I will offer myself in trade for your family. After all, it was my failure to return the skull to the sea that got us into this mess."

"Don't be stupid," I answered, flipping on my flashlight and shining it down the empty tunnel. "If it wasn't for me wanting to get rich quick, none of this would have happened. Besides, what would the professor want with you anyway? He probably doesn't even take vacations."

"I'll bet he does," Vaca argued. "He probably goes to power seminars."

"All this arguing isn't going to get us the skull," Eartha said from her wheelchair. "Does anybody have any other ideas?"

"If Jack would let me finish," Vaca said with a shrug, "I'd tell you the rest of mine."

"All right," I said, impatiently, "I'm sorry. My family's in here somewhere. At least—"

"After I agree to swap myself for your family," Vaca interrupted, "you can make an all-out effort to get back the skull. You know I have powers, and so does the professor by now. I can be of use to him; at least, *he'll* think so. What he doesn't know is that I plan on using my powers to create a distraction so you two can steal the skull."

"Pardon me," I said. "This might be a moot point, but I thought your powers could only be used on somebody *on* vacation."

"Precisely," Eartha agreed with a glint in her eyes. "The professor knows that. But he probably doesn't know that you are still on vacation."

"You call this a *vacation*?"

183

"Technically, yes," Vaca confirmed. "It's not over until you're officially back at work at the plant."

"You mean this nightmare is still my vacation?"

"Jack," Vaca said, "we went through that on the way here. Don't you remember?"

"No," I answered. "I was out of it. What else did we go through?"

Eartha spoke up. "Only that *you* will be of no use to the professor. On the contrary, you're the one who could gain the power before he finds a way to release it himself."

I asked what the chances of that were, and Eartha said that he was getting close to tapping the power. He had been working on a way around the "Aztec only" entry she had placed in the skull, a way to break the bloodline code so that it would release its power without an Aztec descendant looking into the eyes.

The release of energy we had witnessed the last time we were at the cave was an energy trap laid there by Mother Nature to fool thieves. The skull would appear to be releasing positive energy, but then would destroy the recipient—in this case, the high-tech equipment in the cave. The professor figured this out after the lab was nearly destroyed by the flood. Then he launched another plan. After he and Masters managed to get out of the canyon we had lured them into, his research led him to an Aztec descendant, a young boy in town. The professor paid him handsomely for a pint of blood.

He then drained a pint of his own blood and transfused the Aztec blood into his veins. He was about to gaze into the eyes himself.

My jaw dropped and the blood began to drain from my face. "He really is insane," I said, looking at Eartha.

"It may be too late already. Do you think his blood swap scheme will work?"

"Normally it would not," she confirmed, then got a sullen look on her face. "But after that last attempt to gain the power in the skull, it may have been damaged."

"I knew it," I said disgustedly. "I could tell it had been hurt by the tiny fractures inside it."

"Impurities, I'm afraid," Eartha agreed. "Its resistance to

entry may be weakened. The professor's plan just might work.''

"Vaca, what makes you think he'll take *you* in exchange for my family?'' I asked.

"Just leave that to me. Your vacation's not over yet. I've still got some tricks up my sleeve. Now let's get going.''

We proceeded down the tunnel. When we got to the place where the manhole was placed in the ceiling, I could see that we had a new problem. Vaca and Maggie could stand on my shoulders and make it through, and I could jump up and grab the edge of the hole and pull myself up. But what about Eartha? She might fit through, but not her wheelchair. This part of the cave wasn't equipped for the physically challenged.

When I brought up the subject, Vaca turned to me and said forcibly, "It doesn't matter. We can't afford to endanger her life any further. She's too important. She's not going with us.''

"Wait a minute,'' Eartha said. "Why not? I can walk under my own power. I brought my cane.'' She looked at me. "It's on the back of my wheelchair. Let me have it.''

I took it off and handed it to her. "Sorry, I thought it was an umbrella.''

"It doubles as a cane,'' she explained, and with a push of a button on the handle, it shot out a straight, solid oak bar, long enough to serve as a walking stick.

"Now,'' she said, "let's get a move on, before it's too late.''

I was still worried. "But what if we have to get out in a hurry?'' I protested. "Suppose there's another flood, or worse? I've got too many lives on my hands as it is.''

"Believe me,'' she winked, "I can handle it. Besides, I'm not getting out without the skull. I'm going to stay and fight with whatever I have left. Good legs or not. Because . . .'' Her expression hardened, and she gave me an intense stare. "If the professor succeeds with his plan, I've got no reason to go back to the heavens. My fight will have to continue here, in the flesh.''

"But can't you do more from heaven?''

"Some fights have to be waged here on Earth. This one

could last until 2000, when the professor will have to relinquish the power. The Earth could be in a heck of a mess by then.''

''But—''

''Say no more, I'm here until it's over.'' She looked at me. ''Unless a *real* Aztec gains the power. Then I will return to the heavens until the turn of the century, and wait my turn as Earth's custodian again.''

''It will be almost five years until you can intervene. Look, supposing I get the power, can't we make some deal? Some way I can hand the power back to you?''

The Earth shook and some small rocks fell from the ceiling of the cave. ''We'd better get going,'' Eartha said. ''We can talk about this later, *if* it's required.''

''All right,'' I said. ''But promise you won't do anything until we see if Vaca can bargain for the skull.'' When she just looked at me, I repeated. ''*Promise*. You're too valuable to sacrifice. Just stay back unless we need you. Besides, I don't want my wife and daughter exposed to any more danger than is absolutely necessary.''

''Of course,'' she agreed. ''I promise not to get involved unless I'm needed.''

Vaca stood on my shoulders and pushed the rocky manhole cover aside. The way wasn't blocked, so she climbed through. Maggie was next, jumping from my shoulders pretty easily to the upper level.

Then came the hard part. Eartha managed to get atop my shoulders, but she wasn't exactly light. I thought my back was going to go, but just as the strain seemed too much, the crystal pendant around my neck began to glow, pouring soft energy into me that flowed slowly down my spine. It didn't seem to give me strength as much as numb the feeling in my straining back. It allowed me to push Mother Nature up far enough so that she could grab Vaca's hands.

I stooped down, took Eartha's feet in my hands and shoved her through the opening as far as I could. She struggled, but made it upstairs. Then I jumped up, grabbed the edge of the hole, and pulled myself up. It wasn't easy, but soon I was on the next level.

This time there were no multicolored lights or the hum of

electronic equipment in the distance. Behind us the ruptured water tank still lay split open. At the far end of the tunnel above, bright light emanated in the distance. Without further discussion, we began walking.

When we got to the end of the tunnel, I made everyone stay back for the moment as I walked across the corridor, deciding that it was no use trying to hide or sneak up on the professor, since he would surely be waiting for us.

With Maggie joining me at the rock wall, I looked over the edge. The sun streamed down from the slide-away roof, now three-quarters open. It lit up the area below like a harsh stage light and reflected off something beneath me. My eyes had not yet adjusted to the intense sunlight when a voice came up from below.

"Good," the professor began in an eerie, friendly way. "You've arrived. I almost thought you wouldn't make it. Where are the others?"

"We're alone," I said, petting Maggie. I wondered if he was just playing with me, or was so self-confident that he hadn't watched for our arrival.

"Never mind," he said. "We don't need them."

"Where's my family?"

"I thought you'd never ask," he said nonchalantly. "Now we can begin in earnest."

 37

Father Nature

"We're not beginning anything," I said sternly, "until you show me my wife and daughter."

"Naturally," he said with mock casualness. "I would expect nothing less from you than concern for their welfare. But I assure you, harming them is not in keeping with my plans. But of course, that is up to you."

My eyes were starting to focus as I looked down. And

when they did, I saw a much different picture this time of the main room in the cave. Not a single piece of electronic equipment was present anywhere—not onstage, or lining any of the walls. Instead, blank rock face stared back at me. The control room across the way was still there, still covered with mirrored glass.

The stainless steel pedestal that had sat center stage had been replaced by a pyramid that appeared to be constructed of shiny, dense, black plastic. It was twenty feet across at the base, and rose twenty feet high as well. The brushed aluminum stage had been replaced by a white plastic one, built around the pyramid. There was no telling how far below the stage the pyramid descended, but I was sure we were seeing only the very top of it. And I was sure of something else: his power storage center had to be inside it.

The pyramid was made to be climbed, since the edges of the uniform, two-foot black cubes that comprised it, made natural steps.

The capstone had been replaced by a small chrome pedestal, atop which sat a shape that could only be the skull, covered by a fine black silk cloth. I wondered how the cave could possibly have been completely transformed on such a short notice. But I didn't have time to discuss it.

"What have you done with my wife and daughter?" I asked, impatiently.

Wearing a safari outfit, complete with hat, he looked like a diminutive aging anthropologist about to mark his last find for a museum. His seemingly frail, skinny frame was belied by his powerful presence. His body may have been on the way out, but there was fire in his gaze as he motioned for me to descend the rocky spiraling staircase to the bottom of the cave.

"Come," he said like a minister calling sinners to the altar. "Come on down and I will show you they are safe. Bring your animal if you like."

Knowing I could do nothing daring without risking Ellen's and Susie's lives, I glanced quickly behind me. Vaca was waving me off, saying not to go. Eartha just stood behind her, taking it all in, not interfering as promised. I could see by the look on her face that she was a woman of her word. But Vaca was having trouble staying back.

Before she could stop me I began walking down the stairs, winding my way to the bottom, Maggie pulling me with all her might.

Once there we were joined by Ed Masters coming out of the glassed-in control room. A look of forced indifference concealed any feelings he might have had for me. He was wearing a dirty, Mexican peasant shirt and old worn suit pants. Unlike the professor, who was immaculate in well-pressed attire, both Masters and his clothes needed washing badly. Even from ten feet away, he smelled of sour sweat and body odor.

My eyes were back on the professor, no less ominous from five feet away. Black bottomless pits for eyes and a slight sneer seemed to say it all.

He motioned to the mirrored wall behind him. "Your wife and daughter are behind the window," he said with a half smile. "See for yourself."

Maggie began to growl, so I had to restrain her by placing a loose boulder over her leash. She switched to whining, but at least she would be better off, especially since Masters was fondling a Colt .45 that was stuck in his pants. He blocked the door to the control room, and looked like he wasn't going to budge anytime soon.

Catching the professor's nod, I ran over and pressed my face to the glass. My heart pounded in my chest as I expected the worst. But there were Ellen and Susie, sitting comfortably on the floor.

Ellen wore her purple jogging suit, and a relatively happy, if cautious, expression. Much to my great relief, Susie seemed oblivious to their situation, playing innocently in her favorite green jumper. Her wooden train set was spread out on the floor in an open space where computer consoles had once been. She chattered away as she pushed the little train around the tracks.

I glanced around the room. There was a brown stuffed leather couch along one wall, with some blankets and pillows resting comfortably on it. A small oak coffee table against the other wall supported Ellen's purse and Susie's diaper bag.

There was even a box of groceries on the tiled floor, and a brand new Whirlpool refrigerator in a corner in the back.

Seeing that they were in no immediate danger, I asked, "Can they see me?"

"Certainly," he said. "Tap on the glass if you like."

When I did Ellen looked up with an expression of astonishment and relief. She left Susie and ran to the window, trying to touch me through it. She was mouthing, "We're fine. Are you okay?" and "Can we get out of here now?" in rapid-fire succession as she scratched the glass.

A second later Susie was at the window wanting to be lifted up. The look on her face was a priceless treasure as she repeated *Daddy, Daddy* over and over.

"I'm fine," I said aloud. "We're almost ready to go. I'll be there in a minute."

There was a gruff tug at my arm, which I ignored until it came again. The smell told me who was doing the tugging. When I glanced over my shoulder, Masters pulled my arm back and gave an anxious look at the professor.

Deciding not to press my luck, I turned around. "Thank you," I said to the professor, struggling with each word, "for not harming them. Now, what will it take for you to let them go?"

"Treasure has its curse," he replied, glancing up at the cloth-covered skull. "This one, as you are well aware, has been booby-trapped so that only Aztec blood can unlock its mysteries. You are probably also aware by now that my attempt at tapping the skull's powers with my instruments failed. I suspect that it's because the one they call Montuca has set it up that way.

"What you don't know is that I was only attempting to measure the skull's power with my instruments, not transfer the energy to them." He whirled and stared at me. "Instruments and machines should never be allowed to control mankind. They should never be allowed so much power over our lives, over the Earth. But they make excellent servants. Excellent sources of power."

When he uttered the word "power," something strange happened. His irises appeared as small rusty spinning gears, just as the old woman at the cantina had said. Either he wasn't human, or I was losing it. Then the spinning stopped, and he went on to say that a single man or woman was capable of ruling the world. But it must be someone whose vision of the future was true. Someone who was meant to be ruler of the elements. When I started to speak, he waved me off, saying it was rude to interrupt.

This position of power could not be left to just anyone, he informed me. It should only be given to the one that was most deserving—someone who understood and accepted the position of high priest for all mankind. Someone who could be patriarch of this planet—who could serve as Father Nature. This should be the one who had waited; the one who was ready.

Hardwick informed me that my duty was to help *him* re-shape the Earth. It would not be easy and there wasn't much time. But the deplorable condition of the Earth called for drastic action: fires, floods, earthquakes, and even famine if necessary to return the world to its former glory.

Suddenly a look of rage came over him. "Who else has the courage to change this Earth by bringing it to its knees? The entire Earth must be reshaped, using the forces of nature at full power. There is only one who has the courage to restart civilization.

"And then, when the Earth is completely purged of the stupidity that humans have brought with their primitive, mis-guided, emotional love of nature, civilization can begin again. A civilization based not on superstition and tree-hugging fools, but on science and thought, on high technology. That is this planet's future in the universe.

"I, and I alone, will reshape the Earth to restore it to its former glory, to reestablish a new Garden of Eden. A place of technological wizardry. I shall call it the Garden of Instru-ments. This time the apple of knowledge will be scientific knowledge and not spiritual myths. If mankind is to survive into the twenty-first century, it will be only by using technol-ogy, not through bowing to the whims of nature, which must be brought to its knees."

Overwhelmed by his madness, I couldn't say a thing. He truly believed that in order to save the Earth, he must destroy everything Eartha had done. He wanted to set the clock back

to the beginning and create a world based not on the balance
of nature and science, but on science alone. The look in his
eyes said he meant it.

Knowing this, and that his insanity was beyond my argu-
ments, I asked simply, "What do you want from me? You
have the skull."

"Blood," he said passionately. "I want your blood."

"I've been told that you already have Aztec blood in
your veins."

"And I would have used it," he smiled wickedly. "But
why take chances with someone else's bloodline when I am
certain of yours? You, my friend, are my Aztec. Your blood
will enable me to conquer nature. It is your blood that will
save this Earth."

"But—"

"Look at it this way. You will be saving the Earth and
your family at the same time. I intend to make you part of
my new world order. I shall be high priest, and you shall be
my sacrifice to the gods. I will not kill you. You are much
too valuable for that. But whenever I need more blood to tap
the power of the skull, you will be the source. It's ironic,
don't you think? Quartz crystal gave birth to the new electronic age, and now, I shall use the most powerful crystal on
Earth to give birth to an even higher standard of living. I
shall use it to subdue nature itself."

"Then you would use nature against itself," I said accusingly. "You are truly despicable. You are not human. You're
no better than a machine."

"Naturally," he continued, as if I hadn't spoken, "your
wife's blood is of no use to me. But if you refuse, then I
shall be forced to use your lovely daughter."

"You son of a—"

"That won't be necessary," a voice said from atop the
wall. "You touch Jack or anyone in his family, and you'll
have *me* to deal with."

When we looked up, Vaca was staring down at us, shaking
her fist at the professor. There was fire in her eyes, and power
in her voice.

"Ah," the professor said, surprise and animation in his
tone, "let the games begin."

38

Vaca's Battle

As Vaca descended the staircase, the professor had me get Maggie. It took some effort to keep her from taking a bite out of the professor and Masters, but I yanked hard on her chain and pulled her to my side. Vaca was halfway down when the professor ordered Masters to secure me and Maggie behind the mirrored wall.

I was of two minds. I wanted to be with my family more than anything, but didn't want to leave Vaca to battle the professor alone. Not that I could have done anything other than jump on somebody if it came to that, but I felt like a deserter. Still, when Masters pulled and cocked the gun, it assured me that he meant business. It was the first time he had shown any expression since I arrived, but as he led me behind the door to the glassed-in room, a wicked smile formed on his dirty face.

"Looks like the vacation's over, *gringo*. Why don't you join the missus until the blood bank needs you."

I shouldn't have said anything, but I couldn't resist asking, "What's in this for you? Surely you're not content with being the professor's errand boy? What are you, servant to the superstar world destroyer?

"Frankly, I don't see it. So when are you going to knock him off and get away with the skull? If you let me go, it'll be easy for us to take him on together. Besides, I don't have any use for the skull now. I just want my family back. What do you say?"

"Shut up," he commanded, waving his drawn gun at me and Maggie. He pulled back the gun like he was going to hit me on the head with it. "Or I'll be forced to give you a sleeping pill."

"Go ahead if it will make you feel better," I said, taunting

193

him. "But just think about what's going to happen to you when the professor decides he doesn't need a yes-man anymore. Soon as he perceives you as a threat, you're gone. And I'll still be here pumping out blood."

He didn't take any more out of me, just jerked open the heavy steel door and shoved me headfirst into the room. Maggie started to attack him, but I managed to keep her from being shot by getting her in a bear hug as we tumbled through the doorway onto the floor in the next room.

In the split second before he slammed the door shut, I yelled so that Hardwick could hear, "Better watch your backside, Professor. If you think your sidekick Judas here wants to be your undying servant, you'd better . . ."

The rest was silenced by the closing door, but I had made my point. As far as I was concerned, it wasn't even much of a fabrication on my part. For the life of me, I just couldn't see the guy playing second fiddle to a madman. Not when there was so much personal power and potential wealth to be gained.

All of those thoughts dissolved for the time being as Ellen, Susie, Maggie, and I had a hugfest on the floor. Everyone repeated how worried they were about the others amid kisses and twirls and hugs. Susie even said she missed Maggie, but not as much as she missed her dad. We laughed nervously at that, but all of the revelry was cut short by the presence of Vaca at the bottom of the stone staircase, eyes flashing fire at the professor.

Besides a light switch there was an audio switch by the door, so I flipped it on. Vaca's voice came through loud and clear. She had joined the professor atop the stage, next to the black plastic pyramid.

"Okay, Professor, I'll cut to the bottom line. Unless you want this whole place to rattle the Richter scale, I suggest you let everyone go. This matter is between you and me now."

"Sorry, that won't be possible just now," the professor said, sitting on one of the bottom ledges of the pyramid. "It would give you an unfair advantage, I'm afraid. I don't possess *mental* powers. Just a little expertise with machinery. That makes it an unfair fight, the way I see it, unless I keep my hostages for bargaining chips."

He tipped his safari hat back like Will Rogers telling some homespun anecdote. "But I'm not unreasonable." He got a peculiar glint in his eye and said, "I'm sure we can negotiate something."

Vaca began to pace, waving her hands as she spoke. "Here's the deal," she offered. "Plain and simple. Everyone behind the glass goes free, and I walk. I'm not saying I won't come looking for you, but you let everyone go now, and today I go back to town. I'll give you twenty-four hours to tap the power inside the skull. Then, I'm coming after you."

The professor nodded approvingly. "Most generous," he said with a slight smile, "but not quite what I had in mind."

"Then what?"

"I am willing to consider a cease-fire," he said, "under these terms. Since I plan on using Jack's blood, he stays here. You and the others will have safe passage back to town, but Jack must say good-bye to his family. Those are my terms. Take them or leave them ... Unless you've got some better ones," he added with a half smile.

"Matter of fact I do," Vaca finally answered, smiling slyly. "I'll level with you. Jack is not Aztec. He doesn't have one drop of Indian blood in his veins. After he had come this far to save his family, I didn't have the courage to tell him."

Vaca stopped pacing the stage, then turned toward the professor. It was a tense moment, and Ellen and I had our faces pressed against the glass. Maggie's paws rested on the windowsill. We must have looked like fish inside one of those giant water tanks at Sea World.

We were at the mercy of Vaca's words. I tried to bang on the window to get her attention, since I didn't want her sacrificing her life for mine. Ellen, however, thought differently. Not that she believed Vaca was expendable, but preserving her family was uppermost in her mind. She grabbed my hands and held them before I could bang on the glass.

Vaca pulled the picture of my grandparents from out of her front dress pocket. "How did she get that?" I said aloud.

She held it up to the professor. "This was supposed to be proof that his grandmother was Aztec," she said. "But I did some checking that he doesn't know about. This isn't his grandmother; it's his father's nanny. She took care of Jack's dad after Doc's mother died of pneumonia. I was just using Jack as a fall guy. He was merely a decoy meant to throw you off—buy time until I found a way to get the skull. I figured after his blood didn't work the magic, I might be able to step in and get it myself. You might as well let him go. He is of absolutely no use to you."

The professor was thinking, taking all of it in. Vaca sure had me fooled. I couldn't tell if her story was true, or just a fabrication. Was she just playing for time? And what about this crystal around my neck? But one thing was certain. Vaca did have powers beyond her magic tricks—powers of persuasion. This was no ordinary battle of the elements. It was a battle of wits, and she was good at it.

The professor walked over and pushed a small rock that was sticking out of the side wall. A small safelike hatch sprang open. He reached in and pulled out a sealed beaker, filled to capacity with a thick, deep red liquid.

"Suppose I believe this story of yours," the professor said, "and grant Jack and his family safe passage out of here. Then whose blood do I use to gain access to the skull?" He held out the beaker. "The peasant boy's from town? Too risky. No, I'm afraid—"

"*Mine*," Vaca said through gritted teeth. "You use mine." The professor's eyes lit up. This was something he hadn't considered.

Vaca filled him in. "Let's not fool around. We both know I'm a goddess. But look at me. What kind of blood do you think flows in these dark-skinned veins? What kind of body do you think I would take on in order to gain possession of the skull? Actually, the way I planned the whole thing is really quite simple."

Vaca explained that she always took on the form of someone in the locale where she was doing her work. In Mexico, it was only natural that she borrow the body of a young girl. The peasant girl would get it back when Vaca moved on, and never know what had happened.

Since Vaca knew that I was about to discover the skull in the gulf, she made sure her borrowed body was Aztec so that she could gain access to its power.

"You don't seriously think I want to be the goddess of

vacations forever, do you?'' she asked, sounding tougher than she looked. ''This is a nowhere job, not suitable for someone with my, shall we say, aspirations.''

I knew she was lying to throw the professor off the track. I just hoped he didn't realize it.

''Then why let them go?'' the professor asked, taking her seriously and setting the beaker of blood on the ledge of the pyramid. ''Someone with your thirst for power surely wouldn't give it up for a couple of ordinary, middle-class Americans.''

''I may be ambitious,'' Vaca explained, moving toward him until she got face-to-face, ''but I'm not bloodthirsty like you. Let them go, and my veins are yours.'' She held out her arms. ''But decide quick. For the moment I'm feeling sentimental.''

''Goddesses are not allowed to feel sentimental,'' he said with a sneer. ''That's a human trait.''

''I don't know.'' She threw up her hands. ''Somehow, when I saw how innocent he looked with his family, I got to feeling sorry for him. My mistake, I guess. I shouldn't have let my heart get in the way of business. Now, do we have a deal or not?''

The professor wasn't satisfied. ''And just what caused this sudden change of heart?'' he asked.

''Believe it or not,'' she said with a laugh, ''I felt a little guilty. I should have been smart enough to get that skull from you without him. Now I see no need to involve him and his family. This is our fight.''

''Then why not just let me eliminate him? I say you still need him, same as I do. And that you're bluffing so you can have him to yourself as soon as you get out of here. That is, if you make it out alive. I say you're lying. Your blood's no better than mine. All that borrowing-an-Aztec-girl's-body stuff is just another deception. You're human, and you're trying to trick me, hoping I'll let him go. And when I do, I'll find your blood is ordinary, worthless, not even Aztec.''

''Maybe, maybe not. Call me on it if you're big enough. Otherwise . . .'' While the professor thought about it Vaca made a swift move and snatched the beaker off the ledge, then backed away.

"Looks like you've got no choice now. Jack's blood won't open the secrets to the skull, and whatever's in the beaker here is history."

She held out the beaker and let it drop off the edge of the stage. It hit the rock floor below and shattered into a thousand pieces. As the blood seeped into the dirt between the stones, she said, "I'm afraid I'm your last hope, Professor, and your time is up. My offer is closed, so I'll be leaving now. Good luck on gaining access to the skull. You'll need it."

With that she turned, stepped off the stage, and began walking up the ramp. Before she got ten feet Masters grabbed her from behind and wrestled her back. Just as he got her to the bottom again, the ground began to shake, and the room we were in suddenly began to warm up, though there didn't seem to be a heat source anywhere. Small billows of steam began to seep from tiny cracks that formed in the tile floor, and outside in the dirt floor of the main room as well.

Suddenly, everyone's eyes were drawn to the top of the ramp. There was Mother Nature standing at the edge of the low rock wall, pointing her cane at the professor.

"Let her go!" she roared in a voice that was almost too powerful to believe. "Or you will have to answer to me. And I answer to no one on Earth."

The professor looked up and his eyes grew big. "At last," he said with great assurance. "The one I've been waiting for has arrived." He fired a powerful glance at her, and it seemed as if a quiver of dark invisible arrows flung themselves at her. She staggered and grabbed the wall to steady herself.

"So, evil one," Eartha said, "I see you are ready to play." She began to wave her cane in a circle in front of her, and, when she did, it formed a beam of bright, yellow sunlight that shot straight at the professor, knocking him backward away from Vaca.

When he steadied himself he was laughing in a sinister way. "Good," he said, satisfaction in his voice, "you are not an impostor. I may not believe in the magic of mankind and his world, but you are not of it. You have come at last to Earth. But it doesn't need you anymore. You've been superceded by technology. Go back where you've come from, or prepare to battle the Prince of Power."

39
Eartha's Entreaty

"You are not as feeble as you look, old woman," Professor Hardwick said. "So pick your weapon. What'll it be, lightning bolts at thirty paces?"

"Don't be foolish." Eartha planted her walking stick on the ground. "My powers are no match for yours—I have grown weak sitting on the sidelines watching your kind destroy the Earth."

"Then what was that little demonstration? A parlor trick?"

"About all I have left." She shrugged.

"Then why have you come?" he asked with growing disappointment. "Why have you wasted my time? Can't you see I have a world to remake?"

"I won't waste time convincing you that remaking the Earth at the cost of mankind and many other living creatures is the method employed only by a servant of evil, because you're already certain that your end result justifies your drastic and tragic means. You won't be satisfied until you see for yourself that the destruction of nature is not the way to progress. Beings like you have been trying to enslave the Earth for centuries, and there doesn't seem to be any end to it. Unfortunately, even if you are stopped, some other misguided soul will appear to take your place.

"I have grown tired waiting to get my power. Too tired. So, go ahead. Be my guest. Make the world in your image. It is you who will have to live on it—and with millions of deaths on your conscience."

"You are correct," he replied coolly. "My mind is made up. *Someone* has to take control of the elements. You yourself say you are old. It is time for you to step aside.

"This is my world now, unless you intend to fight for it. Frankly, I don't think you can anymore. Go quietly, old woman. Leave while you still can, before my pity is exhausted. I'm sick of the sight of you.''

Eartha raised her cane over her head and held it aloft, as if it were a rifle. ''Yes,'' she said weakly. ''You are correct in that. Therefore, I have come to surrender.''

''No!'' Vaca yelled, but it was too late. Masters put his hand over her mouth and tossed her into the room with us.

Upstairs, Eartha was preparing to descend. ''If you will permit me to use my cane to help me get down the steps,'' she said, ''I will turn myself over to your keeping.''

''I am not an imbecile,'' the professor replied. ''What do you want in return for your surrender?''

''The release of all your hostages.''

''No!'' Vaca yelled again, standing next to me at the glass window. ''Me! You must take me instead!''

Her plea went unnoticed as Hardwick answered, ''You take me for a fool. You know that if I am stripped of my blood supply, the skull is useless to me.''

He waved disgustedly at her and turned away. ''Go on, old woman. Go tell the other gods you've failed to retrieve the skull. I have no further use for you. Go on, get out before I have my servant throw you out.''

Masters still guarded the door, but got a perturbed look at being referred to as a servant. It wasn't enough to move him to action, but it gave me a ray of hope. Yet, something wasn't right. The newly arranged cave still puzzled me.

''Vaca,'' I asked. ''What's going on here? This cave was changed too quickly to be done by human hands. And when I looked into Hardwick's eyes, for a moment they were spinning like gears, just like that old woman back at the *cantina* said. Not to mention the way Eartha talks to him, like he's some kind of evil spirit or something.''

She tried to turn away, but I grabbed her. ''Vaca, who or what is he?''

''All right, there is one small detail I forgot to mention. I was going to tell you the first time we were here, but I didn't want to frighten you off, not when we were so close to tapping the pearl. But now that he's got your family, I suppose you should know.''

''Oh, great! Now what?''

"The professor. I'm afraid he's not just some mad scientist. He's . . . he's a god himself."

"*What*? Which one? The god of mass destruction?"

"Modern technology," Eartha interrupted, staring at me through the glass. "He was created during the industrial revolution to oversee new inventions and scientific progress."

I threw up my hands. "Why didn't you tell me this before?"

"I haven't been in this solar system for nearly five hundred years. When I was away, I was taking care of another planet, getting it ready to support life with what limited powers I have left. I have been back for only a few years, disguised as a political activist, not acting as Mother Nature. When I felt someone touch the skull, it sent a signal for me to return—as Mother Nature. When I arrived, one of the other gods here told me about the professor."

I looked at Vaca accusingly, and she took me aside.

"Yes," she admitted. "I already told you I knew. But I wanted to wait to tell you until Eartha returned to take him on. As I said, I didn't want to frighten you off. We still need you to get Mother Nature's power from the skull, because she promised that if she intervened, as a god she'd have to leave the Earth for another five hundred years. But if an Aztec gains the power in the skull, she'd never be tempted to intervene, because man could save the planet himself."

"But you endangered the lives of my family. How could you do that?"

"Jack, there's a world at stake here. I'm sorry, but—"

"Never mind. It's too late to talk about it. Well, being the god of modern technology explains how he got the lab rebuilt so quickly. But tell me, what are the limits of his power? I must know that much in case Eartha fails and we have to confront him on our own."

"He can only manipulate machinery, not natural resources. And even then only with controls, not with the wave of a hand or twitch of an eye. He is a brilliant inventor, as you might expect."

"This doesn't sound good," I said, shaking my head. "Almost anything can be accomplished by remote control these days.''

''Yes,'' Vaca said slyly. ''But machines do not always work. Electronics is tricky stuff. Signals sometimes get crossed, or jammed, even for him. He is ultimately limited by technology. He has no magical powers, but he's a wizard with machines.

I felt a little bit better, but I still couldn't figure what Eartha was up to. I looked to Vaca for an explanation, but she just shook her head and said she couldn't believe any of it. Something must be up. But what?

Just as the professor began to walk toward the glass room, Mother Nature spoke. ''You are a greater fool than I thought, Professor. You don't even recognize a gift when you see one.''

''Shut up,'' he said, offhandedly. ''I've got work to do.'' He pushed a button on the wall next to the glass room and a drawer popped out. He reached in and pulled out a needle big enough to draw blood from a horse. Then he turned around and motioned to Masters, who opened the door and motioned for me to come forward.

Amid curses and pleas from Ellen and Vaca, I broke away and presented myself at the door. Masters pulled me outside and held out my arm. If I tried to take them on and failed, they might destroy everyone. I rolled up my sleeve.

The professor gave one last look at Mother Nature and moved the needle toward my arm, looking for a vein. He placed the tip of the six-inch needle against a large vein on the inside of my arm and pushed. A sharp pain ran up my arm, and I flinched.

''Thank you,'' he said with a sly smile, ''for contributing to our blood bank.'' He reached for the plunger at the end of the needle to pull it back and draw out the blood.

Suddenly, Mother Nature spoke again. ''His blood is nothing,'' she said harshly. ''Even if he *was* Aztec, it has been diluted many times by the marriages of his ancestors. What's left in his veins isn't enough to power the crystal in a wristwatch.''

The professor stopped but left the needle in. Eartha had gotten his attention. He was noticeably shaken by her statement, and suddenly, angrily, pulled out the needle. "Then I shall take your precious Vaca's blood!" he yelled.

Eartha laughed, tossing back her head. "That waif? You don't believe her story, do you? You said so yourself. Vacation Goddess? You know very well there's no such thing. But you are wrong about one thing. She is a goddess all right. You've been so busy with your plans and inventions that you haven't even kept track of the gods and goddesses. She's a new one, brought on by your technology. She's goddess of industrial espionage. She's come only to steal the skull and sell it. Thanks for locking her up. You saved me the trouble."

I looked at Vaca. She told me in private that none of it was true. Eartha was just saying it to save the rest of us.

The professor looked up, gazing at Mother Nature. "Yes," he said, almost quietly. "I suspected that Vaca was a spy. But I had to be sure."

Finally, exasperated, he said, "Then what? In all of heaven and Earth, whose blood do you have in mind?

"Mine."

Her answer sent shock waves through all of us. We had never even considered it as a possibility.

"*Yours?*"

"I made the skull with my own hands," she said slowly. "My own sweat and blood. Even for me it was a chore. But I have infused it with my own essence and power. If anything can unlock the secret of the skull, it is my blood." She studied his expression carefully for a few moments, then got a funny look on her face, and quickly switched directions.

"I have changed my mind," she said seriously. "Suddenly, looking at you makes me sick. Therefore, I am leaving.

"And as for the others," she said with a wave at us, "I'm afraid my sentimentality for the human race has been sadly misplaced. I should never have gotten involved with man in the first place. My patience has been tried beyond its limits." She turned and began to walk away. "Good-bye, professor. You will die never knowing the power. And the gods will laugh at you when they find out who you let get away. Just remember I will be back in 2000 to claim my world. You probably won't be here; you'll be replaced after this failure. So teach your successor how to defend the world he will have made. That is, if he succeeds.

"But beware," she added, turning and pointing her cane at him. "I will take no prisoners upon my return."

There was a long tense silence, and then, "Wait!" yelled the professor to the empty stone railing above him. "The others shall go free. You have my word on it. They mean nothing to me. They are yours—take them all. Take my servant as well."

Masters had heard enough. "You rotten, back-stabbing traitor," he said, pointing the gun at the professor. "I ought to shoot you right now."

Hardwick turned to face him. They shouted at each other for nearly a minute, almost coming to blows. Then, without warning, Eartha suddenly appeared at the bottom of the stairs. Everyone had been so busy watching Hardwick and Masters argue that no one had seen her slowly descend the steps, using the rock wall and her cane for support. She was now only twenty feet away.

She took the last careful step to the bottom of the cave and planted her feet firmly on the dirt and ground-up rocks. "This is much better," she said with great satisfaction and a broad smile. "When you get to be my age, and in my condition, you work better at close range."

The argument stopped. The professor whirled around, a warm smile on his face. "Excellent," he said. "I knew we could work something out. Now if you'll just—"

"Jack," Eartha interrupted pleasantly, "I suggest you go back inside the room behind you. Things might get a little hot out here."

"Pardon?" the professor asked, still pleased by her reappearance. Then he turned and looked at me. "Of course," he smiled. "Go inside and round up the others. You're going home."

Without saying anything I turned, opened the door, and stepped inside.

"Now," the professor said. "Where were we? Oh, yes. About that blood sample." He looked down at the needle.

"My, there's been some mistake." He frowned. "This isn't the right needle at all. This one's much too big. Masters, how could we treat our guest so rudely? Get me a regular hypodermic needle. Make it a clean one. And get our guest here a chair."

"That won't really be necessary," Eartha said. "I won't be staying that long."

"But—"

"Just long enough to collect what I came for."

When the professor gave her a weird look, as if she were about to renege on a deal, she added, "As I said, at my age I work better at close range."

With that she raised her cane and pointed it at the professor. A blinding flash of sunlight filled the cave, so brilliant that all of us behind the windows went down on the ground to regain our eyesight; even Maggie had her paws over her eyes. The blinding light burned like an extended blast from a camera flashcube. It took a full thirty seconds to get our vision back, but when we did, we scrambled back to the window.

Slowly, the light in the room returned to normal—to just the sunlight overhead shining through the half-open ceiling. Mother Nature was standing there, casually straightening her hair. The skull, covered with the black silk cloth, was still atop the pedestal. But the professor and Masters were gone. Using the cane, Eartha walked over slowly and reached for the doorknob.

The professor came out of the doorway on the far side of the cave. He had exchanged his safari hat for a gas mask. He reached for a button made of rock on the wall next to the door.

"So, I hear it's not nice to mess with Mother Nature," he said. "Well, we'll see about that."

He sealed the gas mask and goggles over his face, then pushed the rock button. Slowly, from several metal vents around the cave, just two feet off the ground, a black cloud began to filter into the room. He pressed another button nearby and the roof panel began to shut.

From the wild look in Hardwick's eyes, and the angry look

in Eartha's as she let go of the door handle to the glassed-in room, it must have been some kind of toxic cloud.

In a minute the main room of the cave was filled with thick, black smoke, but Eartha stood her ground.

Then it was at our door, and heading for the vents.

 40

Full-Scale War

The faint foul odor of toxicity began to drift toward us. Its noxious smell fell somewhere between that of burning rubber and ammonia. Outside the room, Mother Nature stood completely enveloped in smoke. We looked at each other, certain of our unavoidable fate.

"Quick," I said, tearing off my short sleeve khaki shirt, "we've got to get these vents blocked."

There were three vents into the room, all just below the windows at waist height. I ran for the one on the left, shirt in hand. Ellen grabbed Susie's blanket and headed for the middle one. Vaca reached down and took hold of the hem of her peasant dress. Just as she was about to pull it off over her head, something strange happened.

The vents, which blew a constant flow of cool air into the room, suddenly began to pull air out of it. The small amount of black sooty smoke that had filtered in was immediately sucked out, followed by a tremendous hissing sound in the main room.

We looked through the window. Slowly, all of the smoke began to converge where Eartha stood. In a matter of seconds the air had cleared enough to see that she was sucking it all inside her mouth, like a powerful vacuum. Soon the only smoke that remained came out of the vents in the main room. In a minute, that too was depleted and inhaled by her.

When she had taken it all in, her eyes turned the color of red fires. She shot a glance at the exit door on the far side of the lab, near where the professor stood. The heavy metal door tore open, and when it did, she exhaled, pouring a thick tube of black smoke from her mouth right through it. The smoke formed a column and disappeared through a hole in the top of the sky.

After her lungs had been emptied, and the last of the smoke shot through the opening, the hole in the sky closed and the ceiling door slammed shut. She just stood there, firing a cold stare at the professor, who removed his gas mask with a wry smile.

"Very good lung capacity for a woman your age," he quipped with a grin. "But let's see how you handle this."

He pulled a remote control out of his safari jacket pocket and began to work the buttons. There was a strange mechanical sound coming from the top of the stairs, like the sound of machinery moving.

In a few seconds four life-sized robots appeared atop the landing overlooking the lab. They had brushed steel tubes for arms and legs, complete with metallic ball joints at the elbows and knees. Their hands and feet were no more than foot-square clamshell devices, like those you see on earth-digging equipment, complete with overlapping teeth. Their chests were long cylinders filled with electronic circuitry and hydraulic hoses, encased in clear, inch-thick plastic. Video monitors served as heads, mounted on old car springs for necks. Electrical power lines ran up the middle of the rusty springs to the monitors, which played motion pictures of huge earth movers strip-mining and clearing forests. This was soon replaced by the image of the professor's talking head as it appeared below on the floor of the cave, laughing in a sinister mixture of madness and wicked humor.

The robots seemed incapable of quick movement, but, with a plodding effort, they descended the stairs four abreast, taking up the entire width, so that Eartha couldn't get by if she attempted a run for it. The look in her eyes said she had no intention of leaving, though she seemed weakened and dizzy from inhaling the toxic cloud.

She steadied herself on her cane and then raised it up, pointing directly at the advancing column of robotic indifference. Now donning a set of dark glasses, the professor's face still played on their monitors. "Go on, spray us with your sunlight," he said confidently. "We have our sunscreens on."

Just as the words were spoken, the robots were attacked by a powerful wave of bright yellow light. It immediately bounced back with such blinding reflective force that even Mother Nature covered her eyes. The professor just laughed. I shielded Susie's eyes as the rest of us hit the floor.

In a few seconds the light inside the cave resumed its normal level and we all got up again. Obviously, *that* wasn't going to work. Now what was she going to do? We soon found out.

Mother Nature gazed up at the ceiling. The roof began to slide open, again a foot at a time, letting in gushes of light. It still had no effect whatsoever on the robots, who were now halfway down the steps and still coming, playing the smiling face of the professor on their screens.

Then it became clear that letting in sunlight was not Eartha's game at all—for the sky over the dome suddenly filled with ominous, gray rain clouds, turning the cave below into a dark dungeon.

The professor frantically ran back to the far wall near the door and began working the roof controls with his free hand, but to no avail. It stayed open. He went back to the robot remote control in his other hand.

The air grew heavy with tension, silence, and near darkness—the calm before the storm.

Then, without warning, there was a great blinding flash as a bolt of lightning hit one of the robots, sending him crashing down the steps in a heap of smoke and fire.

"Lucky hit," the professor spat out, working the controls wildly. The robots lifted their clamshell shovels over their heads in a protective maneuver.

Another sudden bolt of lightning came crashing down, this time striking one of the robots in the clamshell device, just as the professor had planned. The bolt ricocheted wildly off the clamshell, sending sparks in a thousand directions. One of them hit the observation window just above us and rippled across the glass in an electrical array of splintered light. We had to back up in a hurry as the protective glass heated up and sent thousands of tiny hairline cracks rippling through it, covering it completely with a web of fractures. If it hadn't been for the chicken-wire pattern of metal inside it, the glass would have shattered.

"Okay!" I ordered. "Everyone back. This is too dangerous." Nobody argued, but Maggie barked, whined, and got down low on the floor. We all moved toward the back of the room, where we could watch from a safe distance. At least we hoped it was. I came to my senses for a minute and told everyone to look for a back exit. I pulled my sunglasses out of my pocket and kept watch on the battle outside.

Just as I began to realize that the intensity of the flashing light might make the sunglasses useless, Vaca found enough smoked goggles in an unlocked cabinet to pass around. They were probably no protection against lightning wars, but they were still better than nothing. I told the others to start pushing on walls and floor tiles, knowing there just had to be another way out of the observation room in case of emergency evacuation.

Outside, Eartha was getting in deep. She turned and glanced at me through the million cracks in the safety glass. I could tell she didn't want to risk another bolt of lightning hitting the window, though it looked rather easy to strike the professor with a well-placed bolt. Eartha must have thought it was too dangerous with us in the next room protected by a damaged glass window, and the skull balanced precariously on the pedestal center stage in the lab, for that was the end of the electrical storm.

Overhead, the heavy black clouds burst their seams just as the three remaining robots reached the bottom step, echoing the professor's victory grin on their monitors. But it wasn't over yet.

Rain poured down in torrents, so heavy that it almost knocked over the robots. Eartha stepped next to the window directly in front of me. Since there was a two-foot overhang where the ceiling rolled back against the cave, she remained just out of reach of the rain, though she was clearly getting soaked from the downpour bouncing up from the cave floor next to her.

The professor defiantly stood his ground, pummeled by rain, but unmovable and still working the remote controls.

Then one of the robots was suddenly down, having slipped on the last step, and was unable to get up. He reached up for the hand of another. His comrade stood silently over him, then bent and clamped his wrist with a clamshell embrace to pull up the fallen warrior.

A sudden wind screamed down from above, bringing with it buckets of rain, and knocking the standing robot down on top of the other. Water gushed over them, and in seconds they were swimming vainly in a foot of water, unable to get to their feet. The more they struggled, the more entangled they became.

Just as it looked as if they would make it to their feet in one last desperate attempt, there were flashes of fire inside their chests. Grasping each other wildly, they had effectively severed each other's electrical lines in several places. Having shorted each other out, they collapsed in the water. Their screens went blank.

The last robot kept coming, though much more slowly through the pounding rain. He advanced within a foot of Eartha, and when he did, reached up with an open clamshell shovel and grabbed her by the waist, pinning her left arm to her side. The professor's rain-soaked face flashed a wicked smile on the monitor.

"At last," he said with great satisfaction.

The robot lifted its other arm and opened the claw. Slowly, with a great, rusty creaking sound, it began to close on Eartha's head as she struggled to break free. But it was no use, he had her in his death grip, and was about to crush the life out of her. There was nothing I could do but watch from three feet away on the other side of the glass. I might as well have been on the other side of the Earth.

Just as the mechanical beast's claw met her skull I had an idea. But in the instant before I turned to hurl a chair at the window, Eartha feebly raised her cane with her free right arm and pointed it at the monster's throat.

He was a split second from crushing her skull when she slipped the tip of her cane between his car spring of a neck and shoved it into the electrical conduit that led to his head. He flinched, and it was just long enough.

Eartha lunged her head forward as his iron claw slammed

shut behind it, taking a good clump of hair, but nothing else. She drove the tip of the wooden cane farther into his electrical spinal cord, freezing him in place. The monitor played only the professor's surprised expression as Eartha wriggled free.

When she was completely free, she stepped aside and gave the robot an amazingly gentle shove, as though she were casually shutting a refrigerator door. He fell backward into a foot of water and never got up again.

She lifted her cane to the heavens and the rain stopped as suddenly as it had begun. The clouds blew away and behind them the sun shone brightly again.

"You are everything I've been looking for in a woman," the professor said with amazing affection. "Marry me, and we'll take care of the world together, and I will take care of you."

"Will you never learn?" Mother Nature said, rubbing her waist. "I will never be your concubine. If you could be trusted, we could be partners, but your thirst for power is limitless. Someday, when *you* are brought under control, we can work together to save this planet. But you are too young, too vulnerable, too ambitious. Once, perhaps, you sought to help man make a better world, but now you seek only to make the world in your image, devoid of nature, devoid of life.

"The only life you promote is manufactured in the laboratory. The only knowledge artificial intelligence. As for myself, I seek only to be your equal, not your master. I have returned to balance the scales of nature and technology. To set the world right, before—"

Her voice was drowned out by the wild rush of liquid flowing from the same vents the professor had used to propel the smoke into the cave. In a minute, the foot-deep water on the cave floor was covered with a thick, slimy layer of liquid. Judging by the smell coming through the vents in the observation room, it was crude oil.

Vaca and Ellen reported that they had knocked on every square foot of the room and found no emergency exit or trapdoor anywhere.

"Look again," I commanded, watching as the professor

climbed atop the center platform, two feet above the oil-on-water, and slipped into an asbestos suit he had taken from beneath a loose panel in the platform floor. As he pulled the glass face mask and helmet over his head, he said to Eartha, "Too bad. It could have been a helluva honeymoon."

With that, he pulled a Zippo lighter from one of his pockets and held it out. "Remember," he said, in his crazed and squeaky voice, "only you can prevent forest fires."

He spun the starter mechanism on the lighter and it sprang to life with fire, then he casually tossed it on the oil slick. It immediately burst into flames, spreading almost instantly across the floor of the cave, still covered in foot-deep water topped with a layer of crude.

The three-foot-high flames raced across the room to greet an angry Eartha. "Little boys," she said, raising her cane, "shouldn't play with matches."

Just as the flames eagerly licked the hem of her dress, she brought the tip of the cane down and touched the oil slick, stirring it like an evil potion in a witch's cauldron. The oil and water began to swirl beneath the cane, creating a tiny whirlpool. It was no bigger than the drain of a bathtub, but it pulled the oily mess, fire and all, into it.

The flames drew back from her dress, helplessly sucked into the whirlpool at her feet. Soon, all of the fiery slick and water were pulled down into it, and the floor of the lab was bare again, except for a mixture of rocks and mud. In the spot where the whirlpool had been sat a six-inch drain hole, covered by a round metal gate. Eartha pulled it up with the tip of her cane and an oily rag came up with it.

"Thanks for unclogging my drain," the professor said facetiously. He popped open another panel on the floor of the stage and flipped some switches inside it. All around the room, at two-foot intervals, rifle barrels pushed out of the cave walls. The professor climbed inside the open panel that served as a trapdoor, and closed the lid. The gun barrels adjusted so that they all aimed at Eartha as though she were facing a firing squad.

"It's been fun," he laughed over a loudspeaker, "But now let's see if you can get the lead out."

A quick blast from one of the rifle barrels knocked the cane out of Eartha's hand, breaking off the handle and sending the rest twenty feet away against the far cave wall to the left of the observation room. Just as I thought that the rest of the guns would be let loose, the trapdoor popped open and the professor emerged, holding a black blindfold in one hand.

"How utterly uncivilized of me," he claimed, faking a frown. "As my prisoner, you're entitled to a last request before you face the firing squad. Now, what do you want on your headstone?"

"What's the charge?" Mother Nature demanded, not moving from her spot in front of me.

"I beg your pardon?" the professor asked in disbelief.

"If I'm to be executed, I want to know my crimes. That's my last request. A headstone won't be necessary. Just mark my grave with a newly planted tree."

"Very well, then, I shall tell you," he acknowledged, stepping down off the platform. He stuffed the blindfold into his safari suit pocket, straightening it like a handkerchief and heading for the broken cane. "But let's have no more parlor tricks."

He marched past her and picked up the cane, then tramped back across the muddy floor. He stopped in front of her and held out what was left of the cane as though he was going to give it back. But when she reached for it he broke it sharply over his knee, then tossed the splintered ends and torn umbrella shreds over his shoulder like a king tossing bones to the dogs.

With forced calm, he said, "Even the most casual observer will note that other than sucking the smoke out of the room, all of your power seemed to be concentrated in that cane. Now that it's been destroyed, we should be on a more equal footing. So let's cite your many crimes. And rest assured, you will pay the full price if convicted."

"Enough small talk," Eartha said coldly. "What are my offenses."

"First let me inform you that, in the interest of fairness, you are entitled to a trial by a jury of your peers." He looked around the room nonchalantly. "And I'm afraid that I'm the only peer you've got right now. So I'll just have to be judge and jury . . . oh, and executioner of course."

"If I'm found guilty."

He shook his head. "You *will* be found guilty."

"And will I get *my* say?"

"Of course. I'm not a barbarian, you know."

"Good, but I want a lawyer."

"What?"

She brushed her hair back with her hands. "Only a fool defends herself in court. Ask any lawyer."

"Well, there seems to be real shortage of legal counsel at the moment. Whom did you have in mind, my dear?"

"Jack."

"That middle-class working stiff?"

"I've made my choice."

"Fine!" he bellowed. "The Supreme World Court is now in session. The honorable Jason B. Hardwick presiding. All rise!"

With that, the trial of Mother Nature had begun, and I was in way over my head. What had started out as a battle was now a full-scale war, and I was being asked to take command.

 41

The Trial

"The charges against you should come as no surprise to anyone," the professor said. "They are willful neglect and abandonment of a helpless young planet."

I stood motionless, stunned by what was happening. Eartha spoke to the professor. "I wish to talk to my counsel now," she said. "We need a minute to prepare before the trial begins."

"Very well," Hardwick said nonchalantly, letting his legs dangle over the edge of the platform like a kid sitting on a pier. "You may confer. But he cannot come outside. I don't want to have to keep an eye on both of you."

"What's the matter?" Mother Nature said sarcastically. "Afraid of an old woman and a washed-up wrestler?"

The professor planted his boots on the muddy ground-up rocks beneath the stage. "If you keep wasting my time, I'll be forced to cut to the verdict. Now, do you want to see him or not?"

"Then at least let me in the observation room," she requested, folding her arms in front of her. "Surely you can grant me that much."

Without answering, the professor pulled a key from his pocket and led the way to the steel door that separated us. Eartha moved slowly and solemnly behind him. There was still an air of dignity in her stride, labored as it was. When they got to the door a quick twist of the key by the professor popped the lock. He swung the heavy door open and let her in.

"You have one minute," he said, shutting the door behind him.

I met Mother Nature at the entrance, but Vaca had stepped in front of me. She appeared to be watching the door, as if making sure the professor didn't slam it on Eartha as she entered the room. He shut it behind her with a crisp click, and went back to the stage, fumbling with some controls in one of his trapdoors.

"We haven't much time," Eartha said, "so I'll make it brief. The professor will try to prove the charges against me are true. . . . And Jack," she added, looking at me, "it will be your job to defend me, as you already know."

"But you're much better at this than I could ever be. Why me? Are you stalling, or do you have some plan for getting us out of this?"

"My plan is for *you* to get us out of this."

"But I'm not that good with words! Can't I just wrestle him for your freedom?"

She laughed. "That would be too easy. I'm afraid this will be much tougher . . ." When she read the disappointment on my face she added, "But not impossible. You've got two good weapons. Have you forgotten about all those contracts you've negotiated at work? From what I hear, you're pretty tough. You don't give an inch without a fight. Use the skills you learned from that. And if you get into a tricky situation, use some of your wrestling techniques. Remember how good you are at wriggling out of tight spaces.''

She reached out and took my hands. ''Use your mind as you would your body. Be quick and agile, and above all, don't ever give in. Look for an opening, however slight. The tiniest crack lets in enough light to sustain your vision.''

I felt more like the Karate Kid than counsel for the defense. But what she said was right. I had negotiated some pretty tough business deals at work, and I was pretty slippery when it came to getting out of tough holds, both mental and physical. I had never put the two together consciously, but now that she mentioned it, what I had learned in wrestling had benefited my negotiating skills. Maybe I wasn't a lawyer, but I could still fight when it came to defending my company's position in a contract. I had saved them more than a few times.

Who would have ever thought those survival skills I had developed in the business world would become so important? Much as I disliked it, maybe that job *had* given me something besides grief. It had taught me how to fight for what I believed in, and maybe this fight wasn't that much different— just bigger and tougher. Ironically, all of my past battles may have been leading up to this one supreme moment.

Before I could think about it further, the professor's voice boomed over the intercom. ''Your minute is up. Prepare to defend your illustrious client.''

He had his hand on the door, but Mother Nature requested that she stay inside with the rest of us, so we could all be together.

''Very well,'' the professor said. ''It'll be easier to keep an eye on you. Now, enough small talk. It's time for my opening argument.'' He backed away and stepped up on the stage.

''Ladies and gentlemen,'' he began, motioning to nothing but the rock walls inside the cave, ''in the interest of expediency, I will make this short. Mother Nature''—he pointed toward her through the fractured window—''has been a very poor custodian of this Earth. You can see what she has let happen in the last five hundred years because of her unexcused absence. Look no farther than the headlines. Hurri-

canes, floods, earthquakes, and volcanic explosions abound.
She has also let millions starve by failing to provide them
with adequate means of growing food.

"In short, she is a criminal on the grandest scale. Yet she
feels no remorse; indeed, she only feels innocent. I will prove
beyond a doubt that she is not."

He gestured toward me. "Give your opening statement.
But make it brief."

I wasn't prepared for this, but had to say something. Taking a deep breath, I started pacing the floor. "Mother Nature," I began, "has been unable to defend this world against
the ravages of men and women for the last five hundred years
because she kept her word not to intervene. Besides, humanity has been demanding control of the world for thousands
of years, and for the last half millennium humans have gotten
it. Now you complain that *she* hasn't helped properly, im-
plying that she should correct man's most recent mistakes.
Yet humans want her to stay out of their affairs. Well, you
can't have it both ways. Either she gets to intervene, or humans take the blame. I will prove that it is not Mother Nature,
but mankind, who should stand trial for the crimes against
the Earth for the last five hundred years."

"Very good," the professor said after a silence. "But not
very original. She is on trial here. Not mankind. Let's stick
to the issue. *She* abandoned the Earth, left men and women
to their own devices hundreds of years ago, when they
weren't capable of taking care of themselves.

"She is guilty as charged of willful neglect and abandonment of a poor, defenseless planet. Her actions and absence
prove her guilt beyond a shadow of a doubt. No more proof
is needed.

"And why, you ask, did she leave human beings in the
hour of their greatest need? For no more than to save her
own reputation. She was so disgraced at having conceived a
human child, after a night of drunken revelry, my sources
tell me, with a *mere* human that she chose to hide her face.
That is, until now. She thinks everyone will have forgotten
her stupid affair, and feel sorry for her like she's some homeless old bag lady. Why, she even brought a cane to elicit our

sympathy. That too was a deceit. It was her weapon, which she tried to use to get back her precious skull, but failed.

"All of a sudden, after five hundred years, she doesn't trust humans to run the world anymore. And now that her magic skull has been discovered, she shows up. You might ask, why?

"I say she came back because she doesn't want anyone to have her level of power. She wants sole control over the elements so she can ravage our planet at her whim. Well, it's our world now. We don't need her to control nature. With the skull and technology, we have all the means to do it ourselves.

"Do not be deceived. She did not leave the crystal skull out of the goodness of her heart, as a symbol of her love for Montezuma's priest. She was forced to leave it as part of the deal she made with Zephacan, the god of liquid spirits, I am told, to win asylum from the laughter of the other gods. Leaving the skull with nearly all her worldly powers in it must have hurt a lot for someone used to ruling nature. But it was her sentence for the crimes she had committed. She did it not out of kindness, but out of vanity, to protect her image as faultless, to protect her pride.

"If she wasn't going to help the world, she had to agree to at least leave the power within mankind's grasp. And believe me, she hated leaving the magic here with mere mortals."

He went on with his fantastic story, saying that Eartha knew half a millennium ago that humans could not control the elements, even with the powers in the skull. They were still too primitive, not ready to take the reins. She knew that the power was beyond the ability of the Aztecs, and they would have to call to her for help. Then, she would come back in a blaze of glory to seize the power again, under the guise of helping mortals. No one would remember her failings, her weakness for a man, or her promise of nonintervention. All would be forgotten or forgiven.

It was a clever scheme, and might have worked, except for one small twist of fate: she hadn't counted on Cortés conquering the Aztecs. But when he did, suddenly the skull's powers were in real danger. She knew that men of advanced societies like Spain and Portugal stood a good chance of unlocking the secrets inside the skull, preventing her from ruling the world forever. So she had it buried at the bottom of the sea.

There it sat, quietly hiding her secret for centuries. She had shown up again only to keep humans from having the power that is rightfully theirs—the power to rule this planet properly. For without mastery over the elements, men and women would remain no better than beasts. Yet we were destined to control the elements. And, according to Hardwick, destined to become gods. This was her greatest fear, he told us, to let humans into the closed circle of gods. And they wanted no new members. Even the gods were human once, until they learned the ways of power, according to Hardwick.

"Ways Mother Nature has come to take back," he added forcefully. "Thus keeping humans locked in darkness forever. She has come to steal your future."

He had been pacing the stage, gesturing wildly. It was as if the combined pent-up contempt of centuries that humans had gathered against nature was venting itself through him. He whirled and flashed a bitterly cold stare at Mother Nature.

"Did you not assist in hiding the power from Cortés after you gave the skull to mankind by providing a clamshell to keep it in?"

"Of that she is guilty," I answered, not sure if I was saying the right thing. "But for no other purpose than to keep the power from falling into the wrong hands, the hands of people who would only use it for their own personal gain. Such humans' professed love for nature has been only to control it for their own ends. In reality, they don't care if the Earth lives or dies, as long as *they* are comfortable.

"And now that such people have nearly destroyed the Earth, you, Professor, want to blame the only one who can save it. How convenient, and how wrong." I was starting to get into it. Now I almost welcomed his challenge. It surprised me. I could feel my hands tingle where Eartha had touched them.

The professor countered with the fact that besides leaving humanity defenseless against the elements for the last five hundred years, natural disasters had been going on for millions of years, proving that Mother Nature had destroyed the lives of men and women for eons even prior to the time of the Aztecs. Her legacy was one of mass destruction. He claimed that she exerted mastery over the elements to show her godlike status, which were no more than acts of great ego. She had no real feelings for the fate of humans, other than keeping them out of the kingdom of heaven, the home of the gods.

"What kind of caretaker destroys mankind with famine, pestilence, and flood waters?" he asked, his face afire with anger. "I submit that she was doing a lousy job of caring for the Earth, and was looking for a new world to conquer. Ravaging the Earth had grown tedious and boring for her. Despite the deaths of millions, she feels nothing but boredom and frustration at not having advanced farther—at only being the custodian of this puny planet.

"What do you have to say about that, council for the defense?"

The seed of electricity that had been planted in my hands by hers began to work its way up my arms, then to my chest, recharging my pendant, and spreading until it reached my neck and head. I felt as if I *was* her, standing there defending my actions.

I conferred with Eartha, and came back with my reply, pointing out that she could not be held responsible for the events prior to her liaison with a mortal. That was inadmissible evidence, since no one alive had any proof that she was trying to do anything but protect the planet. I pointed out that most of the professor's wild story about her just wanting to accumulate power to increase her status as a god was pure speculation. The Earth was not an easy planet to care for. Even today it was still settling; volcanos were still active, and tectonic plates were constantly shifting. It was still an unsettled, young world, and difficult to control, even under the best of circumstances. We had to assume that she had at least done her job unless willful neglect of duties could be proved. Inference was not enough for a conviction in any modern court of law.

"Besides," I went on, "it's not possible to command such major forces as earthquakes and hurricanes without some damage. All in all, I think she has done a pretty good job. In fact, the Earth was in excellent shape until mankind got hold of it the last century or so and began wholesale pollution on a grand scale. Surely, Mother Nature cannot be blamed for that.''

Professor Hardwick grumbled, but didn't cut in. Maybe I had him in a good hold. Now, if I could only pin him . . .

''This being the case, the only mistake she has to answer for is the one night of love she has had in millions of years. What is her offense? Simply that she fell in love with a man?

''You accuse her of abandoning the Earth in mankind's hour of need. Yet people have been around for thousands of years. They have had plenty of time to mature into responsible caretakers of this planet. But humans thought nothing of preserving the Earth until just the last few decades. How long will they continue to play the victim while they ruin the world? Is Mother Nature to blame for mankind's reckless and destructive behavior? I think not. Now, even as humans see the consequences of their actions, it may be too late for even Mother Nature to save the planet. And you would deprive her of her birthright.

''She knew that she had erred, if you can call it that, when she fell in love with a mortal. She could not stay on Earth and carry out her tasks without being subject to the ethical argument that she had violated a sacred trust by showing humanness.

''That is her crime!'' I shouted, staring at the professor through fractured glass. ''She knew that she could no longer serve the Earth as a god once she had shown the so-called human weakness of personal love. So she excused herself and stepped down, so as not to bring on ill will by the other gods.''

''She left mankind unprotected,'' the professor spat out. ''And alone to fight the elements.''

I looked at Eartha, suddenly seeing myself in her face, in her eyes. Her touch had taken me over completely; at that moment, we were as one.

''That,'' I said, pointing at the professor, ''is why we are here. There would be no trial. None of this would have happened if she hadn't left behind . . ." I raised a pointing finger at the pedestal. "The *gift*.

"She left the skull. It was supposed to guide us until her return. And it would have, if it hadn't been for the aggression of conquerors who sought to use it for their own gain. It is Cortés himself who should answer for this last half millennium of man's rise to power. But that would serve no purpose. He's only a symbol of *civilized* humanity, conqueror of cultures, enemy of the Earth, seeking not to use the natural resources of the Earth, but to abuse them. His only motives were conquest, fame, and fortune. His only defense is ignorance.

"And now, after five hundred years, the human race has learned nothing." I turned and shot a sharp stare at the professor. "Why, you might as well be Cortés himself. All you want is to use the gift for your own glory, under the guise of a new world order. You're unfit for the power. For you would destroy the world and all the creatures that inhabit it in order to save it. But it will not be much of a world when you are finished. It will be a lifeless, desolate, dead planet, spinning in space.

"And Eartha," I said, with a wave of my hand, "is only guilty of falling in love. Not with a single solitary man, as she claims, but with the whole human race."

"What proof do you offer?"

"The proof stands before you. If her love had been selfish, meant for her lover only, then she would never have come back. She would not be standing before you today. She has come back for one purpose only. To put the world right again. Or let someone worthy do it for her. And you, Professor, are not now, and never will be, worthy to care for the Earth. All you seek is the glory of commanding the raw power of nature. But it will take more than power over the elements to heal the world as it is now. And that is all you offer.

"And what *does* it take? What *is* the magic ingredient necessary to save us all? Love, of course. Love for the Earth, but not for its own sake. It's just a bunch of water, sky, plants, rocks, and dirt. It should be loved as the home of the creatures of this world, especially men and women. Despite their struggles and shortcomings, they are still god's greatest creation, the essence of his image. The love I'm talking about is the unconditional kind. The kind only a parent can know. A mother's love ... The defense rests."

There was a long, tense silence. Then, at last the professor spoke. "I salute you, Jack. That was a remarkable defense for someone so ordinary. Quite eloquent, actually. You can be proud of yourself. You did your best.

"Unfortunately, I am not one who fancies romantic delusions, however pleasant. The Earth, I'm afraid, needs decisive leadership, not motherly love. The jury finds for the prosecution. Now, Eartha my dear, prepare for your death."

He went back to the stage and popped open one of the panels, pulling out a hypodermic needle. "But first," he said with a nasty grin, "we'll need her blood sample."

He pushed some buttons inside the panel. "Don't try anything funny, anyone," he remarked. "The guns are set on ready. Move too quickly, and they open fire automatically. And oh, before I forget, they track everything but me. Seems my body is a few degrees colder than your average human."

He donned a bulletproof vest anyway, and walked over, needle in hand. The door to the room swung open. I wanted to lunge at him, but Ellen held me back. "You've done all you could," she said. "All anyone could do. It's over now. Our fate is in god's hands."

"It was a lousy defense," I complained. "I should have found a way to win. There has to be a way to pin his shoulders to the mat. But now I suppose we'll never know. I've failed."

As Eartha walked through the door, the professor led her to a spot directly center stage, lifted the needle, and shoved it into her right arm. The cave shook a little. Hot air blew fiercely into the observation room for a moment from the vents, but then stilled.

Slowly, methodically, he began to draw back the plunger, filling the syringe.

42

Guns 'n' Mud

When the syringe was full of Eartha's blood, the professor pulled it out and walked away. Just before he got to his array of trapdoors, the cave shook again, this time more violently, and it wasn't letting up. Rocks fell from the ceiling and tumbled off the walls. I pulled everyone back from the window, since it looked like it was going to come crashing down upon us.

The pedestal atop the pyramid swayed back and forth, shaking the shrouded skull with its motions. I took a deep breath as I glanced quickly at the hard plastic base of the pedestal.

Rock crystal was tougher than plastic, but in its weakened condition, the skull could be further damaged if it tumbled from its thirty-foot height. Maybe it would even shatter.

The professor saw it too, and suddenly dashed for the pyramid, some twenty feet away. When he did, the stage shifted slightly, and he tripped, hitting the deck panels and crushing the hypodermic needle in his fist. The syringe broke, leaving Eartha's blood in a small pool by his hand.

The shaking stopped, and the professor got to his feet. Firing an angry glance at Mother Nature, he wiped the blood off his hand. Miraculously, he was only cut slightly on the palm. As a tiny amount of Eartha's blood seeped into his hand, she threw back her head and laughed.

"Enjoy it, Professor. That's all the blood you're getting out of me. Not nearly enough to power the skull, I'm afraid. I suggest you give up. Are you really foolish enough to think all the power I had left was in that old umbrella?"

"That little blood sample was just a test," he said, watching the skull settle on its lofty and precarious perch atop the pedestal. "Now let's see what you're really made of." He scampered quickly to his main trapdoor and popped it open, using the recessed handle built into it, then jumped inside, up to his shoulders.

"Sorry," he said as he lowered the lid, "I'm fresh out of blindfolds right now, but it'll be over before you know it— unless you're faster than a speeding bullet. No, wait, that was Superman. Never mind, he's dead too. Good-bye, I'll be back to pick up your blood in a minute."

With that he closed the lid. A long, tense few seconds followed, while I kept everyone back from the window and told them to get down on the floor, anticipating the fractured window disintegrating and sending glass flying everywhere, followed by volleys of bullets. But before we could even think about it, there were strange splattering sounds coming from outside in the main cave, like someone throwing mud pies.

I stuck my head up and got quite a sight. The soggy mess the water and oil had made of the floor was playing its part in the battle. Huge hunks of mud and rocks were flying. Mother Nature had moved center stage, and was directing mud at almost–bullet speed into the gun barrels. She looked as though she was conducting the Los Angeles Philharmonic without a baton, but it worked, for not a single bullet made it out of any of the barrels. They were clogged to capacity with the muddy mess.

A minute later the trapdoor opened and the professor stuck his head and shoulders out. He had a look of half-crazed but friendly defeat on his face.

"Well," he said, "looks like you've done it again. Of course, it's no secret that you work well with nature . . . but tell me," he added, looking at the panel just below her feet, "how well do you work with plastic?"

Just as he said those words, the floor beneath Eartha gave way and she fell below. There must have been a deeper part of the space below the stage, away from the pyramid, because she disappeared completely. A minute later the sound of an elevator working filled the room, and, much to my great surprise and chagrin, a life-sized clear, plastic cylinder began slowly to rise where she had been standing. It looked like an inverted test tube. Eartha was standing inside it, and she was slowly, painfully gasping for air.

"My god," I said half-aloud. "He's sealed her in plastic. Now she'll surely die. Unless we can do something."

No one else said anything, hardly believing their eyes, except Susie. "Daddy, why is she in there?"

I couldn't answer her. How do you tell a two-year-old that Mother Nature is just about finished? Even Maggie, who had her paws up on the ledge and was whining, seemed concerned.

The professor opened his trapdoor and climbed out. He walked slowly over to the test tube, carrying a battery-operated power drill. "Don't get your hopes up," he taunted us. "I have plans for this, and it's not to make an air hole."

When he got there he placed the drill against the side of the tube and pulled the trigger. The drill sprang to life, whirling against the inch-thick plastic at shoulder height. Inside, Eartha looked on the verge of passing out. A human would probably be able to breathe for a while inside the tube. It would take some minutes to use up all the air, but Mother Nature and plastic are mortal enemies. She was suffocating, and squeezed so tightly inside the life-sized test tube that she could barely move. Her shoulders were pinned squarely against the sides.

Suddenly, the tip of the half-inch diameter drill popped through the inside of the tube, tearing through the sleeve of Eartha's dress and penetrating her left arm where a vaccination mark would have been. Blood oozed out, saturated her sleeve, and ran slowly down the side of the tube. The professor dropped the drill on the stage floor and pulled a new syringe from his jacket pocket, then inserted the needle through the hole and into Eartha's arm. She struggled, but it was useless. She wasn't going anywhere, and appeared on the verge of fainting.

I grew desperate. There was little time and no tomorrow. "Get back, everyone." I grabbed a chair and raised it to throw at the window, but someone had hold of my shoulder just as I was about to let it fly.

"I think we can get out through the door," Vaca said. "I looked at the lock when he let Eartha in here. I think it can be picked. Then the rest of you can sneak out." When I gave her a doubtful look, she added, "Jack, this may be your only chance to save your family. The guns are stuffed with mud.

You might make it to the exit door; it's only thirty feet from here. It's at least worth a try.''

"Do it," I said without hesitation. "We're running on empty as it is."

"Can you really pick the lock?" Ellen asked, standing behind me and holding Susie.

"I think so," Vaca replied. "But I need something to pick it with."

"All I have is my wallet and comb," I answered, noticing that Ellen's purse was open and empty. "There's only the diaper bag."

Vaca looked at Susie. "Can I borrow one of her diaper pins?"

Ellen practically tore Susie's cloth diaper getting the pin off. When she got it unhinged and removed, she handed it to Vaca, who bolted for the door and began picking the lock.

Outside, Mother Nature was almost gone, held up now only by her shoulders squeezed against the sides of the plastic tube. The professor had gotten his blood sample and stuffed the blood-filled syringe into his jacket pocket. Then, out of spite, he pulled a black rubber stopper out of his other pocket. He wiggled it into the hole and tapped it in with his fist until it was sealed shut.

"Relax and make yourself comfortable," he said sarcastically. "This plastic will biodegrade in about ten thousand years. I should be finished with the Earth by then. Goodbye—and I'm sorry it had to end like this. We'd have made a great pair."

He leaned forward and gently kissed the plastic tube that was to be her coffin, then turned and walked away without another glance at her. He climbed back inside his hole and closed the lid.

Vaca had popped the lock. It was time to make our move. She pulled the door open and we all made a run for it. I carried Susie so we could make better time. When we got halfway to the exit the professor popped the trapdoor open and stuck his head and shoulders out. This time he was holding an assault rifle, aimed right at me.

"Stop!" he yelled. "Or the baby gets it."

We stopped cold in our tracks. He ordered us back toward

the observation room, Maggie growling the whole time. He climbed out and moved toward us, motioning us back to our cell with the rifle. Right before we entered the room, Maggie decided she had had enough and bolted for the professor. He raised the assault rifle to eye level and took aim at Susie as I held her in my arms.

I spun away, turning my back to him to shield my daughter with my body. Just as his finger began to squeeze the trigger, a loud pop center stage distracted him. Before he could adjust his aim again, Maggie was on top of him, grabbing at his sleeve. I went for the gun, but never got there. Behind the professor there was a loud hissing sound: the stopper had popped free and Mother Nature had managed to turn toward the hole and was blowing, creating a powerful wind that came screaming out of the hole. When it got outside the tube it spread out, howling like a hurricane. The force was so great that it knocked Maggie off the professor's arm. His assault rifle went flying. The rest of us were pinned to the cave wall by the rushing wind.

The hurricane formed into a small tornado, swirling about the room, releasing us from the cave walls. Once we could move again, we inched our way back toward the exit door.

"What about Eartha?" I asked, not sure of her ability to escape the tube.

"Don't worry about her," Vaca said, over the howling wind. "She can take care of herself."

The wind had blown the black scarf off the skull, and it began to rock back and forth atop the pedestal, slowly at first, but then it came dangerously close to toppling.

The tornado reached the professor and engulfed him, suddenly picking him up and swirling him slowly in its center. His eyes were wild, his expression mad with rage. The tornado and its captive began to rise off the ground and head for the roof. When it got six feet up the professor looked down at Eartha, still blowing from inside the tube.

"Have all the fun you want!" he shouted at us as he spun slowly in the wind. "You haven't seen the end of me. The age of technology has just begun. Prepare yourselves well. For when I return, the Earth will be mine."

The tornado pulled mud and rocks into itself, clouding the

professor in a brown haze. Then it rose through the roof and soon drifted out of sight overhead. It disappeared into the sky, a tiny dot rising in a clear sky.

The wind inside the cave died down and we ran to Eartha. Working together, all of us were able to pull the tube off its base, which was nothing more than a huge black rubber stopper. It really *was* an upside-down test tube. But there was no time for celebration.

The cave rumbled, this time worse than ever. I looked at Mother Nature. "What's going on here? I thought it was all over."

She just shrugged. "I'm afraid I may have started something," she finally replied. "This cave is sitting right on top of a dormant volcano, as you know. At least it *was* dormant. But it's been disturbed by the earthquakes, and I'm too weak now to stop it from erupting."

The cave shook again, and the floor began to crack in several places. Steam rose from the cracks, followed by searing heat. The bottom of the cracks was oozing red-hot lava. The cave wouldn't last much longer.

"This place could go up any minute," I said, watching steam and sulfur gas rise from the cracks. "We'll never get far enough away in time unless . . ." I looked to Eartha for help. She seemed pretty exhausted. "Can you take us out of here on the wind like you did the professor? It may be our only chance at escape."

"I'm afraid not," she said, between gulps for air. "I'm all out of breath."

"Vaca, can you do anything? Anything at all to stall this thing?"

"I'm afraid this is way beyond my abilities."

"Then, let's get out of here before this thing blows!"

Ellen ran for the exit, Susie in her arms. Vaca followed right behind. Mother Nature was still out of it, so I knew she couldn't be of further help. I scooped her up in my arms, running as fast as I could out the exit door and down a long tunnel, dodging rocks and splits in the floor that oozed hot lava and belched sulfur gas. I almost passed out from the heat and smell, but stumbled on.

Maggie ran beside me, barking excitedly. Luckily, there

was a light coming from the end of the tunnel. When we got there, some hundred yards later, we were almost blinded by the bright sunlight outside the car-sized entrance.

There was a new Range Rover parked a few yards away. By the time everyone climbed in, the ground was shaking pretty hard.

"We have a slight problem," I said from behind the wheel. "The professor didn't leave the keys in the ignition."

Vaca raced around to the hood and was inside it in an instant, working to get the Rover going without keys.

Without thinking, I jumped up and ran back inside the tunnel, waves of protests yelling behind me. But it was no use. I had gone mad. We had forgotten the skull, and I just had to retrieve it.

Once inside I raced down the tunnel, dodging rocks and lava-filled cracks. I could barely breathe amid the steam, heat, and foul smell, but I staggered on and entered the main room of the cave. Just before stepping onto the stage I looked up at the pedestal. It was empty. The space where the skull had sat stared back in empty desolation.

With a mighty crack, the stage, pyramid and all, collapsed, crashing into a deep hole beneath it. I stood on the edge of a deep pit, watching the stage, and a huge cylinder-shaped storage chamber beneath it, fall a hundred feet below into a vat of white-hot molten lava tinged with red. Everything sank slowly into the fiery liquid like bones in lye, emitting a foul odor of burning plastic mixed with sulfur.

The blast of heat coming up from below was overwhelming, and I instantly stepped back. I grew dizzy, but held on, staggering for the exit. As I did, the floor of the cave slowly began to crumble behind me as the pit widened its circle.

I stumbled forward, fighting the heat and noxious fumes. As I passed through the door to the tunnel, sweat pouring from my body, the entire floor of the cave collapsed behind me, pulling everything that remained down with it. The control room, the staircase, and the main room were now melting in molten lava. The cave was returning to its natural state, a burning cauldron more powerful than anything man had ever devised.

Just as I was again about to pass out, a cool wind came rushing down the tunnel, drowning me in fresh air. It brought me to my senses and gave me strength. I recovered and ran for daylight, dodging more boulders and cracks oozing hot lava on the floor. As I raced into the blinding sunlight and dashed for the Rover, the tunnel collapsed behind me, burying itself in rock with a thunderous noise.

Vaca was still under the hood, swearing. In the distance a jeep was speeding off toward town, a good-sized driver at the wheel.

 43

The Chase

I climbed behind the wheel just as Vaca fired up the engine from under the hood, slammed it shut, and jumped into the passenger's seat. "Let's go," she said. "If that mountain blows, we'd better be a safe distance away."

There wasn't time to talk about it. I jammed the Rover in gear and spun the tires. Then they grabbed and we raced off into the desert, shoving a dust cloud behind us. I kept driving, and we kept waiting for it to blow, but there was only the sound of the engine racing and the desert wind across the sand. Finally, when we were no more than a quarter mile away, the second hand on our escape clock ran out.

There was a tremendous explosion behind us that shook the ground for miles. When I looked in the rearview mirror, the mountain had blown its top off and was spewing dark, sooty smoke a thousand feet in the air.

Smoke continued to belch out of the top of the mountain, but now there was something else: bright red lava was pouring down its sides. The smoke had cleared enough for us to see that the top of the mountain had been ripped off by the eruption.

"My god," I said, looking back as Susie hid her head in Ellen's shoulder. "That was close. We barely made it."

There was more good news. The smoke was drifting the

other way, behind us across the desert, toward the Pacific, but the erupting lava still sent a shock of heat our way. I kept the gas pedal on the floor, but Ellen had something to ask Eartha.

"Did you have to use earthquakes back there?" Ellen asked. "We almost didn't make it out alive."

"I didn't," Eartha said slyly. "I'm afraid that once the cloth slipped off the skull, it began to release some of its powers as a warning. The sun over the open roof activated its alarm. The professor should have known better than to leave the roof open. It only took a slight breeze to blow the scarf off."

"It looked to me as if his controls jammed when he tried to close the roof," I said, looking at Vaca.

She just grinned. "Machines are sometimes unpredictable. He must have had an electrical short somewhere."

I glanced at her. "Well, anyway. Thanks for the breeze on my way out back there. I almost passed out before that cool wind came up."

"What wind?"

"Never mind."

I turned back east on a path that would intersect the road to San Bajamos and also put me in line with the jeep up ahead, now just a small speck, though it left enough of a dust cloud behind it to follow.

"Slow down, Jack," Ellen ordered. "You're scaring Susie, and we don't have a car seat. It was bad enough you frightened everyone to death by racing back into that cave, but since you didn't come out with the skull, I'm assuming it fell into one of those cracks in the cave floor."

"If it had," I answered, slowing just a little, "whoever is in that jeep wouldn't still be racing for the main road. If my guess is right, that's Masters, and he's got our skull."

"Let him go," she said. "He's not Aztec. Besides, we've had enough excitement for one vacation."

"But . . ."

"Ellen's right," Eartha said from the backseat. "No point endangering the lives of anyone at this point."

"Endangering the lives? Why, it was your skull that got us into this mess in the first place. Now I intend to finish the job. I may be dumb, insane, and foolish, but this crystal pendant on my neck is buzzing. I think it's trying to home in on the mother lode. I'll drop everyone off at a hotel. Without the professor, Masters will be a piece of cake. I figure he's heading for the airport. I'll capture him there.''

"He'll be in an airplane and gone before you catch up to him," Ellen said. "Even if you take us with you. Unless . . ."

"Unless what?"

She looked at me in the rearview mirror. "You stop heading for the highway and cut a forty-five–degree angle toward town. If you do that, at least we'll have half a chance to catch up. You won't even have to speed."

"Of *course,*" I said, turning the wheel to make the angle. "That way we'll cut him off. We're gaining on him now. That old jeep is no match for this baby."

Suddenly, out of the corner of my left eye, there appeared another speck on the horizon, slightly smaller than the jeep, which had grown to the size of an egg. A motorcycle screamed across the desert, kicking up a violent dust cloud as it made a bullet path for the jeep.

"Great!" I yelled. "Who's that? Just what we don't need, competition."

I went back to following the jeep, anticipating his interception by the cycle.

Before we could do anything about it, the cycle had gained on the jeep and sat just off the driver's rear fender. We stayed slightly upwind to avoid being choked in their dust trails. In minutes we were only a couple of hundred yards behind. The jeep must have had engine problems for us to gain on him so fast. I decided to lie back a little to see what developed, figuring one of them would be eliminated shortly. Besides, we had no weapons, unless you count an aging ex-wrestler, a dog, a mother and child, a tired Mother Nature, and a mechanical genius.

"Wait a minute," I said, keeping back a couple of hundred yards. "Vaca, did you somehow jimmy the jeep so we could catch up?"

She just smiled and said, "I am working on my long-distance powers. But to tell you the truth, I think there's sand in the gas tank."

The jeep labored on, the engine cutting out every few yards. The cycle, now fully visible and much louder, had pulled up alongside. It was one of those high-fendered dirt bikes with knobby tires, ideal for the desert terrain. The jeep was horribly outmatched. The bike rider was big and muscular, sporting a red-striped cycle suit and matching racing helmet with visor and mouth filter. He must have thought he was Evel Knievel or something, because he went up a natural rock ramp and flew clean over the jeep, then swung the bike around and pulled up alongside again.

A moment later he had jumped from the bike onto the driver, like some cowboy capturing a bandit in an old Western. But it worked. The cycle fell away in the sand as the jeep skidded to a sideways stop and went up on two wheels, sending a gunnysack with a bowling ball–sized object inside it flying across the desert, but not far away enough for me to make my move. I had too many people in the Rover to protect.

I slammed on the brakes and slid to a stop fifty yards back, safe enough to stay out of immediate trouble, and watched the action.

The jeep came down on all fours and the fight began in earnest. They tumbled wildly on the ground, then got up and took to slugging it out. Both men were socking each other, but Masters wasn't having much luck hitting the cyclist with that heavy helmet on—at least not in the face. Body blows weren't doing a thing to him.

In a moment it was over. The cyclist landed a knockout punch to the jaw and Masters went down. He didn't get up. The cyclist took a long look at us, the Rover reflecting on the dark-mirrored finish of his plastic face guard. Then he turned, walked slowly over to the gunnysack, and picked it up.

I put the Rover in gear, ready to move in on him.

"Don't you dare run over him," Ellen said. "We don't even know who he is."

"Hold your horses," I demanded. "I'm not running over anyone . . . But I'd like to," I added, sensing a familiarity in the air.

The cyclist dusted himself off and picked up his dirt bike,

which looked a little dented, but rideable. He tweaked the front fender and climbed aboard, then kicked the starter.

"We can't just let him get away!" Vaca cried.

"And we're not running him down," Ellen reemphasized. "We're not going to be a party to murder."

"What about the professor?" I asked for some reason. "Eartha, where is he now? This obviously isn't him, but where did your wind take him?"

"Who knows where twisters go," she said with a shrug. "But if you ask me, he's probably somewhere in the Pacific just now."

"The Pacific?" I asked.

"Sure," she answered. "No point polluting the gulf. It's a sacred burial ground for old Aztec artifacts, if I remember correctly."

The cyclist got on and zoomed away, but just as I got ready to put the Rover in gear, he stopped and looked over his shoulder. He turned the cycle around and headed straight for us, a quarter mile away and going pretty fast.

"Brace yourselves, everyone," I said. "We're going to have company."

As the cycle sped straight for the driver's side of the Rover, I waited to make my move until he got too close to swerve into me. But just as he got fifty yards away he swung it around and skidded in a half circle to a stop, skillfully dumping the bike on the sand. He left the bike on the ground and began to walk over, casually swinging the gunnysack in his left hand.

I was about to jump out to keep him from smashing one of the windows with it when he stopped, ten feet away. He set the sack down and reached for his helmet, pulling it off over his head. A bundle of long black hair fell over his shoulders.

"Warren!" Vaca shouted. "What are *you* doing here?"

"Drive on," Eartha said, as if talking to a chauffeur. "We don't need him. I don't bargain with mercenaries. We'll find another way to get you the power."

"But he's no worse than anyone else," I complained loudly, looking in the rearview mirror. "All he wants is money, I'm sure."

"You don't know him," she said gravely. "Now, either you drive, or I walk back to town."

I shut off the engine. "I . . . can't. We've all come too far to walk away now. Besides, you'll never make it on foot. Your legs aren't strong enough yet. Whatever he wants, we'll pay it."

"What he wants," Eartha answered coldly, opening the car door and stepping out, "is me. And this time, I'm not for sale . . . at any price."

With that, she turned and slowly walked off into the desert, laboring with each stride.

 44

With Apologies

A minute later I got out of the Rover and went after Eartha, catching up to her about twenty yards away.

"This is not the time to get weird on us," I said emphatically. "He's brought the skull. Let's bargain for it if we have to. You can't just walk off into the desert. We fought for this, and now it's within our grasp."

When she didn't reply I added, "Look, if you won't help, fine. I'll go back and see what he wants. But why are you getting emotional on us all of a sudden? This is strictly a business deal. Plain and simple."

I threw up my hands. "If you're not going back with us, then at least tell me what's going on. You owe me that much."

She stopped walking and looked me straight in the eyes. "He's not one we can deal with," she said coldly. "That's all I can tell you."

"Why?"

"Just leave it at that. Will you?"

"How can I?" Grabbing her sleeve, I asked, "Okay, so you have your reasons, but if you can't tell me what's going on, at least tell me why you won't barter with him. He's only human, after all.''

She looked away across the desert, watching a slight wind kick up some sand. "That's just it, Jack. He's not."

"Not human? Then what on God's green earth is he?"

"If you must know, he's Zephacan, God of Liquid Spirits."

"What?"

"He is the one who tricked me that night nearly five hundred years ago. The very reason why the Earth is plunged into darkness to this day. He got me drunk, and that's when I grew weak, how I ended up in Montuca's father's bed."

"That was a long time ago," I argued. "Besides, you can't blame others for your weaknesses. I'm sorry to have to tell you this, but it was *you* who got yourself drunk. You were a big girl, even then, I'm sure. You shouldn't blame him for your night of love."

There was long illuminating silence. She got a funny look on her face, like no one had ever said this to her before.

"And another thing," I added. "I mean no disrespect, but by blaming him for your fate, you give him more power than he actually has. No one can force anyone to drink if she doesn't want to. You could have said no, especially a woman of your immense power. You're surely master of your own destiny."

She laughed. "You're a better lawyer than I thought. Only a good attorney could get his client to admit guilt."

"I'm not a lawyer," I corrected, grasping the crystal pendant. "But this piece of quartz seems to clear up my thinking enough for me to see the plain truth. Now, are you coming back, or do you want us to pick you up on the way? You won't get very far on foot in your condition."

"Give me a minute to gather my thoughts. You go and see what he wants."

"Fair enough." I walked back to the Rover, marched around the front end, and stood right in front of Gates— or Zephacan.

"I assume you've come to bargain for what's in the sack," I stated, as if we'd never met.

"Yep," he said casually. "You guessed it, *stranger*. So, what do you suppose it's worth?"

"Not much, unless you're Aztec. What did you have in mind?"

"A chat with a lady," he said, motioning toward Eartha. "That's my price."

"She doesn't want to talk to you."

"I know that. Did she tell you I've been trying to get an audience with her for centuries? A fella can't apologize if there's no ears to hear it."

"You came," I said with disbelief, "to apologize for what you did five hundred years ago?"

Zephacan stated that it was the sole reason he had shown up in the first place. When he learned that the skull had been discovered, he saw it as his last chance to clear things up between him and Eartha. Unless he had the skull for bargaining power, he knew he'd never get an audience with her. He had never intended to sell it to the professor, but when Hardwick approached him with a deal, he got an idea. His apology would be better received, he figured, if he were to discover and destroy the cave. Unfortunately, he got double-crossed before he could do that. His only powers involved making alcohol attractive to mortals, so he couldn't do much when he got hit over the head but go after the professor with the others. He didn't tell Vaca and me any of this because he wanted to present the skull to Eartha by himself. It was a personal thing. He couldn't trust us to let him do it alone. And if he couldn't do it alone, it might only seem like half an apology.

He went on to explain that people are always blaming alcohol for their problems and weaknesses. But in reality it was how it was handled. Like any other thing on the Earth, it was how you used it that decided your fate. Some people are born without the ability to resist its intoxicating effects and become addicted, but that was their cross to bear. His job was just to see that there was plenty of it available for recreational and religious purposes.

I told him he seemed to be doing a fine job on that account, but I wasn't sure Mother Nature would talk to him, though she realized it was her inability to say no that had gotten her in so much trouble nearly a half millennium ago.

"In that case," he said, turning to leave, "I'll be off. Tell the lady the skull will be waiting for her when she's ready to listen."

Not satisfied and through negotiating for one vacation, I asked some pointed questions about the circumstances surrounding Mother Nature's departure five hundred years ago. He told me what really happened. It was what I needed to know.

I ran back and told Eartha all about our conversation, that he was tired of being blamed for everyone's problems, including hers.

"He said you left of your own free will. That the other gods didn't force you out because you slept with a mortal. They mostly didn't care. They didn't make moral judgments about such things. They had better things to do than point fingers at other gods. Is this true?"

"The real reason I left," she admitted, "was because humans had evolved to a point where they thought they could master their own world. Control their own destiny. When men began to set sail for the Americas, they broke the chains of fear and isolation that had imprisoned mankind for eons."

She told me that after discovering the Americas, human beings were not afraid of the world anymore. They began to turn away from nature and to trust their own power. It was a proud moment. And she too thought mankind was ready for the world. But when she saw that humans wished to use their science and technology for conquest of civilizations and plunder of natural resources, she knew they might not have been ready. Yet she knew that if she stayed on Earth, it might slow humanity's progress as caretaker of the planet. She had been caring for the Earth only until mankind became ready to do it for itself. She left because it was time to step out of the way and let humans fulfill their destiny, leaving the skull in her place so that the Aztecs could protect themselves against those who were not ready to care for the planet, but only capable of destroying it. The Aztecs were the hope of mankind then, conquistadors the risk. She did not forsee Cortés conquering the Aztecs, so the skull should not have come to danger.

"When he finally came twenty years later," I pointed out, "Cortés was only a symbol of the new civilizations already alive in Europe. Humans had finally come to the point where they thought they didn't need you." I looked into her eyes. "That's what you hated the most, isn't it? That modern man would figure out how to control the elements and you would not be needed. That's why you left the skull. As a tool and symbol of the power of nature."

"I . . . I love this world," she admitted. "I loved taking care of it. But as you guessed at the truth, sleeping with a mortal made me realize I'd become too attached to the human race. Too involved. I was beginning to feel almost human myself. It was clouding my judgment. It was time to move on. Funny, but I miss caring for the Earth as a parent. I never thought I would miss being a mother to this small planet. Yet, hardly any human even believes I exist these days. Guess the joke's on me. Oh, well," she laughed. "No fool like an old fool.

"Parents' greatest joy is watching their children grow up," she added. "But I couldn't let go. I didn't want to see mankind make it without me. But you have to let go sometime. The skull was my only chance to leave something of myself, my chance to help in my absence."

"It was too soon to let go then," I said. "And too soon now. We still need you. But there is a way. You can still watch your world grow up." I touched her hands. "You can watch through me. And it will be because of your gift. The magic and power you left in the skull will be inside me."

"You mean . . ."

"When I ran back inside that cave, I realized it was for only one purpose, to inherit my destiny. I may be lousy at it and I may be slow to learn, but I finally feel ready to receive the power—your power."

I put my arm around her. "Come on, let's go back. Some-one's got an apology to accept."

Warren had started the cycle, but hadn't put on his helmet or moved from the spot. I could see by the look in his eyes that he had hoped for this moment, waited for almost five hundred years. He shut off the engine and stood beside the bike, gunnysack in hand.

Eartha approached and stopped three feet away, at first not looking at him, only at the ground.

"Mother," Zephacan said, and it surprised me. It sounded like he was her real son. "I have come to apologize. I never meant for this to go on so long. But you . . ."

"The apology is mine," she said, looking up at last. "Jack reminded me that the fault was mine. You've been a good son."

She stepped forward and they hugged. He handed her the gunnysack and stepped back. The big man almost had to wipe tears out of his eyes, but afterward got on his bike and left slowly.

"Call your mother sometime," Eartha said as he rolled away. "It's been good to hear your voice again."

She turned and handed me the skull. "No," she said, answering my questioning eyes. "He's not my son. It's a term other gods use out of respect. All the gods that care for the little things here are like my sons and daughters. Guess I was too ashamed to face him after that night with Montuca's father."

Once inside the Rover, I handed the gunnysack to Vaca, who set it on her lap. "After all this," I said, glancing at her, "you'd better check inside it. I don't think *he* did. Masters may have made off with a dummy just to fake us out."

Vaca opened the top and looked inside. A warm glow of light came pouring out, and the crystal on my neck began to vibrate big time.

"Good," I said. "That answers that. Now, let's get back to town. I've got a date with destiny . . . Wait, I forgot something. Vaca, do you think you can get that jeep running?"

"Sure," she answered. "Now that you mention it. I'll bet there *isn't* sand in the gas tank after all. I'm sure it just needs a carburetor adjustment."

She got out, walked past an unconscious Masters, and pulled the key he had taken from me back at the cave out of his pants pocket. Popping the hood, she spent a few seconds just looking and then got behind the wheel. The engine fired up and the jeep rolled on ahead, running better than ever.

I started the Rover and rolled off, heading straight for the road. No one felt the need to say very much, except Susie, who said she was hungry. We stopped by a little *cantina* once we got on the main highway and ate like wild beasts. Afterward it was getting late in the afternoon, and everyone was pretty tired. Eartha pulled some pearls out of one her dress pockets and paid for all of us to stay south of town in one of those expensive tourist resorts. Yes, it was the Baja Bonita. They were sure happy to see us. We got cleaned up and went swimming after dinner. They even let Maggie in the pool. We took horseback rides at sunset. Afterward, we were too tired to do anything but sleep.

The next morning, after ten, we met Eartha in the lobby. She had a rested look and carried a new wooden cane she had bought from the hotel gift shop. After breakfast it was time to go. There was only one place that came to mind; one place where I could accept my destiny as the new keeper of the elements. Turning north, I headed straight for the old camp, where all of this impossible adventure began. Vaca followed in my jeep.

As I pulled into camp I was feeling a little nervous, but the familiar sight of Mr. Zapata's truck calmed me a little. There were no other vehicles around. That was good. Nice and private for the ceremony of looking into the Eyes of God.

We climbed out of the Rover and approached the beach. Mr. Zapata came walking out of his shack. When he did, Eartha lit up like a lottery winner. "Don't tell me," I said, sensing something in the air, "that he's a god too."

Eartha was barely able to speak, and hardly able to contain her happiness. At last, after a long time, as Mr. Zapata stood before her, she uttered one solitary word. A word that confirmed not only that this was a small world, but an infinitely crazy one.

"Techapan," she said, and couldn't say any more.

45

Coronation

"Montuca's father? For crying out loud," I said, throwing up my hands.

"He's a god now," Vaca whispered, taking me aside.

"Is there anyone around here who's *not* a god, other than my family?" I looked at Maggie, panting as she stood on the sand. "How about you, girl? Next someone's going to tell me you're the goddess of canines? What is this, the vacation spot of the gods?"

"You forget," Vaca reminded me. "You are about to become one of us. We wanted to be here for the coronation ceremony." Just as she uttered those words, a motorcycle came roaring down the roadway, kicking up dust clouds. The helmet looked familiar.

I looked at Ellen, wondering if she would tell me to get back in the jeep and drive all humans home, before she lost me to the boardroom of the gods. She just looked back knowingly.

"Are you going to be all right with this?" I asked. "I can still say no. We can get back in the jeep and head home, try to pretend none of this ever happened."

"Jack, it's too late for that," she smiled. "Besides, I'm proud of you. This world could use a caretaker again. You'll be good at it. You know how to fight. Go on; I won't stand in your way. I'll stand beside you."

"We can still be together," I assured her. "I'm not giving up a family; I'm gaining a world."

"Hey," she joked, "you can be Father Nature, and I can be first lady of the elements.

"There may come a time when your new responsibilities are too great, and our little family unit too small to stand in

243

the way. Just promise you'll be there when we need you most.''

"I wouldn't miss my life with you and Susie for the world. If the job gets too big, I'll abdicate if I have to. I'll find a way to—''

"There is no other way,'' Vaca said behind me. "This is a job for life. You'll just have to live with whatever difficulties come along. Of course, in five years you may be able to renegotiate.'' She looked at Eartha. "If you can get her to come back. But she may not be well enough.''

Eartha was hugging Mr. Zapata, or Techapan as it were. "What are you doing here?'' she asked him. "It's been a very long time.''

"Didn't you hear?'' he asked, hugging her back. "After what happened I was promoted to deity.''

"No one ever tells me these things,'' she said, shaking her head.

"You refused to talk to anyone about it, remember?'' he asked. "Not even a word on the subject. Then you took off.''

"What kind of god lives on an old run-down tourist beach?'' she asked. "After all, I thought that was Vaca's job.''

Techapan reminded her that he had been partly responsible for the birth of a half god in the form of Montuca, their son. And was also responsible for the birth of a legend, the story of the crystal skull. So while she was away, the gods got together and decided to make him the god of lost legends. Since the pearl was just offshore and Techapan received word that it was about to be discovered, he arrived a few months earlier and took up residence to make sure an Aztec discovered it. He looked at me.

"And so you did, but I couldn't leave . . .'' He looked at Eartha. "Until Jack looks into the eyes and assumes the power he deserves. He fought for it, argued for it, was born to it, and now, it's his.'' He looked up into the sun. It was only a few minutes to twelve. "Today is a good day for legends to come true.''

Everyone gathered around in a fifteen-foot half circle as the sun reached high noon in a cloudless blue sky.

I stood in the center of my circle of friends. Vaca handed

the gunnysack to Eartha, who cradled it gently in one arm, and walked toward me slowly with the aid of her new cane. She was very wobbly and nearly collapsed a couple of times. Everyone wanted to run to help her, but she waved us off. She wanted to make it under her own power. It was painful to watch her labored gait, one unsure step at a time. But somehow, she made it, collapsing in front of me. I reached out and grabbed her just before she fell, picking her up until she stood weakly before me.

She handed the sack over and had me bend forward so that she could kiss me on the forehead. It tingled, and made my crystal pendant vibrate with a good feeling.

"With this kiss," she said, "I give you the power to control the wind, the rain, the Earth, the oceans, and fire. Use it well and you will be a great god . . . Good luck," she added, and backed away slowly. This time she motioned for help. Vaca and Ellen rushed to her side, propping her up and walking her back until she was at her spot in the circle, leaning on her cane.

I reached in and touched the top of the skull with my right hand as I held it in my left. My whole hand filled with warmth and energy, and my pendant began to glow with a gentle white light. I ran my fingers gently over the skull inside the sack—the smooth surface along the cranium, its carved teeth, strong jawbone, and, finally, the eye sockets. They were especially warm.

I was getting nervous, and to prevent myself from having second thoughts, I quickly pulled the skull from the sack and let the cloth drop to the ground. There was a series of gasps from the others. I was taken aback by the skull's powerful luminescence, and began to shake a little.

A moment later I was seized by a great desire to drop it in the sand and run, to go back to the life I had known, ordinary as it was, and certainly much safer than the one that was about to come. I began shaking so badly that I almost dropped the skull.

Instinctively, I glanced over at Ellen for help. "Go on," she whispered. "We're all with you. This is what you've waited for. Do it, Jack."

Her glowing insistence was all that I needed, just enough

to push me to action, to see me through this moment of truth, though it was still much bigger than I.

Without thinking about it further, I held the skull out in front of me, marveling at its transparent reflections of sunlight as they bounced wildly off the surfaces. Slowly, I tilted the head back and gazed straight into the eyes.

A wild shock of sunlight caught the sockets and blinded me.

And the vision of Montuca returned.

A month had passed since he had saved the skull from Cortés. He had arrived at the northern end of the gulf, where the coast began to circle toward the long dry Baja Peninsula. His shoulder had not healed. Montuca was weak, the pain was spreading. He knew he would die soon from infection. The skull's power must be saved for someone stronger. But Eartha would have to decide whom. For now, it was enough that the magic's final resting place was not far away.

With great difficulty, he was rowing alone across the gulf. He was only a few hundred yards from the beach when he noticed the men on horses along the Baja shore. As the sun came up behind him, he realized it was too late. The men in helmets were riding toward the boat. They had Cortés's golden horse with them as they entered the water. There would be no escape this time. Only the ocean and the gods could save the magic now.

The heavy round object sat behind him in the boat, tied up in rough cloth. The sound of horses splashing filled his ears and echoed along the beach. The tide was all the way in, so it would take the Spaniards a few minutes to reach him. As they slowed down in the water, Montuca looked over the side of the boat. There was six feet of water between him and the bottom. Not nearly enough, but it would have to do.

Splashing wildly, the conquistadors raised their muskets toward Montuca.

He looked up for the first time. Seeing his face sent a chill down me as I watched the vision before my eyes. For it was my own, only framed with long black hair that flew behind me in the wind.

Then I was in the boat, inside Montuca's body. At that moment, I *was* Montuca, high priest of the Aztecs.

With the sun blasting into the faces of the approaching conquistadors, I seized the opportunity, carefully untying the knotted cloth and slowly lowering the magic over the end of the boat.

The sun drenched the magic before it hit the water. The Eyes of God sparkled brilliantly in the morning sun, sending shafts of blinding light skyward.

I never saw the great ridged jaws open on the bottom of the sea to receive the magic, and never saw the enemy shoot. I only heard the crashing echo of the fire spears and felt the dull thud slam into my chest. As the invisible spears of fire entered my heart, my spirit flew toward the heavens.

The Eyes of God disappeared into the heart of the sea, and lay undisturbed for nearly half a millennium.

The vision vanished, and I was back in the center of the circle, realizing that I had become Montuca for that instant in the vision to complete my initiation into the ways of power.

Shaken, but still standing, I gazed again into the eye sockets. This time there were no visions of Montuca. There was something else, more powerful than any vision before it. The skull became the head of Mother Nature, staring back at me and smiling. It frightened me, and I almost dropped the skull. Then, slowly, her image faded and I saw the elements at work.

Volcanoes erupted and hurricanes blew fierce, horrible winds. Floodwaters covered the Earth, and fires burned all across the land. Earthquakes and thunderstorms passed in front of my eyes. All of this was accompanied by a tremendous surge of power: The power to direct the rain and winds, move the seas, ignite fire and shake the Earth. All of it was at my command, and I was master of the Earth, seas, and sky. A move of my hand and lightning could strike; a nod of my head could start an earthquake.

I felt like someone directing a symphony, changing movements and moods at my slightest whim. It was intoxicating and all-consuming. The whole world bowed to my power. For that moment, I was a god.

With visions of volcanoes and earthquakes playing in my head, I looked out from the center of my world, taking my eyes off the skull for a second to survey my kingdom.

Ellen and Susie seemed very distant, as if unrelated to me. Maggie began to bark, but it sounded faint and far away. I was beyond them now, beyond human. There was a world to rule, and I had claimed my destiny.

Then, just at the height of my glory, Susie's face caught my eye. She was looking at me and crying. I turned away, feeling much too important to tend to such trivial matters as a single baby's cry.

The crying didn't stop, though I commanded it in a bellowing authoritative voice. That only made it worse. As I became almost enraged at this interference with my coronation, I began to lose control. Should I have the wind wipe out her little voice?

As Ellen turned to take her away, Susie fought free and ran to me, begging to be picked up. She was an annoyance that wouldn't go away. Ellen left her there, knowing Susie would only leave forcibly and screaming.

Susie stood on my boots and grabbed for my belt. Then it occurred to me that I should not be so arrogant. People too were part of my kingdom, and I should strive to help them while restoring the Earth to its former glory. I remembered what I had said to Professor Hardwick, that people were the reason the Earth existed. It was their home, first and foremost. Surely, this was my first test.

I set the skull down in the sand and picked up Susie. She hugged me hard and looked me squarely in the eyes. "I want my daddy," she ordered through tears. "I want my daddy."

As the words came out of her mouth, the word *Daddy* seemed a thousand feet high. All of my fatherly feelings began to come back, doing battle with my feelings of power.

Slowly, surely, I began to come back down to Earth, brought there only by the tiny voice of a little girl, a cry in the wilderness of my mind. I followed it, and at last became human again, at least for the moment. There was one final choice to make before the godly power surged again.

Just as I was about to deal with it, a feeling came over me more powerful than any before it, stronger than the feeling of greatness and being ruler over the elements. It started small at first, and then, growing rapidly, moved over me like a wave.

It was the one thing, the only thing that could win me back. In Susie's eyes shone the most irresistible force on Earth: the power of love, human love.

"Daddy," she said at last, and I hugged her hard. Ellen came over and took her, but my mind was already made up. There was no greater feeling than personal love.

I picked up the skull, and walked over to Mother Nature, handing it to her and looking deep into her eyes.

"The power," I said, "is not meant for mankind. We have too little experience and too many desires. You take it. I've had my fling with power, felt its greatness, peeked at the possibilities of moving mountains, flirted with mastery over the elements. It was too much for me. I never wanted power, just a family and a little worldly work to pay the bills."

"But I . . ."

"The skull," I went on. "I secretly wanted to know what face it carried, what features were on its surface . . . It is an exact image of you, a carved replica of your very own skull. You gave the gift of yourself. And now, I'm giving it back. *You* look into the eyes, for they are your very own. Take back the power that is rightfully yours. We still need you."

"You are greater than a god," she said. "You are a true human. Only a true human can give Mother Nature back the power to save this Earth. I accept your gift from the center of my very being. For it is given freely, with honesty—and love."

With that she slowly took her place in the center of the circle and gazed into the Eyes of God. There was a long deep silence, heavy with anticipation. And then the sun caught the eye sockets and shot forth a blinding flash of light. Everyone had to cover their eyes—everyone except Mother Nature.

There was a tremendous thunderclap and the Earth starting swaying beneath us. In the distance, the volcano erupted again, spewing lava and gray smoke a thousand feet high. This was followed by a tremendous whirling wind that formed just outside the circle, as if cutting us off from the rest of the Earth. Beyond it, the world was nothing but a spinning blur of sand in the wind, so thick that it was impenetrable to our eyes.

The rest of us began to regain our vision. Mother Nature was still standing there, staring intently into the Eyes of God. They poured back a steady stream of white light, tunneling right into her wide open eyes.

The light poured into her like white-hot lava, as if someone had captured sunlight in a bottle and transformed it into liquid. It traveled inside her, all the way down to her feet. Slowly but surely, they began to glow with a warm luminescence. The light began to fill up her whole body, climbing gradually up her legs, chest, and finally to the top of her head, as though she was a mold being filled with liquid light.

The air around us was as still as a windless day on the desert, though sand still whirled madly beyond the circle.

Finally, when she was completely filled, and glowing like a white-hot ember, the light ceased pouring from the skull. The transfer was complete.

Still glowing, she set the skull down on the sand. In a moment she began to absorb all of the light inside her, and her skin returned to her natural shade of deep brown.

She went around the circle without the aid of her cane and touched each of us. Her hands vibrated with intense energy, and it made each of us glow for a moment. And there was something else in her touch, something a parent transfers to her child. It was the warm glow of her love. It entered each of us, and was absorbed by our bodies into every cell.

Then, with a gentle wave of her hand, the whirlwind stopped and the world returned to normal. None of us could move for the longest time, or speak. Mother Nature went back and picked up the skull, walked over, and handed it to me. It was warm, but retained none of its power.

"Here," she said. "Find a place for this. It will remind you of this day."

"Nothing will ever make me forget this," I said humbly. "Nothing. Is the Earth safe now?"

"Not yet, but everywhere there are seeds planted in the hearts of women and men. I cannot save humans from themselves, but I will try to do my part. It may not always seem like it, but try to remember that, whatever happens, nature itself is trying to heal the world, balance out the forces that are working to destroy it. A little help from the human race will go a long way toward this end.''

She hugged everyone, filled us with hope, and took Techapan's hand. ''We have much to catch up on,'' she said.

''Yes,'' he agreed. ''But it was worth the wait.''

''How is Montuca?'' she inquired. ''Have you seen him?''

''Yes, he's waiting for us. It's time for a family reunion.''

They walked away down the beach. When they became tiny specks on the horizon, a wind came up and blew sand around them. When it stopped, they were gone. But I swear that just before they disappeared I distinctly saw three specks on the sand.

Warren bid us farewell and sped off on his dirt bike. Vaca agreed, with some prodding, to accompany us as far as Palm Springs, saying her work in Mexico was finished for the moment.

We left the Rover on the beach, climbed in the jeep, and I started it up, rolling away slowly. I stopped at the top of a small rise and looked back. Somehow, the beach had never looked so beautiful, a winding strip of pure white sand caressing the blue-green sea.

I put it in gear and headed for the main road. When I got there I surprised everyone by turning left toward San Bajamos.

''Where are you going?'' Ellen said, though not critically.

''Last time I was in town, I saw a little museum of local artifacts. Mostly old Aztec stuff and a few sacred fish bones. These people are so poor, I'll bet they could use a new treasure. It might help the tourist trade a little.''

46

Snowfall

No one argued that a skull made out of a solid piece of rock crystal was worth a small fortune, even devoid of its powers. And on any other occasion I would have cashed it in and thought nothing of it. But on that day, after what I had experienced, there seemed no other choice than to turn it over to the local community. It also reassured me of what had real value in life. I realized it was the chase, the adventure, and the lure of wealth and power that gave treasure something beyond its cash value.

Getting the skull back had given me something more valuable than money. It gave me back my dignity. I had gotten my second chance in life, and had succeeded, with a lot of help, in wrestling my opponent to the mat. There was no good reason at the time for letting him up again. Sure, a life of leisure, or at least doing the kind of work I wanted, was still very appealing. But the feeling that filled me when I walked into that little Indian museum was far greater.

I would go back to my job, but I would have something around my neck that still glowed, and a fire inside that wouldn't be extinguished by the workaday world.

"You realize," Ellen warned, just before I went through the front door to the museum, "that this is it. You do whatever you want, but once you turn it over there will be no second chance. No taking it back."

"We've got our treasure," I said, looking over at a happy Susie sitting on Vaca's lap and playing with the gearshift. "Let's not get greedy."

Naturally, the curator was overjoyed, thinking I was some great, rich philanthropist from the States. She even wanted to build a special secure wing to display it as a sort of supplement to the Indian Artifacts Museum of San Bajamos. I told her to do what she wanted, left my name and address, and walked out. When I got to the jeep, I had an idea.

Back inside, I asked the elderly, dignified woman if she wanted to know more of the legend that went with it, about Eartha, Montuca, and Cortés. That I would be happy to write to her sometime, just to flesh out some of the details that might be missing.

"Señor," she said authoritatively, "I have a doctorate in Mexican anthropology and mythology from the university. We know there have been other skulls found, all in Central America, but none are as beautiful as this one, and none come with such a legend. It must be something the local peasants have told you. For the legend does not exist outside this village."

"Yes," I laughed. "We *gringos* are suckers for a good story. I have *my* reasons, but why do you think this one is the most beautiful?"

"Look at the cranium," she said, pointing to it. "There's hardly a mark on its surface, or an impurity inside it."

When I bent down to look, it was true. The tiny specks that had formed inside it were beginning to vanish. One of them seemed to disappear right before my eyes. It was nearly transparent, as if it were beginning to heal, though it still had a way to go.

"It is worth a great fortune," she assured me. "We will be contacting you about its new home here, and possible reward for turning it over to the people of Mexico instead of taking it back as your booty. Indeed, *señor,* you must be a saint."

"Not me," I said with a wave good-bye. "I'm just an old washed-up wrestler. Give my reward, if there is one, to your village. People are starving here."

I said my good-byes and marched back to the jeep. Then we were off for the border. I can't say that there wasn't a small part of me that wanted to go back and claim I made a mistake. That I really did need the money and was suffering from a sudden attack of overgenerosity. But I couldn't make myself turn back for anything. The feeling of doing the right thing, however unwise, was just too powerful. As it turned out, my regrets were short-lived.

Once at the border, Vaca got out and walked across. This time we met her shortly thereafter on the other side. They didn't even bother to search the jeep. I didn't think anything about it until we pulled over at that same McDonald's to get some dinner. We pooled all of our resources but seemed to be coming up a little bit short.

"Oh well, Maggie," I apologized, "guess you'll have to wait until I get some cash out of the electronic teller. Unless there's some change in the glove compartment."

Vaca popped open the glove box lid and was showered by a huge cache of perfectly shaped and matched, pinball-sized pink pearls.

"What in the . . . Vaca, what are you doing, practicing your magic?" I asked.

"I . . . I didn't have anything to do with this. Wait," she added, reaching in the back, "there's a pouch in here with a note attached."

She pulled out a hand-sized burlap sack and pulled off the note, which was held there by strings. I read it aloud.

> *Thanks for your help. You are all good children. And Vaca, I know the tourist business can get a little hectic, so I've gained permission for you to take a long vacation, and I mean a real one. Take as long as you like. Tourists can go it alone for a month or two. I've agreed to stay on as long as it takes and try to set the world right again. And judging by the looks of things, that could take awhile, if I succeed at all. Good-bye.*

> *Love,*

There was no signature. She had just drawn a picture of a sunflower.

"Thank god," Vaca sighed. "She's staying on as ruler of

the elements." She opened the pouch and poured something into her hand that only nature could make: a sack full of rare, precious diamonds.

Needless to say, we were overwhelmed, and after lunch and a stop at the electronic teller for Maggie's sake, called work and said I had won the Arizona lottery and wouldn't be back to clean out my desk for a couple of weeks. Then we headed straight to Palm Springs with darkening skies overhead, so that Vaca, and all of us, could have a real vacation.

As Maggie ate dog chow on the floor in the back, I found a jeweler and cashed in the diamonds and pearls. A whopping half million for Vaca, and the other half for us. It took a couple of hours, but he eventually got a check deposited in my account back home. Vaca said I could pay her later, when she came to visit. She also insisted that we take $750,000, and we couldn't talk her out of it.

"You realize," Vaca said, "that nobody will believe any of this at your job."

"What job?" I laughed. "I'm on vacation until further notice."

Just as Vaca was saying her good-byes to us, a strange thing happened. The sky had been growing progressively more gray, and it began to get very cold. Then, much to everyone's surprise, it began to snow. Right in the desert. Something had happened while we were away. October had become November, and now it was snowing, even in the desert.

"Awful funny weather we're having lately," I remarked, with a glance toward the heavens.

"Sure is," Vaca said. "Well, guess this is good-bye then." She stuck out her hand.

"Say," I said, not reaching for her hand, "aren't you on vacation?"

"Sure but—"

"But nothing. You can't sunbathe in this weather. Let's go buy our own motor home, some equipment, get cleaned up, and go skiing. I said I'd teach you, remember?"

"You're crazy," Vaca said, and Ellen confirmed it, but

nobody could think of a better idea just then, so that's just what we did.

We headed up the side of the mountain to Big Bear ski resort, after getting the gear and listening to the radio report that the early snowfall had brought three feet of packed snow, and the lifts were open early this year.

On the way up the mountain it occurred to me that I had gotten everything for our trip except tire chains. Then, as luck would have it, we passed a little hardware store along the side of the road just as it began to ascend the steep part. When we got there, a small, hand-painted sign was stuck invitingly in the window. One I couldn't ignore. It simply said: FOR SALE.

DAVID LEE JONES first discovered Baja while in college, driving down on weekends with buddies to drink too much tequila at the Long Bar in Tijuana. He has since rediscovered the real Baja with his in-laws on October trips to San Felipe. He currently lives and works in Santa Barbara, California, with his wife, their daughter, and their black Labrador retriever. He is the author of two previous fantasy novels, *Unicorn Highway* and *Zeus & Co.*, also available from Avon Books.

AVONOVA PRESENTS
MASTERS OF FANTASY AND ADVENTURE

SNOW WHITE, BLOOD RED 71875-8/ $4.99 US/ $5.99 CAN
edited by Ellen Datlow and Terri Windling

A SUDDEN WILD MAGIC 71851-0/ $4.99 US/ $5.99 CAN
by Diana Wynne Jones

THE WEALDWIFE'S TALE 71880-4/ $4.99 US/ $5.99 CAN
by Paul Hazel

FLYING TO VALHALLA 71881-2/ $4.99 US/ $5.99 CAN
by Charles Pellegrino

THE GATES OF NOON 71781-2/ $4.99 US/ $5.99 CAN
by Michael Scott Rohan

RETURN TO AMBER...
THE ONE *REAL* WORLD, OF WHICH
ALL OTHERS, INCLUDING EARTH,
ARE BUT SHADOWS

The Classic Amber Series

NINE PRINCES IN AMBER 01430-0/$3.99 US/$4.99 Can

THE GUNS OF AVALON 00083-0/$3.99 US/$4.99 Can

SIGN OF THE UNICORN 00031-9/$3.99 US/$4.99 Can

THE HAND OF OBERON 01664-8/$3.99 US/$4.99 Can

THE COURTS OF CHAOS 47175-2/$4.99 US/$5.99 Can

BLOOD OF AMBER 89636-2/$4.99 US/$5.99 Can

TRUMPS OF DOOM 89635-4/$4.99 US/$5.99 Can

SIGN OF CHAOS 89637-0/$4.99 US/$5.99 Can

KNIGHT OF SHADOWS 75501-7/$4.99 US/$5.99 Can

PRINCE OF CHAOS 75502-5/$4.99 US/$5.99 Can